THE
BAD
PLACE

THE
BAD
PLACE

M.K. HILL

HEAD of ZEUS

First published in the UK in 2019 by Head of Zeus Ltd

Copyright © M.K. Hill, 2019

The moral right of M.K. Hill to be identified as the author
of this work has been asserted in accordance with the
Copyright, Designs and Patents Act of 1988.

9 7 5 3 1 2 4 6 8

A catalogue record for this book is available from
the British Library.

ISBN (HB): 9781788548267
ISBN (XTPB): 9781788548274
ISBN (E): 9781788548298

Typeset by Adrian McLaughlin

Printed and bound in Great Britain by
CPI Group (UK) Ltd, Croydon CRO 4YY

Head of Zeus Ltd
First Floor East
5–8 Hardwick Street
London EC1R 4RG

WWW.HEADOFZEUS.COM

For all the Hills and Herods

'Nothing but heaven itself is better than a
friend who is really a friend.'

—Plautus

1

The Thirteenth Day...

Peter Carrington already had a steaming headache when he got the call that those missing kids had been found safe and sound.

'And we've got an address,' one of his detectives said, and hesitated.

'Go on, out with it.'

'It's Jerry Swann's place, guv.'

It took a couple of moments for the name to register above the din of the pub. Carrington wearily pressed his fingers into his eyes. 'Are we sure it's him?'

'There's no question, they all identified Swann as the abductor.'

The detective inspector cursed under his breath. The timing of those kids turning up couldn't have been any worse. Carrington had been on the lash all night. What had been intended to be a single drink after work, just one for the road, had turned into a massive sesh with some of the lads from the station.

Minutes later, he was being driven at high speed along

pitch-black twisting lanes towards the Wallasea Island wetlands, the headlights of the car carving out a narrow path between high verges. Carrington palmed a couple of dry aspirin into his mouth and wound down the window to blast his face with cold air, trying to sober up. He gripped the door handle tightly to stay upright as the vehicle flew around bends.

The car trundled into woods, the headlights jumping, suspension juddering on rough ground, making the contents of his stomach slop and lurch and churn. Acid surged in his throat to scorch the back of his mouth. And when they finally came to a stop, he stumbled gratefully from the car into the chill night.

Following his CID detectives through the trees beneath a silvery moon as wide as a dinner plate, Peter Carrington hoped the assembled officers wouldn't be able to see how ill he felt. He saw lights blazing from an old farmhouse.

'The kids said they ran into these woods and Swann never followed them,' one of his team told him. 'We think he's still inside.'

'Then let's go pay him a visit.'

'But one of the girls still hasn't been located,' said a voice, and Carrington turned to see a young female officer. She was barely even a woman, to his mind; she looked like she should still be at school.

'Did all the children get out or not?' he asked his men.

'According to the kids at the station, they all escaped

and ran together into these woods, but Becky Haskell is unaccounted for.'

'So they got separated.' Carrington nodded into the darkness. 'Hardly surprising, it's as black as the ace of spades. The girl is probably still wandering around somewhere.'

'But, sir,' the uniform insisted. 'The children are in shock, their recollections of what happened are confused, what if they're mistaken?'

He considered the girl. 'How long have you been on the force, dear?'

The girl swallowed. 'A week, sir.'

A probationary PC, a bloody sprog! Carrington, who had been a copper since before this little girl was even born, felt his headache crank up a notch. This investigation was going to come back and bite him on the arse, he felt it in his water, and he wasn't in the mood to be interrogated by some upstart who had been on the force for all of two seconds.

'What's your name?'

'Chancellor, sir.' She swallowed. 'WPC Chancellor.'

'I like your attitude, Dawson, very admirable.' Carrington appraised her; she was a pretty girl, he'd give her that much. 'I've no doubt you'll climb the ladder soon enough, you being a female and the world being what it is these days, and that right now you really want to help.'

'Absolutely, sir,' said the girl.

He stepped close, and the way she flinched when she

got a rancid blast of his beery breath gave him a little bit of satisfaction.

'It's going to be a long night, sweetheart, and I could murder a nice cup of tea.' Carrington winked at the other detectives. 'So, be a love, pop back to the station and make us all a nice flask.'

The guys from CID sniggered and the girl's cheeks reddened. With embarrassment or anger, Carrington couldn't tell – and didn't care. He had wasted enough time and had a job to do.

'Let's get this over with.' He walked towards the farmhouse. 'I met Swann, trust me, he ain't going to give us any trouble, the man wouldn't say boo to a goose.' He clapped an armed officer on the shoulder. 'You're with me.'

The interior of the farmhouse was as grim and dilapidated as the exterior and he felt his shoes stick on the tacky hallway carpet. His colleagues moved quietly upstairs and into a kitchen on the left.

'Jerry Swann,' he called. 'Are you here? It's Detective Inspector Peter Carrington from Essex Police, Jerry. We'd like to talk to you.'

He walked unsteadily along the narrow corridor beneath the sallow light of a single bulb, crooked shadows conspiring with his headache to give it a lopsided aspect like a Krazy House at a funfair, and tried not to brush his shoulders against the curling wallpaper covered with ancient framed photographs. The overpowering smell of damp and drains made him gag. He sensed the armed officer at his shoulder.

'Jerry!' Carrington stopped. He heard something coming from ahead. Voices.

At the end of the corridor was an open door, with dark steps leading downwards.

'Torch.' He gestured to the officer, and a light winked on behind him, revealing a set of stone steps. Someone was crying below – it was a girl's voice – and his stomach churned.

Heart pounding, Carrington took the worn, slippery steps carefully, making sure to hold on to the wall. At the bottom, he signalled to the officer to stay out of sight.

Then he walked into the cold, dismal basement, squinting into the glare of light from the naked bulb in its ceiling cage, and saw the wiry figure of Jerry Swann standing against the far wall. He was holding a knife to a teenage girl's throat.

'Jerry.' Carrington stepped forward, toeing a dirty blanket on the concrete floor. Knowing there was an officer with a weapon outside the door, he opened his arms so Swann could see he was unarmed. 'Come on, son, let's talk about this.'

The detective ran his tongue along his parched lips. He wasn't a man who was ever lost for words – everyone knew he could talk the hind legs off a donkey – but the sight of the girl in Swann's grasp was a shock.

'And you'll be Becky,' he said softly. The girl's eyes

bulged with terror, *please help me*, as Swann's trembling hand held the long, glinting blade to her white neck. 'Don't you worry, dear, we're all going to walk out of here soon enough.'

'Stay back!' yelled Jerry Swann. 'You keep away!'

'It doesn't have to be like this, Jerry. Let the girl go so we can discuss everything, man to man.'

Carrington heard a flutter of fear in his own voice. His vision was blurred, sweat was pouring into his eyes despite the cold of the basement, and he wiped it away with his sleeve.

'You-don-unerstan.' Agitated, Swann moved from foot to foot, pulling the girl with him. But his words were almost unrecognizable because of the tears and snot now pouring into his mouth. 'I-do-i-fo-er!'

'Sorry, Jerry, I didn't catch that.' Carrington was desperately playing for time. He wished he knew the right thing to say; that his mind was clear, and he hadn't stayed in the pub for so long. 'Slow down, son, take all the time you need, tell me again.'

But Swann kept crying. The girl's petrified gaze never left Carrington's face. Knife pressed to her throat, her body juddered, and her mouth was open wide in a silent scream.

Carrington wanted to make her feel better, convince her she was going to be safe, but all he could do was gently wave his fingers as if to say, *everything's going to work out.*

'Jerry, please, put the knife down and then we can have a proper chat. You can tell me anything you like, but let's not do it like this.'

'I-doin-fo-her!'

'Say again, Jerry!'

Swann roared. 'I'm... doing it... for... her!'

When Carrington looked into the man's small eyes, swivelling crazily in their sockets, he saw fear and desperation.

'The girl doesn't deserve this.' Seeing Jerry Swann hesitate, Carrington stepped forward. 'Put it down.'

Swann looked in shock at the blade, as if he had realized for the first time it was in his hand, and began to lower it.

Carrington dared to breathe. 'That's right, Jerry, just put it on the floor.'

But then the armed officer stepped into the room with his weapon raised and Swann cried out in alarm. The knife flashed back in front of the girl's face.

And in that instant Peter Carrington felt the situation slip out of his control. 'No, no – no!'

He stumbled forward in a panic.

Swann clamped a hand around Becky's forehead and yanked it back, exposing her soft neck. He shouted across the room. 'This is for *you*, my love!'

Carrington flung out an arm—

'Jerry, no!'

—as the glinting blade jerked across the girl's throat.

2

Twenty-Six Years Later

'Perhaps we should eat soon, before it gets too late.' Karin straightened the cutlery on the table, adjusted the place mats. 'Just give her another ten minutes.'

'Nice spread as usual, Karin.' Paul was the only person who ever made a point of thanking her. 'Is there anything I can do to help?'

She tossed him a box of matches. 'Do you mind lighting the candles?'

All Karin had to do was get through tonight, they'd have their usual reunion dinner, and then she'd let them all drift from her life. There was no point in their meeting any more. None of them had anything in common except that *one* thing that happened to them. The evenings were usually tense, and no one even pretended to enjoy themselves, except for Paul, who spent the whole night vainly attempting to encourage some kind of ridiculous camaraderie.

It was crazy that they still even had these reunions. Psychologists had suggested it when they were all too young to know better. They shared a bond, the shrinks said, nobody outside of their group would ever understand the sickening ordeal they had suffered. Coming together regularly to remember their shared trauma, to remember *her*, would help them heal.

Heal, Karin thought. *As if.*

The four of them would never heal – they were losers, rejects, misfits. And Lydia, when she eventually arrived, was in a worse state than any of them. Well, Karin would feed them all one last time, and then they could all finally go their own way. There was no rule to say that just because one awful thing happened to them a long time ago, they had to keep returning to it again and again, like an animal licking a festering wound.

The evening would unfurl exactly like every other year. Michelle would look down her nose at everyone; Paul would bang on about his *faith*; Simon would hardly utter a word; and Lydia would take them all aside, one by one, and ask to borrow money.

'It's really not on, Lydia should be here by now.' Michelle poured herself another glass of wine. 'Some of us have responsibilities. I've a multi-million-pound business to run and can't stay out all night. I imagine she's probably off her face on smack or whatever and has completely forgotten.'

'She doesn't do that any more, she's clean.'

Michelle snorted. 'If you believe that, you'll believe anything. What does our chatterbox friend think, is she going to turn up?' She waited for Simon to answer, but he just shrugged. 'Don't you worry about replying, darling, we don't want your powers of conversation to peak too early.'

'I'm uncomfortable being judgemental about Lydia,' said Paul primly. 'She needs our love, not our criticism.'

'So sorry, Paul.' Michelle smirked. 'I must have missed that lesson in Bible class.'

Paul ignored the jibe. 'She won't let us down, but maybe we should do the toast now, just in case.'

They all gathered behind the chair that would remain empty for the evening – because it always did.

Six places set – but only ever the five of them in attendance.

'To our absent friend.' Paul lifted his glass. 'You're in a better place, but you will always remain for ever in our hearts. God rest your soul.'

'To Becky,' they all said.

Karin dropped her gaze to the floor, unable to look anyone in the eye. After a moment's tense silence, Michelle reached for the wine and Paul chatted to Simon, who stood – as always – near the door. It wasn't unusual for him to slip away early without saying goodbye.

Pretending to arrange napkins, Karin watched these sad, broken people. They may all have survived that ordeal, but none of them had come out the other side of the experience intact. None of them, her included, had gone on to enjoy anything remotely like a normal life.

Simon was a solitary wanderer who disappeared off the grid for weeks, sometimes months, searching for solace in distant places. Paul was a charity worker who had battled desperately to find meaning in his life, finally announcing that he had become a born-again Christian. To look at her you'd think blunt, forceful Michelle, with her expensive clothes, thick mask of make-up and towering bouffant of hair, was every inch the successful businesswoman. She lived in a big house along the coast, had a flash car, enjoyed luxury holidays. But Michelle was a three-time divorcee with a drink problem, and behind her brittle exterior she was as emotionally insecure as the rest of them.

And Lydia was… it was difficult to know where to even begin with fragile, damaged Lydia.

As for Karin herself, well, things hadn't worked out the way she expected. 'I'll heat up the food.'

In the kitchen, she pulled silver foil off the lasagne and placed the dish in the oven.

'I don't know how you do it.'

She turned to see Michelle in the doorway, a large glass of wine pressed to her chest.

'Do what?'

'I don't know how you put up with her.' It was still early, but Michelle was already slurring. 'Oh, I know what you do for Lydia. Giving her money, running around after her like a headless chicken. Mark my words, darling, she's going to bleed you dry.'

'Pass me those plates.'

Michelle picked up five plates from the counter and handed them to Karin, who placed them in the microwave to warm, and continued.

'Let me give you some advice. Mollycoddling Lydia is a waste of time. She's all take, take, take. Tough love is what she needs. Sooner or later she's going to fling your friendship back in your face. She's that type, she'll always be that type. But you know that.' The doorbell rang. 'Speak of the devil.'

Karin called, 'Can you get that, Paul?'

'Or maybe,' Michelle lifted the glass to her lips, 'there's some other reason you keep her close.'

Karin looked up sharply, just as they heard a commotion in the hallway. They headed out to see Lydia pressed against the wall. She was sobbing, hands lifted to her face, as she fended off Paul's attempts to calm her.

'What's going on?' asked Karin. 'What's happened?'

Paul stepped back. 'I don't know, she's upset.'

Pressing the wine glass against her cheek, Michelle leaned against the door frame. 'She looks how I feel.'

Lydia moaned.

'If she's upset, we should take her home,' said Simon.

'How about we all go home?' suggested Michelle.

Lydia's scrawny body, her stick-thin legs, were smothered by the giant parka she wore. Her long, lank hair stuck damply against her wet cheeks. Her tears soaked into the matted faux-fur lining of the parka's hood. She cringed as if she was scared of being struck.

'I saw it… We have to help…'

'What did you see?' Lydia slid down the wall, pulled her legs to her chest, as Karin kneeled in front of her. 'Someone get tissues.'

'We've got to help her!' Lydia gulped down big, juddering breaths, as Paul rushed away. 'We have to!'

Karin tried to lift Lydia to her feet, her malnourished frame was as light as a feather, but was shoved away – 'No!' – and she crashed against a side table, causing a vase of flowers to smash to the floor.

'What's wrong with her? Is she on drugs?'

'Please, Michelle,' said Karin. 'You're not helping.'

Sobbing, Lydia wrapped her arms tightly around herself.

'I don't need this madness in my life.' Michelle took a swig of wine. 'It's just not healthy.'

'Where's your compassion?' Paul was returning with paper from the bathroom. 'Lydia needs our prayers.'

Michelle gave him a withering look. 'Stuff your bloody prayers. We've all had our demons, Paul, but some of us have managed to make something of our lives. Once upon a time you were a gobby little shit, now you're a self-righteous little shit.'

Paul flapped a hand at her. 'You're not very nice.'

She placed her long nails to her chest. 'I'm truly heartbroken about your opinion of me.'

'Guys, let's not fight,' said Karin.

And then Lydia let out a piercing scream that shocked everybody into silence.

'You're not listening to me!' She looked at each of them in turn – at Karin and Simon, at Paul and Michelle – and her eyes were wide with fear. 'We have to help her, she needs our *help*!'

'Who does, Lydia?' asked Karin softly.

'The girl.' Lydia let out another sobbing gasp. 'The one who was taken.'

'Who was taken, Lydia? What's happened?'

The terrified look on Lydia's face sent a chill down Karin's spine.

'He's back.' Her eyes bulged in terror. 'Jerry's *back*!'

3

Arriving at the speed-dating, Sasha Dawson took off her wedding ring and dropped it in her pocket – leaving it on would send *all* the wrong signals.

She parked her Spider in the car park behind the pub, applied lippy in the rear-view mirror, tugged a brush through her silver hair and climbed out to a chorus of squawks from the noisy gulls gliding on the thermals high above the seafront.

'Lovely evening!' Sasha gave a big smile to the doorman who let her inside.

The interior was dark and shabby, and a smell of vinegar and ketchup lingered. Among the round tables arranged in a loose semicircle, a scattering of men and women waited for the event to begin.

At the bar, Sasha ordered a Coke with ice and lemon, pointedly ignoring the attentions of two men to her left. Lips pursed in an arrogant pout, a faint smile playing across his rugged face, the taller of the two was a handsome black guy. He nudged his friend and said, loud enough for Sasha to hear, 'There's plenty of talent here tonight, some right crackers.'

The shorter Asian man smiled, embarrassed. Sasha turned her back on them just as a figure, face hidden beneath a hoodie, slipped in a side exit at the back of the room.

'Hello, madam!' A small, curvy woman, with a head full of white-blonde hair, perfectly straight white teeth sparkling in her fake-tanned face, and wearing a dress shimmering with a million sequins, came over. 'I'm Lolly!'

'Hi, Lolly, I'm Sasha. You look nice.'

Lolly beamed with pleasure at the compliment. She spoke with a bubbly estuary accent. 'And you're totally stunning for an older lady, you don't mind me saying, I bet you're going to be *very* popular tonight! Ready, Sasha?'

'As I'll ever be.' Sasha's thumb rubbed guiltily against her naked ring finger. 'I'm a bit nervous. It's been a while since I've done anything like this.'

'Just be your fabulous self.'

'That one...' – Sasha nodded at the man who had spoken at the bar – 'is too cocky by half.'

Lolly followed her gaze. 'Craig, you mean? Don't worry about him, he fancies himself something rotten. Anyway, chin chin!'

She raised a glass of tonic water and Sasha clinked her Coke against it. A bell dinged.

'Are we ready to start?' Everyone gathered round while a woman explained the rules. 'I want all the ladies to take a table and a gentleman will talk to each of you. Have a chat, get to know each other. When I ring this bell after three minutes,' – she struck it again just in case anyone was still unclear what it sounded like – 'all the gentlemen will move to the next table in a clockwise direction, and so on. There are pencils and score sheets in front of you, ladies, and when we're finished, I'd like you to tell me which of the gentlemen you'd be interested in seeing again.'

'Good luck, Sasha.' Lolly sat to her left. 'Knock 'em dead!'

'Are we all ready?' The woman rang the bell, just as the man who had slipped in at the back of the pub took off his hoodie to reveal a loud Hawaiian shirt, and stepped forward to join the fun. 'Happy romancing!'

The first man to sit in front of Sasha was the Asian guy from the bar. He squirmed in his chair, his gaze roaming everywhere but never quite landing on her face.

'What's your name, sweetheart?' she asked.

'Ajay.'

Bless him, he looked terrified. 'Why don't you tell me a bit about yourself, Ajay?'

'I had a turtle once.' His face reddened. 'When I was a kid.'

It wasn't much to work with, but it was a start. 'What was his name?'

'Frank.' Ajay searched the ceiling. 'And I had a guinea pig called Marmite.'

Sasha saw the man in the Hawaiian shirt chatting to Lolly. 'Anything else, Ajay?'

'I like sports and eating healthily. I'm a very spiritual person, I meditate. I try to hit the recommended daily intake of proteins and fats, although it's true to say the data changes regularly.' Sasha felt sorry for him, he looked like he'd rather be anywhere else. 'After all, we only have one life and then we're dead.'

'You're quite right.'

'So I think it's important to look after your mind, body and soul.'

'That's so true.' Sasha was struggling with Ajay's intensity. 'Do you want to ask me any questions? My name, maybe?'

He looked surprised. 'What's your name?'

She smiled sweetly. 'Sasha.'

'What's your favourite colour, Sasha?'

'I'm glad you asked me that.' Finally, here was something she could work with. 'I have several. Cyan, mauve, I'm partial to aquamarine.'

Ajay thought about it. 'Aquamarine is good.'

The bell rang – 'All change!' – and Ajay stood.

'Thank you,' he said. 'Have a nice evening.'

When he walked to the next table, she picked up the pencil to give him a score, but thought better of it.

Then the man in the Hawaiian shirt dropped into the chair, swinging one tattooed arm over the back, opening his legs wide – manspreading, she believed was the term – and favouring Sasha with an excellent view of his groin. Middle-aged, thickset, hair slicked back by lots of product.

'Now *you* look interesting.' Sasha leaned forward. 'What's your name?'

'Darren.' The man's legs opened and closed like a pair of elevator doors. 'Call me Daz.'

'Hello, Daz, I'm Sasha. Tell me about yourself.'

He grinned. 'I'd rather we talked about *us*.'

Sasha gasped. It was an audacious start.

'I'll be honest with you, Sasha.' His knees snapped together so that he could swing closer to the table. 'You're not my usual type, you're probably a decade older than I'm used to.'

Sasha smiled sadly. 'Devastated.'

'But when I saw you earlier, I knew *immediately*, I said to myself, Daz, there's something about that woman. She's got a...' Wiggling fingers heavy with jewellery in front of his face, he struggled to conjure the exact word. 'A twinkle.'

Sasha listened gravely. 'Do I really?'

'You got a way about you. A mystery. Despite the...' He grimaced at her unexpected shock of long white hair.

'Go on,' she said.

'Wanna know what I'm thinking?' Darren gestured around the pub. 'This whole event is a big fat waste of time. It's a charade.'

Sasha blinked. 'Is it?'

He jerked his head, *come closer*, and Sasha leaned in. Darren picked up the sheet of paper and tossed it over his shoulder.

'You don't need to mark a stupid scorecard, because our attraction is obvious. We're like two ends of a magnet, me and you, compelled to attract. I see the desire in your eyes.' His hands framed her face in the air. 'Your beautiful eyes, which are like two hazel windows to your soul.'

'Oh, Daz.' Sasha swallowed. 'And what do you see in my windows?'

'I see a sensitive, sophisticated woman with womanly needs and appetites. You've got a thing for me.' His eyes fastened on hers, tongue sliding slowly along the length of his top teeth. 'And, no bullshit, I've a serious thing for you. So let's get out of here, let's go somewhere more… intimate.'

'I'd love to talk to you more. I know just the place we can go.'

Darren gave a satisfied grunt. 'Now we're talking.'

His hand crept across the table, but she coyly moved hers into her lap.

'Let's go to the station,' she said.

'The Station.' Darren narrowed his eyes. 'That a trendy new bar, is it?'

'Oh, Daz, you've been to the police station many times.' The bell dinged and Sasha made a sad face. 'Time's up, I'm afraid.'

Darren turned to see everyone in the pub staring at him. The men and women sitting down, the guy behind the bar, the doorman who had slipped inside.

'Shiii…' He jumped out of his seat and raced towards the door. But before he'd managed to get two yards, half a dozen plain-clothed police rushed at him from every direction. Darren lashed out and an officer went down. Lolly leapt across her table to land on his back, yanking his arm behind him and slamming his face into the diamond-patterned carpet.

'Get off me!' he screamed.

'Stay still, mate,' she warned him.

'Darren Gary Walters,' said DC Craig Power, hauling him to his feet. 'I'm arresting you on suspicion of aggravated theft and assault with intent to rob. Robbery, burglary and attempted murder. You do not have to say anything, but it may harm your defence if you do not mention, when questioned, something which you later rely on in court. Anything you do say may be given in evidence.'

'You're a difficult man to find, Darren,' Detective Inspector Sasha Dawson said as he was pulled upright. 'We thought we'd never catch up with you.'

Darren had been on the run since taking part in a series of Post Office robberies. With a network of known associates across the county to hide him, he'd gone underground. But he had a weakness for the ladies: he couldn't resist turning on the charm at clubs and pubs, and the regular speed-dating event at The Crown was a favourite hunting ground.

'Your long-suffering wife suggested we'd find you here, Daz, she's a bit fed up with your roving eye,' she said. 'Take him away.'

'You were terrific, Sasha,' said DC Lolly Chambers as they walked towards the car park.

'I enjoyed that.' Sasha marvelled again at the young woman in a figure-hugging sparkly dress who had floored a man twice her size. 'Remind me *never* to mess with you, Lolly.'

Behind that winsome Essex Girl exterior, all glittery lipstick, false lashes and bronzer, was a tenacious and capable officer.

'I'm out tonight,' the detective constable said in her cheerful sing-song. 'Might as well since I'm all glammed up. You have a nice evening.'

'Good work,' Sasha called to Ajay, who was talking to the officer who had stood outside the pub pretending to be a doorman.

'Sorry.' He blushed. 'I kind of froze in there.'

'You did magnificently,' she lied. 'Got anything planned?'

'Picking up Scott from his Caribbean Fusion cookery course, and then we'll probably grab a Pilates class.'

Sasha was fishing for her keys when she saw DC Craig Power finishing a call on his mobile. He walked over with his usual rolling swagger.

'Nice work, Craig,' she told him.

'No problem,' he said, peering towards the sea, which thrashed against the shingle on the beach. Approaching seven in the evening, it was still bloody hot, another scorcher. Southend-on-Sea, along with everywhere else in the south-east, had been basking in a relentless spring heatwave.

'You out on the town tonight, too?' she asked.

He took out a packet of cigarettes. 'We've had a report of an abduction in Alexandra Road. I thought I'd check it out.'

'That's out of your way.' She watched the red tip of his fag fizz when he dragged on it. 'Give me the address.'

'Are you sure?'

'No, I'm not. I really want to soak in the bath and grab a glimpse of my kids – I'm reliably informed I've two of them – so just say *yes, Sasha*, and walk away before I change my mind.'

Craig nodded. 'Thanks, boss.'

'You're welcome.'

He saw the way her eyes followed the coiling plume of smoke dancing on the breeze and offered his cigarette between thumb and forefinger.

'I shouldn't, I really shouldn't.' She shook her head, she had given up months ago, but was still buzzing from the arrest, and one tiny little puff wasn't going to do any harm. 'Oh, go on then, just don't tell my kids!'

With a furtive look round – an old habit from when

she used to have a secret smoke up the end of the garden – she inhaled deeply. The smoke filled her head. She exhaled into the clear blue sky and handed the cigarette back as the nicotine rushed along her bloodstream, making her feel slightly giddy.

She smiled. 'So, Craig, I'm a right cracker, is that right?'

Loosening the knot of his tie, DC Power peered over the top of his fag.

'I was merely getting into character, ma'am, playing a role for the benefit of the operation. I would never have the insolence to call a senior-ranking officer a cracker.' He began to walk away, but turned, and there was a devastating glint in his eye. 'Even if, hypothetically, she was.'

'Goodnight, Craig,' she said cheerfully.

When he walked off, Sasha took her wedding ring from her pocket, and slipped it back on her finger – where it belonged.

4

Sasha Dawson waited patiently for Lydia to pull together her chaotic thoughts. 'It must have been a terrible shock for you.'

'Yeah, I was in bits.' Despite Karin's attempts to get her to take it off, Lydia looked hot and uncomfortable in her massive parka. Shadows fell across her gaunt face in the lamplight. Her eyes, puffy from her earlier crying, darted regularly to Karin for support – *don't worry*, Karin smiled, *I'm here for you* – and back to the police-woman. 'Shouldn't you be writing this down?'

Hands clasped in her lap, Sasha sat on a dining chair, which had been moved into the living room. 'I will, but first I want to hear in your own words what you saw. Take your time, nobody's in any rush.'

'You say that.' Michelle checked her watch. 'But it's not like we all need to be here.'

Karin shot her an annoyed look and Michelle shrugged.

'There was this girl standing on the corner of the

street.' The tendons in Lydia's hand slid beneath the skin as she gripped a phantom mobile. 'She was looking at her phone.'

Sasha studied Lydia again, her thin, unnourished hair, the way the skin stretched tightly across her pock-marked face. 'How old was she, would you say?'

'I dunno, she was a teenager, fourteen, fifteen. They all look the same at that age, don't they?'

'Can you describe her, Lydia?'

'She had a short skirt on, and these cool trainers, which were really white. Blonde hair to her shoulders, one of them shiny jackets, you know, like they all wear.'

'And then what happened?' asked Sasha.

'There was a noise behind me.' Lydia glanced again at Karin for encouragement. 'And a van passed me. Well, I didn't think anything of it, but it stopped further up, next to the girl, and then she was gone.' She clicked her fingers. 'Just like that.'

'Gone?'

'She seemed to tip forward, like she'd been pulled into it.'

Bum perched on the edge of the chair, spine perfectly straight, Sasha crossed her legs. Her lean body broadened to wide hips. A coil of hair from her long wavy bob – prematurely icy white – bounced across her eyebrow. She lifted it clear with the tip of one slim finger to reveal the sharp point of a widow's peak against her olive skin. She smiled encouragingly at Lydia, and it occurred to Karin that the entire time she had been here, that gentle smile – by turns concerned, encouraging or sympathetic – never left her oval face.

'Have you had any other reports?' Karin asked. 'Did anyone else see anything?'

'We'll have officers knock on the doors of the houses along the street. It's possible someone else saw the… incident. But until a girl fitting that description is reported missing, there's not a lot we can do. At this point, a crime may have been committed, or it may not.'

'What if it's him?' Lydia looked anxiously at Karin. 'What if he's back?'

Michelle made an exasperated noise. 'Get a grip, Lydia.'

But Sasha Dawson must have sensed the change in atmosphere in the room because she turned in her seat to look closely at them. At Karin, and Michelle clutching her glass of wine; at Simon, beside the door; and Paul, his small hands folded in front of him. Karin saw the policewoman trying to work out why they were all so familiar. She had seen that same look many times.

'I imagine it must have been a shock when Lydia turned up and told you what she saw,' Sasha said to nobody in particular. 'Were you having a party?'

'Just a meal,' Karin said. 'We get together occasionally.'

'And has one of you gone home?' Sasha nodded at the dining table. 'There are five of you, but six places set for dinner.'

Michelle sipped her wine, said, 'I can see why you're a detective.'

'We always leave an empty place,' admitted Karin. 'One of us... can't make it.'

Sasha Dawson's smile drifted. 'So you're all friends?'

Michelle snorted. 'Oh, we all love each other to bits.'

Breath caught in the detective's throat. 'You're those children who were taken to the Bad...'

'Oh, you might as well say it,' said Michelle. 'We were the kids from the Bad Place.'

'I was *there*,' said Sasha. 'The night you escaped. I was at the station when you were brought in.'

Michelle snorted. 'What, were you on work experience?'

'I'd been on the force all of a week. I was there when Becky Haskell was...' There was an awkward silence. 'I've often thought about you all.'

'Can we go now?' Michelle drained her glass. 'I have to get home.'

Sasha cleared her throat, getting back to business. 'The incident Lydia saw was around the corner, so if the rest of you were here and didn't see anything, there's no reason for you to stay.'

Michelle didn't need telling twice. She pulled on an expensive cashmere coat. 'Well, I'd like to say it's been fun, but I can't.'

Paul took Lydia's hands in his. 'I'll pray for you.'

'Pray for that poor girl instead, yeah?'

'And for her, too. Take care, all.'

'Yeah.' Michelle rolled her eyes. 'Can't wait.'

'Thanks,' said Simon, avoiding everybody's eye as he left.

In the hallway, Karin opened the front door and her guests stepped out into the warm evening.

'I'm happy to stay.' Paul looked with compassion at the others. 'If you need me.'

'I think DI Dawson is nearly finished.'

'Take care of yourself.' He kissed her cheek. 'Same time next year, I suppose.'

Karin smiled at the inevitability of it. They would all meet up again, because these people were the closest thing to a family she had, and because some people could never escape each other's orbit.

'Bye,' she called to Simon, but he was already striding down the path.

'I don't want to go home,' Lydia said when Karin went back into the room. 'I'm all agitated now.'

'You know you can stay. You're always welcome.'

'I might go up now, yeah? I'm shattered.'

When Lydia went upstairs, Sasha stood, tugging her skirt back into place over her knees. 'Do you think—'

'That she saw someone getting abducted?' Karin listened to Lydia thumping around above them. 'We have these reunions once a year to remember what happened to us, and every year I think, never again. But it's important to remember that we were the lucky ones.'

'Lucky?'

'We came home.'

Sasha glanced again at the six places set at the table.

'But these nights stir up a lot of emotions.' Karin sat heavily in a chair; it had been an exhausting couple of hours. 'And Lydia's... fragile, she finds these evenings particularly stressful and upsetting. So, yes, I think she was mistaken. I'm sure she saw something – a van stopping sharply, even a girl climbing in – but an abduction? I don't think so.'

'And when she said, *he's back...*'

'She was talking about Jerry Swann, the man who abducted us. But as we all know, that's not possible.' Karin began to clear the table. 'I'm sorry if you came for nothing.'

'Better safe than sorry.' Sasha Dawson looked like she was about to tell Karin something... but lifted her nose. 'Do you smell burning?'

The stench hit Karin's nostrils just as brown smoke tumbled from the kitchen and across the ceiling. An alarm filled the room with noise.

'The oven!' Rushing into the kitchen, Sasha stood on a chair to wave a tea towel beneath the smoke detector, and Karin pulled on oven gloves to lift out the blackened, smoking lasagne and dump it in the sink.

'Oh dear,' said Sasha. 'It's just as well everybody's gone home.'

When the detective left, Karin opened windows to let

out the smoke. She took the plates from the microwave – her best china would go back in the cupboard for another year – and binned the salad.

Above her head, a floorboard creaked. Karin stopped to listen.

'Lydia?' she called, going into the hallway. 'Is that you?'

Karin jumped when she saw Lydia at the top of the stairs, her features mostly hidden in the dark.

'I hope you didn't say mean things about me,' said Lydia. 'Cruel things.'

'I would never do that.'

Lydia's eyes glinted down at her, and then she dissolved into the shadows on the landing.

Karin went back next door, just as a message dropped into her phone.

When she saw it, her heart leapt with hope – and fear.

I ♥ U
BeXxx

5

The First Day...

Nobody even noticed when a stranger climbed into the minibus and drove them to the Bad Place.

It was pandemonium inside, and stifling hot. The air-conditioning wasn't on because the youth worker who was driving them had jumped out to nip to the toilet in a pub across the road. The interior was rank with the heavy musk of body odour after a day in the sun. All the kids were sweltering in their T-shirts and jeans.

Becky and Karin were sitting in the back row discussing everything under the sun, enjoying each other's company, the conversation jumping from one subject to another: the boys Becky fancied at school, her favourite boy bands, a sparkly nail varnish she'd discovered.

Paul's hand swung suddenly over the top of the chair in front of Karin and swiped at her head, giving her a shock, and Becky launched herself out of her seat to try to slap him back. The second time he appeared, Becky was ready with her fists clenched. 'I mean it, Paul, leave us alone!'

In the row ahead of Simon and Paul, Michelle was

nodding to music on her headphones, while Lydia watched gulls swoop to the pavement on the seafront to grab morsels of food.

That was when the driver's door opened and someone climbed in and turned the keys in the ignition. The engine roared and the minibus swung away from the kerb.

'Seriously?' said Becky when Paul reappeared over the back of the seat, looking to make more trouble. 'If you lay another finger on either of us I will *destroy* you.'

Becky raised her eyebrows in a steely challenge, ready to teach him a lesson. Karin loved the way Becky's eyebrows arched like fighting alley cats.

Paul froze, weighing up the odds, and then waved her away, as if he couldn't be bothered. 'You're lucky this time,' he said. 'I'm going to let you off.'

Becky made a sarcastic face. 'Yeah, big man, we're *so* lucky.'

Simon laughed like a drain, because he knew Paul didn't fancy messing with Becky. Karin's heart swelled with love for her friend, because Bex didn't take any shit from anyone, certainly not some divvy boy like Paul. Karin didn't care that she felt sick from all the sweets and fizzy drinks she'd consumed, and that it was sweltering in the vehicle, because she was with Becky. She dreamed they would be best friends for ever, and they would take the same exams at school and get the same grades, so they could go to the same university to study on the same course, and live together into old age.

Rain clouds rolled in over the sea, but the streets were still packed with sightseers and holidaymakers, as the minibus turned north past the town centre and picked up speed. Nobody noticed they were going in the wrong direction, or even that the man driving them wasn't Greg, the volunteer from the youth club, until Becky saw how his hair hung lankly over his ears.

'Who is that?' She prodded Paul, but he was too busy lunging back and forth, avoiding Simon's playful punches. 'Who's driving us?'

And when the others finally saw it wasn't Greg, but somebody else completely, nobody was too concerned. Greg had gone home, they thought – he'd been taken ill, or there had been a change of plan and they hadn't been told – and another driver had stepped in to take his place. All they could see was the back of the man's head, and an occasional flash in the rear-view mirror of the orange lenses in his glasses.

The two boys thought it was a big joke.

'Hey, fella, who are you?' Paul made a funny remark about the man's hair and everyone laughed. But the driver didn't respond at all.

'This isn't the right way,' said Simon as the minibus passed the designated drop-off point and headed out of town towards Rochford. 'Where are we going?'

Seated behind the driver, Michelle told the others in a low voice, 'I don't recognize him, he's not from the club!'

Becky reached over to tap her on the shoulder. 'Tell him he's going the wrong way!'

'Excuse me, but this isn't the way!' Michelle told him, but he ignored her.

'Tell him again,' Becky insisted. 'Find out who he is!'

And this time Michelle leaned forward between the front seats to get his attention. 'Excuse me—'

She screamed and fell back in her chair.

'What is it?'

Michelle turned to the others. 'He's got a knife – a big knife in his lap!'

They all huddled together to talk, trying to work out what was going on, hoping that Michelle was mistaken, or that she was joking. But they knew she wasn't, because she was weeping with fear.

Sitting quietly at the back, forgotten in the heat of the moment, Karin's eyes lifted to the rear-view mirror and the man's orange lenses briefly met her gaze.

'Let us out!' screamed Michelle. 'Let us out now!'

Her panic frightened the others as the minibus headed further into the countryside. The man drove calmly, hands placed on the wheel at ten and two o'clock, pulling up slowly at junctions and lights, staying within the speed limit. Becky beat on the window when a vehicle came the other way – *help us!* – but it whipped past in an instant.

And after their initial terror, all the kids could do was sit stunned and bewildered as the road narrowed and the lanes became more twisted and the minibus drove into the countryside, past fields and meadows. Then tall trees loomed on either side of the road, their reflections climbing the windscreen, and a low, red sun emerged from the clouds to flash behind the trunks.

If any of them had been thinking straight, they could have made a note of the few features of the flat landscape, the way the last rays of sun sparkled on the surface of the River Crouch; or the name of one of the country pubs they passed; or they could even have tried to memorize the turns the vehicle made, left and right and left again, down a lane where a tractor was crashed into a ditch, along a bumpy rutted track, past a burbling stream. But everyone was too disorientated to track their progress – and too scared. Not even Simon knew what to do.

And then the minibus swung down a darkened lane barely wider than a pitted pathway. The clawed fingers of the bushes on either side scratched at the windows, pressing so close that it would be impossible to turn the vehicle or even reverse. The kids bumped up and down in their seats as the vehicle hit one deep hole after another, and emerged into a clearing to park outside an old farmhouse at the edge of a thick wood.

The man cranked the handbrake, killed the engine. His neck was slick with sweat, the shoulders of his shirt dark with damp where it pressed against the leather of the seat. The kids watched with a sick fascination as he took off his glasses to wipe them on his shirt.

Replacing the glasses on his nose, he turned to face them – they gasped when he lifted his hand to reveal the blade – and nodded at the door of the farmhouse.

'I'm going to let you out and you'll walk inside one by one. But if anybody tries to make a run for it or makes any trouble,' – he jabbed the knife, making them all scream – 'I'll kill every single one of you.'

6

This is how the day always began. With a big, scream-ing row.

Sasha listened to the yells and shouts, the doors slam-ming, the floorboards pounding above her head. She was going to get dragged into it any moment... now...

'Muuuum!' shouted her daughter. 'Tell him to leave my stuff alone!'

'I didn't take your stupid hairdryer,' her son bellowed. 'I don't want your dandruff blowing all over me!'

Angel screamed in frustration. It wasn't difficult to light a fire under her fragile emotions and Denny knew how to strike the match. Sasha went to the bottom of the stairs. 'Hurry up, please, I have to go!'

Her thirteen-year-old came downstairs, his thick mop of hair swinging across his eyes. Sasha grabbed his school tie to yank his face close to hers.

'Breathe,' she said.

He opened his mouth wide and let out a foetid breath.

'Yuck! Go and clean your teeth.' She spun Denny around and pushed him up the stairs, her son trudging away like a condemned man to the gallows. 'And brush your hair!'

In the kitchen, she took a last gulp of tepid coffee and chased a shoe around the tile with her foot.

'Got a fiver?' Denny came back into the room. There was little evidence to suggest he'd made any attempt to brush his hair; it stuck up every which way.

'What do you need it for?'

'We've got a geography field trip today so I need to buy lunch.' He lifted her purse from her bag. 'I told you about it.'

She grabbed the purse out of his hand. 'You didn't tell me about it.'

Denny rolled his eyes. 'I did.'

'Don't act like a sulky teenager, Denny, you're better than that.' She pulled out the single note. 'I've only got a tenner.'

He took it quickly. 'That'll do.'

'Don't snatch.'

Her son lifted a remote at the TV on the wall and the room was filled with the sound of screeching tyres, explosions and gunfire. Cars leapt about on screen, defying all gravitational logic. Sasha could barely hear herself think.

'That's an awful lot of noise first thing in the morning.'

'All my friends are watching it.'

Sasha sipped her coffee. 'Is it age appropriate?'

'There's no fucking in it, if that's what you mean.'

'Excuse me?' she asked sharply, as Kev walked into the kitchen. Her husband was still in his pyjama bottoms and the T-shirt he slept in. There was the lingering ghost of a sleep crease on one unshaven cheek.

'Shouldn't you be dressed by now?' Sasha asked as he poured coffee from the pot, but he trudged out without replying.

Angel appeared at the door with her hands on her hips and said, as if the world was about to end, 'My hairdryer is gone!'

She was wearing her school uniform, at least, but in the last few months some kind of diabolical transformation machine had been at work on her appearance. Every day there was some alarming new change. A little more make-up was applied, her hair dyed more luridly or moussed higher into the stratosphere, ever longer lashes obscured her eyes. Lately, she'd been talking about getting her tongue pierced. Sasha yearned to take her daughter shopping, to encourage her to buy something *nice*, but knew Angel would have an almost allergic reaction to every item she suggested.

'Denny's hidden it!' She tugged at her hair, almost in tears. 'Look how frizzy it is!'

'I didn't touch it.' Denny spooned cereal into his mouth. 'I wouldn't touch your skanky stuff with a bargepole.'

'*I* used it,' said Sasha, and her daughter let out a deafening scream. 'Mine isn't working. I must have put it in my bedside drawer by mistake. I'm sorry, Angel.'

'Don't touch my things!' Her daughter's voice lifted shrilly over a burst of automatic gunfire on the television. 'Don't. Touch. My. Stuff.'

'Don't be a bitch all your life.' Denny favoured his sister with a charming smile. 'Take a day off.'

'I'm going to be late for school!'

'I did try to tell you.'

Sasha watched Angel run around banging cupboard doors, shouting where's the milk, where's the cereal, not the one with the berries, I hate the berries, the *other* cereal, the one I like, where is it? Denny had hidden the Special-K box at his feet and Sasha picked it up and placed it on the counter, and her daughter poured some into a bowl.

'Careful, Angel.' Denny smirked. 'You look like you're putting on weight.'

His sister fretted endlessly about her spoon shape, her thick tummy and wide hips, and reared away from the bowl as if it was a spitting cobra. 'I'm not hungry!'

'Don't be ridiculous.' Sasha glared at her son and mouthed the words: *not helping!* 'You need to eat breakfast.'

Angel stormed to the door. 'I'll get some at school.'

'I should give you a telling-off for being so mean to your sister, Denny, but because you're at a *difficult age*, trapped in that terrible limbo between being my beautiful little boy and a moody, surly teenager, I'm going to let you off this time... on one condition.'

'Yeah?' he said warily. 'And what's that?'

She held out her arms. 'Give your old mum a cuddle.'

He grimaced. 'No chance.'

'You give me a cuddle,' she commanded. 'Right now!'

'Mum!' Angel called from the hallway. 'Dad's in the living room being weird – again!'

'I've got to go.' Sasha leaned in to kiss the top of her son's head. 'You're a good boy, despite all the evidence to the contrary. I'll get back early tonight, I *promise*.'

Denny cringed beneath her touch. 'Whatever.'

In the hallway, Sasha pulled on her jacket, and swerved into the living room. 'Kev, are you going to be – what are you doing?'

He was standing behind the curtain, peeking out. 'I'm looking out the window. Can't a man look out his own window?'

'You're not, though, are you? You're spying.'

'Yeah.' He didn't take his eyes off the street. 'That too.'

'Those ironed shirts are in the wardro… Kev, are you listening to me?'

He didn't turn. 'Look at this.'

'I've got to go. I'm late for work.'

He beckoned her over, and when she went too close to the window, pulled her behind the curtain. 'Careful, he'll see you.'

'What am I looking at?' she asked, staring at the empty street.

'Here he comes!' He teased back the curtain. 'Watch.'

Sasha saw their neighbour carry cardboard boxes to the recycling bins that had been pulled on to the pavement ready to be collected. He flung open one of the lids and started stuffing the boxes inside.

'This is fascinating, Kev, but what am I looking at?'

'That's our recycling bin. He's using *our* bin.'

'Kev.' Sasha made a face. 'Who cares?'

'That's our recycling bin!' he said indignantly. 'If Nelson keeps filling it with his crap, then there's going to be no room for *our* rubbish. And look, he's putting in plastic. You're not allowed to put plastic into the recycling.' He wagged a finger. 'That's a no-no.'

'What does it matter?' said Sasha. 'Kev, this has got to stop.'

Kev and Sasha got on fine with their neighbours on the right, another middle-aged couple with children. They went next door for summer barbecues and parties, and fed the cat when the family were away. But Kev had got a bee in his bonnet about the guy who lived to their left. When the man had moved in, Kev had made a point of introducing himself. Her husband was a big bloke – with a nose twisted almost circular, broken many times when he was still boxing, a tat on his bicep, a shaved head – and it was obvious that their new neighbour didn't like what he saw.

The man said his name was Nelson.

'Nice to meet you, Nelson.' Kev offered a hand but the guy stared, nose in the air, and told him Nelson was his surname, his first name was Stuart. Now, when he came round to complain about something – the noise made by their kids, the tree in their garden with the roots he worried was damaging the foundations of his house, the wind chimes that Kev bought just to drive him crazy, and which Sasha made him remove because it kept *her* awake at night – Kev made a point of calling him Nelson just to wind him up. *Hello, Nelson. Alright, Nelson? Nice day, Nelson.*

'It's the principle,' whispered Kev about the recycling. 'He wouldn't think twice about complaining if *we* did it.'

Sasha found herself whispering too. 'Don't you think you're a little bit obsessed?'

When Nelson glanced up, Kev tugged Sasha out of sight. She was tired of skulking around her own house.

'Where are you going?'

She was exhausted and the day hadn't even started yet. 'To work.'

But when Sasha got to the front door, a shadow fell across the stained glass. Someone was coming up the path.

'Mum!' she said, when she opened it.

Her mother lifted a trolley case inside. 'Put the kettle on.'

'What are you doing here?' Sasha double-checked to make sure her father wasn't following; wracked her brains to remember if she had made some kind of arrangement for her mum to visit. 'Where's Dad?'

In the kitchen, her mother fastened around her waist the apron that Sasha never wore, and looked grimly around the messy room, with its abandoned boxes, mugs and toast.

'Oh dear.' Ursula dropped her slippers to the floor and scooped the cat from the counter, where it was lapping milk from a cereal bowl. 'I came just in time.'

'Mum,' Sasha asked again. 'Where's Dad?'

'He's at home.' Ursula reached for the kettle. 'I'm going to live here now.'

Sasha blinked. 'Excuse me?'

She felt a breeze ripple into the kitchen. The front door was open, someone had gone outside.

Ursula waved vaguely at the sink. 'I can't even think about it until I've had a cup of tea.'

'Mum, I have to go to work.'

'Don't you worry about me,' said her mother sadly.

Sasha didn't have time for this. 'We'll talk when I get back tonight.'

Raised voices came from the front and when Sasha got outside, pulling her car keys from her bag, she found Kev arguing with their neighbour.

'You're out of order.' He stood in the middle of the street in his pyjama bottoms, jabbing a finger at the bins. 'That's your one, this is ours!'

Sasha turned to see Angel and Denny watching incredulous, her mother coming outside. A couple of neighbours observed the argument unfold; a passer-by lingered.

Nelson was trying to get a word in edgeways, but Kev had worked himself into a temper, and was taking the cardboard out of the bin and throwing it about.

'You're a total embarrassment!' Angel screamed at her dad and ran inside, but Kev was too busy shouting at Nelson to notice.

Sasha didn't know what had got into him lately, wished they had time to sit down together to discuss what on earth was going through his head. And then there was whatever the hell was going on with her mother...

Her phone buzzed in her bag and she fished it out, saw her detective sergeant's name on the screen.

'Ajay,' she said quickly.

He must have heard the commotion in the background, and said uncertainly, 'Everything okay?'

'Of course.' She waved at her mother to take Denny inside. 'Sorry, I'm running a bit late.'

'It's not that.' What DS Ajay de Vaz said next made the blood freeze in her veins. 'A girl's gone missing.'

7

Standing on the pavement in front of the house, Sasha gestured to the uniformed officer outside, *give me a moment,* and took out her mobile.

The call rang three times and dropped to voicemail.

'Dad, it's Sasha. Pick it up, I know you're there.' She was fully convinced he was standing right next to the phone, listening to her. 'Pick up the phone, go on, pick it up. Pickitupickitupickitup.'

She twisted away, just in case the uniform was earwigging.

'Alright then, I don't know what's going on with you and Mum, but whatever it is, it's very silly, and you should both know better. Give me a call, please,' she said and added, 'I love you.'

She dropped the phone in her bag and went to the door of the bland new-build house in the suburb of Eastwood. The estate, up by the airport, couldn't have been more than a decade old.

'Remind me of their names,' she asked the officer quietly.

'Alan and Jessica.'

The Mannings' living room was neat and impersonal, most of the space taken up by a big leather sofa and a low coffee table with a bowl of fragrant potpourri on it. On the wall was a colourful canvas image of Alan, Jessica and their daughter, Sammi. The little girl was only seven or eight in the photo, which had been taken in a professional studio. The family lay face forward on a rug, Sammi snug as a bug between mum and dad, a big grin on her face.

Alan Manning had put on a bit of weight since the photo was taken and his hair had thinned. He paced in an oversized cardigan, jowls trembling as he scowled at his mobile. Perched on the sofa, Jessica Manning watched him tensely through bleary eyes.

'Nothing,' he told her. 'It's still switched off.'

'Try it again.'

'If it was off a second ago, it's hardly likely to be switched on now.'

'Mr and Mrs Manning.' Sasha stepped forward to shake hands. 'I'm Detective Inspector Sasha Dawson.'

Jessica jumped up. 'You've found Sammi?'

'I'm sorry, no.' Sasha smiled sadly. 'I'm here to ask you a few questions.'

Sasha would have to be careful about what she told the parents. Their fifteen-year-old daughter hadn't been seen since the previous evening, but there was still no serious evidence that she had been abducted. As the attending officer, Sasha would fill out a Missing From Home form, a risk assessment that Sammi had gone missing in suspicious circumstances. Then it would be up to her boss, DCI Vaughn, to decide what, if any, resources should be put into looking for the girl.

But in Sasha's experience there was still every likelihood Sammi would walk in the door safe and well, and admit she'd stayed overnight at a friend's house. Frantic with worry, her parents would go ballistic, there would be harsh words, and then they'd all weep with relief. Sasha had seen a similar scenario unfold many times before.

Usually, a uniform would speak to the parents – the visit of a senior officer like Sasha could make the Mannings more anxious – but she had been rattled by last night's report of an abduction and wanted to talk to them herself. The witness was an emotional wreck, but Lydia Tide – a former abductee herself – had been convinced she saw a girl being bundled into a van. Sammi's subsequent disappearance was an uncomfortable coincidence.

The girl certainly didn't fall into any of the high-risk categories of kids who tended to go missing. She lived in a respectable middle-class home, she wasn't homeless or living in care, or involved in gangs, and she wasn't previously known to the social services.

The parents told Sasha that their daughter had left the house at six the previous evening, while Alan was still at work and Jessica was in the kitchen. Her mother heard the door slam. Phoning around later, piecing together her movements, they established that Sammi joined a group of girlfriends hanging out on the High Street for an hour.

'Her friends said she got a text and left them.'

'A text – who from?'

'We don't know.'

'Did you argue with Sammi last night, did she leave the house upset?'

'Is she punishing us, do you mean?' Jessica perched again on the sofa to rub her hands up and down her shins. 'We'd had words earlier because she'd earned a detention for talking in class, she can be a chatterbox in lessons, but it was hardly a row, certainly nothing that would make her storm off and not come back.'

'Which school does she go to?'

'Hanley Cross.'

'There's no easy way to ask this, but does Sammi... get *down* at all, or anxious?'

'Does she get depressed, you mean? She's a happy girl, the life and soul.'

'And has she ever been absent from home before?'

'What is this *absent* word?' said Alan Manning. 'She's not absent, that makes it sound like she's standing outside the room, she's *missing*.'

Sasha ignored his testy response. 'Can you tell me what she was wearing?'

Jessica closed her eyes, trying to remember. 'She usually wears leggings and a loose top, but she was in her room until she went out, so I can't say for sure. Her silver puffa jacket is gone.'

Sasha didn't like the sound of that. Lydia had said last night that the girl she saw being abducted had been wearing something shiny.

'We've rung her phone constantly since last night,' said Alan. 'But it's switched off.'

'You've spoken to her friends.'

'And friends of friends, and parents of friends, we rang and rang. And, before you ask, we've searched everywhere in the house and walked round the neighbourhood. We went to the youth club she used to attend, and looked at her Instagram.' Alan's frustration boiled over. 'Frankly, I don't understand why you're sitting here talking to us when you could be searching for her!'

'What will you do next?'

Sasha could see the desperation in Jessica's eyes, which were red from tears and a lack of sleep. The last thing she wanted to tell the Mannings was that she was going back to the office to fill out a form that *may* release resources to begin the search for their daughter.

She clicked her pen top, thinking of a careful reply, but before she had a chance to speak, Jessica blurted out, 'You must think I'm a terrible mother, allowing Sammi to go out without even knowing where to.'

'I've children of a similar age to Sammi.' Sasha smiled kindly. 'They're in and out of the house, half the time I don't where they are. And teenagers change their plans all the time. You think they're one place, and they pop up somewhere else.'

'That's what's happened.' Alan took his wife's hand. 'She's stayed at a friend's.'

'On a school night?' said Jessica incredulously.

'Children go missing every day of the week, and I'll tell you what usually happens. Nine times out of ten they return home, or are located unharmed, within forty-eight hours.'

At that moment they heard voices on the doorstep. The Mannings stood, hoping Sammi was about to fly inside. Instead, the PC poked his head in.

'Excuse me, ma'am, there's someone here to see Mr and Mrs Manning.'

A woman barged past the officer. In her cashmere coat and kitten heels, the expensive bag hanging from her shoulder, she was instantly familiar to Sasha.

'I came as soon as I could.' The woman embraced Alan and then hugged his wife, but Jessica's arms stiffened at her sides. 'You must be going out of your minds!'

Jessica's voice lifted irritably. 'What are you doing here, Michelle?'

She was the woman who had stood, bored, at the back of the room last night while Sasha had spoken to Lydia

– another of the abductees who had been taken to the Bad Place as a child.

'I came to tell you I will do everything in my power to ensure that poor girl is found. As you know, I've plenty of contacts in business, on the council and in the press. I will turn this town upside down to get her back. I will not stop until Sammi is found.' Michelle gave Sasha a cursory glance. 'I'll make sure the authorities find her or, I swear to God, I will make merry hell.'

Jessica stared at the floor, her face like thunder.

'Thank you, Michelle,' said Alan quietly.

Only then did Michelle turn to Sasha, her eyes lifting immediately to Sasha's white hair, because everyone clocked the hair first. Standing close, Sasha wondered if she could smell alcohol on Michelle's breath. She'd been drinking the previous evening, but it didn't smell like the stale funk of the night before, instead the sharp tang of spirits consumed this morning.

'Have we met?' Michelle asked.

The last thing Sasha wanted to do was alarm the Mannings by telling them that a girl had been seen getting bundled into a van the previous night, not when there was still every chance Sammi would return home of her own accord.

'Michelle, isn't it? DI Sasha Dawson.'

'Wait.' Michelle's eyes flashed in recognition. 'You were there last night.'

Jessica and Alan watched in bewilderment. 'You know each other?'

Sasha said urgently, 'I wonder if I may have a quick word with you outside.'

But Michelle turned back to Alan and Jessica. 'You must be terrified after what happened to that poor girl.'

The Mannings stared, bewildered, and Sasha went quickly into damage-control mode. 'That's not really very helpful, we don't yet know if—'

'What poor girl?' Jessica asked. 'What's she talking about?'

'A girl was kidnapped last night,' said Michelle. 'Thrown into a van and driven off at high speed.'

'Oh my God.' Jessica whirled on Sasha, her voice rising hysterically. 'Why haven't you told us this? How could you keep it from us?'

'We have a single witness to what may or may not have been the abduction of a girl.' Sasha darted a fierce look at Michelle, who seemed completely unconcerned about the havoc she had caused. 'The witness admits she may have been mistaken.'

'Yes,' said Michelle, finally backtracking. 'Lydia isn't the most reliable of people at the best of times.'

'You were there?' asked Alan.

'I was in the room when she spoke to this officer about it, yes, but take it from me, Lydia is more than capable of making up some silly story.'

'But a girl was taken!'

Alan helped Jessica back to the sofa and she sat with her head in her hands.

'It's a possibility.' Sasha was annoyed at being put in a difficult position. 'But I must stress it's no more than that.'

'I tell you what.' Michelle clapped her hands together. 'Why don't I go and make us all a nice cup of tea?'

'Why is she here?' Jessica asked her husband sharply when Michelle left the room. 'How does she know what happened?'

'I phoned work this morning to say I wasn't coming in, and must have mentioned that Sammi hadn't come home.'

They heard Michelle banging open cupboards in the kitchen next door.

'You work with her?' Sasha asked Alan.

'I'm Ms Dormand's office manager.'

'They actually started the business together years ago.' Jessica shot her husband a dark look. 'But now she bosses him around. He's the backbone of that company, it would fall apart in an instant if he wasn't there. I don't know how many times I've told him to leave, and she's always here interfering in our lives.'

'She's been good to us,' Alan insisted. 'She's Sammi's godmother, it's only natural that she's going to be concerned.'

'It's not appropriate for her to be here.'

'Underneath the sharp manner, she's a good soul.'

'I want her gone,' snapped Jessica.

'You heard what she said, she's got all sorts of useful contacts.'

'She'll do what she usually does and make everything about her. Sammi's missing but don't worry because Michelle is all over the papers – again!'

Sasha said, 'I'll ask her to leave.'

Michelle came back into the room empty-handed and said, 'I'm sorry, I couldn't find the teabags.'

'They're in the cupboard,' hissed Jessica. 'With the mugs. In a pot with the word TEABAGS written on it in giant red letters.'

'I didn't see it.' Michelle eyed Sasha. 'Maybe you or one of your officers could do it. Just to let you know, I've asked someone from the local paper to come along, and they'll get the word out.'

'That's not very helpful until we're absolutely certain there's cause for concern,' said Sasha. 'Sammi's only been absent since—'

'There's that word again,' said Alan. 'She's not absent, she's *missing*.'

A phone rang in Michelle's Prada bag, the familiar barking chorus of 'Who Let the Dogs Out' filled the room, and she took out her Samsung. 'I'm going to have to take this. There's been a mix-up at work. If Alan was there, it never would have happened.'

When she spun out of the room again, Jessica began to weep. 'I just want my baby home.'

Sasha walked outside, shielding her eyes against the sun rising in the clear blue sky. It was going to be yet another hot day. A single puff of white cloud hung suspended on the horizon. An airliner, sleek like a needle, took off from the airport in the distance. She saw Michelle pacing the pavement, giving someone a piece of her mind on the phone.

But all Sasha could think about was that odd, unlikely connection.

Michelle was there last night when Lydia described an abduction she said she had witnessed – a girl bundled into a van. And now here she was a few hours later when a girl – her own god-daughter, no less – was reported missing.

Abducted.

The same thing that happened to Michelle all those years ago.

8

'Morning, morning!' Sasha walked into the Major Incident Team's suite of offices at the police station on Victoria Avenue, regally twirling her fingers. 'Please don't get up, not on my account.'

'Hi, Sash,' called Lolly Chambers. 'You're looking a billion dollars.'

'Bless you, Lols.'

Sasha mostly wore the same black trouser suit or jacket and skirt combo from Marks and Sparks every day, but this morning the addition of a smart fitted shirt and dark slim tie, and a pair of shiny black-and-white brogues, gave her a two-tone look.

She dumped her bag and shrugged off her jacket, draping it over the back of her chair. While she waited for her computer to wake up, she rearranged a few things on her desk to her satisfaction – her pot of pens, the photo of her kids, a ball of coloured rubber bands – and kicked her feet out of her shoes. From the bottom drawer she took a packet of salt and vinegar crisps and opened it, absently snacking while she typed in her password.

'You're going to ruin it.' Ajay de Vaz picked up the jacket from the floor where it had fallen and hung it on a coat stand. 'Sorry about last night. The last time I intentionally flirted with a woman I would have been blackout.'

She popped a crisp into her mouth. 'You were kind of intense.'

'The occasion got to me. My wheelie bin goes out more than me.' He shrugged. 'Tell me about Sammi Manning.'

Sasha gathered her thoughts. 'The parents are going out of their minds with worry, but Sammi doesn't appear to be in a vulnerable, high-risk group.'

She checked her phone – it was approaching midday – and hoped that by the time she'd finished the risk assessment, Sammi would already have returned home. Call it magical thinking, but stranger things had happened.

'I sense a *but* coming on.'

She picked up a biro and tapped it against her chin. 'What do you know about the Bad Place?'

'I saw the film about it on Netflix.' Lolly Chambers spun in her chair. 'It's brill, but a bit disturbing.'

'I don't have a television,' Ajay told her. 'But everyone knows about the Bad Place.'

'To think, I wasn't even *born* when it happened,' said Lolly.

'But of course you weren't.' A day didn't go by when

Sasha wasn't reminded she was years older than most of the youths in the office.

'And it all happened in Southend!' Lolly pronounced it Sarfend. 'Who'd have believed it?'

'By the way, don't think I've forgotten your promise.' Ajay stabbed a warning finger at Sasha's packet of Walkers as if it was strychnine. 'Those are no good for you.'

Ajay was always going on about her diet and lack of exercise, and it was true that she could eat more healthily. She worked long hours, often under great pressure, and ate crap all day; had promised him more than once to swap the unhealthy snacks for fruit or nuts.

But when he tried to snatch the bag she whipped it out of his reach and shooed him away. 'Let me get on.'

'Wait, you don't have a television?' Lolly shook her head in disbelief as Ajay passed her desk. 'That's just *weird*.'

Clicking open a browser with the only two fingers that weren't sticky with salt, she typed in 'the Bad Place'. A list of articles filled the screen. Sasha read the various reports, familiarizing herself with the official facts of the investigation.

Twenty-six years ago, six teenagers from a local youth club were sitting in a minibus on the seafront, waiting to be taken home after a day trip. The youth worker who accompanied them jumped out of the vehicle to go to the toilet. When he returned less than five minutes later, the vehicle was gone.

There was a nationwide hunt for the six:

Karin McCarthy.

Michelle Dormand.

Becky Haskell.

Paul Ferdinand.

Simon Parkin.

Lydia Tide.

Six children were taken that day... But only five came back.

Sasha felt a personal connection to the events of that tragic night. She had just joined the force as a probationary PC when the kids – filthy, malnourished and terrified – were brought to the station following their escape. Karin, Paul, Michelle and Lydia; Simon had been taken to hospital.

Sasha desperately wanted to put an arm around them all, but the kids were hurried into separate interview rooms. Even at the time she didn't like how they were treated, and in the aftermath it became clear that investigating officers initially suspected the teenagers of making up the abduction, believing the whole thing was an elaborate teenage prank. Sasha only had to look into the traumatized faces of those kids to see that wasn't true.

For a couple of minutes, Karin McCarthy was left in a corridor outside an interview room, and Sasha was told to wait with her. She was struck by how small Karin seemed. Sasha was only a few years older than her, still just a teenager herself, but Karin looked many years younger as she sat staring at the opposite wall.

A lost and broken little girl.

Sasha lifted her eyes to the ceiling now, trying to remember what she had said to her.

You're safe now, something like that. *You're safe and sound.*

But Karin had just stared at the wall.

Then Sasha had told her... that's right, that's what she'd said, it came back to her now... she had touched the back of Karin's hand and said, *we'll find Becky, I promise, she'll be safe.*

And when Karin finally turned to look at her, her gaze was so full of misery and anguish that it sent a chill down Sasha's spine.

Then the door to the interview room had opened and a CID detective had told Karin to come inside. The girl had obliged, head bowed.

Within the hour, Sasha was travelling with other officers to the farmhouse, where the confrontation with Jerry Swann ended in a fiasco. In interviews, all the kids had confirmed that Becky was right behind them when they all escaped, that she had fled into the woods, but when Senior Investigating Officer DI Peter Carrington and his team went inside, she was discovered in Jerry Swann's clutches.

Sasha was waiting outside when officers went into the building. She heard faint screams, shouts – a gunshot.

And then awful silence.

Confronted by police, Swann had slit the girl's throat, then rushed with the knife at Carrington – and was shot dead. The coroner ruled that he had in effect committed suicide by attacking the detective with the blade raised.

The last thing Swann had said as he killed her was, 'This is for you, my love.'

Sasha burned with shame at the memory, even all these years later. She had given Karin false hope that her friend was alive.

We'll find Becky, I promise, she'll be safe.

Sasha could only imagine the heartbreak Karin felt when she discovered Becky had been brutally murdered.

Unable to explain how the girl was in the basement, detectives had theorized that she had stumbled in the dark and been recaptured by Jerry Swann. Psychologists fiercely debated Swann's last words and pronounced that he'd developed an obsession with Becky and killed her in a twisted act of love. But questions were immediately asked about why the kids weren't found earlier – just the day before, detectives had visited the farmhouse as part of door-to-door enquiries – and people demanded to know why Swann, who fitted the classic profile of a disturbed loner, wasn't on their radar. The decisions made by Carrington were debated in the press. Basic procedural mistakes were revealed to have been made in the investigation, culminating in a tragic confrontation, and Essex Police's reputation took a battering.

Investigative procedures were tightened and Carrington took early retirement. In effect, he jumped before he was pushed. The gossip around Victoria Avenue was that he left the force a broken man, haunted by the death of the young girl in his arms.

Coverage of the case gripped the nation; it was all anyone could talk about. The hunt for the missing kids had dominated the news 24/7. Reporters from across the world flooded into Southend.

And Swann's crime was cemented in infamy when it was given a name, thanks to a photograph taken at his ramshackle home. His dilapidated property was called Baden Place. But when a journalist took a photo of the burnished name plate above the front door, the 'en' in Baden was hidden by a creeper. The image became notorious across the world, and the farmhouse became for ever known as 'the Bad Place'.

Sasha's mobile rang, making her jump. Cleaning her sticky fingers with a wet wipe, she fished the phone out of her bag. 'Hi, Mum, how's things?'

'The place is a tip,' said Ursula. 'I don't understand how you can live in such a state.'

Sasha squeezed the phone between her shoulder and her ear as she typed 'Bad Place images' into the browser.

'If it's so terrible, don't let me stop you getting out the vacuum.'

'I have already, as you well know, and the hoover bag is packed as solid as your father's bowels.'

Sasha winced. 'There are some bags in the cellar.'

'I'm not going down there,' said Ursula dismissively. 'The steps are too steep. I'll be discovered hours later, groaning on the floor like those silly grannies in adverts for panic buttons.'

'Then put your feet up. Kev can get them when he gets home.'

Sasha scrolled down dozens of images of Swann's remote farmhouse. Saw police vans and crime scene tape; the overgrown entrance to a lane; an aerial photo taken above the countryside, a big red arrow pointing to Swann's home on scrubland at the edge of a dense wood.

'I can't live in a mess,' said Ursula. 'That may be what your dad desires to do in his remaining days, but it's not for me. I'll go and buy some.'

More images. A pair of overweight detectives outside the house; men and women in forensic suits. Sasha remembered standing at the perimeter of the crime scene as support vans and emergency vehicles came in and out. It was a long and exhausting shift, the black night fading to drab grey morning, and she didn't leave the scene till noon the following day.

'Why don't you do that?' said Sasha. 'And get yourself a nice coffee.'

'Why would I want to waste money on a coffee when I can have a perfectly good cup here. You're basically paying for froth.'

There were photos of the kids the morning after they had escaped the Bad Place. Gaunt, dirty, with wide, frightened eyes. Sasha recognized Michelle and Karin, Lydia and Paul. And there was a school photo of a pretty girl in a smart school uniform – Becky, the girl who didn't get away.

Then Sasha scrolled down to three images of a shy-looking man in glasses with orange lenses, and leaned back.

'Are you phoning for any reason, Mum?'

'Have you by any chance spoken to your father?'

Finally they had arrived at the real reason for her call. She would never admit it, but she wanted Sasha to act as intermediary.

'I haven't had the time.' It was a lie, but she didn't want to say her dad had refused to answer the phone. 'I'll try later, I promise.'

'What time will you be coming home?' asked Ursula. 'Because your family need to see you.'

Oh God, she had promised Denny she would get home at a decent time, but her hopes of keeping that promise were fading fast. Not her first parenting fail and certainly not her last.

'Got to go, Mum, I'm late for a meeting!'

Sasha killed the call and threw the phone across the desk, peering at the photos of the man in the tinted glasses. Jerry Swann. Loner, abductor, murderer.

The first image was a head-and-shoulders photo ID taken at a warehouse he had once worked at. His face was soft and featureless. Badly cut hair billowed over his ears but lay flat and lank on the top of his head. Ginger fuzz curled over his upper lip, and his weak chin barely seemed to protrude from his neck.

The next photo was taken at a company Christmas party. White tinsel and paper chains hung in a canteen. In the foreground, a gang of drunken men and women laughed and leered at the camera. Jerry stood at the edge of the image watching them, the camera flash bouncing on the coloured lenses of his glasses so that his eyes seemed to blaze with satanic fury. In stark contrast, the rest of his bland face was blank, immobile; he didn't look happy or sad. He was just *there*, ignored by everyone.

And there was one final photo of Swann, sitting self-consciously in a deckchair. Oversaturated polaroid colours gave the image a feverish, hallucinatory quality. His chest was bare in the sun and his white legs, protruding from tiny shorts, twisted tightly around each other.

Swann was a nondescript man, the kind of fellow you wouldn't glance at twice in the street, yet he had joined the pantheon of notorious monsters who fascinated the public. Countless books had been written about the Bad Place, all of them regurgitating the same few facts. There had been an award-winning novel, a stage adaptation, even a graphic novel. An American TV movie had transplanted the drama to Minnesota.

Only the other month Sasha had seen advertised a documentary, *Return to the Bad Place*, which dramatically reconstructed the story. The only abductee interviewed was Michelle Dormand, who, according to her website, was also available for TV and radio appearances, celebrity openings and conference events. The child who had encountered Jerry the most was Karin McCarthy. She had reportedly spent hours alone with the killer, but she had always refused to tell her side of the story, despite being offered huge amounts of money to reveal all.

Swann had been cold in the grave a long time. But last night, Lydia Tide had voiced a fear that he had returned. She was convinced he had snatched a teenage girl off a quiet street in Southend, two and a half decades after his apparent death.

And the abducted girl could be Michelle's goddaughter, who was barely eighteen months older than the kids who had been abducted all those years ago.

This is for you, my love.

Sasha realized she had been hunched over her computer for an hour. A group of people were laughing on the other side of the office and she wanted to join in the fun, but she couldn't rid herself of the feeling that something awful had happened to Sammi Manning.

That she had been taken to a Bad Place.

The only thing Sasha could do was fill out the risk assessment and hope that history wasn't repeating itself. She opened the online form on her computer.

'Sasha?' Craig Power flicked his tie over his shoulder to lean in close, resting his knuckles on the desk, his bulging biceps twisting beneath his tight shirt. The smell of aftershave was overpowering.

'Blimey, Craig.' Sasha flapped a hand. 'Do you shower in that stuff?'

'A van's been found abandoned at the edge of town. With clothing inside.'

She pushed her chair away from her desk. 'What clothing?'

'A silver puffa jacket.'

Sasha felt fear flutter in her gut.

Stuff the risk assessment.

9

That was the moment Sammi Manning's disappearance officially became a missing person investigation.

'Sammi left home just after 6 p.m.' Sasha moved back and forth across the office space, making sure everyone in her team could hear her properly. 'We know she went to meet friends from school who were hanging around on the High Street not so very far from here, and she sat with them for over an hour. Then she got a text, she didn't say who it was from, and left soon after. We'll be getting her phone records soon and hopefully that'll shed some light on who she was meeting. A neighbour saw a girl fitting Sammi's description waiting on the street at ten to eight. We know she climbed into, or was *forced* into, a white van within ten minutes of that sighting. The van was found abandoned this morning in North Shoebury, with Sammi's silver puffa jacket inside.'

'The owner?' asked someone.

'Reported it stolen from Canvey yesterday morning,' said Craig.

'A forensics team is working on the van,' continued Sasha. 'So the question is, who did Sammi arrange to meet in Westcliff? And is it the same person who abducted her?'

'A boyfriend?' asked Lolly. 'She was going to see another mate?'

'Maybe it's a random abduction,' said Craig. 'Someone driving along, waiting for an empty street and a vulnerable kid.'

'It's a possibility.' Sasha stopped in front of the whiteboard where she had neatly written a timeline. 'We've a lot to do, lovely people, so let's get going.'

Most of the rest of the day was spent bashing the phones and drawing up the main lines of enquiry, as Sasha put in place her investigative strategy. The vehicle had been moved to the station and a forensic team was swarming over every inch of it, photographing, bagging evidence, searching for prints.

She spoke to the county's search advisors. A PolSA search was being organized for the Westcliff street where Sammi had been snatched, and the surrounding tangle of streets near where the van was abandoned would be meticulously combed for evidence, and CCTV footage collected. Door-to-door interviews in the neighbourhood where Sammi was last seen were due to begin imminently.

A Family Liaison Officer was assigned to Alan and Jessica Manning to keep them informed on the progress of the investigation, and to help the parents cope with the trauma of the disappearance of their child. But the FLO would also provide Sasha with information about Sammi's relationship with her parents and feed back personal details that could shed light on her disappearance.

Officers were currently at the Manning household, bagging up some of Sammi's belongings – notebooks, a diary – and taking away her devices, a laptop and tablet, which would be sent to Chelmsford for examination by the Digital Forensic Unit.

Sasha faced a long afternoon holed up in the meeting room adjacent to the Major Incident Team suite of offices. On sunny days it got insanely hot in that glass-partitioned room so the door was propped open with a chair, to little effect.

There was a strategy meeting with the Essex Police Missing Person Liaison Officer and the Missing From Home Manager, and Sasha spoke with county social services. More comfortable padding about the office in her bare feet, she left her shoes under her desk.

Someone did a coffee run and brought Sasha back a milky latte, her third of the day. She finally managed to eat lunch in the middle of the afternoon, wolfing down a coronation chicken sandwich, another bag of crisps and, in an attempt to convince Ajay she was eating more fruit, some red grapes.

Late afternoon, Ajay and Lolly drove to Sammi's school to talk to the kids who had sat with her outside the Victoria shopping centre, and spoke to other school friends about the people Sammi knew, and her state of mind.

Craig dropped Sammi's phone records on Sasha's desk and she flicked straight to the last message she'd received before she'd left her friends.

It said:

> Please meet me 1 more time

She replied:

> leave me alone

And then, a moment later:

> Please meet me and I will leave you alone I promise
> 8pm Churchill Road

Sammi's last text:

> ok

'The phone?' Sasha asked, pressing a biro against her chin.

'It's a prepaid number, a burner.' He edged his bum on to the top of her desk. 'And it's not pinging anywhere. Switched off, like her own phone.'

'Up!' She raised her palm sharply upwards and he

lifted a buttock so that she could rescue papers from beneath it. 'So she definitely went to meet someone.'

Craig tapped his chin. 'The pen.'

Sasha removed it from her face. The pen was leaking ink everywhere and she dumped it in a bin. She reached into her bag for wet wipes and a compact, peered into the tiny mirror to smear away the ink on her chin, thought she'd got all of it. She jutted out her jaw for Craig to inspect. 'How's that?'

Craig examined it from every angle. 'Got it.'

He hovered, looking like there was something else on his mind, but she checked the task list on her notepad – Sasha was big on lists and religiously ticked off each task as it was completed – and saw she needed to speak to Vaughn. She had written in brackets: *(wear shoes)*.

She slipped them on and rapped on the door of his office. 'I was wondering whether we should organize a press conference?'

'Are you asking me or telling me?' DCI Claude Vaughn was an intimidating man who expected clear decision-making.

She hesitated. 'I think we should.'

The chair's springs creaked in protest as he shifted his large frame. 'When were you thinking?'

'As soon as possible,' she said. 'Tomorrow, if we can.'

Sasha gave him an update on the search for Sammi, and about the texts the girl had exchanged with her mystery correspondent. 'There's still a possibility she's gone off with someone voluntarily. She's fallen head over heels and they've run away. I don't personally believe it, but if that's the case she may not have realized the alarm she's caused.'

'It's your call, Sasha.' Vaughn laced his fingers over his bulging stomach. 'If that's what you want to do, and think it will help, go for it.'

'I do.' She nodded, but wondered if it was the right thing to do. Barely a day went by when Sasha wasn't second-guessing her own decision-making process, when she didn't feel up to the job and worried she was going to get found out at any moment and marched from the building. 'I'll get on to the press office.'

'By the way.' Vaughn lifted a finger to his face. 'You've something on your chin.'

When she walked back into the main office, past the bleeping phones and clacking keyboards, Craig Power was still orbiting her desk.

'Boss,' he said. 'Got a moment?'

'Give me a sec, Craig, just let me... do... this.' She thumbed the screen of her phone to send a message to Kev, asking what time he was going to get home, fully expecting him to ignore it. The days when they bombarded each other all day with texts because they couldn't bear not to be in contact – when it was a thrill to know they were always thinking about each other – were long distant. The message flew away with a *whoosh* and, satisfied, she slapped the phone down. 'What can I do for you?'

'Why am I here?' he asked.

'Well, that's a big question, Craig. I think we all ask ourselves that sometimes.'

He loomed over her, his tall frame obscuring her view of the rest of the office. Craig Power was a talented young detective who had transferred from South London several months ago. He was one of those people who could be absolutely charming when he chose to be, but who was also under the impression he was God's gift to policing. He dragged his heels at the bread-and-butter stuff, the phone-bashing, the slow accumulation of data mined from various sources, all the desk work that was absolutely vital to bringing an investigation to a successful conclusion.

Craig preferred old-fashioned police legwork. He liked prowling crime scenes, interviewing, following up leads around town. Seated at his desk for too long, chained to the phone, he became irritable, even confrontational with other members of the team – but rarely with Sasha, Craig was far too sensible to piss off his line manager. She'd see him scowling at his monitor, one leg restlessly beating an impatient tattoo on the floor. His frustration reminded Sasha of Denny, who would get ill-tempered if he couldn't get to the park regularly for a kick-around.

'DS de Vaz and DC Chambers are out interviewing.

Meanwhile, I'm stuck here.' He gestured at his desk, where he'd been compiling an up-to-date list of local CCTV cameras.

'Don't get neggy, Craig.'

'Get one of the civilians to do it. We've got a misper out there, and you're not playing to my core strengths.'

It was on the tip of her tongue to tell him that his core strength, as far as she could see, was being a pain in the arse.

'Newsflash, Craig,' she said quietly, 'a lot of police work is boring, monotonous, repetitive, and absolutely crucial.'

Exasperated, he returned to his desk, heaved himself into his chair. Sasha liked Craig, he had a great future ahead of him if he lost the attitude, but she didn't like it when he acted like a sulky child. She already had a pair of those at home.

The evening sky was stained a golden and red by the time Ajay and Lolly came back to the office. They were giggling about something, which annoyed Craig. Ajay came over to Sasha's desk with packets of seeds and nuts and dried fruits and placed them in front of her, just as she was finishing a call to one of the force's press people about tomorrow's media event.

'The next time you're hungry,' he told her as she listened on the phone, 'just eat a handful of these.'

She pressed a hand over the mouthpiece, the press manager still speaking in her ear, and poking at the spongy fruit, whispered, 'Your husband is a saint for putting up with you.'

'I'm really hurt, Mrs Dawson.' Ajay made a sad face. 'I'll be over there at my desk, crying my eyes out.'

Late at night, when she ticked off her last task, she finally thought about going home. Most of her team had already left, only Ajay and Lolly were still at their workstations. Sasha was shattered, her joints stiff from hunching over her computer, and her eyes were sore from the stark fluorescent lights. But she was still gripped by the uneasy feeling – that same feeling she had every single day – that there was something desperately important she had left undone.

'Lolly, Ajay, it's ten to ten.'

'Cowboy time!' said Lolly.

'Get yourselves home, we've another big day tomorrow.' Neither of them had to be asked twice. 'Ajay, do me a favour when you get in tomorrow. There was a detective inspector who worked here a long time ago, a man called Peter Carrington, can you get me his contact details?'

'The Bad Place guy.' He made a note of his name. 'Sure thing.'

When they had gone, Sasha took one last look at her emails and saw the press office had sent a link to footage provided by the Mannings, which was going to be released to the press after tomorrow's press conference. When she clicked on it, she saw it was video, taken eighteen months earlier, of Sammi on stage at a school talent show. Sitting in a soft island of light from the desk lamp, Sasha watched the whole performance.

The girl stood awkwardly on stage, looking terrified in front of a packed audience of parents, her palms anxiously rubbing together. A guitarist began to play and the video pulled sharply into a close-up of Sammi, who sang the first trembling verse of 'Bridge Over Troubled Water'. Conscious of all the mums and dads in the audience, her eyes were lifted to the ceiling, and her performance was fragile and full of nerves. In truth, her singing voice wasn't the best, but it was delicate and heartfelt, and her vulnerable rendition suited the melancholy song. Growing in confidence, maybe even enjoying herself, Sammi's eyes closed as she became lost in the performance.

At the end, when the last note had died away, and following a moment of appreciative silence in the hall, Sammi received hearty applause from the audience, and she allowed herself a small smile before she ran off stage.

The video finished, all Sasha could hear was the sound of the traffic passing on Victoria Avenue below. She turned off her computer, laced up her shoes, pulled on her jacket, and thought again about the Bad Place...

The abduction two decades ago of Karin, Lydia, Simon, Michelle, Paul and Becky.

Twenty-six years ago, Sasha had sat beside Karin in an empty corridor in this very building and told her that Becky would come home.

We'll find Becky, I promise, and she'll be safe.

But she never came home. Her reassuring words had proven to be a lie. Thanks to police blundering, Becky died in a pool of her own blood on a cold cellar floor.

But Sasha was in charge now. She finally had a chance to make up for the hollow words she had spoken to Karin many years ago.

She was going to bring Sammi home.

10

It was a quarter to eleven when she got home. She hadn't even yanked the key from the door when her children came thumping down the stairs towards her.

'She won't let me go on my game until I've tidied my room.' Denny's eyes bulged with indignation as he tugged at her arm. 'I tidied it last week!'

'She's driving me crazy!' Angel was almost hysterical with self-righteous emotion. 'She took my phone off me. It's an infringement of my human rights!'

'Back off.' Sasha kicked off her shoes so violently they almost went into orbit. 'Wait, why aren't you both in bed?'

'Why is Nan even here?' cried Angel. 'Just tell her to *leave*!'

Sasha managed to get into the kitchen, placed her bag on the counter. 'She's your grandma and she's going to stay here for a few days.'

'She can stay tonight and go tomorrow, no longer than that!'

Sasha just wanted to get to bed, had to be up again

first thing. She looked around the room, with its sleek fitted cupboards and long central island, and barely recognized it. Usually, every counter was covered with cereal bowls, abandoned all times of the day and night, and licked dry by the cat; random slices of bread, a litter of biscuit wrappers, dumped apple cores and empty yoghurt pots; discarded school books, and clothes. But tonight the room was spotless.

Sitting massaging her toes, she noticed with alarm that her daughter was putting on a pair of trainers. 'Where do you think you're going?'

'Out,' said Angel, as if the answer was obvious.

'Not at eleven at night, you're not.'

'I'm going to the park. Nan said I couldn't, but now you're back, it's fine.'

'Angel,' Sasha insisted, 'you're *not* going out.'

'I'm just meeting friends!'

'It's nearly eleven, it's a school night, you're not going out, end of.'

Angel yanked off her trainers and threw them across the room. She stomped out the door, yelling, 'You're just as bad as your mother!'

'Can you get my Xbox controller off Nan?' pleaded Denny.

Sasha jabbed a finger up the stairs. 'Bed!'

When Ursula walked into the room, Denny hot-footed it out.

'Anybody would think they were trying to avoid me,' her mother said drily. 'Would you like a tea?'

'I've had a long day,' said Sasha. 'I'm going to bed.'

'Is this usually the time you get home of an evening?'

'No, Mum, it's not.' Sasha flicked through the post. 'But a girl went missing today, and it's been kind of busy.'

Ursula thought about it. 'That's no reason for you to neglect your own family. I'm sure the parents of that girl, whoever she is, would understand.'

'The parents are very upset and rightly so.' The mail was all junk and she dumped it in the recycling. 'Besides, I suspect Denny and Angel prefer it when I'm not here.'

'And no wonder.' Ursula pursed her lips. 'They have the run of the place, they sit on their phones day and night and eat rubbish.'

'Kev gets back early for the kids.'

'Does he now?' said Ursula. 'It's not like you'd notice.'

Sasha couldn't meet her mother's disappointed gaze. She often worked long hours – during a major investigation it was unavoidable – and the last thing she needed was her mother reminding her of the fact. Every. Five. Minutes.

These days, everyone in her family seemed to stay in their own personal space, even when she was there. Angel and Denny kept to their own rooms, or never looked up from their phones, and Kev barely seemed to interact with any of them any more. Sasha was terrified that it was all her fault.

Back when the kids were younger, it didn't matter how draining her work was – her days were often filled with the upsetting consequences of abuse and violence, she was forced to process some very grim stuff – she couldn't wait to get home. She'd hear the screams and laughter of her children from the garden gate and go indoors to discover Kev rushing up and down the stairs dressed as a pirate, his face slathered in make-up, chased by Denny and Angel... and Jake toddling behind.

The place would be like a war zone, there would be toys strewn all over the floor – action figures, lightsabers, dolls, those lethal bricks of Lego that buried themselves painfully into the soles of your feet – and pillows, throws and duvets hurled everywhere.

'Help me,' Kev screamed as he rushed past her, pretending to be terrified of the kids in pursuit. 'I'm done for!'

Then he'd fall accidentally-on-purpose and disappear under a pile of giggling arms and legs.

Or, other times, she'd come home to find them all watching a film and discussing it. Going into great detail about a character's superpowers, the science of floating poo in zero gravity, or the particular breed of a talking dog.

'Everybody having fun?' she'd ask and they'd glance

up and sing, 'Hello, Mum,' happy to see her home, and then resume their discussion.

Or they'd all be playing a board game, or on a console together; doing a puzzle; kicking a football in the garden, Kev picking up the kids and swinging them off the ball so that all she saw were her children spinning in the air like helicopter rotors.

Kev was a good dad, Kev was a *great* dad, and the kids loved him.

And when the children had finally been packed off to bed, the two of them would sit together in the garden drinking a glass of wine and sharing a crafty fag, and Sasha would get off her chest all the upsetting things she had seen and heard that day. There were some details she could barely bring herself to utter out loud, it made her too upset, but he'd hold her hand across the table and listen. And when she'd told him about whatever cruel so-and-so she'd arrested that day, or about the nauseating violence against innocent people she'd had to deal with, she'd finally be able to unwind and they'd sit together, enjoying each other's company long into the night.

She and Kev thanked their lucky stars that they had each other and three beautiful kids, and they honestly believed that nothing bad would ever – could ever – happen to any of them.

But that was when they had three children, not two.

And now Kev was... what exactly was going on with her husband?

He always used to be so active, so full of life. When he and Sasha first dated, he was a semi-pro boxer, a decent featherweight. He played football with his mates every Sunday morning, the odd round of golf; he went sailing and fishing. Kev loved a night down the pub, or going to gigs at the Cliffs Pavilion. But he didn't do any of those things now. It was like he was becoming cast adrift from his family. When he wasn't fixating on his cold war with their neighbour, he seemed to drift in and out of the house, going to work and then coming home to hide away in his 'study'. He seemed intent on avoiding them all, even his own children.

And Sasha couldn't remember when there had last been any activity between her and Kev in the bedroom department...

Her mother said, 'I spoke to Stuart today.'

'Who's Stuart?' Sasha was confused by the sudden change of conversation.

'The nice man next door. I apologized for what happened. He was very shaken about it.'

'Please stay out of it, Mum.' The last thing Sasha needed was for Ursula to wade in making everything worse with their neighbour. 'Maybe instead you could tell me what's going on with you and Dad?'

Her mother blinked, as if she had no idea what her

daughter was talking about. 'You have something on your chin, what is that, a bruise?'

'It's ink. Don't change the subject.'

Her mother rolled her thumbs in her clasped hands. 'I think your father and I have come to the end of the road.'

Sasha stared, incredulous. 'Fifty years of marriage and you're just going to throw it all away?'

'I feel like a new start.' Ursula shrugged. 'Better late than never.'

'What does Connie say?'

'I didn't want to trouble her, your sister would be very upset.'

Sasha had to stop herself laughing. Her sister was completely oblivious to the emotional needs of anybody else.

'I'll leave as soon as I can,' said Ursula. 'I'll find myself somewhere cheap to rent... or a hostel, perhaps.'

'Don't be ridiculous, I don't mind you being here.'

'I do,' said Denny, walking into the room. He opened the cupboard where they kept all the snacks and found it empty. 'Where have all the crisps gone, and the biscuits?'

'I've moved them,' said Ursula. 'According to the *Mail*, childhood obesity is a real problem these days.'

'Denny, get to bed.'

When he left empty-handed, Sasha said, 'Thanks for fat-shaming my son.'

'I know you don't want me here.' Ursula's eyes began to mist over. 'And your father certainly doesn't want me back home.'

'Of course he does.'

'Oh, you don't have to lie to me.' Her mother was always indefatigable, and Sasha was shocked to see her so forlorn. There was little sign of the iron certainty that made Ursula Chancellor so impervious to life's slings and arrows. 'I know I can be a difficult person to love.'

'Stop it,' said Sasha softly. 'Tell me what's going on?'

Ursula stood wearily. 'I understand it's hard having an older person in the house. We get under everybody's feet. We don't mean to, we mean well, but after a certain age we're of no use to anybody.' She sighed. 'I'll leave first thing.'

'You can stay as long as you like.'

Her mother said she was going to bed, but ended up fussing around the kitchen, and Sasha went up instead. In the bathroom, she brushed her teeth, wiped off her make-up and peed.

She undressed in the dark bedroom, plugged in her phone, slipped on the T-shirt she slept in. The curtains were pulled but when her eyes adjusted she saw Kev asleep in bed. She leaned close to his face, heard his breath, which was flat and slow, and saw his eyes fluttering beneath the lids.

Climbing in, she pressed herself against her husband's

back. It was still so stifling and she felt immediately uncomfortable, knew she wouldn't be able to snuggle against him for long.

'Kev?' She squeezed his shoulder. 'Can we talk? About this morning, about... everything?'

He grunted, half asleep. 'Tired... tomorrow.'

'You promise?' she asked.

He murmured a yes, but then his breath flattened again into sleep.

Sasha touched his cheek, whispered, 'Who are you and what have you done with my husband?'

11

Sasha drove her Spider Veloce along the esplanade beneath a sky that was a perfect, unblemished blue. Her beloved Spider was knackered now; it had exhaust and suspension problems, and a rusty floorpan, and she very much doubted whether it would survive another MOT, but it was perfect for mornings like this. She could put the top down, pull on her sunnies and let the breeze cool her face on the drive into work.

To her left, the sea glittered in the sun. White fingers of surf crawled placidly up the beach. Tourists were already up and about, wearing football shirts, shorts and sliders. Club crests inked on their calves, ice creams in hand, they pushed baby buggies and prams towards the pubs along the seafront to grab a full English and an early morning pint. Some of the men already had their tops off, revealing angry red shoulders and brown bellies that poured over the elastic of their shorts like tarmac from a tipper, and the women had rolled their bikini tops as far below their tan lines as they dared.

Sasha drove past the abandoned, boarded-up leisure centres with their peeling pink stucco walls; past the Sea Life Centre and the Kursaal estate; the fish-and-chip and kebab shops; and all the new-build apartments with their big glassy windows facing the estuary. The air was thick with the sweet smell of burned sugar from the concession vans selling candy floss and doughnuts.

Usually, she'd turn up towards the station on Victoria Avenue, but this morning she was making a short stop further along the Western Esplanade.

Pulling up at a red light along Marine Parade – Southend pier, the longest in the world, stretched a mile out to sea ahead of her – she closed her eyes for a moment to enjoy the warmth on her face. As soon as the car stopped moving, the dry heat of the morning quickly began to envelop her. It was going to be another hot day, maybe the hottest yet. The arcades were already open and the din of music and electronic sounds, the rings and whooshes and whistles of hundreds of machines, rolled across the street.

Tapping her fingers on the wheel to 'Back for Good' on the radio, her phone rang on the seat beside her. Sasha turned down Magic and put the phone on speaker.

'Sasha,' said Vaughn. 'Do you want me there?'

He meant the press conference with the Mannings, which was scheduled for eleven.

'Don't worry, I've got it covered.'

She recognized someone she knew walking past. It

was the mum of Angel's best friend, Tilly. Or, at least, her best friend until recently. Angel had other mates now, a whole group of noisy girls, her *squad* as she called them. Sasha didn't like the new crowd much, they were loud and brash, and totally different from Tilly, who always seemed so sweet and placid. Sasha missed the days when Tilly and Angel were inseparable.

Sasha pressed on the horn, trying to get Tilly's mum's attention. She didn't know her well, but she was a bubbly woman; they'd met socially a couple of times a year or so back in the day, had even spent an enjoyable night down the pub. For one frustrating moment, her name escaped Sasha. Rowena, Roberta…

'Rachel!' It popped into her head. 'Hold on, Vaughn – Rachel!'

When Tilly's mum looked in her direction, Sasha called, 'Hi! How's Tilly doing?'

But Rachel walked straight past. Sasha was certain they'd made eye contact, but she must have been mistaken.

'It's your call, Sasha,' said Vaughn. As senior investigating officer, Vaughn should probably even make the appeal himself, but he was happy to step back and allow Sasha to run the investigation as she saw fit. Vaughn – nobody called him by his first name, Claude, which he hated, not if they knew what was good for them – was a highly experienced officer, and Sasha regarded him as a friend and a mentor. If Vaughn gave you advice you listened carefully, and if he blew his top you kept your head down. 'Good luck and let me know how it goes.'

She turned the radio back up, drove on towards Westcliff, singing along to 'Torn', and slowly passed her mum and dad's apartment on the first floor of a seafront block. The sliding balcony door was open wide, letting in the light and sun – the white gauze curtain billowed in the breeze – and she saw a newspaper and an empty glass on the coffee table outside.

She parked the Spider and jumped out to buzz the intercom at the entrance, but her dad didn't answer. Sasha stood below the balcony. Usually, he'd be sitting in the lounger in a pair of long shorts, a floppy hat and nothing else, letting the sun soak all day into his skinny body, while her mum moved about inside, tidying and cleaning. Since his retirement, it was all he wanted to do. In the summer, he'd take up his position before breakfast, watching the world drift past, and remain there until the very last rays evaporated from the sky, then head off to the pub. It seemed to Sasha that Alec Chancellor wouldn't be content until every inch of his body was covered in melanomas.

It was no wonder her mum was so frustrated. When he'd retired, Ursula had imagined that she and Alec would see a bit of the world. She had talked exotic cruises, minibreaks at stately homes, retreats and spas, new life experiences in the twilight of their years. Instead, they'd downsized from their big family home in Shoeburyness to this modest one-bedroom apartment on the seafront, where her husband sat about from dawn till dusk.

'Come on, Dad!' He was up there, she was certain, listening to her behind that rippling curtain. 'Let me up, I want to talk to you.'

But she had a busy day on the cards, Alan and Jessica Manning's press conference was this morning, and she didn't have time to play silly games.

'Right!' she called up at him. 'You need to grow up!'

And then she jumped back into her Spider and drove to Victoria Avenue.

12

Working with an Essex Police press officer, Sammi's parents wrote a statement, which Alan rehearsed. He read it again and again but stumbled every single time, rushing some words and mispronouncing others. The press officer suggested a few simple breathing exercises as Sasha sat spinning her fingers in her lap.

She heard the press pouring into the small conference room next door, grabbing seats, setting up equipment. In a few short minutes there would be lights and cameras and microphones, all pointed at the Mannings.

'Thanks, Bronwyn,' Sasha said to the press officer and turned to Alan and Jessica. 'I'll make a short statement first, and then I'll ask you to appeal directly to Sammi. Don't worry about making mistakes, just do your best, you're not actors, you're real people in a very upsetting situation. Then we'll take one or two questions. If you don't feel comfortable speaking, I'm happy to field those. But I ask you to leave any that are about the search to me.'

Jessica Manning listened very carefully to what Sasha had to say and then burst into tears. 'I can't do it!'

Alan put his arm around her shoulder. 'It's going to be okay.'

'Everyone is going to think it's us. People will be watching and they'll be waiting for us to crack and confess that we did away with our own daughter!'

It was true that the police often organized press conferences as a way of putting parents in the spotlight if they were suspected of involvement in the disappearance of their own children, but that wasn't the case here.

'The press and public are absolutely behind you,' said Sasha, 'and this is the best way to get the message far and wide. Appeals like this have proved very successful. If Sammi is with someone voluntarily, she may not have realized the chaos she's caused. She'll see on the news how upset you are, and it'll make her think twice about staying away.'

The door opened and Lolly slipped into the room. 'Ms Dormand is in reception, she says she was invited to the press conference.'

Surprised, Sasha looked at the Mannings, and Alan admitted, 'I asked Michelle to come.'

'You asked her?' Jessica stiffened. 'Why in God's name would you do that?'

'Because she's a local celebrity of sorts and I think she'll help get us publicity.' He squeezed his wife's hand.

'Also, I think she has a right to be here, she's very fond of Sammi.'

Jessica smiled sourly. 'Whatever you say, Alan.'

'She's only trying to support us.'

'If Michelle clicks her fingers, you jump.'

Sasha didn't much like the sound of having Michelle Dormand in the room; she'd be a distraction they could do without. But Alan Manning wanted Michelle there, he was already a nervous wreck, and she didn't want to undermine him any further.

She walked Lolly to the door and whispered, 'Put her by the wall, so that she's not too conspicuous.'

Lolly gave a thumbs-up to the Mannings – 'Good luck!' – and left.

'We can do this,' Alan said, but Jessica was clearly irritated, and Sasha hoped the tension between them wasn't obvious in front of the media.

Camera flashes popped, shutters whirred and phones and tablets were held aloft, as soon as they walked next door. Sasha led the Mannings to their seats behind a table on a raised platform at the front of the room, the giant Essex Police insignia emblazoned on the wall behind them.

The room was packed with reporters and journalists. Broadcast cameras on tripods stood like sentinels at the back of the room.

To her credit, Michelle didn't make any attempt to

draw attention to herself. She sat very still at the end of one row, bag crushed in her lap, never taking her eyes off Alan and Jessica. But it didn't take long for some of the veteran journalists to recognize her, and news of her presence flew around the room. Reporters whispered among themselves; the atmosphere in the room was electric.

'Thanks for coming. I'm Detective Inspector Sasha Dawson.'

Sasha made a short statement about Sammi's disappearance and then introduced the Mannings.

'What can you tell us about the van you discovered with the item of Sammi's clothing in it?' called one reporter.

'We'll be taking questions later,' said Sasha. 'But I'll answer this one now. The vehicle was stolen two days ago from outside an address on Canvey Island and we're currently carrying out forensic tests on it. As soon as we have more information we'll get it to you.' Sasha turned to Alan. 'But now Mr Manning would like to make a direct appeal to Sammi.'

He picked up the written statement with a trembling hand.

'Sammi, if you're watching this somewhere, your mum and I ask you to come home.' Alan spoke in a monotone and Sasha felt the press grow restless. 'If you've... if you've run away...'

Then Alan came to a decision and put down the

statement. 'If you're in any kind of trouble, we don't care what it is, we just want you home. Your mum and I… we're not angry, we're just very upset. If you don't want to come home…' His voice was growing in strength, becoming more impassioned. 'Then please, *please*, contact us to tell us you're okay. Ring us, me and your mum just want to hear your voice, or you can ring the police if you prefer. We want to know you're safe. And if you're being held against your will, then I want to appeal directly to the person who is holding you…'

He dropped his gaze to the table, trying to compose himself, and the room filled again with the click and whirr of camera motors and flashes, as the media captured the strain and anguish on his and Jessica's faces.

'Sammi is our little girl and we miss her deeply. Maybe you're a parent yourself – if you are, you'll know what we're going through right now. I ask you, I *implore* you, to look into your heart. Please… bring our baby back to us.'

Sasha felt tension crackle in the room. Ignoring the written statement, speaking from the heart, was the best thing Alan could have done. He'd made a direct plea to the kidnapper. His raw emotion was dynamite. Nobody – not even these hard-bitten journalists – could fail to be affected by Alan and Jessica's agony. The press conference couldn't have gone better. She'd take a couple of questions and then it would be over.

But then Michelle stood.

She turned to the assembled media, and the cameras and microphones immediately swung in her direction. 'You know me and you know what happened to me.'

'Ms Dormand,' said Sasha. 'I'm going to have to ask you not to interrupt.'

But Michelle ignored her. 'And *I* have an announcement to make.'

Alan and Jessica turned in alarm to Sasha.

'Ms Dormand.' Sasha leaned again into the microphone. 'I don't think—'

The press crowded around her. One man thrust a recorder in her face. 'What's your connection here, Michelle?'

'I'm the girl's godmother,' she said loudly, 'and Sammi is very dear to me, *very dear*. She's a beautiful young woman and so full of the joys of life.'

Lolly Chambers sidled up and touched her arm, trying to guide her to the door, but Michelle yanked away her elbow.

One of the reporters insisted, 'Let her speak!'

Her team looked at Sasha, bewildered, *do we close this down?* But Sasha shook her head. The last thing they needed was for Michelle, a family friend – the girl's godmother! – to be wrestled out of the room in front of the national media.

'Which is why…' – Michelle spoke slowly so all the

reporters could write down every word – 'I'm offering a reward to anybody who comes forward with information leading to Sammi's safe return.'

'Let's get you next door,' Sasha said to the Mannings, and was about to lead them away when Jessica screamed across the room at Michelle.

'Leave us alone!' The reporters turned to stare. 'Why don't you get out of our lives? She's my baby, not yours, she's mine!'

Michelle turned crimson. The phones and tablets moved back and forth between the two women, greedily capturing the confrontation. And then Jessica pushed along the table past Sasha, followed quickly by her husband.

Sasha gestured to Ajay to bring Michelle next door when she was finished giving her own chaotic press conference, and when she walked into the adjoining room, she found Jessica slumped, inconsolable, in a chair, Alan trying to placate her.

'I'm sorry about that.' Sasha was ashamed. 'We should never have allowed her to be here.'

A minute later, Michelle came in with Ajay and Lolly.

'I want her out!' Jessica stood. 'I want her gone!'

Michelle held her head high. 'I just want to help find Sammi.'

Jessica went to her. Sasha and her officers tensed; the last thing they needed was a physical confrontation.

'You can't bear it, can you? You can't bear the fact that she's *ours*. If you had any dignity you would go away and leave us alone.'

'Jessica, please...' pleaded Alan. 'She means well.'

'If she wants the best for Sammi, she should just leave us alone. All these years later and she's still hanging around like a bad smell. Buying Sammi's love, taking her shopping for things she knows full well *we* can't afford to buy her.' Jessica's face twisted with fury. 'You have no shame.'

'I've only ever wanted to help you,' said Michelle.

'We don't need your help, we've never needed your help. Let's not pretend you're doing this for Sammi – this is all about what you want. When Sammi comes home, when our little girl comes back – and she will, I'm sure of it – I forbid you to see her. Alan is mine, Sammi is *mine*.'

Michelle looked at Alan for support, and he said timidly, 'Thank you for everything, Michelle, it's not that we don't appreciate it—'

'Oh, stop being so weak,' spat his wife. 'Stop indulging her!'

'—but we think it's best if you stay away from now on.'

Alan reached for Jessica's hand – and she took it.

'We're going home,' Jessica told Sasha.

'DC Chambers will make sure you get a car.'

Jessica walked to the door, but then retraced her steps

to Michelle. 'Why my little girl? That's what I want to know, why was *she* taken?'

'You can't possibly think I had anything to do with it?'

'I'll tell you what I think. I think you and those other *freaks* from the Bad Place are tainted, cursed, *that's* what I think.' Jessica spoke with a quiet viciousness that made Michelle flinch, and then she and Alan left the room.

There was a terrible silence as Michelle dug in her bag for a hankie. Sasha offered tissues from a box and Michelle pulled out a couple.

'I'll wait till the press has gone.' Michelle dabbed at her eyes, smearing the black rivulets of mascara running down her face. 'And then I'll go.'

'I'll get you a car.'

'My BMW is in the car park.'

'If there's anything I need to know about your relationship to the Mannings,' said Sasha, 'now is the time to tell me.'

'There's nothing.' Michelle waved her away. 'I don't want to talk about it.'

'We should at least discuss what just happened.'

'If you want to talk to me, arrest me.' Michelle lifted her hands in exasperation. 'Lock me up, interrogate me, otherwise I'm going to leave.'

'Nobody's talking about arresting you,' Sasha said. 'I just want to clarify a few things.'

'Not now!'

Michelle Dormand, it seemed to Sasha, wasn't a person who much liked being asked to do something she didn't want to. She left the room briskly, reappearing in the doorway a few moments later.

'I'm lost,' she said. 'How do I get out?'

On the way to the exit, Sasha tried again to ask about her relationship with the Mannings, but Michelle ignored her.

Sasha touched her Essex Police ID on her lanyard to the pad beside the exit. It unlocked with a click, and she pressed the push bar to open it. Michelle stomped towards her BMW, heels clipping quickly on the hot concrete, fishing frantically in her bag for her key fob. Sasha was just about to go back inside when she saw Michelle take something off the windscreen – a piece of paper – and read it. She looked around the car park.

And then collapsed to the ground.

Sasha ran towards Michelle, placing her in the recovery position as other people rushed over to help. As they slowly brought her round, she saw the sheet of paper flutter away in the breeze, sliding beneath cars. She chased it across the car park and stamped her foot down to capture it.

When she picked it up, she saw written, in thick black capitals:

5K. THE USUAL PLACE

13

'She's my girl,' said Michelle, placing a tissue to her nose and blowing. 'Sammi is my baby.'

'You're her godmother, of course you're going to be upset.'

'You don't understand,' Michelle said. 'She's my *daughter*, my flesh and blood.'

Sasha glanced up at Lolly just in time to see her jaw snap shut.

After fainting in the car park, Michelle had declined to go to hospital, insisting she was fine. 'It's been an upsetting day and that note was the final straw.'

'Why don't you go and get Michelle a hot drink?' Sasha said to Lolly. When the DC reluctantly slipped out the door, Sasha waited patiently while Michelle shoved the soggy mess of tissue in a bin.

'You see, me and Alan had a fling. It was a long time ago, well, over fifteen years, obviously. It's difficult to believe now, but Alan was almost handsome back then, and really not so boring. He was a good listener and... he was there. I meet many men and they're all so unreliable, but Alan has always been my constant. I think a little part of him is still in love with me, the poor thing. Anyway, things just happened. It didn't last very long. Between you and me, he was absolutely useless in bed, but he was kind and tender and just what I needed at that time. And, of course, would you believe it, I became pregnant. I never thought I would have kids, never wanted them.' She gave Sasha a brittle smile. 'People don't like it when you say that.'

Lolly returned and placed a white coffee on the table. It had come from the machine, so there was a swirling lump of foamy scum on the top, and Michelle pushed it away.

'I don't drink coffee, caffeine dries the skin. Do you have a chamomile or peppermint tea?'

Lolly picked it up again. 'I'll have a look.'

'Alan and Jessica had been trying for a baby with no success – she has twisted tubes, nobody's supposed to know that – and when she'd *finally* calmed down, we all realized there were benefits to the situation. It was agreed that I would give them... the baby. I thought I'd never see her again, my Sammi, I thought I'd never want to, but it was so hard. I found myself wondering *what if*. And in recent years, yes, I've been going there a lot, playing the fairy godmother, taking her shopping and for spa treatments. Jessica hates me taking an interest, but Sammi's a lovely girl and a lot of fun, unlike her so-called mother.' She ran a finger along the bottom of a teary eye. 'What a lovely young person she's grown into.'

'Tell me about the blackmail,' said Sasha. 'How long has it been going on?'

Michelle shook her head. 'Six or seven years, something like that, I can't even remember. The first note I was sent said they knew all about Sammi and that they'd go to the press about it. This was back when I had a proper profile. Now I'll get a note maybe once or twice a year. There'll be a figure on it, and I'll pay it and forget all about it until I receive the next one. They're usually placed under the windscreen or posted through my letter box.'

'You make it sound like something you live with.'

'It feels like a part of my life now. I just pay it. The amounts are always modest, a couple of thousand here and there, silly money really.'

'Why do you pay?'

'I'd like nothing more than to tell the world that Sammi's my daughter. But I made a promise to Alan and Jessica. It would break Jessica's heart if Sammi found out. And what if she rejected me? She may never want to see me again – I can't take that chance.'

Sasha slid her hands between her thighs and leaned forward. 'I'd like you to think very carefully before you answer this next question, Michelle, because Sammi's safety may depend on it. Do you think the blackmailer could be the same person who took her?'

Michelle looked surprised. 'It never occurred to me.'

'Who knew about your pregnancy?'

'A number of people knew back then, I suppose, I was showing for quite a while, but I can't remember who.'

'What about your husbands?'

Michelle said bitterly, 'I never told any of them about Sammi, mostly because they were never around long enough. They've only been interested in my money. I know it's crazy but...' She was about to say something but stopped herself with a dismissive flick of a hand, making her bracelets jangle. 'It's nothing.'

'Go on,' urged Sasha.

'The other night, Lydia was convinced Jerry Swann is still alive... what if she's right, what if it was all a lie, a cover-up? What if Jerry really got away, and now he's come back and taken Sammi?'

'Jerry Swann died a long time ago, Michelle. His body would have been autopsied and cremated.'

'Then he has family, an accomplice,' she said impatiently. 'Otherwise, why would this happen again? To me, to someone I love – my *daughter*! Somebody needs to explain that to me!'

Lolly returned with a herbal tea and Michelle snapped, 'Take that away.'

She rooted in her bag and took out a half bottle of vodka, unscrewed the cap.

'I'm afraid you can't drink that here,' said Sasha.

Michelle snorted. 'After the day I've had, I'm afraid I don't give a shit.'

She took a long swig and shut her eyes, placed the back of her hand to her mouth for a moment.

Sasha watched her. 'When will the blackmailer be expecting the payment?'

'This afternoon,' said Michelle, replacing the vodka in the bag. 'There's a usual place I leave it. But I suppose you'll probably want me to refuse to pay this time.'

'Oh no,' said Sasha. 'You're going to pay the money as usual. And we'll be there when you do.'

14

S itting at her desk, Sasha spied Vaughn's giant figure
striding through the room. He gave her the briefest
of glances and disappeared into his office.

'Wish me luck,' she said under her breath. Lolly gave
her a look, meant to be sympathetic, which only fuelled
Sasha's anxiety. She picked up a slim folder from her
desk and knocked on his door.

'Come in.' Vaughn nodded to the chair in front of his
desk. He picked up a remote and pointed it at a television
in the corner. The screen flared into life and there, on a
rolling news channel, was the press conference in all its
hideous glory. Sasha saw the reporters pressing around
Michelle, pointing their recording equipment in her
face as she announced, 'You know me, and you know
what happened to me.'

Michelle spoke about the reward money and the
cameras swung greedily back and forth between her and
the Mannings, who looked shocked and upset.

'Do we have to watch it?' said Sasha. 'I don't need to
see it again.'

But Vaughn didn't make any attempt to turn it off.

'Here comes the best part.'

The cameras whipped back again just in time to see Jessica scream at Michelle and scramble along the table to get out of the room, followed by Alan and Sasha. Cringing, Sasha reached down to massage one ankle so she didn't have to look at the screen, and realized she was barefooted.

'You want to tell me what the hell happened there?' Freezing the image of Michelle with her mouth open, Vaughn threw down the remote. 'It's all over the television and radio. It's trending on Twitter and other social media sites.'

'I suppose you could say that where a missing girl is concerned, all publicity is good—'

'*I'm* talking.' He climbed out from behind his desk and began to pace. 'We're a laughing stock. The Super is almost deranged with anger. The Baden Place connection is making everyone upstairs nervous. It wasn't exactly the force's finest moment, a girl was murdered in cold blood because of police bungling. And you gave that Dormand woman a platform to remind the whole world.'

'I made an error of judgement, Vaughn. She should never have been allowed to attend the press conference. I've let you down.' She stood. 'And if you have no confidence in me, the best thing is that I step aside and allow someone else to run the investigation.'

'Don't be ridiculous,' he snapped. 'And sit down. We can't *both* walk around the office.'

'Thank you, Vaughn. If you think I'm up to it, if you still have faith in my abilities, then I'm happy to stay in charge, so thank you.' Sasha realized she was unable to stop all the words pouring from her mouth. 'That's good. Yes. Thank you.'

'And for God's sake stop fishing for reassurance.'

'Sorry.'

Vaughn sighed. 'Look, Sasha, you're a decent detective, nobody's going to tell me otherwise.'

'I'll be honest with you.' She grimaced. 'That sounds an awful lot like a backhanded compliment.'

Like anyone else who cared deeply about her job, Sasha was the first person to rebuke herself when she made a mess of things, and this morning's fiasco – and that wasn't too strong a word for it – had shaken her confidence. The appeal to find Sammi Manning was entirely lost in the frenzied coverage of Michelle's outburst. A young girl's life was at stake and the thought that she could have put her in further danger made Sasha feel sick.

The DCI nodded at the phone. 'I'm sick of taking angry calls from the Super and the Chief Super and they're sick of taking calls from the Chief Constable's office. So give me something, anything, to show you're making progress on this thing.'

'Michelle is being blackmailed,' Sasha said quickly. 'She's the missing girl's biological mother. She had a fling with Alan Manning and Sammi was conceived. She gave the baby to him and his wife to bring up as their own. Straight after the conference, Michelle received another blackmail demand.'

'And you think it's connected to the abduction?'

She opened the folder and placed copies of the news articles about the Bad Place on his desk, and a photocopy of the blackmail note.

5K. THE USUAL PLACE

'The odd thing is, Sammi was snatched a street away from where Michelle was meeting the other people who were abducted with her all those years ago. The kids from the Bad Place.'

'Don't call it that.' Vaughn dropped unhappily into his chair. 'It was called Baden Place.'

'Yes, Baden Place, of course. They have a kind of reunion every year.'

Vaughn picked up the note. 'So this could be from the same person who's taken Sammi Manning?'

'It's possible.' She placed her elbows on the edge of his desk and watched him read it. 'The blackmailer may have decided that they're not getting enough bang for their buck and decided instead to abduct her daughter.

But there's no reference to Sammi, and a sheet of notepaper shoved under a windscreen wiper is pretty low-tech in this day and age.'

'Five grand doesn't seem like much of a ransom demand.'

'Michelle is going to take a package of money to the usual drop-off this afternoon. As soon as someone tries to collect it, we'll move in.'

'Okay, keep me across it.' More calm now, Vaughn settled back. 'How's DC Power settling in?'

'Honestly? I like him but it's been a bumpy ride so far. Craig blows hot and cold. He also has a tendency to rub people up the wrong way.' Craig's arrogance and Big City attitude, the way he talked constantly about all the exciting investigations he worked on at Brixton, name-checking gangsters and crime lords, went down badly here on the Thames Estuary, where things moved at a slower pace. 'I don't understand it, he came highly recommended by the Met.'

'Course he did, they probably wanted him off their hands. Power sounds like me when I was his age. I was desperate to make my mark, too. Let me know if you want me to have a word.' He thought of something else. 'And how's that husband of yours?'

'Kev?' Sasha smiled blandly. 'He's top of the world, as always, and the kids are doing great.'

A few months back, Sasha and Vaughn and their other halves had gone to a swish restaurant. It was an enjoyable evening, the food was good, if pricey, but she and Kev were intimidated by Vaughn's wife, Miranda, an effortlessly glamorous lady.

Vaughn and Miranda had two adolescent sons who were tall and handsome, athletic, polite and both on track to attend Oxbridge. Sasha tried not to compare her own children to others, but Denny and Angel weren't what anybody would call academic. Getting them to put down their phones and pick up a book was like getting blood from a stone.

'It's a digital world now,' Denny had teensplained to her when she'd tried to impress on him the importance of learning and books in general. 'It's all about music, games and movies. Reading is for *old* people – the over 25s.'

She certainly didn't want to be one of those demanding 'tiger mums', pushing and cajoling her kids to study 24/7, but the worry gnawed at her that she wasn't home enough, or emotionally and physically available to them; that she didn't support them enough with their schoolwork or encourage them to do more extracurricular clubs and events. But the reality was, her work was all-consuming.

Vaughn led her to the door. 'You're not going to find the girl by running yourself into the ground. Look after yourself. Manage, sleep, eat, don't try to do it all by yourself.'

'I will.' Karin's dismal stare all those years ago popped

into her head once again; it was the look of a child who had been to hell and back. 'I'm afraid for Sammi, Vaughn.'

'I know you are,' he told her.

'I really need to bring her home safe and well.'

'Which is why you're exactly the right person to lead this investigation.' His endorsement was like a dopamine hit – it instantly made Sasha feel better. He swung open the door and she was about to leave with a spring in her step when he pointed at her feet. 'And Sasha, I've told you before, wear shoes the next time you come into my office.'

15

They sat on the bench beneath trees at the edge of the park, Craig with his arm stretched stiffly behind Lolly's shoulder, heads close together, as if they were a canoodling couple.

A few wispy clouds drifted slowly across the sky thanks to a stuttering breeze that was a welcome relief on another day of unrelenting heat. Near the entrance, someone was using a portable barbecue, which was against park regulations. Wasps and flies buzzed around the mouth of a smelly waste bin beside the bench.

'Get closer.' Lolly was enjoying Craig's obvious discomfort, and she swung her leg over the top of his. 'You've got to make it look real.'

'Just for the record,' Sasha's voice crackled in Craig's earpiece, 'you make a lovely couple.'

Sasha was watching them from an observation point in a bedroom of one of the terraced houses on the far side of the green. Craig couldn't tell which one; all he could see was a row of dark, blank windows reflecting the sun.

There were other officers nearby, too. The park keeper who repeatedly swept the same portion of pavement on the other side of the green was a surveillance officer, and so was the pizza delivery guy enjoying a fag break on the railings. There was even a drone if they needed it, Sasha told them, although she was reluctant to use it in case it spooked the target.

Craig wondered how long he was going to have to sit there, with Lolly Chambers practically draped all over him. He shifted uneasily, feeling the weight of her leg on his.

'You're meant to be in love, Craig,' said Sasha, 'smile a bit more!'

Lolly resting her head on his chest was the last straw. 'Do you really have to do that?'

'What's your girlfriend like?' she asked.

'She's a model,' he said. 'And actress.'

Lolly lifted her head, impressed. 'Is she famous?'

'It's only a matter of time, she's picking up a lot of heat in the industry.'

'I bet she's beautiful. When do you see her?'

'She's based in London, that's where all the work is, and we're both busy people.'

'You must miss each other a lot. It must be hard for you both.'

'It's hard for me,' he said, 'being stuck in this dump.'

'Oh.' Lolly sat up straight. 'Don't you like it here?'

He snorted, as if the answer was obvious.

'Sea, sand, sunshine. What's not to like?' Lolly watched a plane disappear silently over the top of the trees, a pinhead of light in the sky. 'Listen to how quiet it is here. In London it's all noise, noise, noise.'

Annoyed that he had been positioned too far from the drop-off point, Craig scanned the park. 'Some of us want to go where the noise and excitement is.'

'I like to see the good in people, Craigy,' she said, offended. 'But you make it difficult sometimes. Southend ain't the most glamorous place. It ain't as exciting as your London, mate, but some of us like it that way. My friends are here, and my family, and I don't like people being nasty about it.'

Lolly Chambers was usually a cheerful little thing, he couldn't remember her ever being in a bad mood, and it amused Craig to see her all riled up. Red spots appeared on her cheeks, her threaded eyebrows leapt up her forehead.

'A piece of advice.' He rotated his ankle to get some circulation back into his leg. Was it his imagination or was she pressing down harder on his thigh on purpose? 'If you want to move up the ladder, then you're going to have to think bigger than the seaside, know what I mean? Don't be a tourist in your own life.'

'Oh, you're so clever, Craigy,' she said sarcastically. 'If that's what you think, then why are you even here?'

'I saw an opportunity for advancement and I took it. But don't worry, I'm not going to be here for long. It's a stepping stone for me. What I really want to do is join the National Crime Agency.'

'You do realize, Craig, that I can hear everything you say?' said Sasha in his earpiece.

'Ouch.' Lolly laughed, but she kept her leg hooked over his and he didn't tell her to remove it.

Sasha told all the officers positioned around the park, 'Here she comes.'

When Michelle Dormand walked along the pathway on the far side of the green, heading towards the bin, Lolly turned to watch.

'You're going to give us away!' Craig said.

'I'm watching out the corner of my eye.' She flashed him an angry glance. 'I know what I'm doing, fanks.'

'She's dropping the money in now,' said Sasha, as Michelle paused at the bin to push a brown envelope into the slot, then walked quickly out of the park.

'I hope the target comes soon,' he muttered.

'Me too, mate!'

They sat in tense silence for another ten minutes. Craig couldn't help noticing the way Lolly's full lips were pressed together in a terse pout beneath her ski-jump nose.

Then he felt her stiffen as a figure walked purposefully across the grass. It was a tall man in camo trousers, heavy boots and a fleece. The sun was behind him, making the detail of his face a blur, no matter how much Craig squinted.

'Now you're looking!' complained Lolly as he tracked the man's progress towards the bin. 'He's going to see you.'

'I got this,' he said.

'Look at me instead, because we're meant to be in love.'

Annoyed, Craig looked into her eyes – they were a vivid pale blue surrounded by an ocean of white – and her gaze was unflinching. One moment became another moment, and then a bit longer than that, and then Craig said, 'He's gone past.'

'Yeah, thank God,' she told him, but they were still looking at each other. Then they both reluctantly turned away to watch the man arrive at the bin. He circled it nervously, glancing around the park.

'Wait for it...' warned Sasha's voice. They watched him crouch at the slot, whip out the envelope – and walk away.

'Strike, strike, strike!' commanded Sasha and the surveillance officers moved swiftly towards the man from all over the park. Lolly jumped from the bench in pursuit, and Craig stood – and nearly fell over.

'Son of a b-!' The weight of Lolly's leg had made his go dead. Craig stumbled after her, pounding his foot down hard to get the circulation going, but he was already losing pace with the others, when all he was focused on was making the collar himself. Pins and needles shot up and down his thigh as he limped along, but he kept going.

The target saw the officers closing in from every direction and vaulted over a railing and out of the park, heading towards a tall fence at the end of a row of gardens. He hooked his arms over the top and swung out of sight. A couple of officers took a run at it, but didn't manage to get over and slid uselessly back down.

'Go around the side,' shouted Craig, leaping the railing and racing towards the fence, gaining momentum, feeling his leg coming back to life – and sensing an opportunity to make his mark.

He took a running jump at the fence. Heaved himself up and over, falling into a rose bush on the other side. Thorns tearing at his face and arms, he scrambled to his feet, ran across the garden. The spray swishing from a rotating sprinkler system cooled his face.

Craig ran at the next fence, hauling himself over. He stumbled over a child's plastic pedal car, just about landing upright, and his right foot sank into a cold paddling pool.

The top of the head of the man he was pursuing was just visible in the garden ahead as he lunged at the next fence. But it was old and rotten and crashed to the ground beneath him, sending him tumbling into the next garden.

A yapping dog ran from a back door; Craig glimpsed a brown thing with short legs rocketing towards him, and he picked himself up and went for the next fence. The dog leapt at his leg and tore his jeans, the growling animal hanging at his ankle until he finally managed to shake it off. He twisted over into the next garden, where he trampled through the flower beds. The target was already climbing over a wall ahead.

Adrenaline kept him going. He reached that last brick wall and managed to scramble up it. His fingers straining to get a grip, feet scrabbling to find purchase on the dusty brick.

Exhausted, he fell in a heap on a grass verge, found himself back on a street. The guy was still ahead of him, limping down the middle of the road – he'd done himself some damage. Craig pressed his hands into the grass and staggered to his feet. He heard voices behind him, officers rushing around the corner.

Long legs pumping, letting out short, sharp breaths, sweat pouring down his back, Craig was determined to get to the man first. This was why he'd become a copper, not sitting in a bloody office all day.

He was gaining on the target. And then a car came down the road from the other direction, and it screeched to a halt in front of the man, who fell against the bonnet and rebounded off it, landing lightly on his feet, and ran back towards Craig, who was ready to charge him to the ground.

But the man swerved at the last moment, Craig misjudged his momentum, and they clashed shoulders. He spun in the air and rolled along the road, and by the time he came to a stop, Lolly was grappling with the guy, pressing his face into the tarmac and handcuffing him.

Within moments, he was surrounded by other officers.

Craig picked himself up from the floor, smacking gravel off his grazed palms.

'You were lucky,' he told Lolly. 'I did all the hard work.'

'It's about being in the right place at the right time, mate.'

Arriving on the scene, Sasha was panting from the exertion. She placed her hands on her knees, getting her breath. 'Give me... a minute.'

'You do not have to say anything.' Lolly pulled the man to his feet. 'But it may harm your defence if you do not mention when questioned something which you later rely on in court. Anything you do say may be given in evidence.'

Finally straightening up, Sasha looked at the man, and her eyes opened wide.

'It's you.' She shook her head in amazement. 'I know you.'

16

They placed him in Interview Room 2, let him stew there for a while. Simon Parkin looked older than his forty years. As long as you didn't look closely at his stained teeth, he was handsome still, with tangled, curly hair bleached by the sun, and a strong jaw covered with patchy tufts of blond. But his face was ruddy, blotched, the result of a life spent outdoors. Deep crow's feet crinkled the skin around his eyes. His scruffy clothes were old and functional and looked like they needed a good wash.

Hands laid flat on the interview table, he smiled faintly at a top corner of the room, as if his physical form was sitting in the nondescript space, with its four uncomfortable plastic chairs, square table and recording equipment, but his mind was somewhere else. In all the time they'd stood there watching him, a good few minutes, Simon's gaze hadn't shifted from that corner, the distant smile hadn't left his face.

'Simon was at the reunion dinner for the kids from the Bad Place, along with Michelle,' Sasha told Craig as they watched him through the one-way window. 'I can't remember him uttering a word.'

'Guy's a total space cadet,' said Craig.

As a detective inspector, Sasha didn't tend to interview suspects, she left that to lower-ranked members of her team, but they both knew she was going to make an exception for Simon. When they went inside, Simon's gaze didn't drop from the ceiling. Sasha sat opposite him while Craig leaned against the wall. He stepped away to get a better look at whatever Simon was staring at, but didn't see anything to his satisfaction.

'What are you looking at?'

'Silver clouds drifting across a gibbous moon.'

'Course you are,' said Craig.

'How are you, Simon?' Sasha laid a folder on the table. 'Remember, you have the right to a lawyer. We can get the duty solicitor, or there may be someone you want to bring in.' Simon shook his head. 'Is there anyone we can phone to let them know you're here?'

He thought about it a moment and then said, 'Karin.'

'Karin McCarthy, yes? We'll let her know.' Sasha made a note of it and said, 'I'm afraid we don't have an address for where you live.'

'I don't have one.'

'You don't have a permanent address?'

He shook his head.

'Okay, Simon, let's start with why.' He gazed over Sasha's shoulder at the drab blue wall, and she again had the sense that his body was in the room, but his mind was roaming free somewhere. 'Michelle estimates that she's been blackmailed to the tune of maybe eighteen to twenty thousand pounds in the last seven or eight years. Is it you, Simon, who's been blackmailing her?' His eyes met hers very briefly, and they were full of hurt. 'Can you tell me why?'

'He's homeless,' Craig said when Simon didn't answer. 'So of course he needs the money.'

Simon's attention whipped to Craig. 'Money is the last thing I need. I've no interest in it.'

'Good for you.' Sasha bit thoughtfully on the lid of her pen. 'That's very laudable. But you can understand my confusion, then. If you have so little regard for money, why on earth are you extorting it from Michelle?'

Simon sat back in his chair and sighed. 'I've admitted it, it was me, what else do you need?'

'A teenage girl went missing two nights before you demanded money off Michelle.'

'Okay, wait.' Simon's focus snapped back into the room. 'I've got nothing to do with that.'

'You've admitted to blackmail, which means you know she is the girl's biological mother. That's a hell of a coincidence, Simon. What are we meant to think?'

He scraped his fingers through his hair. 'You've got it wrong.'

'Then tell me where I'm wrong. Maybe it's time we got you that lawyer?'

'No,' he said. 'I want Karin in here.'

'Karin's not a legal representative, so I'm afraid that's not going to happen.'

'I thought Michelle was your mate,' said Craig, dropping into a chair. 'You often go about blackmailing mates?'

Simon shrugged. 'We knew each other because of… what happened to us a long time ago. But she's not my friend. I don't *do* friends, friends just hold you down, they make you immobile, they lock you into a single place, a single linear reality.'

'I'm gonna be honest with you,' said Craig. 'You've totally lost me there.'

Simon counted off on his fingers. 'Think of all the things that hold you back from discovering your true self. Husbands, wives, children, work, relationships, colleagues, possessions, homes, rent, mortgages, bills, pets, holidays, insurance, tax, cars, computers, social media, phones, *friends*. All that stuff is like a weight, it tethers you down, and before you know it you're stuck in one place, unable to move freely. The seaside, the village, the city, wherever. I've spent a lifetime trying to have a simple existence unencumbered by all the shit that buries us. Right now, I can go anywhere I want, when I want. Feel the wind against my face on a clifftop, swim in the sea, climb a mountain, watch the Northern Lights. I go where I fancy.' He pointed at each of them in turn.

'You get to spend all your days sitting in this cramped little room. Me, I'm free.'

Craig frowned. 'Not right now, you're not.'

'How do you know about Michelle's personal situation?' said Sasha.

'She told me years ago at one of the reunions, she was so drunk she probably didn't even remember afterwards.'

'It's a pity,' said Sasha.

'What is?'

'Whether you regard her as a friend or not, she thinks of you as one.'

Simon looked away. 'We meet once every year, and that's it. We're very different. She needs lots of *stuff* to validate her life, and I need nothing.'

'You both experienced a terrifying situation, doesn't that count for anything?'

'The Bad Place, you mean?' Simon laughed bitterly. 'Let me tell you about that. That cellar was the best thing that ever happened to me. I became very ill down there, I could have died. After a while I would have been forgotten. And it made me realize it's nice to be forgotten. After the Bad Place, I felt free to just... fade away. I didn't need a warm bed to sleep in, or hot water, or central heating, all I needed was to disappear. I had an epiphany – I could go anywhere I wanted, and nobody would care. My favourite thing is to pitch my tent in the middle of nowhere and sleep beneath the stars. Nobody knows where, nobody cares.' His gaze drifted back to the ceiling. 'That's me, that's what I'm about.'

'Is that where Sammi is, Simon?' asked Sasha. 'In the middle of nowhere?'

He looked shaken. 'I told you, I don't know anything about that.'

'Was that a blackmail note you left on Michelle's windscreen, or a ransom note?'

'It wasn't a ransom note.'

'Then why are you blackmailing her?'

Simon blurted out, 'Because he asked me to.'

'Who's *he*?' Sasha leaned forward quickly. 'Who asked you to?'

He didn't answer, but Sasha saw a muscle twitch anxiously in his jaw.

Craig followed Simon's gaze over his shoulder. 'Maybe you should think about getting a lawyer now. Or the only moon you're going to be staring up at is Albert the Con's hairy arse from the bottom bunk.'

Simon's attention snapped back to Sasha. 'I want to speak to Karin.'

Sasha smiled gently. 'I'm afraid that's not going to be possible.'

'Get her here and I'll tell you why I've been blackmailing Michelle.'

'Why?' Sasha asked. 'Why is it so important to you that Karin comes here?'

He thought about it and then said quietly, 'Because she's my friend, the only one I've got.'

17

It was the last lesson of the day at River Hill School, and the final bell couldn't come quick enough. Karin felt the buzz in the room, heard the whispers.

'And, of course, the Stasi had many prisons where they locked up their political prisoners, innocent people who were degraded and subjected to intense psychological and physical abuse.' She turned to the presentation on the whiteboard. 'These places were little more than dungeons.'

'Excuse me, miss?' called one of the kids. 'Do you have one of those?'

The chatter in the class grew more excited. Ignoring it, Karin picked up a textbook. 'So if you'll turn to page—'

'Have you got one of those, miss?' repeated the pupil, and she turned to see Charlie, one of the jokers in the class, with his arm raised.

'Charlie.' Karin felt queasy. 'Do you have a question?'

'Have you got a dungeon at your house, miss? Is that where you're keeping that girl?'

The class erupted in raucous laughter and Charlie leaned back, satisfied with the hilarity he'd caused.

'That's enough.' Karin waited until everyone had quietened down, but she knew they were waiting to hear what she would say in response.

People in the staff room knew who she was, of course they did, but it had been a long time since anyone had mentioned the Bad Place – to her face, at least. Now, the abduction of Sammi Manning, and Michelle's connection to the girl, had dredged up the whole thing again. The Bad Place was once again on everyone's lips. Her pupils hadn't even been born when it had happened, and were oblivious of Karin's history, but they knew now. They talked about it behind her back, giggled behind their hands when she passed in the corridor. And the teachers, too. Karin couldn't help but notice the way her colleagues glanced at her in the staff room, as if she were suddenly a stranger.

Maybe if she answered any questions her pupils had, if she was honest with them, the whole thing would blow over. At least she could try to shoot down some of the more outlandish rumours that were circulating. So she lifted herself on to her desk and faced the class. 'Is there anything any of you want to ask me?'

'Is it true, miss?' asked a girl at the front. 'Was you kidnapped as a girl?'

Karin nodded. 'Yes, it's true.'

They all started chattering, excited at hearing the truth straight from the horse's mouth.

'And one of the other kids died, that's right, innit?'

'That's right, she was called Becky.'

'What happened, miss?'

Karin folded her arms. 'Myself and five other children were abducted by a man called Jerry Swann. He took us to a farmhouse and we were held captive in a cellar for two weeks, with very little food or water.' She left out the part about the long nights she spent alone with Jerry. 'We all managed to escape but Bex... Becky was grabbed by our abductor. And when the police got to the house, she was... killed.'

One of the kids made a slitting motion across his throat.

'Holy shit,' said another kid. 'It's like a movie!'

'So that's why you've got a dungeon in your cellar.' Eager to get more attention, Charlie raised his voice. 'Because it makes you feel at home!'

There were giggles and gasps, and Karin glanced up at the clock, hoping for the bell to ring.

'I heard you got loads of kids locked up down there. The ones who got their homework in late, innit.'

Everyone roared, except for a boy called Lucas, who doodled on a piece of paper at the back of the class.

'That's enough now.' Karin clapped her hands, trying to reassert her authority, but everyone ignored her, and she knew she was on the verge of losing control of the class.

'Was you abused?' called someone. 'Did he stick his thing in you?'

Karin waited till the noise died down. 'He never touched us, not like that, but it was a very frightening thing to happen.'

'Was Becky your friend, miss?' asked a girl.

'Yes.' Karin swallowed. 'She was.'

'Do you miss her?' asked the girl.

The class went very quiet. Karin felt a knot of emotion in her throat. 'Very much so.'

'Maybe if I don't behave,' shouted Charlie, 'I'll disappear too!'

The kid rolled his shoulders, grinning, drinking in all the laughter.

Lucas didn't even look up from what he was doing when he said, 'Just like your dick disappeared years ago.'

The class roared and Charlie looked furious. 'Fuck off, Lucas!'

But Lucas smirked at Charlie, who jumped up. Lucas stood too, and the boys stood nose to nose at the back of the class. Karin felt her phone buzz in the back pocket of her jeans.

'Stop it, the both of you,' she told them. 'Or you'll do detention!'

But neither of the boys listened, they were too busy staring each other out. Charlie scowled, trying to look menacing, and Lucas stood grimly calm as they locked eyes. The other kids cheered and hollered.

Karin reached into her pocket and took out her phone, hoping it was another teacher offering assistance, and saw the message on the screen:

i miss U ♥ ♥

BeXxx

Shock nearly knocked her off her feet.

Another message. Another message from... it just wasn't possible. Someone was playing a sick joke.

Charlie shoved Lucas in the chest, Lucas shoved him back harder. Karin stared at the message again, the phone shook in her hands – she couldn't think about it, not now – and slammed it down on the desk.

She stepped forward as the bell rang and pulled the two boys apart. 'That's enough! Both of you!'

'I'm going to leave you two weirdos here.' Charlie stepped towards the classroom door. 'You deserve each other.'

When he and the other kids had gone, Lucas stuffed his exercise book into his backpack.

'Thank you for trying to help,' she told him.

'It was my pleasure, miss,' he said, 'because Charlie is a total prat.'

Karin liked Lucas, he was a popular kid, well-mannered and a good student, and she didn't want him to get into trouble. 'But please stay out of it.'

The door was open and she saw pupils streaming along the corridor, some of them taking the opportunity to gawp in at her. What she had told her class would be spreading around the school already. Maybe she should make a statement in assembly.

Lucas was just about to leave when she asked, 'Is everyone talking about it?'

'Pretty much.' He shrugged. 'But there aren't many who think you have anything to do with that girl getting kidnapped, just the usual thickies.'

She sighed. 'Well, that's a relief.'

'Don't worry, miss,' Lucas said with a smile. 'I don't believe it.'

She was gathering up her things, intending to study the message as soon as he had gone, when her phone rang. She picked it up, turning away so Lucas didn't see her hands tremble. She didn't recognize the number on the phone and her immediate reaction – her desperate hope – was that it was Becky calling.

Because she was alive.

But it couldn't be, she knew that. It just wasn't possible. *Was it?*

She held the phone in her fingers.

'Miss?' asked Lucas. 'Aren't you going to answer it?'

She looked up sharply. 'See you tomorrow, Lucas.'

He saw the tension on her face and reluctantly left the classroom. When he had gone, her thumb hovered over the screen.

She was afraid to hope that it could be her. There was so much she wanted to say to Becky, that she needed to explain...

She pressed the button. Put the phone to her ear.

'Yes?'

'Is that Karin...?' The woman's voice was deep – and familiar. Becky would be older now, a grown person, and she'd sound like this...

'This is DI Sasha Dawson.'

Karin realized she'd been holding her breath and exhaled slowly.

'Yes.' She closed her eyes. 'DI Dawson, of course.'

She'd been utterly deluded to even think that... for one stupid moment she'd let herself believe the impossible.

Of course it wasn't Becky. It could never be Becky. Because she was dead, she was surely dead.

'Do you mind coming into the station?' said the detective.

'I don't understand.'

'Simon Parkin has been arrested, it'll be easier to explain when you arrive.'

'Simon?'

'He's asked to see you.'

Karin told Sasha Dawson she was on her way and

tidied her things. And when she pulled her bag over her shoulder, she looked at the message again.

i miss U ♥ ♥
BeXxx

It seemed impossible. But sometimes, surely, miracles *did* happen.

Becky was back.

She had returned.

18

Accompanied by Craig, Karin spoke to Simon in the interview room, which gave Sasha the opportunity to catch up on a few things in the office. A string of urgent emails had arrived, including the details of the calls swapped between Sammi and the mysterious burner phone prior to her disappearance, and she clicked it open.

A total of fourteen messages were sent over several weeks, four months ago, but they were all short statements, curt and anonymous, *please meet me at such a place, at such a time*, as if the mystery correspondent was careful to avoid any personal details; and Sammi, probably under instruction, had replied in terse textspeak, *ok, c u.*

'Lols,' Sasha called across the office, 'I'm mailing you a list of locations Sammi met her mystery caller, in Westcliff, Leigh and Priory Park. See if you can get any CCTV coverage on those dates and times.'

Then she listened to a phone message from a man who

said he was the son of Peter Carrington, the detective who had led the search for the missing teenagers during the Bad Place investigation. Ajay had found a contact number for Ian Carrington, who had phoned Sasha directly. He said his father was living in a nursing home and that she was very welcome to visit him, but that he would have to be in attendance. If Carrington Senior was still the charming individual she remembered from her single encounter with him on the night of Becky's murder, she would welcome his son being there. He gave her the address and told her tomorrow morning would be a convenient time to visit.

As soon as she heard that Karin had left the interview room, Sasha pulled her jacket from the back of her chair and went downstairs.

'Michelle doesn't want to press charges,' she told Karin when she met her in reception, 'she says Simon isn't well.'

'He's had mental health problems in the past.'

'It's in nobody's interest to keep him locked up, so we're going to release him on bail. Simon has given us an address he says he'll be staying at, a cousin's house, but it's important he resides there, Karin, and doesn't try to leave town.'

'I just don't believe Simon could do it, blackmailing Michelle like that.'

'Do you want to get a drink? A café's just opened over the road, and I could murder a coffee.'

At the café, Sasha ordered a cappuccino, and an Earl Grey for Karin. She took pity on a sad-looking pastry imprisoned beneath a cloche and liberated it. She took the drinks outside to a table on the pavement.

Stirring her coffee, Sasha took the opportunity to have a long look at Karin. She was a handsome woman, tall and solid, but she didn't make any particular effort with her appearance. She didn't wear make-up and her hair was tied back in an unassuming ponytail. She was polite but sat with her eyes mostly lowered, absently pulling the ends of her hair, and the way she considered Sasha's questions very carefully before answering revealed a coolness, almost a frost, at her core. Sasha sensed Karin expended a lot of energy keeping people at a safe distance.

When the pastry arrived, it glistened with sticky, calorific moisture and unless Ajay had a pair of binoculars trained on her from one of the station's windows – which wasn't entirely out of the realms of possibility – Sasha was determined to enjoy it away from his judgemental stare.

'You don't realize how much I'm looking forward to this.' She licked sugar off a fingertip. 'Tell me about Simon and Michelle.'

'What about them?'

'Do you know the nature of the blackmail?'

Karin nodded. 'I can guess. The missing girl is her daughter.'

'You know?'

'Michelle wasn't very discreet back in the day, we all knew.'

'Simon doesn't seem to me the kind of person who would blackmail her.' Sasha broke off a piece of the pastry. 'I'm sorry, do you want some of this?'

Karin shook her head. 'I'm as shocked as you are.'

'And then there's the fact that Sammi is missing. That's the kind of coincidence I really don't like.'

'Simon's not one for keeping up with the news, he wouldn't have known that the kidnapped girl is Sammi Manning.'

'And he told us he's not interested in money.'

'When we were kids, it was obvious that his parents were loaded and he was destined for a very comfortable life.'

'How well off?' asked Sasha.

'Enough to live in a big house along the coast with its own tennis court and swimming pool, and to go to an expensive private school. And for his parents to provide him with a trust fund. But they died when he was in his early twenties and Simon divested himself of his inheritance. He gave all his money away to good causes, or to relatives. A lot of people came out of the woodwork back then, but he didn't care, he just wanted rid of it. He now lives off the charity of those same people, the ones who continued to hang around, at least. He has quite a little network of people who let him sleep on their sofas.

He's stayed with me once or twice, but never for long. He'll stay a few nights and then disappear again, for weeks or months, and that's the way he likes it.'

'Where does he go when he disappears, what does he do?'

'He travels about the country, always walking or hitch-hiking somewhere, wherever his fancy takes him. He'll get a job labouring or picking crops. Then he pops up here again, I guess because it's where he grew up – he's like one of those fish who always return to where they were spawned. And when the wanderlust hits him he'll disappear again.'

'So my problem is this. A girl goes missing.' Sasha popped the last piece of the pastry into her mouth and chewed. 'She's abducted in front of Lydia and then it turns out that not only is the girl Michelle's daughter, but she in turn is being blackmailed by another of your... group. That's a lot of coincidences.'

Karin nodded thoughtfully. 'Yes.'

'I spoke to one of our profilers about the kind of person who would abduct a child. They tend to be men with few friends, and who have trouble forming relationships with adults. They're outcasts with a lack of social skills. People like Jerry Swann. And that's also how Simon defines himself, Karin, as a loner. He's a man who goes off on his own for weeks, for months on end, he encourages his own isolation from people.'

She dabbed at the last crumbs of cake with a forefinger. 'Simon's never married, has he?'

'I've never married, Lydia's never married, Paul married for the first time four years ago.' Karin frowned. 'Simon couldn't do something like that.'

'You didn't think he was capable of blackmail.' When Karin turned away to watch the traffic flashing past, Sasha tried a change of tack. 'You know, we met, you and I. On the night you escaped. I spoke to you briefly, but... you were in shock.'

You're safe now.

Karin met her gaze for a long moment. 'What was I like?'

'You were scared, in shock, and no wonder. A lot of mistakes were made that night, and in the investigation, and I'm very sorry about that.'

'It's not your fault.'

'That pastry hit the spot.' Sasha pushed the empty plate away and twisted a serviette around her sticky fingers. 'Lydia said she believed Jerry Swann had come back, and Michelle mentioned the same thing to me. Is that what you believe, Karin, that Jerry has come back from the dead?'

Karin smiled thinly. 'Maybe it's not Jerry who's come back.'

'You mean Becky?' Sasha couldn't tell if she was joking. 'Why would she do such a thing if she were alive?'

'Maybe she's angry with us because we escaped and she... was caught by Jerry. I wouldn't blame her.'

All these years later and Karin was still nurturing her survivor's guilt, thought Sasha, and probably always would. 'I'm sure she would have been relieved to know you were safe. What was she like?'

Karin's eyes lit up. 'She was my best friend in all the world. I had a lot to thank her for. I wasn't a very confident person, my home life was a mess, both my parents were alcoholics, my dad had left home, and I had difficulty forming relationships with people, particularly kids of my own age. Her friendship was literally the best thing ever to happen to me. I clung to her like she was driftwood on the ocean. And her parents were very kind, too, they treated me like a daughter. When things were bad at home, I often slept over at her house.' She smiled. 'I remember snuggling down into the covers in her bed and imagining that her room, her home, all of it was mine; that her happy family was my family. So I lost Becky – but I also felt like I had lost more, I had lost a lifeline out of my own unhappy childhood.'

She dragged her bottom lip under her top teeth, momentarily scraping all the colour from it. 'Bex wasn't a saint, she could be maddening, she always had to get her own way, always had to be the centre of attention, but she was my love. The way she died was... sickening. I wonder all the time what she would have done with her life. A lot more than the rest of us, that's for sure.

Becky would have had it all, no question about it. The perfect family, the perfect home, the perfect career.'

'Michelle's very successful.'

'She tries to convince everyone that she has it all, but Michelle's as fragile as the rest of us... survivors. None of us... me, Simon, Paul, Michelle, Lydia... none of us are what you would call balanced individuals.'

Sasha nodded. 'And is there a Significant Other in your life, Karin?'

'Not even close.' Karin shrugged. 'I've never been interested.'

'You're well out of it,' said Sasha, thinking about Kev's recent behaviour, but Karin's smile stiffened and she realized it must have sounded flippant. 'I'm sorry, I didn't mean—'

'You don't have to apologize. Do you have kids?'

'Three.' Sasha lifted her coffee cup to her mouth before she quietly corrected herself. 'Two. We have two.'

'I like my life. I like being... independent.' Sasha sensed there were few people in Karin's life she could talk to; few people in her life, full stop. She was probably as much of a loner as Simon. 'I'm not looking for a relationship, I'm happy in my own company. There are men I see for... convenience, but I prefer being on my own.'

Sasha, who had always been surrounded by family and friends, listened, fascinated, but then her phone rang, and she answered it.

'Yes, Craig.' Karin watched the early evening traffic

rushing past until Sasha finished her call and dropped her phone in her bag, saying, 'Simon just spoke to my DS and he confirmed he doesn't get the money from Michelle for himself, but someone else. Jim Haskell.'

'Oh, yes.' Karin's face darkened. 'He's Becky's brother.'

Sasha recognized the surname. 'Do you know him well?'

'No, he... doesn't like me, or any of us, very much.'

Sasha Dawson drained her coffee. 'You know another thing about child abductors, Karin? They get a compulsion for it, they can become... addicted to the act. We don't know if Sammi is safe, we don't know how long she has before this person does it again, but I'm not going to let what happened to Becky happen all over again. I need to find her.' A minibus approached, travelling towards Priory Park. 'Where is she, Karin, where is Sammi?'

'I don't know.' Karin watched the minibus full of laughing children speed past. 'All I know is, wherever she is, she'll be absolutely terrified.'

19

The Second Day...

They clung to each other, their fingers slippery with heat and sweat, despite the cold of the basement.

It had sunk in now. They were trapped in this cold place below the earth, in a room filled with shadow. The feeble light from the one naked bulb, protected by a twisted wire cage, barely reached as far as the room's four walls. The dank brickwork was slimy to the touch and greasy water trickled in one corner. Plaster had fallen in chunks to the floor, and damp stained the remaining clumps that clung to the brick. A snaking network of wires and rusting pipes raced across the rotting beams above their heads.

A jumble of stiff, musty blankets lay in a cardboard box sagging with mildew. The basement stank of blocked drains. But the concrete floor was perfectly smooth, as if it had been recently laid, and, except for where the plaster had fallen, swept clean.

Above their heads, they heard footsteps clatter back and forth, the tinny chatter of a radio. A boiler groaned and pipes shuddered.

The kids soon lost track of how long they had been down here. It could have been hours or days. The last thing the man did before he slammed shut the heavy wooden door was demand they give him their watches, and there were no windows so no natural light penetrated the cellar to tell them if it was day or night.

He had marched them inside, roaring at them to *move, move, move*, poking and jabbing the knife and ordering them down the stairs. As soon as they were all inside, the door slammed.

A lock snapped on the other side.

'Someone will come and find us,' Simon said as they huddled together to soak warmth and comfort from each other. 'The police will know we're gone, they'll be looking for us.'

'But what if they don't?' whispered Michelle. 'What if they can't find us!'

'This ain't good,' said Paul, pacing. 'I've got to get home.'

Karin didn't know Paul very well. He was immature for his age, a bit of a joker, and consumed by a frenetic energy – always fighting, running, playing, putting on silly voices, making silly faces – but his bottom lip quivered now.

'You don't understand,' he said anxiously. 'I've got to get back.'

'Maybe the man is nice and it's all been a big mistake!' said Lydia.

'He said he'd kill us!' Michelle snapped.

For a long moment, all Karin could hear was their laboured breathing in that cold room underground.

Lydia turned to Simon. 'What do we do?'

Karin wanted to know what he was going to say, everybody did. If anybody knew what to do, it would be Simon. He was tall and powerful for his age, a rugby player, with that quiet confidence that posh people had, and really clever. But Simon didn't look too good. His face was pale, his eyes flicked restlessly across the bare brick, and his mumbled answer didn't make them feel better.

'We've just got to... sit tight. They'll come for us, probably.'

Lydia said, 'I'm hungry.'

'Is that all you're worried about?' Michelle asked, incredulous. 'That you're hungry?'

'Leave me alone!'

Paul said, 'I've got to get home.'

'We've all got to get home, idiot!' shouted Michelle. 'We're all scared!'

Paul burst into tears. 'I'm *not* scared!'

'I am,' Becky told them quietly. 'And it's alright to be scared, it's only natural, because we're in big trouble here, really big. But do you know what?' She looked at each of them in turn, and Karin took strength from the fact that Becky turned to her first. 'We're all going to get out of here, isn't that right, Simon?'

He blinked. 'Yeah.'

'Shush!' Becky lifted a finger to her lips. 'Listen!'

Upstairs, the radio went off. Any minute now, Karin knew, and the man would be coming down. Everyone looked at Simon, still convinced he was going to take charge of the situation.

'It's a mistake,' repeated Lydia. 'Yeah, that's what's happened, he's picked up the wrong kids.'

'We've got to show him we're not scared.' Becky got everyone to hold hands again. 'And that if he lets us go, we won't say a word to anyone.'

'I won't!' cried Lydia. 'I won't say anything!'

'He's not going to hurt us,' said Becky.

'How do you know that?' Michelle hissed. 'You just don't know that!'

Karin's left hand hurt. Trying to wring out every last bit of comfort and reassurance from her grasp, Paul was squeezing too hard. Cobwebs trembled in the draught coming from the ragged black holes where pipes disappeared into the walls.

They all felt a terrible foreboding and pressed tightly together. Karin felt the clammy skin on their foreheads, the smell of their hot, greasy hair. Looking down at the smooth concrete, all she could see was their scuffed trainers.

And then Lydia broke the circle. She raced to the far wall and sank down, folding her legs to her chest and wrapping her arms tightly around them. The remaining kids stared at Simon, waiting for him to do something.

They heard slow, steady steps on the wooden stairs leading down to the basement – *bang, bang, bang* – and then the lock turned in the door.

'Just let me do… the talking.' Simon looked sick. 'Just let me—'

But when the heavy wooden door opened, they weren't prepared for the furious scowl on the man's face as he ran inside, jerking the knife.

'Over there, all of you! Where I can see you!'

They abandoned the circle to flee to the wall where Lydia huddled. The man lurched forward, moving around the cowering kids, jabbing the knife close.

They cringed against the brick, sobbing. The man flicked the tip of the knife towards the corner, making them crawl on their hands and knees towards it. Expecting to be killed at any moment, they curled there. He pushed his glasses up his slippery nose with a forefinger, an oddly delicate gesture, and Karin saw how his head shook in a nervous tic.

'You are guests in my house. That means you do as I say, you follow my rules. You have good reason to be scared, because I'm not a good man, I'm not… normal. And if you don't do what I say, this is what you'll get!' He made a stabbing motion with the knife. 'Say, yes, Jerry!'

'Yes, Jerry!' they all cried.

'Nobody can hear you here, you're miles from

anywhere. The only person who's going to hear you scream is me, and if I do, I'm going to come down – and one of you will suffer, is that clear?' His top lip curled in a snarl. 'Yes, Jerry!'

'Yes, Jerry,' they chorused.

'You live here now,' he told them. 'You'll sleep down here, there are blankets, I'll bring a bucket so you can do your business. You'll have water, food.'

'I'm hungry,' wailed Lydia.

'Shut up!' Jerry jabbed the knife.

Karin saw Simon lying flat on the floor, his face pressed against the concrete, his eyes shut. To her astonishment, she heard Becky's soft voice.

'May I speak, please?' Jerry stepped back, and she said quickly, 'We're not going to say anything to anyone, Jerry. We haven't seen anything and we think we should go now… We won't say a thing!'

Jerry took out a handkerchief and dabbed at his forehead.

'We won't tell.' Becky's voice was soft and persuasive and Karin knew that if anyone could convince him, it was her friend. 'You have my word. Do it for me, Jerry. *Please*, Jerry.'

Jerry blinked. 'Do it for you?'

And then he lunged, lifting the knife above his head and stabbing it down at her. Everybody screamed, certain Becky was about to die and they would be next, until Karin saw the blade crunch into the wall above her head, heard the clink as pieces of brick and mortar rained down on them.

'This is what I'll do for you. This is what you're going to *get*! *This! Is! What!*' He stabbed and yelled, '*You'll get!*'

Nobody dared to open their eyes until they heard the door slam and the lock click, and were sure Jerry was gone. And then they all lay huddled together, weeping.

20

Jim Haskell opened his front door to Sasha Dawson and Craig Power looking very jolly and relaxed in a summery shirt, which billowed over a bulbous belly, long flowery shorts and yellow flip-flops. He held a pitcher of Pimm's, which was crammed with fruit and ice.

'I don't usually answer the door with a big jug of alcohol in my hand, so count yourselves lucky!' If he was at all fazed by the sight of two police officers on his doorstep, he didn't show it. 'Come in! Come in!'

'Who is it?' called a woman from the garden, where Sasha glimpsed a paddling pool, heard children's squeals and splashes.

'Marco!' shouted one kid.

'Polo!' shouted the others.

'It's no one, luv.' Jim's voice boomed down the hallway and he opened the living room door to guide them in. 'Won't be long, save me some of those hot dogs, yeah?'

'I hope we're not interrupting anything,' said Sasha.

Through a patio door, she could see half a dozen kids sliding in and out of the pool, shivering with delight, while a woman sunned herself in a lounger.

'The nippers have some friends round, so it seemed a good excuse to have a nice drink.' Jim shut the door. 'We're sun worshippers here and soaking up the last rays of the day! Nothing like a bit of Vitamin D to revitalize the soul! Lovely!'

The room was big and spacious, two knocked together, and filled with a pair of large sofas in shiny red leather and one of the biggest TVs Sasha had ever seen.

'Sit, sit.' Haskell clapped his hands as if they were party guests. 'Can I get you anything?'

'You're Becky Haskell's brother,' Sasha said.

'That's me, luv.' He fetched a glass from a cabinet. 'I've just made this Pimm's and it'll be a shame to let the ice melt, so you'll have to excuse my indulgence. I expect you won't partake because you're on duty, I know that from the films.'

He poured the Pimm's, and ice and fruit – sliced strawberries, apple, blackberries – slopped into the glass. On a sideboard was a digital frame where the photo image changed every few seconds. Sasha saw Jim's family on holiday, at a zoo, a kid's birthday party. But there was also a whole shelf dedicated to his sister, Becky: relaxing at home, sitting on a pony as a little girl, and that familiar image of her in the neat bottle-green school uniform, the portrait likely taken days or weeks before her untimely death. She gazed imperiously at the camera, a pretty, confident girl on the verge of womanhood.

'You know Simon Parkin, Mr Haskell.'

'For my sins.' Jim raised the glass. 'Cheers.'

'He's been arrested for blackmailing Michelle Dormand, who you'll also be aware of, and Simon says he's been doing it to get money to you.'

Jim took a long swallow of his drink, the ice shifting in the glass as he tipped it to his mouth, and smacked his lips. 'That's just what the doctor ordered on a hot day like this. Beautiful, love the stuff.' He grimaced. 'Yeah, Simon gives me money, he helps me out financially from time to time, but that's because he's minted, right.'

Sasha watched a wasp land on the sticky lip of the jug. 'Why does Mr Parkin give you money?'

'Because he's a good soul who likes to help me and my family.' He glanced towards Becky's photo. 'I lost a beloved sister, my kids never got to know their auntie. I guess he feels guilty about what happened. I'd no idea that's how he got the money.'

'Guilty about what?' asked Craig.

Jim dug a finger into his mouth to dislodge a piece of fruit pulp from his back teeth. 'That he lived and she died.'

'May I ask what you need the money for?' said Sasha.

'Things.'

'Things?'

'You know, the essentials. Furniture, a car, a summer

house, the occasional holiday. I like to take the family somewhere nice.'

Sasha looked around the big room at the PlayStation and Xbox beneath the TV, the Sonos sound system, and the leather sofas, which looked brand new; at the digital photo display, where images revolved of the Haskells on sandy beaches, ski slopes, at an ancient Asian temple and Universal Studios. All wearing nice clothes, designer gear. She thought of Simon, pounding a solitary coastal path with barely a penny to his name.

'You get away a lot.'

'Travel is good for the soul,' Jim said. 'But, you know, expensive.'

'Why would Simon give you the money to pay for stuff like that?' asked Craig, incredulous. 'Holidays, a new shed.'

'A summer house,' corrected Jim. 'Because Simon is an honourable man who believes he is at fault for how my sister died. She was the best sister a man could ask for, a truly beautiful soul.'

'You'll be aware that Simon gave away all his money years ago.' Sasha smiled sweetly. 'You've been exploiting him.'

'That's not right.' Uncomfortable, Jim cleared his throat. 'There's no law against one man giving another man charity out of the goodness of his heart. As I say, I had no idea how Simon got the money. I can't believe you've come here, into the sacred space of a man's home, into the bosom of his family, to make accusations.' He drained the dregs of his glass and crunched on the ice. 'It's a disgrace, is what it is.'

'How do you know Simon?'

'I've got to meet most of that Bad Place lot down the years in my attempts to get justice for Becky. I found that Simon in particular was very troubled. He thinks he's a free spirit, a bird soaring in the sky, all that hippy nonsense, but the truth is, he's never got over her death.'

Sasha frowned, barely able to hide her disbelief. 'And you had no idea he was getting that money, thousands of pounds over a number of years, by blackmail?'

'On my kids' life,' he said gravely, refilling his glass from the jug, 'I presumed it all came from his own pocket. Shocking, really.'

He was lying, Sasha could see that, and behind his jolly facade she sensed his contempt for Simon. She recalled how Karin had said he didn't like her or the other kids from the Bad Place.

'Jim.' A woman poked her head in the room. 'Would your guests like a cup of tea or coffee, or something stronger?'

'Nah, luv.' He winked at Sasha. 'Not while they're on duty.'

Jim's wife looked at the visitors uncertainly. 'Is everything alright?'

'Everything's hunky-dory,' he said quickly, but she hesitated in the doorway. 'These nice people are police officers. We're talking about Becky, luv, about what happened to her.'

'I saw about that missing girl on the news,' she told them. 'It's been a very bad time for Jim. It's made him very distraught, he can't sleep.'

Jim stared into the bottom of his glass. 'It's brought it all back, for sure.'

'Let's hope that Sammi is found sooner rather than later.'

'Yeah, and that the cops make a better fist of it than they did when Becky was murdered in cold blood.'

'I should get back to the kids,' Jim's wife said.

Her husband nodded at the empty jug. 'A refill would be nice.'

'Not right now, Jim.'

When she had gone, Jim turned back to Sasha and Craig and said gravely, 'And now it's happening again.'

'Excuse me?'

'A young girl goes missing and she's connected to that lot.' He went to a cabinet and flung it open, revealing a stack of files and folders. 'I spent years trying to get you police to reopen the case to discover how my sister was the only one not to escape that shithole farmhouse.'

'Jerry Swann recaptured her during the escape from the house.'

'Look at this.' Jim picked up a cheap-looking plastic trophy sprayed in faded gold and turned it in his hands. 'Not much to look at, is it, but my Becks was proud of it. It's an athletics trophy. She was in the school team, she could run like the wind, that girl. There's not a hope in hell Swann would have caught her. As I understand it, Simon could hardly move, he had to be carried out of that place. It don't make sense that Swann caught Becky, of all people. He was a disgusting man, a monster, and the first thing I do when I open my eyes of a morning is thank the Lord he's rotting in the grave, but then I start wondering all over again about what happened that night. And still, all these years later, it don't make sense. Something *stinks* about the whole thing.'

He took a thick folder from the cabinet. 'These are all the letters I've written down the years to Essex Police, the local MP, the Crown Prosecution Service and Uncle Tom Cobley, to get an inquiry started. Hell, I've written to all the prime ministers. Useless, every one of them!' He dropped the heavy bundle with a bang on to a coffee table. 'My sister was a beautiful human being, a wonderful sister and daughter – her death destroyed our parents – and she deserves justice.'

'Jerry Swann is dead.'

'I ain't talking about Jerry bloody Swann,' he said with a sneer. 'I want to know the truth about what happened that night. Why she didn't get out.'

When he scowled, all the tremendous resentment Jim Haskell felt for Karin, Simon and the other kids from the Bad Place was revealed.

'Where were you the night before last, Mr Haskell?'

Jim laughed bitterly. 'Oh, so now you're accusing me of that poor girl's disappearance? I was here at home. On my own, as it happens, because the wife was visiting her mum with the kids. But I never took that Sammi, why the hell would I? I can't bear it that another girl is missing, all those bad memories coming back. You should be looking for her rather than pestering an innocent man.' He snorted. 'Oh yeah, and I saw that farce of a press conference. You people couldn't organize a piss-up at a brewery.'

Sasha blushed.

'Why would I let another girl suffer the way my sister did?' he continued. 'Go on, search the place if you like, be my guest.'

'That won't be necessary.'

Jim went to refill his glass but remembered the jug was empty. He sighed. 'This stuff goes down too easily. I'm going to have to make more now, so if you're finished, maybe I could get back to my family. Sorry I can't be of greater help.'

Sasha nodded at Craig – there wasn't anything else to say – and Jim led them to the front door. His twisted grin couldn't conceal the bitter anger beneath.

'I'm a bit tipsy now, sure, but you mark my words. That missing girl, that Sammi, I hope to God she's okay, but something is going on, and it's got something to do with those so-called survivors. You both have a nice day.'

Jim Haskell slammed the door in their faces.

21

When Sasha got home late again, Denny was lying on the sofa playing a game on his phone.

Only a few months ago he'd have leapt into her arms and bombarded her with excited chatter about the events of his day. But tonight he barely looked up, muttering 'Alright?' as his thumbs raced across the device. His attention was completely focused on it, his face so close to the phone that Sasha worried his forehead would somehow become fused with the screen.

'Where's your dad?' she asked.

Music and sound effects filled the room. '*Denny*, where is he?'

'I don't know, upstairs – aargh!' he screamed suddenly.

'What's happened?' she asked in alarm.

'I got killed! Stop talking to me,' he shouted, 'I can't concentrate!'

She ignored the outburst, too shattered to argue. Every day, rampaging teenage hormones transformed her children's previously angelic personalities in all kinds of new and challenging ways. It seemed to her that teenagers could be frustrating, playful, cheeky, vulnerable, evil, cold, loving, saintly – and occasionally hateful – all within the space of a few seconds. It was exhausting.

'Where's Nan?'

'Next door. At Nelson's.'

She couldn't believe her ears. 'At—'

But Denny got up and stomped out of the room.

Sasha flung down her bag and climbed to Kev's study. They called it that, but Kev had never studied anything in there, except possibly the sports pages, and her children avoided it like the plague. It was basically a spare room with a desk in it and an old desktop computer that nobody used any more because they all had laptops and tablets, and where they dumped old schoolwork, and all the stuff they didn't know where else to put.

There was also a sofa and a television, and Kev's precious collection of vinyl. He used to love listening to his music, but she couldn't remember the last time she'd seen him cleaning or rearranging his records. The curtains were closed and the room was shrouded in darkness, the only flicker of light coming from the television, and it took Sasha a few moments to see him sprawled on the sofa.

'Hiya, I'm home.' She pawed unsuccessfully at the wall, trying to find the light switch. 'What are you doing?'

'Watching television.'

'I can see that. What I mean is, why are you up here…
again?' When he didn't answer, she asked, 'What's wrong
with you, Kev?'

'Nothing's wrong.' He didn't look up at her. God
forbid anybody in this house should make eye contact.
'Why should anything be wrong?'

'Did you fix the kids' dinner, have you even spoken
to them all night?'

'Your mother is here, she made them dinner.'

'What's going on, Kev?' She came inside, but still he
didn't look up. 'Please, let's talk about this. Don't make
me have to stand in front of the television.'

His tired eyes finally lifted to hers. 'I've had a really
long, shitty day at the office and I can barely think
straight.'

'Denny and Angel may like to think they're happy to
do their own thing, but they need you, Kev.'

His eyes flashed, as if to say, *it's late at night, what's
your excuse?*

She wanted to tell him about Sammi Manning, the
teenager she feared had been snatched and held against
her will by a sick monster. It occurred to Sasha that she
hadn't even spoken to him about the disastrous press
conference. There was a time when Kev would have been
the first person she'd have talked to in the aftermath. In
her shock and embarrassment, she would have needed to
get her bearings, and he had always been her compass,

nobody else would do. The old Kev would have said exactly the right thing to make her feel better, he would have done everything in his power to lift her, to reassure her she hadn't made an almighty cock-up. But – and this was the worst thing – it never even crossed her mind to call him about it, and that broke her heart.

His focus drifted back to the television. 'I've been shattered recently, there's lots of shit going on at work.'

She walked in front of the TV, trying to ignore the forced laughter of the studio audience behind her, to force him to meet her gaze.

'Things will sort themselves out soon. I'll be better tomorrow, I'll… Let's talk then.'

'You say that every day, you say we'll talk about whatever it is that's going on, and it never happens. We're like ships in the night, Kev. Not just you and me, but Angel and Denny, too. Our family feels like it's falling apart, and we've got to fix it, all of us.' His refusal to engage with her was infuriating. 'Have you at least apologized to Nelson after what happened yesterday?'

'Why would I do that?'

'Oh, I don't know,' Sasha said, annoyed. 'Because you're a grown man, because it's the right thing to do. You totally over-reacted, you know that, right?'

'When has he ever apologized to us about anything?'

'I don't care what Nelson does.' Putting him on the spot was getting her nowhere, so she tried to appeal to the social Kev of old. 'Tell you what, if things aren't so great at work, why don't you invite some of your colleagues over?'

Time was – she was clinging to the past again – they used to love having dinners and parties, and the house seemed full of people every weekend. Kev was the King of the Castle, the life and soul.

But that was before what happened to Jake.

Since their youngest had died, a lot of things had changed. A lot of old behaviours, the glue that bound them together, were gone. Invisible threads had been pulled; the dark matter that kept her and Kev in orbit around each other had somehow loosened, and she was terrified that they were drifting apart.

Hugging the cushion to his chest, Kev peered warily over the top of it. 'A lot of people you knew from there have moved on. It's a new crowd now.'

'Then it'll be nice to meet them. It's been a while since we've had a party. We should both invite people from work. Come on, it'll be fun.'

He didn't reply, and she felt downcast, was relieved to hear the doorbell ring. 'I'd better get that.'

She went downstairs to open the front door, and her mother walked in.

'Ah,' said Ursula, 'so you're home.'

'Denny said you went next door to Nelson.' Sasha followed her into the kitchen where her son was still on his phone. 'What do you think you're doing?'

The last thing she needed was for her mum to charge

in and make a difficult situation with their neighbour even more unbearable.

'Building bridges,' said Ursula, tying the apron around herself.

'Here's a thought, Mum.' Sasha's irritation got the better of her. 'Maybe you could build a few bridges with your own husband before you begin diplomatic negotiations with next door.'

'Stuart is a very sensitive man.' Ursula grabbed the phone out of Denny's hand and dropped it in her apron pocket.

'Hey!'

'I told you to stop playing it before I left and you didn't listen,' Ursula told him. 'But now I'm back.'

'Mum!' Denny jumped up and down flapping his arms, but it was late, her son's eyes were red with tiredness, he was totally wired from the countless hours of screen time, and Sasha was kind of relieved her mother had taken the decision into her own hands. Let Ursula be the bad guy for once.

'Denny,' she told him, 'your nan's right. It's time for bed.'

He stomped off and pounded up the stairs as loudly as he could.

'We had a lovely long chat,' said Ursula.

'Mum, Nelson is not our friend and I'd rather you didn't go there to make matters worse.'

'Oh, I did quite the opposite. I said very nice things

about you and Kevin, I think I made him see you in a totally new light.'

The phone was still burbling in her mother's apron pocket. Sasha could hear music and explosions and other sound effects coming from it.

'He's compiling a dossier about us to send to the council. Every time he hears a noise through the wall, whenever one of us coughs or farts, he writes down the date and time. Denny and Angel can be noisy, that's teenagers for you.'

'That doesn't seem like him at all.' Ursula didn't look convinced. 'Why would he do that?'

'Because he's a problem neighbour, Mum, a busybody, a troublemaker who delights in complaining about every little thing. That Denny's football comes over his fence, or that our tree blocks his light, no matter how many times we prune it back. Whatever we do is never good enough, because that's the kind of man he is.'

'I'm sure you have him all wrong. We had a lovely chat.'

'Mum, I forbid you to talk to him.' God knows what personal details Ursula had told Stuart Nelson over tea and biscuits. 'Please don't speak to him again.'

'I'm not sure I like being told what to do in my own home.'

'Ah!' Sasha wagged a finger. 'But this isn't your own home, is it? And are you ever going to tell me why you've left Dad?'

'You don't want to know.'

'Believe me, I do.'

Ursula thought about it. 'He's having an affair.'

'Shut the f... ront door!' blurted out Sasha, because her mother didn't like it when she swore. 'Dad wouldn't do that.'

'Nobody knows what that man is like.'

Sasha waved her off. 'Not Dad.'

Ursula pursed her lips. 'There are things I could tell you about your father that would make your hair curl. He's got up to all sorts in his time.'

This wasn't a conversation Sasha relished having, not this late, not after a long, stressful day. Basically not ever. 'I'll go and see him tomorrow. We'll get it sorted, we'll get you home.'

'I'm not sure I want to. I'm going to bed.'

Sasha pointed at the pocket of Ursula's apron, where Denny's phone continued to blast out noise. 'In which case, you may want to turn that off.'

Surprised, Ursula took it out and turned it over in her hands, trying to work out how to switch it off, until Sasha took pity on her and powered it down.

'By the way, Angel doesn't want to go to school tomorrow.'

'What's wrong, is she ill?'

'You're the detective,' said Ursula tersely as she left, '*you* ask her.'

'Welcome home, Sasha!' she muttered to herself as she trudged back upstairs.

Knocking on her daughter's door, she heard a whimper in response, which loosely translated meant she was allowed to enter.

Before she was even inside, Angel said, 'I'm not feeling well. I've got a fever.'

Sasha sat on the edge of the bed and felt her forehead, which was slightly clammy. But it was stuffy in the bedroom, all the windows were closed. 'You look okay, sweetheart.'

'I'm not, I'm really not, I feel like I'm burning up.' Angel spoke with an exaggerated gruffness. 'I'm dizzy, and I've got the squirts.'

'Then maybe you should stay at home tomorrow.'

'Yeah.' Angel grimaced, as if she was doing her best to cope with the fever burning inside her. 'I really think I should.'

Sasha saw her daughter's eyes were red and swollen – she looked like she'd been crying.

'Let's get some air in here.' Sasha opened a window. 'You will talk to me, won't you, if there's anything on your mind?'

Angel promptly burst into tears.

'Oh, baby.' Sasha took Angel in her arms, held her tight. 'What's happening?'

'Idontwanttogotoschool.' Angel's words tumbled out quickly, and Sasha gently asked her to repeat what she'd said. 'I feel really uncomfortable there, anxious, it's really... not nice. Tilly, she's—'

'What?' Sasha asked sharply. 'Has something happened between you?'

'It's... not been nice,' said Angel. 'It's just, I don't want to see her.'

Sasha's heart leapt. 'Is she bullying you?'

Her daughter began to cry. Between sobs, Angel spoke about nasty texts and messages on Snapchat – cyberbullying! – and intimidation. Sasha was shocked. The idea that Tilly was bullying her daughter made her blood boil. She took out her phone and scrolled through her contacts for Rachel's number.

'What are you doing?' asked Angel.

'Calling her mum.'

'Please don't!' Angel practically launched herself at the phone. 'I'd die!'

'I'm going to speak to her, Angel. You were always such good friends with Tilly, I don't know what's got into her.'

'Promise me you won't phone her,' wailed her daughter. 'Just leave it!'

'No wonder her mum blanked me in the street this morning. God knows what Tilly must be telling her.'

'I know, right?' Angel threw herself down on the bed and pressed her face into the pillow. 'I used to think she was really nice.'

'Have you spoken to your dad about this?'

Angel made a face. *As if.* 'He's off with the fairies!'

And that made Sasha even more annoyed with Kev. Because the old Kev would have been thunderstruck to discover his little girl was being bullied and would move mountains to get the situation sorted. He'd phone the school to try to find a solution, yes, but also demand to know how teachers could let such a thing happen in this day and age. It broke Sasha's heart to think that Kev probably hadn't even noticed that his daughter was unhappy. But then it occurred to her that *she* hadn't realized anything was wrong either.

'Please tell me I don't have to go to school tomorrow,' begged Angel. 'I really don't want to!'

'You don't have to go to school tomorrow,' Sasha told her, and she held Angel tight, mortified that she'd let her down.

22

The best part of the day for Karin was when she could come home, lock the door, and shut out the rest of the world till morning.

And she needed to be alone more than ever tonight. Down the years, the number of people who recognized her, the ones who glanced at her in the street or muttered as she walked past, or even stopped to ask for a selfie, had dwindled. But now, with Michelle's connection to Sammi Manning revealed – that disastrous press conference had been all over the news – people were talking all over again about the Bad Place. Travelling home on the bus, someone had stared at her, their curiosity tinged with suspicion, and Karin had got off as soon as she could. All the old feelings of shame and guilt were back, those same feelings she experienced in the aftermath of the Bad Place, when she felt everyone could see right into her soul.

And then there were the texts from Becky…

Ignoring her own dark reflection in the kitchen

window, she took a ready meal from the freezer, put it in the microwave, and turned the dial to defrost.

The texts couldn't have been from Becky – because Becky was dead, she was surely dead. But a small part of Karin, the part that still ached every day for her friendship and love, hoped desperately they could be from her.

She took out her phone and looked again at the last one…

i miss U ♥ ♥

BeXxx

When she'd eaten, Karin went upstairs. She changed out of her work clothes and hung them in the wardrobe. Someone was shouting on the street below and she tensed – it surely couldn't be long before the first journalist turned up on her doorstep – but the voice receded. She padded naked along the landing and turned on the shower, leaving the phone on the sill where she could see it. Turning the temperature as high as she could, she stepped into the fierce jet of water and braced her hands against the tiled wall, stood under the searing hot spray, let the heat soak into her skin, into her bones, until she couldn't bear it any longer. Afterwards, she towelled off, dabbing gently at her flushed, angry skin, and climbed into a T-shirt and pyjama bottoms.

Downstairs, she placed the phone on the arm of the sofa and watched a film, too anxious to change the

channel in case she stumbled across a news report about
Sammi Manning. Letting the movie carry her away, for
an hour she actually forgot about Becky.

Until a text dropped into her phone, startling her.

She grabbed the mobile, read the text – it wasn't from
Becky. Instead, it was from one of the men she occasionally met, no strings attached, a married guy called Louis.
He was coming into town on a business trip tomorrow
night and did she want to hook up? She hesitated,
replied that she did. The message flew off.

Karin wondered if Becky would contact her again and
immediately chastised herself for even considering that
it could be from her friend, as if she could have returned
from the dead all these years later. But she couldn't stop
herself any longer. Her fingers flew quickly across the
screen as she tapped in a message.

Are you there?
Karin xxx

Three dots began to pulse at the bottom of the screen,
indicating that someone was replying. The dots danced,
someone was writing, writing...

...

...

...

Karin stared, hardly daring to breathe. Expecting a reply to appear at any moment… any moment…

And then:

> Why dont u ♥ me? 😢😢
>
> BeXxx

Karin swallowed, confused. She would never stop loving Becky. Her thumbs twitched across the screen as she typed:

> But I do! XXX

Then a bang on the front door made her jump.

Going into the hallway, she saw a distorted figure framed in the coloured glass of the door. Light from a nearby lamppost cast a shadow against it. It was someone slim, a woman. Karin hardly had visitors, and never at this time of night.

It just wasn't possible. There was only one person she wanted it to be.

Only one person.

Karin was excited – and terrified.

After all these years, Becky had come back to her. She typed quickly, breathing hard.

> Are you here? xxx

Sent the message. Waited for the ellipsis to jump.

...

...

...

And a message came back.

do U want me 2 b?
BeXxx 😻😻

Karin sat on the stairs, staring at the blurred figure on the other side of the door. What would she say to Becky? After all these years, how could she possibly explain?

She felt dizzy with hope, sick with fear.

Unsure of whether to let Becky in… or keep her out.

The figure loomed closer to the door, the features undulating behind the rippled glass. Karin saw a sharp nose and cheeks, clawed hands pressed against the glass.

And then the figure shouted, 'Let me in, yeah, I see you!'

Lydia's voice broke the spell.

Karin slumped with disappointment – and relief. She got up off the stairs, took a moment to compose herself and opened the door. Lydia slipped inside and shot into the living room, tugging at her hair.

'Are you okay, Lydia?' asked Karin.

'I am, as it happens, yeah.' Lydia's head jerked in a nod. 'I'm totally okay, I think so.'

Karin watched her pace anxiously. 'Are you sure, because—'

'I've come to tell you something, yeah?' interrupted Lydia. But her attention was grabbed by the television. She laughed miserably at something happening on the screen.

'Lydia…' Karin picked up the remote and turned it off. 'What is it you want to say?'

'Thing is…' Lydia rubbed her hands together. 'I don't need you any more. Thank you for everything that you've done and stuff, but you don't need to do any more for me, because he loves me now and he wants to be with me.'

Lydia was in a manic mood and Karin knew to tread carefully. 'Okay.'

'He says you're no good for me and I have to stay away from you.'

'Who?' Karin perched on the sofa arm. 'Who are you talking about, Lydia?'

'My boyfriend.'

'You've got a boyfriend,' Karin said in surprise. 'That's nice. What's his name?'

'Matt.'

'Matt.' Lydia's relationships tended to be short and unhappy. She attached herself to a motley collection of addicts, thieves and thugs who usually got her more deeply involved in petty crime and encouraged her addiction, or took what little money and belongings she had and disappeared, never to be seen again. 'I'm pleased for you, Lydia, I really am. But where did you meet him?'

'He's in my drug support group. I met him at the drop-in.'

Karin smiled. 'Perhaps I could meet him.'

'Why?' Lydia said sharply. 'Why do you want to do that?'

'Of course I want to. I'd love to meet the man who's made you so happy.'

'That's right, he loves me!' Lydia folded her arms across her bony chest. 'He says he's going to take care of me. He's going to take me away so we can start again, just me and him, but not around here, somewhere else. We're going to get married and have kids, yeah, we're in love and there's nothing you can do about it.'

'I'm glad you're happy, Lydia,' said Karin with caution. 'Of course I am. Why don't you sit down?'

'I don't want to. He's had his problems, like I have, but he's a good man. He loves me, he says so. He's the one, definitely, yeah.' Lydia picked at a dirty nail. 'But he asked me about you.'

Karin felt the first stirrings of panic. 'Why did he ask about me?'

Lydia looked away. 'He *knows* all about you, and he says that you're toxic, that's the word he used. Toxic.'

'What does he know about me, Lydia?' asked Karin.

'He says you just want to keep me close, because...'

She stepped forward. 'Because what?'

Lydia's eyes darted around the room. 'He says you're scared of me.'

'Why would I be scared of you, Lydia?'

'Because I *know* things, things about, about... what happened.' Lydia swallowed. 'You know, at that place.'

Karin pressed her hands beneath her armpits so that Lydia couldn't see them tremble. 'What did you tell him, Lydia?'

'We tell each other everything, yeah? *Everything.*'

Karin tried to smile. 'I'd like to meet him.'

'I bet you would,' Lydia said. 'You'd love to meet him and tell him nasty things about me, tell him lies to chase him off, so he'll never want to see me again.'

'I would never do that.'

'I've always been a burden to you. Someone to be put up with, to be kept happy, kept *close*. That's what Matt says.' Agitated, she paced around the room. 'He says you're only my friend because you have to be. But we're in love, me and him, and you can't stand it!'

Karin stepped closer. 'I'm worried about you.'

'You have no right to be worried about me, yeah, because I don't belong to you!' Lydia's eyes flashed triumphantly. 'Matt loves me, he really does!'

'Will he look after you, Lydia, care for you? I hope he does.'

'You're always twisting everything!' Lydia threw up her arms. 'To keep me close, control me!'

Karin frowned. 'How long have you known him?'

'He takes me to nice places.' Lydia was becoming hysterical. 'He treats me like a proper person, a lady, not someone to be kept down and pitied. Sit, Lydia, heel, Lydia!'

'I'd love to meet him.'

'You're jealous, that's what you are, and you want to get rid of him!'

'It's only natural for me to want to meet him,' said Karin. 'I want to make sure he's going to look after you.'

Tears fell down Lydia's cheeks. 'You want to scare him away!'

Karin's phone *dinged*, a message had arrived, her heart leapt, she wanted to reach for it immediately, but Lydia rushed to the door. 'Lydia, wait!'

But Lydia flew out of the house, the front door juddering against the wall as she flung it open, and ran down the path.

'Lydia,' shouted Karin. 'Please, come back!'

When she had disappeared, Karin went back inside and snatched up the phone.

> u dont ♥ me no more
> BeXxx 😟 😟

She was desperate to call her, to hear Becky's voice. But

she knew it wouldn't be possible. If it was really Becky, if it was her, she would have rung already. She would have come to Karin and let her explain what happened, how everything turned out the way it did.

But she dabbed at the screen with her thumbs. Making a mess of the text, correcting, writing it again.

I do. I still love you.

XXX

The ellipsis pulsed...

...

...

...

u got a nu ♥ now...

...

...

...

An image dropped into her phone and Karin expanded it and saw a photo of herself sitting talking with the policewoman, Sasha Dawson, at the café on Victoria Avenue. The shot was taken from across the street. They were leaning across the table towards each other in what looked like an intimate way. Karin felt sick.

And then another message arrived:

do u ♥ her more than me? 😳😳

Karin typed:

No! XXX

And waited...

...

...

...

Watching the ellipsis pulse and pulse and pulse, until the reply came.

😈😈😈

23

The following morning, Sasha drove past her parents' apartment and saw that the balcony door was open, the gauze curtain billowing in the breeze coming in off the sea, and her father was sitting in the lounger. He wore his usual pair of cargo shorts and a floppy hat to protect his thinning scalp from the sun. His face was hidden behind a pair of binoculars he was using to watch a tanker nose along the estuary. Sasha was surprised to see a beer can at his feet and checked the time on her phone. It wasn't even nine.

Parking on the esplanade, she stood below the apartment block and called up several times – 'Dad, Dad!' – before the old man finally heard her. 'Let me in!'

Alec Chancellor climbed from his chair and went inside. Reappearing a moment later, he threw down keys, which bounced on the pavement at her feet.

Climbing the stairs to the apartment, Sasha let herself inside. The place looked like a bomb had hit it. Her dad's clothes were flung everywhere and the combined kitchen and living room was covered in mess. There were dirty plates lurking beneath the sofa and clothes flung over every piece of furniture, newspapers and magazines strewn across the floor. Her mother would demand an immediate divorce if she saw it in such a state, or more likely drop dead on the spot.

Sasha had never liked this flat. Her parents' old home had been spacious and full of character. Yes, she felt a yearning nostalgia because she'd grown up there, but this new-build was poky and nondescript in comparison. She understood how they would want to downsize after retirement, but Sasha didn't know why they'd choose to live here. There was that sea view, admittedly, with its glorious golden sunset – that's what they were paying for – but the footfall on the pavement below was relentless.

'Honestly, Dad.' Sasha leaned over to kiss him on his wrinkled forehead. His face was so leathery that his flat, bristly moustache was almost invisible on his brown upper lip. 'You're living like a teenager!'

'Yeah.' He settled back in the lounger. 'This is the life.'

She picked up the can, which was half full. 'And drinking lager first thing!'

'I can do whatever I like now,' he said with genuine enthusiasm, 'there's no one to boss me about.'

'Come on, Dad.' Sasha pulled up a garden chair, taking off her shoes and resting her feet on a metal rung of the balcony. 'What's going on?'

He scratched his bony chest, in no hurry to answer. 'You don't know what it's been like for me. The strain of it all these years. Married to that woman.'

'You don't mean that. You're perfect for each other.'

'Are we really, though?' Alec shrugged. 'It was alright when I worked, we hardly saw each other then. In fifty-odd years I hardly missed a day of work. I did all the hours I could so that you kids wouldn't go without. I wanted you and your sister to have the best of everything.'

She squeezed his hand. 'You did.'

'And the only thing that kept me going was the dream that one day I'd be able to put my feet up. But your mother won't get off my case. She's on at me all day with a never-ending list of things she wants me to do – tasks, errands, projects – and I've had enough. This worm has turned.'

Chin lifted in defiance, he squinted out to sea.

'Dad.' Sasha shifted uncomfortably, unsure of how to broach the question on her mind. 'Mum says… Mum says you're having some kind of fling… well, an affair, with another woman.'

'Ha!' Alec lifted the can to his lips. 'A chance would be a fine thing! Your mum is going senile. She just can't bear it that I like to go down the pub of an evening, have a couple of pints. And yes, Annie is there.'

Sasha gave him the side-eye. 'Annie?'

'She's a fine woman, Annie, you'd never know she

has a bus pass. She's kept herself in tip-top shape. She's got a great pair of pins, still. She likes a laugh, enjoys a pint, and likes to watch the Blues play. She's fun, Annie, and I like her company. And she's got a great pair of pins.'

'Yes, you mentioned that.'

'But your mum thinks there's something funny going on with me and her.'

'And is there?'

'Nah.' He waved her off. 'The lead went from my pencil a long time ago.'

Sasha held up a hand to say, *stop*. 'Dad, please.'

'It's the twenty-first century, Sash, a man should be able to enjoy the company of another woman without everybody getting the wrong end of the stick.'

'I just want you to be happy, you and Mum. You can work this out between you, surely?' She thought of her own stuttering relationship with Kev. 'You can't just throw away five decades of successful marriage.'

Trouble was, her parents were both belligerent. Her mother would return home in a heartbeat, and her father would gladly take her back, but each of them expected the other to make the first move.

'Talk to her, at least. Iron out whatever nonsense is going on between you.'

'It's too late for that,' he said indignantly.

'Everyone loves you, because you're a kind and lovely person. All I want is for you and Mum to be happy, together or apart.' She took his hand in hers and rubbed it with her thumb. 'But, you know, preferably together.'

She felt his attitude soften. Then it was only a matter of waiting for his reply.

'If she wants to come back, that's up to her,' he said finally, picking up his beer. 'But I ain't gonna beg.'

24

Sasha drove to the edge of town and parked her Spider beneath a tree outside a brown brick building with a colourful mural on the front. The Tarpley Care Home was the only building in a wide, leafy road. The gulls soared listlessly beneath the pounding sun. The pavements were already heating up, the sky was an unblemished blue, and it was a relief to walk into the pleasant air-conditioned reception.

She didn't relish the prospect of meeting Peter Carrington again. She remembered encountering him briefly on the night of Becky Haskell's death many years back. She didn't recall what he'd said to her on that busy and traumatic night, but had never forgotten his intimidating and arrogant manner.

Carrington was a big beast in the force back then, one of the alpha males in CID, and had built a formidable reputation as a detective. But he was already a man running out of time. Rumours circulated that he had a drink problem and his mistakes during the Bad Place investigation, including his tragic confrontation with Swann, a man he had even spoken to during a door-to-door search, saw him forced into early retirement.

Carrington wouldn't remember her, she was just a lowly WPC twenty-six years ago – back when there were still WPCs – and she had no intention of jogging his memory.

A tall man in a navy jacket, jeans, and battered boating shoes without socks was talking amiably to a receptionist as she came in.

'The window doesn't shut properly, is it something we can get sorted?' He scraped his long blond fringe back over his head. 'I'd be very grateful if we could.'

'Leave it with me, Mr Carrington.'

'Thank you.' He was a rugged-looking man like his father, but well-spoken and polite. 'You're very kind.'

'Ian Carrington?' asked Sasha. 'That's good timing. I'm Sasha Dawson, we spoke on the phone.'

'Sasha!' He greeted her like an old friend, with a firm handshake. 'I'm sorry, *DI* Dawson, it's good to meet you.'

'Sasha's fine,' she said. 'Thanks for seeing me.'

'You're very welcome. Dad is on the second floor.' He led her to the elevator and they stepped inside. There was barely enough space for the both of them; Ian Carrington seemed to suck up most of the lift. Stabbing the button to close the door, he apologized when he elbowed her. The door trundled slowly shut.

'I have to say I'm fascinated by your request to see Dad. I suppose it's about the Bad Place.' He waved a hand at her obvious discomfort. 'Oh, I'm used to it. Nobody's ever wanted to see him about any of the investigations he brought to a *successful* conclusion. Baden Place is the only one anybody ever wants to discuss.'

'I'm not here to rake over old wounds, but the case has certain threads that connect it to something I'm working on now.'

'The abduction of that girl. I saw the news, and the press conference. I wouldn't have liked to have been in your shoes afterwards.' When she looked uncomfortable, he laughed. 'Don't worry, we're no strangers to bad press around here.'

When the lift door opened, Ian pressed himself against the wall to let her out first, and they walked along a carpeted hallway. 'Second door on the left.'

'How long has your dad been living here?' she asked.

'Three years now, he's been very frail,' he said. 'Particularly since the stroke.'

'The stroke?'

Ian knocked once on a door and went inside, saying brightly, 'There's someone come to see you, Dad! A detective! I bet that takes you back!'

With obvious affection, he kissed the top of the head of an old man who drooped in a wheelchair at an open window, just as Sasha had kissed her own father earlier. Ian fussed around him for a few moments, smoothing his white hair, removing a blanket from his lap. 'We don't need this, it's baking!'

But Peter Carrington didn't react at all; it was impossible to tell if he even knew his son was there. A thin, hunched man, he stared into space with moist, empty eyes. His mouth was slack and drool dribbled down the creases in his jaw. He was nothing like the big, vital man Sasha remembered. Ian pulled up a chair beside his father to dab the damp corners of his mouth with a tissue.

The room was bright and filled with the vivid sunshine that poured in the window and made the floating dust motes and summer pollen sparkle. There was a cabinet full of battered paperbacks, police textbooks and tidy rows of framed photographs.

'Hello, Mr Carrington,' she said. 'It's good to meet you.'

'What was it you wanted to ask Dad?' When she looked at the old man doubtfully, Ian smiled. 'You'll have to ask me, I'm afraid, but I can assure you, he's told me everything about the Bad Place – everything that he knew.'

Occasionally the old man's mouth jerked, and Ian kept turning to his father, smiling at him encouragingly, as if he still had hope that Peter would shrug off his affliction and join the conversation. Sasha considered whether her own children would be as attentive when she was as old and infirm, whether they would change her incontinence nappy and straighten her wig, and decided it was best not to dwell on the matter.

'The girl who's gone missing,' she said, glancing at the family photographs, 'is the god-daughter of one of the kids who was abducted by Jerry Swann. Her name is Michelle Dormand.'

'I saw that.' Ian clicked his fingers, trying to place her. 'Michelle was Becky's best friend, yes?'

Sasha realized that, despite his eagerness to help, Ian probably didn't know as much about the Bad Place as he claimed – he was clearly a people pleaser – and that she'd wasted a journey.

'No, that was Karin.'

'Ah.'

She saw a photo of Peter Carrington that looked like it had been taken at a police do when he was in his pomp. Barrel-chested, with a thick mane of black hair swept back over his head, Peter wore an expensive-looking three-piece suit and a white shirt. The knot of his silk tie bulged ostentatiously, and a chain with the initial 'P' framed the neck of his flamboyant waistcoat. He wore a big, complacent smile, and his blue eyes flashed.

She could only imagine the way those eyes widened in panic as Jerry Swann pulled the knife across Becky's throat.

This is for you, my love.

Other middle-aged men surrounded him in the photo. Carrington's team looked as thick as thieves, and gazed at him with obvious devotion. His *boys* – because in those days it was invariably men who worked in CID

– loved and feared him in equal measure. Carrington was a big personality from an age when SIOs ran teams as they saw fit, when investigative strategies were a reflection of their own personal style and experience, before a series of high-profile misjudgements and mistakes, the Bad Place investigation among them, led to police procedure becoming more formalized.

There were other photos, too. There was Peter, his wife and a teenage Ian in a rowing boat on a lake. The resemblance between Peter and his young son was striking.

'Nice photo,' she said, holding it up.

'It was taken on Windermere in happier times, before Dad was... let go. And before the press and the conspiracy theorists got hold of him.'

Sasha put down the photo. 'Conspiracy theorists?'

Ian rolled his eyes. 'People demanding to know the *truth*.'

'The truth?'

'Oh, you know.' He rubbed the top of his father's hand. 'There are people who believe all kinds of nonsense. That my father and Jerry Swann were members of a satanic cult and were secretly working together to enslave children; that a Masonic cabal within the police covered up the whole thing; that Swann now lives with Elvis above a launderette in Woking. Trust me, I've heard every conceivable variation on the theme. There are some disturbed people out there.'

'Blimey,' said Sasha. 'Even now?'

'There's a hard core of true crime buffs who are still fascinated by what happened, isn't that right, Dad?' He glanced at his father. 'We get all kinds of nutters with the strangest ideas trying to sneak up here, but they're usually intercepted in reception.'

'Your poor dad.'

Ian shrugged. 'He's oblivious to it all, lucky thing.'

'It's nice here,' she said, looking around the bright, airy room. 'And your father seems well cared for.'

'He's comfortable, aren't you, Dad, we've been very lucky in that respect.' The old man's mouth spasmed and his tongue bulged momentarily between his teeth, but no noise emerged. 'He's a brave soldier.'

'When did he...'

'Have the stroke? Four years ago. It's a cruel thing.' He nodded at the photos. 'As you can see, he was a vibrant man, full of energy and vim. He was always the biggest man in the room, but he was never the same after he was thrown under the bus. He was a good policeman, with a fine record of service, but there was a lot of pressure on him to find those kids. He simply didn't have the proper resources, and he just didn't catch any breaks.'

He hesitated, realizing Sasha was police.

'Dad tried his best, DI Dawson. But when it was revealed that he had spoken to Jerry Swann on his own doorstep, the press went for him like a pack of hungry wolves. All of a sudden, every little thing that went wrong in the investigation was his fault. Dad was a convenient scapegoat. He didn't deserve that.'

Ian reached out to wipe gunk from the corner of his father's eye with a thumb. 'It's a terrible shame. I come to see him as much as I can, twice a day if I can, and we'll chat. I love our chats.' He winked. 'They're a bit one-sided, mind.'

Sasha checked the time on her phone. 'I'd better go.'

'Oh, I thought you wanted to ask some questions?'

'I think I've kept you both for long enough.'

The more Sasha thought about it, the more it was unlikely the abduction of a teenage girl could have anything to do with the disappearance of six kids two and a half decades ago. All she had done was waste precious time that could have been spent coordinating the urgent search for Sammi.

'Goodbye, Mr Carrington,' Sasha said, but the old man didn't give any indication he had heard her, or even that he knew she was there. Her own single memory of the man may not have been a positive one, nor would she wish this kind of affliction on anyone in their last days, but he was lucky to have a son so devoted.

'I'm sorry I wasn't much help,' said Ian. 'But if you need any information, do come back.'

Her phone rang in her bag as she went back to the lift.

'DI Dawson,' she said, answering it.

'It's Ajay. We've found something on Sammi's computer.'

'What?' she asked.

'Images,' he told her. 'And you're not going to like them.'

25

'The photos are clumsy glamour shots. It's cheap and tawdry stuff, but nothing hard-core.'

'Hard-core or not, she's a vulnerable fifteen-year-old.'

Sasha clicked on the dozen images on the screen. Of Sammi posing in her bra against a wall, or with her hands cupped across her naked breasts, or sitting in her knickers in a wicker chair. She was doing her best to smile, but it was a thin, faltering thing, and her eyes were full of guilt and shame. It was clear she didn't want to be posing for those shots.

'They were found buried in an applications folder on her laptop,' Ajay told her.

Sasha examined the images. There was nothing to suggest where the photos were taken. All she could see was that wicker chair, and a plain white wall behind.

'Do we know where they came from?'

'They were sent to her by email.'

'So we can trace the email address back to the sender,' Lolly suggested.

'If only it were as easy as that. It was sent via an

anonymous email system, it's impossible to know who sent it. But the Digital Forensic Investigator is coming in from Chelmsford, one of the new guys apparently.' Ajay frowned at his watch. 'He should be here by now.'

'I hope he's showered, at least,' said Craig, and they all turned to him in surprise. 'Come on, you know what these techie blokes are like. He'll be barely out of nappies, with long, lank hair and zits on his zits. He'll stink to high heaven. They may know how to find their way around a computer, these guys, but most of them are barely acquainted with a bar of soap.'

'Remind me to book Craig on to a diversity course ASAP,' Sasha told Ajay.

Craig nodded sagely. 'Just you wait.'

Ajay saw an old gent in a cardigan, cord trousers and a shirt and tie wander aimlessly around the office, and poked his head out of the meeting room. 'Excuse me, can I help you?'

'I think someone's expecting me. I'm Anthony Eden.' The old man peered over the top of his half-moon glasses. 'I'm the Digital Forensic Investigator.'

'Of course you are,' said Craig with a frown.

After introducing himself to everyone, careful to re-peat his name every single time – *Anthony Eden, Digital Forensic Investigator, Anthony Eden, Digital Forensic Investigator* – he placed a battered leather satchel on the table and took out a packet of Percy Pigs, a folded copy of the *Telegraph*, the crossword completed in small, precise handwriting, and an angling magazine. Finally, after all that, came a slim silver laptop.

Lifting the visitor pass that dangled on the end of his lanyard away from the keyboard, Anthony floated a crooked finger across the trackpad to reveal a screen full of incomprehensible data.

Sasha glanced at her watch and asked cheerily, 'What have you got for us, Tony?'

He stood to inform her gravely, 'It's Anthony.'

'Sorry,' said Sasha. 'Quite right. Anthony.'

Lolly covered her mouth with a hand: *you got busted.*

'Now then.' Anthony took a moment to frown at Sasha's bare feet. 'I'm afraid I can't tell you who sent the photos to the young lady if that's what you were hoping. But the good news is that the images were taken on a digital camera that contains Exif metadata.' Ajay nodded, already way ahead of them. 'That stands for exchangeable image file format.'

'And what does that mean?' asked Craig.

'Exif data contains information about the photo itself,' said Ajay. 'Format, date and time, camera settings, any copyright information. And geotagging.'

Lolly's eyes lit up. 'GPS coordinates of where the photo was taken.'

Anthony held the packet of Percy Pigs towards her. 'You've just earned a prize, young lady.'

She put her hand in the bag and popped the sweet

into her mouth. Anthony turned the laptop towards Ajay, who scribbled down the coordinates on a notepad and rushed out of the room, headed towards his desk.

'Whoever took these photos probably didn't even know that data was being captured. It's so difficult not to leave a trace on the world these days.'

'To be honest, you're not what we were expecting,' Sasha told him.

'Oh, you thought I'd be some young long-haired fellow in a Metallica T-shirt, I get that all the time.' He glanced at her white hair. 'But they haven't got rid of all us old folk yet.'

'Quite.' Sasha smiled tersely, not altogether sure whether the suggestion was that *she* was also over the hill.

Moments later, as he offered around the last of his Percy Pigs – *treat yourself, take two!* – Ajay returned with a copy of the printout he'd taken from Google Maps, an aerial shot of a home in an ordinary suburban street in the east of town.

'Let's find out who lives there.' Sasha clapped her hands, feeling that familiar excitement of a new lead.

But Ajay had already done it and handed her his notebook. 'This is the address and the name of the householders, courtesy of the electoral register.'

Anthony packed away his laptop and his other bits and pieces while they all tensely looked over Sasha's shoulder.

'You've got to be kidding,' she said, looking at the names of the registered householders on the page.

'Who is it?' asked Lolly.

Sasha nudged Craig and went to the door. 'Come on, Powerman, here's your chance to get out of the office.'

26

All Paul Ferdinand's digital devices – his phone, laptop and tablet – were seized, and officers searched every inch of his home for Sammi Manning. That same wicker chair, the one she had been photographed in, was found in a spare bedroom, an image of Jesus Christ now hanging on the white wall behind it. Sasha didn't think Sammi was likely to have been kept captive in Paul's family home, where he lived with his wife and two children, or locked in the shed at the bottom of the garden, but stranger things had happened.

'He volunteered at a youth club Sammi attended until five or six months ago,' Ajay told Sasha on the way to the interview room. 'According to her parents, Sammi used to love going there, but she went off it suddenly. They just thought she'd outgrown it.'

'More like she wanted to avoid Paul Ferdinand.'

'How the hell did he manage to volunteer?' Craig clapped his hands down his sides. 'What about the Criminal Records Bureau check?'

'The CRB check only works if you have previous. Paul has never been in trouble with the law.' Sasha let out a long breath and glanced at her phone to see a missed call from Angel's school, River Hill.

'You need to take that?' asked Craig.

'It can wait.' She put the phone away. 'Okay, let's go in, shall we?'

Again, Sasha accompanied Craig into the interview room. Sammi Manning had been a misper for going on three days and Paul was their best hope to bring her home.

'What am I going to tell her?' Paul whined as soon as they walked in. 'What will I tell my wife?'

Taking a seat, Sasha dropped a folder on the table.

'This interview is being recorded. I'm Detective Inspector Sasha Dawson. Also present is Detective Constable Craig Power. Please state your full name and address and date of birth.' When Paul had done that, she confirmed the date and time. 'At the conclusion of the interview, I'll give you a form that will explain the procedure for dealing with this recording and how you can access it. You're being interviewed under caution, Paul. You do not have to say anything, but it may harm your defence if you do not mention when questioned something which you later rely on in court. Anything you do say may be given in evidence.'

Paul squirmed in the chair. Always a slight figure, he looked even more diminished. His face was a sickly green. Sasha took from the folder the copies of the images of Sammi Manning.

'I'm showing Mr Ferdinand the photographs of Sammi Manning found on her computer. Did you take them, Paul, were you the photographer?' She neatly lined up the images in front of him and he nodded. 'Out loud, please.'

'Yes I did,' he croaked. 'And I will never forgive myself.'

'Your house is being searched. We'll be looking on all your devices.' She checked her notes. 'You have a tablet and a smartphone, a desktop computer, and also a couple of digital cameras, is that correct? So what else will we find on those devices? More of the same? Other indecent images of children, hard-core stuff, perhaps?'

'There'll be... other photos of...' He pressed a hand hard against his chest. 'Yes, there are others.'

'How many?'

'I can't remember, exactly.' He closed his eyes. 'Dozens, perhaps more.'

Craig leaned forward. 'Of Sammi?'

'There are other girls too.'

'Taken by you?'

'No.' Paul's hands trembled violently. 'Those were the only ones I took... but there are other images, yes.'

'And where did you get those, Paul?'

'Someone I know online. Someone with... similar interests.'

Sasha gathered up the photos. 'Go on.'

'We discuss things, we have, uh, common interests, and he told me how to go about... taking my own.'

'And who is this person?'

'We met in a chat room.'

'This person told you how to groom a child,' said Craig shortly, and Sasha gave him a warning glance, *calm it down.*

Paul looked like he was about to cry. 'You don't know how sorry I am.'

'Did you tell him who you were interested in, Paul?' asked Sasha. 'Did you name Sammi or the youth club?'

'He's the one who suggested she liked me, he's the one who said that she was... interested, and he told me how to make the most of my friendship with her. He was very... persuasive.'

'Friendship.' Craig's voice dripped with disgust.

'You keep saying *he*, Paul,' said Sasha. 'Give us a name.'

'I don't know his real name. He seemed to know about me and who I was. I'm just presuming it's a he, it's got to be, hasn't it? It's always men who like to...' His voice trailed away. 'Look, I made a terrible mistake, but I really need to go home now.'

'Have you physically touched her, Paul?'

'Never, I swear!' A gasp of despair made him shudder. 'I made a mistake, I've admitted it, please may I go?'

'Paul, a mistake is forgetting to buy milk or leaving the oven on.' Sasha leaned forward slowly, as she imagined a judge passing sentence would do. 'What you've been doing – making pornographic images of a minor – isn't a silly mistake. It's a serious crime, and it's going to ruin your life and the lives of the people who love you.'

'May God forgive me.' His face crumpled. 'What is my wife going to say? What am I going to tell Megan?'

'How many times did you text Sammi, Paul?'

'I really want to help, but my head is swimming.'

'You bought a phone specifically so you could arrange to meet her.'

'I don't know why I got the phone now. There was a reason.'

'How many times did Sammi go to your house?'

'Just a couple. She came round for a cup of tea. The first time we sat and chatted.'

'About what?'

'About how difficult she found it at school. She asked my advice about some problems she was having, and I spoke to her about Christian values.'

Craig pressed fingers into his eyes and rubbed.

'And the second time?' said Sasha.

'I asked her to pose for photos, *nice* ones, I'm a keen photographer.' Paul shifted miserably in his seat. 'It was never my intention to... but things went too far, somehow I got her to take off her... I'll never forgive myself for asking her to undress, but I never touched her, you have to believe me!'

'Here's what I'm thinking, Paul,' Craig said suddenly. 'If you're the kind of man who could groom a girl, convince her to come to your home, persuade her to strip, then I'm thinking you're the kind of man who would go further.'

'No!'

'You probably couldn't help yourself and you touched her, or assaulted her...'

'No, no, no!'

'Raped her.'

Paul began to cry. 'That's not true.'

'But then you got scared, as well you should. You realized taking those photos was going to get you sent to prison. You would spend the rest of your life on the Sexual Offenders Register, you'd lose your wife, your kids, and your good name among all your church friends. Megan isn't going to forgive something like that, how the hell could she, and she'd certainly never let you near your own children ever again.'

'That's not—'

'But the only person who knew what you did, the only one who could tell anyone, was Sammi. She'd tell people about the calls, the assignations – hell, you sent her the *photos* – maybe she had already decided to tell her parents. So you went and did something really stupid, even by your own standards, Paul. You arranged for her to disappear. You waited till you had a bulletproof alibi, the dinner with Karin and the others, and then you got someone to snatch her off the street. Maybe one of your creepy online buddies.'

Paul lifted his hands to his face. 'That's not... no, it's not...'

Craig was about to let rip again, but Sasha touched his arm, and he leaned back in his chair, frustrated.

'Why on earth did you send those images to her?' Sasha said quietly. 'What were you thinking?'

He whispered, 'I wanted her to see what a beautiful person she was.'

Sasha thought again of the video of Sammi singing – the way her fingers nervously rubbed her palms as her fragile voice entranced the audience, the way you could hear a pin drop when she had finished – and she had to take a moment to swallow the anger she felt surge inside her.

'Tell us where we can find her, Paul.'

Eyes lowered to the table, he shook his head. 'I would never...'

'Help us bring her home before this all goes too far.'

He whimpered. 'It's not me.'

'When you saw it was Sammi who had gone missing,' said Craig, leaning forward again, 'didn't you think to come forward to tell us about your... relationship to the girl? You must have known we would find those photos?'

'I was scared and confused. I deleted the images.'

'Nothing gets deleted, Paul, not really,' said Sasha. 'Anyway, we've already got all the information we need to prosecute because the metadata on the photos you sent to Sammi told us everything. That the photos were taken on your camera, and posed in your house, in your wicker chair.'

Paul said something Sasha didn't hear and she asked him to repeat it.

'It was a wedding present,' he said dismally. 'The chair.'

And then Paul squeezed his eyes shut. His shoulders heaved as he wept.

'Where's the burner phone you used to call her on the evening she disappeared?' asked Sasha.

'I don't even know what a burner phone is.'

'It's a pay-as-you-go, Paul, often used by people who don't want their calls to be traced.' She opened the folder and took out a copy of the texts sent between the two phones when he was in contact with Sammi, then placed them in front of him. 'Tell me if you recognize these texts.'

He glanced at them. 'I sent those, yes, but I threw the phone away months ago.'

'Except it was used on the night she went missing. She

received a call from that same number at 7:08 p.m.'

She opened the folder again and took out the texts sent on the night of Sammi's disappearance.

Please meet me 1 more time

leave me alone

Please meet me and I will leave you alone I promise 8pm

Churchill Road

ok

'Soon after that last message was sent, she went to that street and was abducted. You'll see the mobile number is the same as the one you used to communicate with her all those months ago, which makes it, by your own admission, your phone.'

'No.' He shook his head fiercely and for the first time she sensed a little steel in his response. 'I threw it out weeks ago. It was a relief to get rid of it. *I* never contacted her the other night.'

'Where did you throw it away?' asked Craig.

'The bin outside my house.'

'What time did you arrive at Karin's that night?'

'At seven thirty,' Paul told Sasha.

'Twenty minutes after the texts were sent to Sammi. And the four of you – Karin, Simon, Michelle and yourself – were in Karin's house when Sammi was bundled into a van. Lydia saw it happen. And since then I've discovered connections between Sammi and Michelle, and

Sammi and you.' What Sasha didn't say was that Simon had already been interviewed. 'There's a connection between what happened at Baden Place, and Sammi's disappearance, I'm sure of it. Tell us what it is, Paul.'

His voice rattled with tears and snot. 'I did a bad thing, and I will pray for forgiveness from God for the rest of my days, but I swear I had nothing to do with her disappearance. I threw the phone away.' He held out his hands in pathetic appeal. 'Please, I just want to go home.'

'I'm going to ask you one more time, Paul. Where's Sammi?'

'On my wife's life, on the lives of my children, I've no idea where Sammi Manning is. But she's in my prayers.'

'Yeah.' Craig stood. 'If I were Sammi, I'd tell you where to stick your prayers.'

Sasha watched Paul's shoulders heave as he wept again, trying to guess the nature of the slender thread that connected what happened to him and the other survivors at the Bad Place to the disappearance of Sammi Manning.

27

The Fifth Day...

It soon became clear that neither of the boys was going to help them escape.

Paul spent most of the time crying in the corner, but everyone had hoped Simon would protect them all. He was tall for his age, physically strong, and the only one who could possibly put up a fight if Jerry attacked them.

But Simon became more withdrawn as the hours and days went by. He stared at something crawl across the brickwork, something only visible to him. His pale complexion was clammy, his T-shirt drenched in sweat, and he became sick, as if whatever writhing phantoms he saw on the walls had made him ill. Curling up on the floor, he seemed to go into a kind of trance.

Jerry came into the room every day to throw food on the floor, little more than scraps. He waved the knife and warned them all to stay back, those orange lenses swinging angrily around the gloomy basement as if he was deciding which of them to kill first. Maybe it was just her imagination, she prayed it was, but Karin thought his gaze lingered on her. When Becky tried to tell Jerry that Simon needed a doctor, he ignored her. Slamming the door behind him, they heard the lock snap into place.

On the fifth day – or it could have been during the night, it was so difficult to tell – Becky sat beside Simon on one of the rough blankets as he shuddered with a fever.

'What can we do to help?' she asked him.

'I'm s-sorry,' he said through chattering teeth.

'You don't have to be sorry about anything. But we're worried about you, Simon, we need you.'

'The walls.' His voice was faint. 'Please... the walls.'

She leaned closer. 'I can't hear you.'

'I can't be here... in this place.' He grimaced in pain. 'It's th-the walls, they're too close, I can't b-bear it.'

Karin watched Becky stroke Simon's arm and felt a shameful burst of jealousy. He was in a bad way, she saw that, but Karin needed Becky's comfort too. Just because she wasn't ill or crying her eyes out every two minutes didn't mean she wasn't petrified; she needed her friend's love and attention just as much. And she didn't like to think about the way the man called Jerry kept looking at her...

Paul was sobbing again, and Lydia looked over and made a face at Becky. *We need you.* Paul was often hysterical with tears, and the last thing they needed was for him to start screaming. If he did, maybe Jerry would make good on his threat to kill them. Becky wearily climbed to her feet and walked over to crouch in front of him.

'Everyone is going to be so happy when you get home,' she told him.

'You don't get it,' he wailed. 'My father is going to be angry!'

'Of course he won't, he can't wait for you to come home!'

But his face crumpled with misery. 'He's going to be so mad.'

Like the others, Karin couldn't get her head around it. They were captives, and may never get home, they could be kept here for ever or killed by Jerry Swann, yet Paul was worried about his father's reaction.

'None of this is your fault,' said Becky.

Paul wrung his hands. 'He gets really mad if I get home late, or if I don't keep my room tidy, or do my home-work, he's always mad!'

'At least you've got one,' Michelle told him. 'Karin's dad pissed off years ago.'

Karin blushed with shame and Becky shot Michelle a look, *please be quiet!*

'Your dad may get angry sometimes,' Becky told Paul. 'But he won't this time, I promise. He loves you, he wants you back, and when he sees you he's going to give you a big hug. We're all going to go home soon and get on with our lives.' She held up a finger. 'Here's an idea. We should all say what we're going to be doing in ten years, and then we can all meet up and see if it came true. I'll start… I'm going to be a vet and look after sick animals. Or a marine biologist at the Great Barrier Reef. What about you, guys?'

Lydia shrugged. 'I haven't really thought about it.'

'There must be something you want to be doing in ten years?' Becky asked her gently. 'You can tell us.'

'I'll have a boyfriend, I guess.' Lydia frowned. 'And he's going to be tall and handsome and powerful, you know, like a fireman. We'll probably go out for two years and then get married, and we'll have a big house, with lots of rooms and a garage, and at least three kids – all girls, I don't want boys – and I'll dress them nice, but not the same, they'll all be different, and we'll go on holiday in Lanzarote every summer, to this resort I've been to, me and mum went there once. I'm going to stay at home so I can get involved with the school and spend time with the girls. I'll help them with their homework.' She gave an embarrassed smile. 'Well, I'll try, but the thing is, they'll be cleverer than me, a lot smarter. And they'll each play a different instrument, a cello, a violin, a guitar, and there's going to be a dining room with a table big enough for a five-thousand-piece jigsaw and we'll have a shaggy dog called Otis and a cat called Simba. And a blue Volkswagen.

'I'll probably take a part-time job in a charity shop on the High Street, but I'll always be home in time for school pick-up, and I'll take my kids to clubs and playgrounds and to those special cafés where you can paint mugs and they'll have a season pass for Alton Towers. Oh, and we'll spend months deciding which characters they'll dress up as in book week, so that they have the best costumes. I'll look after them all week, but on Sundays I'll stay in bed and Rich, that's my husband, will bring me a cup of tea, and toast and jam, and I'll lie there listening to the kids practising their instruments. I'll just lie there and...' She stared at the brick wall. 'Yeah, I'll enjoy the lie-in, just that one day a week.' She remembered the others, finally, and squirmed. 'You did ask.'

'That's really lovely, Lyds,' said Becky. 'And I bet it all comes true.'

'I hope so. You can all come and visit us, if you want. It's a big house.'

Becky turned to Michelle, who was slumped against the wall. 'What about you?'

Michelle shook her head. 'I don't know.'

'You must have some idea what you want to do.'

'My mind's gone blank.'

'Just tell us what you want to have in ten years' time?'

'Everything,' Michelle said sharply. 'If we get out of here I'm going to make sure I have *everything*.'

'You can't have everything,' said Paul.

'No, you're right,' she said with venom. 'I'm not going to have everything, because what's the point of us all getting our hopes up, we're all going to *die* down here.'

Paul's pursed mouth began to tremble.

'Of course we aren't,' Becky said. 'Please don't say that. Look, you're upsetting Paul.'

'I don't care about Paul!' Michelle swiped the tears angrily from her own eyes. 'He's not the only one who's allowed to get upset. And stop telling everyone what to do all the time, *let's talk about this, let's make-believe about that, let's stay positive*, it's doing my head in. I don't remember anybody putting you in charge!'

They all sat in tense silence. But Karin hadn't yet told them her dream for her own future, which involved her and Becky living together, and she wanted the others to hear it too. She wanted them all to know about it.

'I haven't done mine yet,' she said.

'No one wants to do it any more,' Becky told her.

'But I want to say it.'

'For God's sake, Karin!' Becky snapped. 'Nobody's in the mood!'

Karin felt a burning shame like a sharp pain in her chest, as if someone had pushed a hot nail into her heart, and she went to sit on a blanket on the other side of the room. She didn't know how long she'd been there, staring at the cold concrete between her legs, when she sensed someone sit beside her.

'I'm sorry I shouted.' Becky put an arm around her. 'I didn't mean it, it's just, Simon's not well, we're all scared and hungry and tired.' Karin heard a quiver in

Becky's voice. 'I'm trying to do my best, but it's so *hard*.'

Karin had upset Becky, when what her friend needed more than anything right now was her unconditional love, and it made her feel wretched.

'I'm sorry,' she muttered. 'I'm useless.'

'Oh, darling,' Becky said. 'You're not useless.'

'I am.'

Becky pressed her forehead against hers. Karin closed her eyes, drinking in the moment.

'You're not.' She felt Becky's warm breath on her face. 'You're an amazing person, Karin, you've just got to believe it. I'm scared, too, but I've got to get us all through this.' She laughed bitterly. 'Why does it always have to be me. It's like at that party when Tanya was sick all over the sofa, guess who had to clear it up!'

Karin's stomach clenched. 'Tell me what you want me to do.'

'When the time comes, you'll *know* what to do. We're going to get us all out of here, Karin. We will, somehow, me and you, okay?'

Karin reached for her hand. 'I'm going to get you out.'

'I know you will, my darling.' Becky kissed her. 'You're already helping me by being here.'

Karin swallowed. 'What party?'

'What?'

Karin searched Becky's face, looking for reassurance. 'What party was Tanya sick at?'

Becky smiled. 'You know, Julie's sleepover.'

'Julie had a sleepover?' asked Karin.

'Yes.' Becky looked embarrassed. 'I forgot you weren't there. I only went because I thought you'd be going!'

Karin knew Julie liked Becky, and sometimes she'd find them sitting together in the canteen. When she approached the table, Julie would make a face at Becky, like, what does *she* want? Karin knew she'd never be invited to one of Julie's stupid sleepovers, or anywhere else, because she didn't fit in with those girls, the ones who thought they were cool and who looked down their noses at everyone else. She didn't mind Becky going to the party, of course she didn't, but she didn't understand why Becky hadn't told her.

'No,' said Karin. 'I didn't know about it.'

'I wouldn't have gone if I thought you weren't going to be there, honest. I'm so sorry, Kaz, I should have told you. Do you forgive me? I really couldn't bear it if you didn't forgive me.'

'Of course I do,' said Karin.

Then she let Becky take her in her arms and hold her. 'Thank you, my darling, thank you so much.'

And they sat together like that for a while, and Karin felt a bit better – but then they heard footsteps pounding downstairs. The lock snapped, the cellar door was flung open, and Jerry Swann ran in. Everyone, except Simon on the floor, pressed themselves against the walls.

'You!' The blood froze in Karin's veins when Jerry pointed at her. 'Come with me!'

She shook her head, terrified.

'Where are you taking her?' Becky raced forward. 'Please don't hurt her.'

He pointed the knife into Becky's face. 'Keep your mouth shut or I'll tear your throat out!'

And then Jerry grabbed Karin's wrist and dragged her away.

She felt his fingers dig deep into the flesh of her arm as he pushed her out of the door and up the stairs.

28

At lunchtime, Karin had to get out of school, away from the noise and crowds, the whispers and glances. Sometimes she sensed a phone being lifted behind her back and guessed her image was being uploaded on to social media. She knew the hashtags:

#BadPlacebitch
#Jerrysgirl
#RememberBecky

She should take some leave, until the whole thing blew over, until Sammi came home and the news juggernaut rolled on to something else. She loved her work, teaching was her lifeline, and her year eleven pupils were about to sit their exams. She wanted to support them, but didn't want to be a distraction.

So she went for a walk, moving at speed down side streets where she knew she wouldn't bump into any school kids or her colleagues, gripping the phone in her pocket in case she received another message from *her* – she'd not received any more texts from Becky since last night but Karin lived in hope, even all these years later she still had hope – and then headed back, feeling the exercise had done her good.

She came out on the main road that led to River Hill School, saw the gates up ahead, and found herself surrounded by groups of school kids coming out of newsagents' and cafés, eating burgers and chips from polystyrene tubs, and walking back to school for the afternoon. A couple of her pupils waved. A car slowed; the parent at the wheel gave her a cold look.

Someone called her name – 'Karin!' – and she instinctively stiffened, but turned to see Simon trotting towards her on the pavement.

'What are you doing here?' she asked him in surprise.

There was a bulging rucksack on his back, a sleeping bag rolled beneath it. 'I wanted to say goodbye.'

'What are you talking about?'

'I'm getting out of here,' he said. 'I'm leaving.'

'You can't,' she told him. 'You're on bail. You have to stay at your current address, it's the law.'

He looked up and down the road, as if expecting a police car to pull up at any moment. Karin had no idea where he would go; he probably didn't either.

'I made a mistake. I tried to help Becky's brother, I thought I was doing the right thing, but he was using me. Michelle didn't deserve that. It's this place, this town. I can't think here, Karin, I have to get away.'

'I really wouldn't do it, not with everything that's happening. The police told me Paul has been arrested, he... took photos of the girl who went missing. He's probably going to be charged.' But Simon looked adamant, and she asked, 'Where will you go?'

'Somewhere quiet, somewhere nobody will recognize me. Overseas, maybe.' He shook his head. 'I'm not coming back.'

'They'll find you, they'll bring you back. You'll go to prison for breaking the terms of the bail. And then you won't be able to go anywhere. They'll lock you up, Simon.'

He frowned at the pavement. A group of pupils walked past, looking at them curiously. 'Hello, miss!'

'We can't talk here.' She was worried for Simon's state of mind. If he went to prison, if he was jailed, she knew it would break him. She remembered his fevered writing on the floor of Jerry Swann's cellar, remembered how sick he had been in confinement. She had to talk him out of running. 'Let's go to—'

He held up his hands to stop her. 'I've been thinking about it a lot and I've made my decision. I need to go. I did a bad thing to Michelle and I can't forgive myself. I can't stay here, I need to get my head straight.'

'Please,' she begged. 'Don't run away. Even if what you did was wrong, you did it for what you believed were the best of reasons, and I think even Michelle will understand that. Becky's brother, that Jim – he was using you, Simon, manipulating you. He's an angry man who has always blamed us for what happened to Becky.'

'You're not going to change my mind. We won't meet again.'

She felt helpless. 'You know, every year when we all get back together, I think that's it, it's the last time, I don't want to see any of you ever again. Every year I vow never to do it again and I always do. And now look, you're making the decision for me.'

He gave her a big hug. It was the first time they had physically touched for maybe twenty-six years.

'I'd be grateful if you didn't tell anyone you saw me.'

'I'm going to miss you.'

'Hey, miss!' called a voice. Distracted, she looked across the street and saw Lucas, his face obscured every few moments by the cars that whipped past.

'Who's that?' asked Simon.

'A boy from my class.'

Lucas stood at the edge of the pavement trying to get across, impatiently waiting for a gap in the stream of traffic. One, two, three vehicles passed. And then a gap opened up and he stepped off the pavement—

Just as a car screeched to a halt beside him and someone jumped out. Lucas staggered back, confused by the figure in a balaclava who stabbed something into his arm.

Karin watched in horror, trying to see what was

happening as cars roared past, one after the other, obscuring her view.

'Stop him!' Karin screamed. 'Stop him!'

Lucas's legs buckled and his limp figure was gathered up by the masked figure. Karin only saw flashes as he was lifted into the back of the car, watched by a bewildered group of children. Then the figure, face hidden, ran to the driver's side.

But Simon pulled back his shoulders, letting the heavy backpack fall to the pavement, and ran into the road. A car skidded to a halt in front of him, horn blaring, and he rolled across the bonnet in a fluid movement, landing on his feet. Simon grabbed the figure as he was climbing behind the wheel, but the driver punched him low in the gut. The wind knocked out of him, he doubled over. The figure lifted a leg and kicked him into the road.

Karin watched helplessly as Simon flew into the path of a van. There was a sickening crunch as he was hit at high speed. The van skidded left and right as the driver panicked, smashing into parked cars. Glass exploded, metal screeched, alarms shrieked. Simon spun in mid-air, rolled along the road – and lay still.

The car taking Lucas accelerated away down the road; Karin heard it skid around a corner and out of sight even above the sound of screaming children. She ran to Simon, who was splayed in the middle of the road.

'Someone call an ambulance,' she shouted at the crowd of kids. 'Now!'

Simon wasn't moving, she couldn't find a pulse.

Happening again; it was happening again.

29

Simon was taken away in an ambulance and the street cordoned off so that officers could search for evidence. Lucas's school bag was collected, but the syringe witnesses had seen the driver use to subdue him wasn't found.

The teenagers who had seen the incident were interviewed at the school and offered counselling. One pupil had filmed the abduction taking place on his mobile, but much of the action was hidden behind busy traffic. There was a clear view of the vehicle, a blue Mazda, but the driver who bundled Lucas inside was mostly obscured by passing vehicles and the jerky movements of the kid holding the phone. He and his friends gasped in excitement and disbelief when Simon was struck by the van. Other witnesses confirmed that the car's number plates were hidden.

A child rescue alert had already been issued; local taxi drivers and other emergency services were notified. Local radio and TV networks made appeals. Patrol cars combed the streets and a helicopter sent from the police air base in North Weald flew over the town. As Sasha stood in the middle of the street barking into her mobile, she could hear its low throb disturbing the quiet of the afternoon, occasionally glimpsed its hard silver body glinting against the sun as it hovered in the distance, monitoring traffic, watching for suspicious activity, for that Mazda.

As news of Lucas's abduction spread around the school, causing fear and upset, the decision was made to send pupils home for the rest of the day. Parents were contacted by text and asked to collect their children, and it was requested they didn't come by car. Pupils whose parents weren't able to come early were discouraged from going home alone and required to wait in the school hall. Staff were under strict instructions not to allow kids to leave with anybody unfamiliar.

Sasha spent most of her afternoon moving back and forth between the crime scene and the school, coordinating the search for the vehicle and the missing boy. She eventually managed to sit down with Karin in the headmaster's office and they discussed the sequence of events: Simon's arrival and Lucas's appearance, his abduction.

'Tell me again about the driver,' said Sasha, encouraging Karin to dig a little deeper for detail. 'It was a man, you said?'

'I think so.' Karin was still shaken. 'He was tall, with

broad shoulders. But he was across the road, it all happened so quickly, and there was so much traffic, so I couldn't see properly. He wore a balaclava. Look, can we speak again later, I really need to see how Simon is doing.'

'I won't keep you much longer.'

Karin stood, frustrated. 'I don't even know where he's been taken.'

'He's at University Hospital,' Lolly said from the doorway.

'Why did Simon come to see you?'

Karin looked uncomfortable at Sasha's question. 'We discussed what was happening with Sammi's abduction... and the news about Paul.'

'His rucksack was found on the street,' Sasha said. 'He looked like he was about to leave town. You know he'd be violating his bail conditions.'

'I don't know anything about that.' Karin moved towards the door. 'I'm sorry, there's nothing more I can say that I haven't already told you. I have to go.'

'I can drive her,' Lolly said.

'Don't worry, I'll take Karin myself.'

Sasha had been expecting to visit Lucas's parents, a task she wasn't looking forward to, but Ajay and Craig said they would go in her place so that she could continue to coordinate the search. But Sasha wanted to talk more to Karin about the abduction and she'd be able to do that on the way to the hospital.

When they walked into the corridor, groups of school kids were heading to the hall, some of them energized and laughing, delighted at getting an unexpected afternoon off; others were in tears.

Outside, tempers frayed as a group of parents confronted school staff. Sasha and Karin saw Jim Haskell in the thick of it, despite the fact that he had no kids at the school. He was angrily berating a teacher, but when Karin walked past, he nudged some of the parents, and they all glared at her.

Sasha spotted Denny with his mates, a pair of white earbuds draped over his shoulders. Sasha had already phoned Angel, who told her in a faint voice – to emphasize the indisputable fact of her illness – that she was in bed watching Netflix.

When Sasha called, Denny came over. 'They're sending us home, some kid got snatched outside. What are you doing here?'

'What do you think I'm doing here?' she said. 'I'm working.'

Sasha couldn't help herself, she reached out to tousle his hair. Embarrassed in front of his friends, Denny reared back. 'Don't!'

'Do you know the boy, Lucas White?'

He shrugged. 'Not really, he's a couple of years above me.'

'Denny, make sure you and your friends go home together. Stay in a pack.'

'We were going to head to the High Street,' he told her. 'To hang out.'

'Stay at home and *chill*.' Denny grimaced at her embarrassing uncoolness. 'Glue your eyeballs to your phone, knock yourself out on some funny YouTube videos, dancing cats, whatever, but do your old mum a solid, watch them in the garden.'

'Like I need your permission to go on my phone.' Denny rolled his eyes, playing to the crowd. 'Anyway, there's already been one kidnapping today. The chances of there being another one are astronomical.'

His mates laughed.

Denny smiled at Karin. 'How are you, miss, alright?'

'I'm good, Denny,' said Karin. 'Thanks for asking.'

When he shuffled off, Sasha called after him, just in case he didn't get the message the first time, 'Straight home!'

'I didn't realize Denny was yours,' said Karin. 'He's a nice kid.'

'Yeah,' said Sasha, grateful for the validation. 'Sometimes.'

When they got to Southend University Hospital, Lydia and Michelle, who had been told what happened by Karin, were already sitting in the Emergency Department. Lydia was rocking backwards and forwards, and Michelle was awkwardly patting her arm, not trying very hard to comfort her. She jumped up as soon as she saw Karin and Sasha.

'Is there any news?'

'Lucas hasn't been found, I'm afraid, but we're doing everything in our power to—'

'I meant about Sammi,' Michelle said sharply. 'I know you're keeping Jessica and Alan informed, but nobody tells me anything.'

'No,' admitted Sasha, 'but I can assure you we're working on a number of avenues of enquiry, and have prioritized strategies that—'

'Please!' Michelle held up a hand. 'Talk like a human being.'

Sasha nodded. 'You're quite right, I'm sorry, I—'

'What about Simon?' Karin asked, taking the heat out of the situation. 'Have they said anything?'

'Nothing.' Michelle glanced towards the doors where the paramedics had wheeled him in to surgery. 'We don't know what's happening.'

Sasha's phone rang again; she had been unwilling to answer it while Karin was in the car, and needed to stay in touch with her team in case there were any developments.

'Excuse me.' She took the phone from her bag and, despite seeing the caller ID, said, 'I'm going to have to take this.'

'When are you home?' asked Ursula as Sasha walked towards the automatic doors at the entrance.

'Not now, Mum,' she said. 'It's not a good time.'

'It's a simple question and doesn't take any time at all to answer.'

'I'm very busy,' Sasha insisted.

'Five, six?'

'It's going to be difficult tonight.' She lifted her eyes to the ceiling, counted slowly to three, and then said, 'If I'm honest, I'm probably going to be very late.'

Her mother tutted. 'You can't work yourself into the ground every night.'

'Something's happened and I'm going to have to stay to—'

'I was hoping to make it a surprise, but I may as well tell you now. We're all going to have a barbecue, spend some nice family time together. If you're not here, it'll be spoiled.'

'That's very sweet of you, Mum,' said Sasha, 'but you should have checked with me first. Another child has gone missing.'

'I saw that,' said Ursula dubiously, as if the whole thing was fake news.

'As you can appreciate, I've got a lot, and I mean a *lot*, to do here.'

'Hold on a moment.'

Sasha heard a door slam at the other end and Ursula's muffled voice asking Denny why he was home so early. She heard him say 'A kid got kidnapped', as if it happened every day, and thump up the stairs.

Ursula came back on the phone. 'Please try and get home by seven or you'll ruin everything.'

'Mum.' Sasha was getting frustrated. 'I told you I'm not—'

But her mother had already rung off. Sasha gurned angrily at the phone, just as Karin and Michelle came over with a doctor, who introduced himself as a trauma consultant.

'Mr Parkin is in a very bad way,' he told Sasha while the others listened grimly. 'He has physical injuries to his pelvis, spine and ribs from the point of impact, multiple internal injuries, and, I'm afraid, considerable swelling on the brain.'

'Is he in any condition to talk?' Simon was the only person who saw the abductor up close and may be able to provide vital descriptive details.'

'He's unconscious,' said the doctor. 'He's been given a sedative and a paralytic to prevent movement, and we've placed him on a ventilator.'

'And when will he be conscious?'

'Not until we can bring the swelling down. A day or two, certainly not before that.'

'Thank you,' said Sasha, and the doctor strode away.

'Simon is not my favourite person at the moment, I can tell you that, but I would never wish anything like this on him.' Tears filmed Michelle's eyes. 'Paul, on the other hand, can rot in hell for what he did to Sammi.'

Sasha watched Michelle walk away, guessing that she was going to lock herself in a cubicle to gulp down vodka.

Karin glanced over to where Lydia was rocking on the seat. 'Lydia came to see me last night.'

'Okay.'

'She said she was seeing somebody, she had a new boyfriend. I got the sense he had been asking about Simon and Paul and Michelle… and about me. About what happened to us all.'

'You think he has some kind of agenda?'

'It just seems odd that this man has come into her life out of nowhere. If she had known him for any length of time she would have told me about him before, unless he asked her not to. She said she met him at the drug drop-in centre where she goes for group counselling, it's in Basildon. Lydia is fragile, always has been, and I'm worried about what he's been asking… and what he's been putting into her head.'

'Let's go and talk to her.'

Sasha and Karin went over to the corner where Lydia was sitting.

'What?' Lydia stared at them. 'What's going on?'

'Tell Sasha what you told me last night.' Karin perched on the seat beside her. 'About Matt, your boyfriend.'

'What's it got to do with him?' Lydia reared away from her. 'You leave him out of it. He ain't got nothing to do with this, yeah, any of it!'

Sitting down opposite, Sasha smiled. 'I bet he's really nice, Lydia. What's his surname?'

'What's his name got to do with anything?' Lydia began to rock anxiously. 'Why did Karin tell you about him, why is she being so nasty?'

Karin was about to speak but Sasha gave an imperceptible shake of her head, *let me do it*.

'Karin told me he was asking questions about you, about what happened at the Bad Place.'

'Why can't he? Everyone wants to know about that, like, all the time.'

'There's no reason he can't, but a girl has gone missing, taken in front of you, Lydia, and now one of Karin's pupils has been abducted in front of her, and Simon is badly injured. It's my job to speak to as many people as possible so I can tick them off my to-do list. I'd just like to have a quick chat with Matt to rule him out of any involvement.'

'He's not involved, yeah,' Lydia insisted. 'Because he loves me, he told me so.'

'Of course he does.' Sasha nodded encouragingly. 'So let us all put our minds at rest.'

'Foster,' said Lydia. 'His name is Matt Foster.'

'Do you have a number for him?'

'He's got nothing to do with it.' Lydia was rocking harder. 'You've got it all wrong. If you speak to him he won't want to be with me no more, he'll leave me.'

'Why would he do that?'

'For bringing him into the whole thing. He don't like the police.' Lydia took a cheap mobile from her parka pocket, rubbing her thumb along its worn plastic casing as she considered whether to give Sasha the number. 'I'm meeting him later on the seafront. I can ask if he wants to speak to you, if you want.'

'Why don't we come with you and I can speak to him, then we'll be able to leave him alone, how does that sound?'

Lydia reared away. 'Why would you want to do that?'

'To save time. I'll have a brief chat and then I can eliminate him from our enquiries.'

Lydia blinked. 'Eliminate him?'

Sasha smiled. 'Figure of speech.'

'I'll ask him,' said Lydia, and began to punch in a number on her phone. 'See if he's happy about that, yeah?'

Sasha placed her hand gently on Lydia's. 'There's no need to disturb him, I'll just come along, have a quick chat with Matt and then go.'

30

They stood waiting beside one of the food concessions on Marine Parade. The street was filled with tourists enjoying sea and sun after a blow-out lunch, families heading to Adventure Island, or to catch the train to take them along the pier. Sasha sipped on a bitter coffee, waiting for the man called Matt Foster to emerge from the crowd.

'He should be here by now.' Lydia frantically searched the crowd, wiping the sweat off her forehead with the sleeve of her parka. 'He said to meet by this van, but he must have changed his mind, yeah, he don't love me no more.'

'Why don't you take that off?' asked Karin, tugging at the heavy coat, but Lydia jerked her arm away.

'Leave me be!'

Sasha tipped the rest of the coffee away on the sandy pavement and binned the cup, took out her phone to check her messages. She saw a missed call from Ajay and rang him back, and he told her Lucas's parents had been informed of their son's abduction.

'They're terrified, of course they are, Sasha, but...' He hesitated. 'Am I on speakerphone?'

'No.' She kept her voice neutral in front of Karin and Lydia. 'You're okay.'

'The first thing they asked was whether we believed Karin was involved in his abduction. They have some pretty strong opinions about her and demanded she's questioned as a suspect. The Bad Place has been linked too many times in the news with Sammi's disappearance.'

'I see.' Sasha smiled when Karin glanced at her. 'Thanks, DS de Vaz, keep me informed of any other developments, and I'll be back soon.'

She killed the call, but saw the voicemail sent this morning from River Hill School, before Lucas's abduction, and listened to it. It was from a teacher who identified herself as the school's head of pastoral care, whatever that was, asking Sasha to come in tomorrow morning for an urgent meeting. The teacher didn't want to go into detail over the phone, but was clearly calling about Tilly's bullying of Angel. They were on top of the situation, at least, and Sasha hoped it would soon get sorted.

Dropping the phone in her bag, she clapped her hands, ready for business. They'd been waiting nearly twenty minutes now. Sasha considered returning to the station; this Matt character could wait till another time.

But then a group of teenagers sauntered past, laughing

at Lydia's crumpled parka, her dirty old trainers and pale, pinched face.

'Look,' one of them called, 'it's Skeletor!'

Lydia reacted angrily. 'Get lost!'

'Piss off, weirdo!' The group began to taunt her.

'Don't you talk to me like that, yeah?' Lydia surged forward. 'I'm better than you!'

'Hey.' Karin tried to pull her back. 'Just ignore them, Matt's going to be here soon.'

But the kids were dancing about, giving Lydia grief, making her more upset. Karin asked them to move along, but they ignored her.

'Calm down, you old witch, or you're going to have a heart attack!'

'You're nasty!' Lydia's face twisted in fury. 'You should be ashamed!'

Deciding to bring this situation to an end, Sasha rooted in her bag for her warrant card. She held it out stiffly, movie style, so they all copped an eyeful.

'Jog on,' she told them.

They laughed at her white hair. 'You're late for bingo, Grandma!'

But the kids lost interest and walked off, just as Sasha's attention was grabbed by a figure in a hoodie approaching along the seafront. Karin grabbed her arm.

'It's him,' she whispered. 'He took Lucas!'

Sasha felt a flutter of apprehension. 'Are you sure?'

'He's dressed in the same clothes, it's the same man.'

The figure stopped further along the pavement, his face lost in the dark of the hood, as Sasha tried to get Lydia's attention.

'Is that Matt?'

Lydia's face lit up, and she called, 'Matt, Matt!'

Seeing that Lydia wasn't alone, the man hesitated, and turned back the way he had come.

'He hasn't seen us!' cried Lydia.

'Oh, he's seen us alright,' said Sasha, shoving her bag into Karin's hands. 'Call my office, Detective Sergeant de Vaz, he's in my recents!'

Then she began to trot towards the figure, meaning to follow him. The crowds thickening around her, she weaved in and out of the families walking along the pavement. The hooded figure walked quickly into the road, crossing towards the arcades and gift shops, sliding between the crawling traffic, and Sasha kept pace, until the man began to run – and disappeared into an arcade.

Following him in, it took her a moment to adjust to the cacophony of noise and light as she made her way along a narrow corridor of machines; the slots and games, dozens of them, flashing and whirling and whooping at full volume. Every fruit machine and video game hurled out deafening music and sound effects – crashes and gunfire and explosions and bleeping melodies and the electronic clatter of cascading coins – so loud that the pop song playing full blast on the speaker system was lost in the discordant din.

There were kids running about, and parents feeding money into the slots, as Sasha scanned along the aisles, to her left, to her right, examining all the people, moving down one row of machines and up another, turning full circle, worried that she'd lost him.

She headed towards the back of the arcade where there was often a rear exit that led directly to the car park behind the parade. A kid pointed a yellow rifle at a screen and a horde of zombies exploded with sickening screams. *Game over!* A racing car roared around a virtual racetrack and flew off the road, exploding into a million pieces. *Game over!* A jangling bank of fruit machines seemed to shimmer and shake as lights raced up and down their metal casings. *Win! Win! Win!*

She could barely hear herself think as she tried to find the guy. She went down one aisle – it was a dead end – and doubled back, and the next aisle was also empty. The tannoy blared but the voice was distorted. Pressing deeper into the room, Sasha raced down another aisle, the only one left – and hit another dead end. She was about to turn—

But her arm was yanked painfully behind her back and she was pushed forward. Slammed head first into a machine. Her forehead hit the glass of the screen, the noise was deafening against her ear, manic lights exploded in her vision. All she could see was a blur of red and yellow and blue. The symbols on the screen, fruits and numbers and coins and dollar signs, spun and stopped, spun again.

A hand grabbed a fistful of her hair to shove her into the machine again, and then her thoughts became sluggish and the strength ebbed from her legs. Her body wanted to slide to the floor despite her best intentions to stay upright, but the hand kept her pressed against the side of the machine.

'You're going to be sorry!' She felt hot breath on her ear and a voice hissed, 'You'll know the truth about her!'

And then she was released and Sasha flopped on to the carpet beside the machine and lay there, struggling to find the strength to get to her feet.

Disorientated, the world flashing and whirling above her, noise and light detonating inside her head.

31

Crouched in front of Sasha, the paramedic said, 'How many fingers am I holding up?'

Sasha blinked. 'Fifteen.'

The paramedic shook his head gravely at Vaughn.

'Oh, come *on*,' said Sasha. 'I was joking. Someone with a sense of humour can't possibly have concussion, I'm perfectly fine. Help me up, please, I need to get back to work.'

Vaughn climbed on to the back of the ambulance, where she was sitting on a trolley. 'No, you're not, you're going home.'

'Any dizziness or ringing in the ears? Do you feel nauseous?' asked the paramedic.

'I heard bells,' Sasha said, 'but that was probably the fruit machines.'

He tried to ask her another question, but Sasha ignored him, climbing from the ambulance with as much dignity as she could in front of hundreds of tourists. As far as she was concerned, the angry bump on her forehead looked worse than it actually was.

'Vaughn, really, there's too much to do, I need to get back—'

'It wasn't a suggestion, Sasha, I'm *telling* you, go home.'

'There's CCTV along here,' she said, pointing at a camera on the top of a street lamp. 'He'll be captured on those.'

'Look who you're talking to.' Vaughn pointed to his own face. 'I know all that, we'll get the footage, and tomorrow morning I'll want a description of your attacker.'

'Lydia will be able to give you a proper description,' she said, feeling excitement that they could finally have a breakthrough. 'And she has a number for him.'

They looked over to a patrol car where Lydia was sitting in the back talking angrily to Karin, her face a mess of tears and snot. 'She's in considerable distress, we're not going to get anything from her tonight.'

'Tomorrow, then,' Sasha insisted. 'As soon as.'

'Go home.'

It was nearly six now and still as hot as hell. The pounding rays of the sun felt like a furnace inside her skull. Bloody hell, she thought, will this heatwave ever end?

'I'll take a couple of painkillers,' she said.

'Stay away from aspirin,' said the paramedic, closing the ambulance doors, 'as that can cause internal bleeding. And if you suffer from vomiting, seizures, loss of consciousness or abnormal motor function or speech, then attend the ED.'

'Thank you,' she said and turned back to Vaughn. 'You're not going to replace me when I go home? It's not an excuse to get me out of the office? I mean, Ajay's very good and sooner or later he's going to want to step up but—' She felt a sharp twinge in her temple that made her lift her hand to her head, but then pretend to bat a fly off her fringe. 'My God, it's still really hot, isn't it… where was I… Uh, I feel a lot of threads are coming together, Vaughn. Trouble is, now Lucas White has been taken, and—'

'I'm not going to tell you again, Sasha,' snapped Vaughn. 'Go home or I will *definitely* replace you.'

Sasha saw Craig talking to another officer and motioned him over.

'Lydia met Matt at a drug support centre she attends in Basildon. I'd like you to go there to find out who he is.'

'By the time we get there it'll be closed.' He looked at the angry bump. 'Are you sure you're okay?'

'Go first thing. I'll be coming in to work tomorrow morning and hopefully by then everyone will have stopped gaslighting me.'

'Tell me again what he said to you, this man,' said Vaughn.

'He told me we'd discover the truth about her.'

'About Lydia?'

Sasha looked again at Lydia getting emotional in the car, and Karin beside her with her head bowed.

'Maybe,' she said thoughtfully. 'He said, *you'll be sorry*, just before he smashed my head against the machine. I don't imagine it was a threat against me specifically, maybe he meant he was going to harm the missing kids.'

'So you definitely think he's the abductor?'

'I'm convinced of it,' she said.

'Either way it doesn't sound good.' Vaughn hooked a finger at a PC. With officers moving between the school and the incident room, local resources were already stretched to breaking point. 'I'll get someone to drive you home.'

'No need, my car's parked behind the arcades,' she said.

He laughed in her face. 'Good try. You can pick it up tomorrow morning.'

'Okay,' she said. 'But I'll definitely be in first thing, because I'm fine. Look at this.' She lifted a hand, intending to show how steady it was, but when it trembled, she dropped it, explaining, 'That's shock, not concussion.'

Minutes later, she was travelling home in the back of a car, trying not to shut her eyes, because every time she did she heard Sammi Manning's fragile voice, saw her singing on stage; the girl looked like she was weeping, and it made Sasha feel nauseous. When she got home and let herself inside, she smelled cooking meat and wondered if it was a sign she was having a brain haemorrhage.

'You're home!' Her delighted mother came to meet her, a packet of salad in her hand. 'I'd almost given up on you.'

'What's going on?'

'I told you, we're having a barbecue.'

Oh God, she thought. 'I'm really not in the mood, Mum.'

It was bad enough being sent home. She had a headache, yes, but it wasn't like she had double vision or couldn't remember the names of her children. But she was there now, and wanted to get an early night so she was fighting fit tomorrow morning. Two children had been abducted and she didn't feel like sitting around making *happy-happy* with Ursula.

'It'll do you a world of good.'

She followed her mother into the kitchen where Ursula took a cold bottle of white from the fridge to pour Sasha a large glass.

'Not for me.'

'If you don't care to join in,' her mum said in a voice dripping with disappointment, 'be my guest, go to bed and we'll have all the fun without you.'

Sasha saw the meat Ursula had bought for the barbecue on the counter. Plates of uncooked pork chops and sausages and steaks and chicken legs and beef patties, enough to feed an army.

'I've put Kevin to work.' She looked up from halving

burger buns and gestured outside where he was firing up the grill. 'And I'm doing the salad.'

She saw the bump on Sasha's forehead and reached out to touch it. 'What on earth happened?'

'Ouch!' It hurt when her mother pressed her fingers to it – *what was she thinking?* – and Sasha swatted her away. The last thing she was going to do was tell Ursula she had been slammed head first into a fruit machine. Her mother would only complain again about her job – 'it'll be the death of you' was a favourite phrase – or more probably tell her off for hanging around the arcades. 'I fell on the stairs at work.'

'Then you should sue.' Sasha picked up the glass of wine and Ursula took it from her. 'Maybe you shouldn't drink in your condition.'

'It's just a bruise.' Sasha decided that if they were going to have a barbecue, then what she really needed was a tiny sip – painkillers be damned, if she ended up insensible by the end of the evening, then all the better – and snatched the glass back. 'What do you want me to do?'

'I don't want you to do anything,' said her mother. 'Just go outside and plonk yourself in a lounger and leave everything to me.'

Unused to having leisure time forced upon her, Sasha instinctively took out her phone to check her emails.

'No, put that away. You're going to eat and drink and relax. Actually, you can give me that.'

Sasha laughed. 'I'm not a child, Mum, I'm not going to give you my phone.'

'I take it there are people in the office, working hard to locate those children?'

'Yes, but—'

'Then, no buts, give.' Ursula held out a hand. 'You can have it back in a couple of hours, by which time you won't care to look at it. Until then, you're forbidden to use it.'

Sasha reluctantly handed it over. 'This is totally unnecessary.'

Ursula slipped the phone in her apron pocket and started buttering a heap of rolls.

'How many people have you invited?'

'Oh, did you want people here?' asked her mother. 'I thought we could keep it small and select. But Angel has invited some friends – I must say, she seems to have perked up since this morning.'

Sasha sipped her chilled wine, just what the doctor ordered, as Angel came through the kitchen with a group of her girlfriends – ''lo, Mrs Dawson!' they all shrieked – and ran up the garden, where her mother had placed cushions and throws on the ground.

'Glad to see Angel's feeling better.' Sasha nodded at the meat. 'You do know she's a vegetarian these days?'

Ursula smiled tersely. 'We'll see about that.'

'Cheers,' said Sasha and she lifted her glass.

'Down the hatch,' said Ursula and sipped her own

wine. It was good of her mother to do this, really, and Sasha would do her best to put Sammi and Lucas out of her mind for the evening.

She watched Kev flipping burgers as he sang to music on the radio and did a bit of dad dancing, well aware that Angel's friends were taking the piss. They gave him grief about his moves and he answered back, in good spirits. He seemed more like his old self as he pushed meat and veggies around the grill. Giving a man bits of flesh to cook clearly had some mysterious recuperative effect.

'As soon as they pick up those tongs,' said Ursula, as if reading her mind, 'it stops their minds churning.'

'What are you talking about?'

'He's struggling, surely you can see that?'

'He's just...' Sasha tried to capture the right word, but what was it? Quiet... reserved... 'A bit preoccupied.'

'He's depressed, is what he is.'

Ursula saying the D-word shocked Sasha, who had pussyfooted around the idea without ever daring to utter the word herself. Part of her expected Kev to snap out of his funk at any moment and – what, come to his senses? It was almost inconceivable that her happy-go-lucky husband could be depressed. Down in the dumps, yes, a little bit blue, under the weather, maybe even at a push... *sad*. But her mother was absolutely right, there was no other word to describe it. Kev was depressed, that's exactly what he was.

And the truth jolted her, because Kev had always been the strong one, the cheerful one, the one who took life by the horns.

He'd helped her through the darkest days, when Jake died. When a driver lost control of his car while they were on a trip to London. Sasha had gone into a shop with Denny and Angel, one of those places where they sold fancy notebooks and stationery, while Kev waited outside with Jake because the damned buggy – which was the width of a lorry, and laden down with bags of shopping – wouldn't fit through the door. She remembered touching the page of a diary, remembered still the pale, smooth pulp of the paper beneath her fingertips.

And the moment her hand lifted from that blank page, her life was changed.

She heard a crunch in the street, the ground judder, the buzzing vibration of the window, and then a single moment of ghastly silence before the other customers gasped. Outside, Kev roared in terror. Blood shrieked in her veins, and in that instant her DNA was for ever scrambled, rearranged.

A driver had lost control. His car mounted the pavement.

Something was lost. Her boy, her youngest.

And she was never the same person again. In those early days, she didn't think she'd ever survive his loss. For weeks, she barely had the strength to move from the bed. She was gripped by a numbness, a paralysis.

She couldn't sleep, couldn't eat. She cried all the time. It hurt to open her eyes and to close them. The world was sluggish, drained of colour and energy. Her grief was a physical pain. She relived the agony he must have experienced again and again, it kept her awake long into the night and it was the first thing she imagined when she woke after a few hours of fitful sleep. Some days, all she wanted to do was curl into a ball and forget all the people who loved her, the people who needed her.

Sasha believed she would never be able to face the world again, but she did, and she had Kev's strength and attentiveness to thank for that. He would hold her until she fell asleep, or bring her other children to her, when all she could think about was that she would never hold Jake in her arms again. He let her mourn for as long as she needed, and after a few months that all-consuming grief began to abate. Life went on, she found her feet. She planted one foot in front of the other, and then the other – and her life resumed. She didn't forget, she could never do that, but the world kept turning.

But she realized now that she had taken Kev's own strength for granted. Something was eating away at him. When the party was over, she'd speak to him about it, force him to discuss whatever it was.

And then the doorbell rang. Sasha put down her wine to answer the door, but Ursula hotfooted it around the counter and shoved the glass back into her hand. 'You go and *relax*!'

Sasha followed her, curious to see who had arrived, and when the door opened, she couldn't believe her eyes.

32

As soon as Karin felt his body judder and he moaned, she pushed him off. Louis lay on the bed staring up at the ceiling, getting his breath back, and she sat up to look around the floor for her underwear.

'That was good,' he said, 'but it always is.'

His knuckles brushed against her spine, so she lifted herself from the bed to slip her knickers on. What she wanted to do was lie on the tangled sheets and let him hold her for a few minutes more. But that wasn't the deal she'd made with herself, that's not how it worked. When it was over, when they were both finished – whether it was Louis or one of the others – she just wanted to get out of there.

Particularly tonight. He'd been tense in the bar, as if he was building up the courage to say something. Whatever it was he wanted to say, she didn't want to hear it. Karin reached for her phone on the bedside cabinet and checked for messages, but there was nothing from Becky.

'You've been looking at your phone all night.'

She pulled on her jeans, then dropped to her hands and knees to search for a shoe that had been kicked under the bed. 'Have I?'

He propped a pillow behind his head. 'Going already?'

'Looks like it.' She was eager to get out of that hotel room before he got dressed and insisted on leaving with her. 'Things to do.'

'Look, Karin, there was something I wanted to—'

'*Don't.*' Pulling the shoe out, she looked over the top of the mattress.

Louis made a face. 'You don't know what it is yet.'

'Whatever it is, I don't want to hear it.'

He plumped the pillows behind him. 'I'm splitting up with my wife.'

'None of my business.'

He was married, of course he was. That was the only reason they were here. Sometimes she needed to be close to another human being, she needed a release, someone to fuck, and to give herself permission to hold, and be held by, another human being, no strings attached.

The other men she saw were also in long-term relationships, they had partners, families, mostly businessmen from London or elsewhere, whose work brought them occasionally to the Essex coast. Sometimes when they were here, they gave her a call. She'd meet them for a drink, or a meal, and then they would go to a hotel room. And as soon as they finished, she would leave.

They'd split the cost of the room, and the food and drink – she insisted on it. The men weren't interested in anything more, and that suited Karin just fine. And if she didn't see any of them for months, she'd go to a bar and pick someone up. A seaside resort like this, there were always plenty of men happy to oblige. She'd bring them to this hotel, or one just like it. She never, ever took them home.

Louis was a handsome man, and he was good in bed, but she was going to have to ditch him, because lately he'd been giving off too many vibes. She'd catch him looking at her with a searching expression on his face. She suspected he wanted something more. He liked her too much.

'I told her there was someone else,' he said. 'Someone I can't get out of my head.'

'Then you were mistaken. Because that's not what this is.'

She was annoyed that he was spoiling everything, that he was asking for too much. He knew the rules, she had been very clear with him, it was a relationship of convenience, and she thought he understood that. He should just accept it for what it was. Karin quickly gathered her things and pulled on her jacket. But one arm was turned inside out and she struggled with it.

He placed his hands behind his head, stretching on the bed. 'We could have more, if that's what you—'

Her phone vibrated, and letting the sleeve drop to her side, she pulled the device quickly from her jeans, heart racing. But it was a text from Lydia.

Soz i shouted

XXX

Louis saw the disappointment on her face. 'Expecting a call from anyone special?'

Ignoring him, she forced her arm violently into the sleeve. 'I don't want more, I just want this. You've always known that.'

'That's me told, then.' Louis swung his legs over the edge of the bed to pull on his boxers. 'And it's a shame because I like you, Karin. I'm sorry to be a disappointment, but there it is.'

'You don't know me. We see each other once in a blue moon. We have a drink, a laugh, and we have sex. And it works, it *worked*.' When he didn't reply, she added, 'And if you knew me more, you wouldn't like me.'

'I've seen the news, Karin, I even saw that stupid movie.' She stared, shocked that he knew who she was. 'But don't let one thing that happened to you a lifetime ago define who you are. The truth is, I like you too much.'

'This...' She gestured around the room. 'It's not real life.'

He came to her – she should have just walked out

as soon as he started talking – and cupped her cheek, and for a split second she instinctively pressed her face against the warmth of his hand.

'I like you, Louis,' she said, 'but... you should stay away from me.'

'I was hoping I could do just the opposite.'

'Honestly, you don't want to know me.'

'Give me one reason why.'

'Because I'm not a good person.'

'Oh, well, we'll have to disagree about that.' He took his shirt off the back of a chair. 'I've just gone and ruined everything, haven't I?'

Karin went to the door and opened it, and he sat on the bed.

'Where are you going?' he said, but immediately held up a hand in apology. 'It's none of my business.'

'I'm sorry,' she said. 'I've got to see somebody.'

'Can I call you again?' he asked and she hesitated in the doorway, torn about how to respond, wanting to say, *yes, I want you to, because I like you too*, but instead she left without saying a word, slamming the door hard behind her.

33

Their neighbour, Nelson, stood on the doorstep, clasping a cheap bottle of wine.

'Stuart!' Ursula greeted him like an old friend. 'So glad you could come!'

'I hope I'm not too early. This is for you.'

He handed her the bottle and came inside, nodding warily at Sasha. 'Thanks for inviting me.'

'You are *very* welcome,' said her mother quickly. 'Let me take you outside, Kevin will be thrilled you're here.'

Sasha stood mesmerized as Ursula took Nelson into the garden, and saw how stunned Kev was to see him. His eyes met Sasha's through the patio window and she shook her head. *I have no idea what's going on.*

She saw her mother talking to them both, probably reading them the riot act. Her husband's head dropped as he listened, and Nelson held out his hand – and Kev took it. Nelson moved closer to the barbecue, looking at what was cooking, and then the two men started discussing it. When Ursula came inside, she looked very pleased with herself.

'So that's what this is all about, it's an excuse to invite Nelson.'

'They'll be fine now,' said Ursula, emptying the bag of salad into a colander and taking it to the sink. 'All I needed to do was engineer an excuse to get Stuart here. Everyone's friends now.'

They watched Nelson and Kev talking about the meat. Kev showed him the marinade. After a couple of minutes their ceasefire was confirmed when Kev handed Nelson the tongs. Their neighbour immediately took the opportunity to prod and poke at the meat, and Kev came inside to the fridge, took out two bottles of beer.

'Everything alright?' Sasha asked over the rim of her glass of wine.

'Yeah.' He nodded cagily. 'So far so good.'

He walked back outside and handed one of the bottles to Nelson.

'I've got to admit it, Mum, you've played a blinder,' Sasha said and Ursula preened. 'Maybe you could sort out the Middle East next.'

'You don't get to my age without learning a thing or two about men.' Her mother rinsed the salad. 'Life's too short to hold silly grudges.'

'You should take your own advice and go home to Dad. I went to see him today.' Sasha's visit to her father first thing seemed like a million years ago now.

Ursula opened a cupboard to find a bowl. 'Is that right?'

'He's waiting for you to come home.'

'Did he say that?' Sasha frowned, *not in so many words*. 'Our marriage isn't big enough for the three of us.'

'He told me this Annie person is just a friend.'

'Your father has told me a lot of things down the years,' her mother said darkly, 'and I've learned to take them all with a pinch of salt.'

'Like what?' asked Sasha.

'I'd rather not talk about it, I was hoping we could all have a nice evening.' Sasha had known hardened criminals give up their secrets more easily. 'And besides, I'm happy here.'

Bloody hell, thought Sasha, she's here to stay.

'Go, relax,' said her mother.

So Sasha went outside to lie on the lounger. She was at a loss to know what to do without her phone to fiddle with. Angel was with her friends at the top of the garden, rolling around on the nest of cushions, and Sasha saw Denny with them too. It was good to see Angel enjoying herself; it broke Sasha's heart to think what she must be going through at school, and hopefully the whole sad situation would get sorted tomorrow.

Maybe it was the shock of the attack, or the painkillers, or the pills and wine combined, but she felt a swell of emotion at the sight of her two precious children larking about on the lawn. And then Sammi Manning's fragile singing voice popped into her head again, like a guilty earworm, and she thought of Lucas White, too, and gave silent thanks that Angel and Denny were safe.

You'll know...

She shifted uneasily on the lounger. Sammi was missing, Lucas was missing. She really wanted to be at the office, but she also knew in her heart that she was no good to anyone right now. She would get into work early and wouldn't rest until both kids were brought home.

... the truth about her.

She sipped the wine and raised her face to the dying rays of the setting sun; the heat was comfortable now and her headache was fading. She felt herself relax for the first time in days; was even glad her mum had confiscated her phone so she wasn't tempted to look at it.

Sasha listened to the men discussing the barbecue grill, a big beast of a thing Kev had bought himself a year back. Nelson was asking questions about it and Kev pointed at all the different dials and switches. Then they started talking about Southend United. Sasha wouldn't have guessed their stroppy neighbour was a fan, it was funny what you learned when the barriers came down.

They were laughing about something, and she remembered when they used to do this all the time, she and Kev. They'd invite friends and work colleagues around for a barbecue and they'd eat and drink and sit in the garden till the early hours in the soft flicker of tea lights, chatting and laughing, the baby alarm propped on the table. Those were good times, long before Nelson lived next door and banged on the wall every two minutes.

Ursula came outside to look at the kids. 'They're going to ruin those cushions if they keep throwing them about like that.'

'Leave them be,' said Sasha drowsily, but her mum was already marching up the end of the garden to try to get the girls to put on After Sun. Sasha watched as she squirted a puddle into her hand and tried to smear it across Denny's face. He was desperately fighting her off, his voice lifting in distress, while the girls giggled.

Feeling quite exhausted now, Sasha slipped her sunnies over her eyes. She heard Kev say, 'Another beer, Stuart?' and then go inside. The fridge door opened and shut, and then Kev came out to lop the caps off the bottles with an opener that was built in to the side of the barbecue.

Dislodging the heel of one shoe with the toe of the other, she let them both slip off the end of her feet and clop on to the patio, pulled her skirt further up her thighs. She closed her eyes, enjoying the buzz of wine in her veins, the smell of the sizzling meat, and the laughter of the kids. Kev and Nelson were laughing, too. Somehow the conversation had turned to local bars and clubs. She was surprised that Nelson even knew about any of them, and chided herself again for making so many presumptions about him. She had to get used to calling him Stuart now, she supposed.

Sasha reached for her glass and took a final sip. In the

circumstances, she shouldn't have any more. Then she laced her fingers across her stomach and let her body slide in the lounger. The laughter of the two men and the raucous conversation of the kids became an inaudible burble. Her limbs grew heavy and her breath flattened. Something buzzed in front of her face and she woke up groggy; she must have drifted off for a couple of minutes.

'I don't know how I had the stamina when I was young,' she heard Kev say as he placed chops on the grill. The marinade spat. 'In those days I'd think nothing of drinking till dawn and then heading straight to work.'

'Maybe,' Nelson said, 'your child's death was a wake-up call.'

Kev said, 'What did you just say?'

'Your son was killed, isn't that correct?'

Sasha's eyes snapped open.

'What the hell,' said Kev, pointing the tongs in his face, 'has that got to do with anything?'

'I was just—'

'I was drunk, that's what you're implying?'

'I was simply making a point that these things often make us think carefully about how we choose to live our lives going forward,' said Nelson. 'In a more moral way.'

Kev's temper could go from nought to sixty. Knowing she had to intervene, and quick, Sasha struggled to right herself in the lounger, but it was too late. Kev's face contorted in rage, and he threw a punch. Nelson fell across the table, causing her glass to smash on to the patio.

She scrambled out of the lounger.

'Kev! Get inside!' Her husband pressed forward, aiming to get another punch in at Nelson, and she pushed him away. 'Now!'

Scrabbling around on the floor, Nelson put his hand to his bloody nose.

'He hit me! He hit me!'

Ursula was beside him in a second, offering kitchen roll. The kids stood at the top of the garden watching; one girl was filming it on her phone. Kev dropped the tongs and, ignoring the food that spat and hissed on the grill, stormed inside.

34

Austin was sitting in his usual place on the railing outside the estate before midnight. He was enjoying a smoke, listening to the quiet roar of the night, when he saw his bruv Roy in the gloom of garages beneath the concrete walkway, yakking to a woman who stood in the shadows. Roy kept looking in his direction, and Austin knew it was only a matter of time before he came up. Sure enough, a couple of minutes later, Roy loped along the path.

'Got a lady wants to talk,' Roy said with a wink. 'And she looks loaded.'

'Yeah?' Austin watched the woman pacing. 'If she wants to talk to me, she knows where I'm at.'

Roy shook his head. 'She's nervous, bruv.'

But Austin was comfortable on the railings where he could see in every direction. The last thing he wanted to do was head down into that piss-stinking place, where someone could put a knife to your throat and rob you of your hard-earned, or handcuff you and throw you in the back of a patrol car, and you wouldn't know a thing about it until it was too late.

'If she wants to buy from me, she's got to come here. It's so dark down there she could be wearing a fucking police helmet.'

Truth was, Austin was sick of being patronized by middle-aged professional people. You got a lot of them in the summer, all those respectable nursery school teachers and advertising executives and artisan bakers. They'd all get together for a drink, and the sun and the prosecco would go to their heads and they'd start talking about the good old days, before they were saddled with a house full of kids, a cockapoo and a crippling mortgage on a holiday home in Portugal, back when they were young and went to festivals to get off their tits. They'd get this drunken idea that they wanted to recapture those glory days, so they'd ask around in a few pubs and stumble across Austin's name. And suddenly they were parking their 4x4s at the edge of the estate in the dead of night, all these idiots in summer shorts, crocs and bum bags, pissing their pants at the excitement of buying a bit of weed or coke.

Sometimes they even left their brats watching Peppa Pig in the back of the vehicle while they nipped over to Austin. It made him laugh. You could bet that if any of the people who lived round here got caught taking their children to a drug deal, those kids would be taken into care faster than you could say Pablo Escobar.

But these liberals, the lifestyle coaches and marketing assistants and yoga teachers, software engineers and occupational therapists, all thought it was a game, a bit of fun.

'What's she after, anyway?'

'Smack, innit, which is why she don't want to be seen.'

Austin didn't much fancy moving from this safe, comfortable place. He was of the opinion that if she needed it so much then she could come to him. However, it was also true to say that he was feeling the pinch right now, on account of owing some dangerous fellas a bit of dosh.

'I think she'll pay big, man,' added Roy, who knew how to press his buttons. So Austin sighed and jumped off the railings.

The woman was standing against a wall, near the sallow glow of the single overhead light that still actually worked down there. Austin had to admit she was a brave lady for coming alone to this dirty, stinking place at – he looked at his phone – nearly midnight; brave or desperate. She was fit too, now he got a closer look, a milf.

'My bruv tells me you're after something,' he told her.

The woman folded her arms, wary. She wasn't like some of the other well-offs who came to see him, dizzy with excitement at meeting a dealer, and acted like they were his friend. Austin had enough friends as it was, people he'd grown up with on the estate, and didn't need the friendship of some soppy dork with an online antiques business. He could see this woman just wanted to get the deal done and get away.

'I need... heroin.'

'Yeah?' Austin went through the motions of appearing to be offended. 'And what makes you think I can get you something like that?'

'I heard it was you,' the woman said. 'Yes or no?'

He sucked through his teeth. Most of his customers were careful to stay polite, but this woman was straight to the point, and he respected that. That didn't mean he was going to give her an easy ride.

'Heard that, did you?' The way she was dressed, the nice clothes, expensive jeans and shoes, a scarf round her face, something didn't add up. 'And what would someone like you want that for?'

The three of them tensed when a siren screamed in the distance, the woman waiting till it had receded. 'I need it... for a friend.'

He smirked. If he had a pound for the number of times he'd heard that phrase, he'd be able to knock off early.

She kept her distance, ready to flee if the situation turned bad. Fact was, if Austin decided to get nasty, she didn't stand a chance. Not that he would; attacking potential customers wasn't a good idea when you were trying to build a profitable business.

'You've been misinformed, someone's winding you

up, I don't sell shit like that, so sling your hook.' He rapped the back of his hand against Roy's chest. 'Come on, bruv, let's go.'

The woman looked almost relieved and began to walk away. 'Thanks for your time.'

'Wait,' said Austin.

Things had been tight lately, he owed people he really didn't want on his case, and he considered her carefully. She was familiar to him somehow. He wracked his brains, trying to work out if he'd maybe seen her around the estate or at court, or even the local cop shop. If she was undercover police, he was totally fucked.

'I can do you a deal, maybe,' he said. 'But it'll cost you double the usual price. Because you don't look like the usual skank who comes looking for product. You seem like a nice lady, and if you're so intent on fucking up your life—'

'It's for a fr—'

'Friend, right.' He lifted a finger. 'If you want the product, if you want it bad enough, then you're going to have to pay me what I want.'

The woman looked away, thinking about it, but he knew she'd pay.

She nodded. 'Whatever you say.'

He felt a little sad for her, but only for a moment. Because at the end of the day she was no different from any of the other middle-class day-trippers. She was the same as the artisan bakery guy, the advertising dude, and that woman who took the under-nines to the swings. For Austin, these people were all just customers with deep pockets.

'It's not for me,' she said again.

'Yeah.' He yawned. 'I don't care.'

Austin nodded to Roy, who ran off towards the estate to get what she wanted.

'Let's get down to business,' he said.

35

'It was just a silly argument.' Ursula sat on the sofa in the early hours of the morning. 'Can't you pull any strings?'

'No, Mum,' snapped Sasha. 'I can't, not if I want to keep my job.'

'It was just a suggestion,' said Ursula, making a disappointed face, and tightened her fingers in her lap.

Sasha wished her mother would go to bed, but the old woman had insisted on sitting up until Kev came back home from the station – *if* he came back home, he could remain in the cells until morning. But then Ursula's head turned at the sound of a car idling outside. A moment later, the front door opened and her husband walked in. He stood in the doorway, nodded wearily, and then disappeared. Sasha jumped up and followed him.

'Kev, talk to me,' she said as he started to walk upstairs. 'What happened?'

He waved her off. 'It was nothing, I was stupid.'

'It wasn't nothing, you punched our neighbour.' Sasha

lowered her voice, conscious that Nelson could be listening on the other side of the wall. 'Are you being charged?'

'Cautioned. I don't think he's going to take it any further.'

'What a relief.' Ursula blew out her cheeks in the doorway.

Sasha followed him upstairs to get away from her mother.

'Is that it?' She was tired of seeing him walk away. 'Is that all you have to say?'

'I'm going to bed.'

'Kev.' She took his arm on the dark landing, making him face her. 'I think you need to speak to somebody, a doctor.'

'It's late, I've work tomorrow.' He wouldn't meet her eyes. 'Can we—'

'No!' she hissed. 'No, we can't talk about it tomorrow, I want to talk about it now, Kev. Right now!'

'I'm shattered,' he said. 'And want to go to bed.'

She felt all the emotion of the day press against her chest. When he tried to walk into the bedroom, she stepped in his way, determined to get him to open up to her. 'Why won't you talk to me? Kev, please, I'm worried about you.' She could cry. 'It's me, you can talk to *me*.'

His breath rasped heavily. She waited, heart pounding in her chest.

'You heard him.' His voice was a fragile whisper. 'You heard what he said, as if Jake's...' Tears welled in his eyes and his voice faltered. 'As if it was my...'

'Come on, Kev.' She placed a hand on his chest, feeling all her love for him flooding back. 'You can tell me.'

And then Denny's bedroom door opened and her bleary-eyed son appeared. 'I'm trying to sleep!'

'Denny.' Sasha fought to keep the impatience out of her voice. 'Go back to bed.'

'You're being loud!'

Kev pushed past Sasha and slammed shut the door to their bedroom. She knew when she went in later he'd already be asleep, or pretending to be.

'Get back to bed,' she told her son.

'Is Dad alright?' Denny asked, an anxious quality to his voice.

'He's fine,' she told him softly. 'It's been an upsetting day.'

In the bathroom, she splashed water on her face. The bump on her head looked red and angry. She gingerly poked it, and it stung. When she got back downstairs, Ursula was sitting with her hands in her lap.

'Go to bed, Mum.'

'I can't sleep now.'

She fell into an armchair, pressed her fingers to the closed lids of her eyes. Thinking about Kev, thinking about her mum and dad, and about Angel getting bullied at school; about Sammi and Lucas, wondering where they were, imagining their terror. She was letting them down, letting them all down.

'Would you like a cup of tea?' asked Ursula.

Sasha didn't even open her eyes. 'Besides everything else that's happened, what I don't understand is why you would tell our neighbour, a man who hates us, intimate, personal details about our lives?'

Ursula looked uncomfortable. 'I thought it would break the ice.'

'Break the ice,' Sasha repeated, incredulous.

Sasha waited patiently for an apology to come from her mum but knew she wasn't going to get one. Not from her mother, not in this life. Instead, Ursula picked up her empty mug and left the room.

Sasha jumped up to follow her into the kitchen. She felt her anger building, knew she had to be careful because she was spoiling for a row. 'That man has been trouble ever since he moved in.'

'That's the difference between us,' said Ursula, rinsing the mug. 'I see the good in people. But in your job, with all the criminals and ne'er-do-wells you meet, you see too much of the worst of human nature. It's not good for your soul.'

'Leave my soul out of it. You told our troublesome neighbour the most private, upsetting thing about us, about... Jake. Information he couldn't wait to throw back in our faces.'

'I'm sorry if I've stuck my nose in where it's not wanted.' Her mother placed the mug upside down on the draining board and began to rinse another one. The kitchen was spotless, you'd never have known they'd had a barbecue only a few hours ago.

'For God's sake, Mum,' she snapped. 'Tidy up in the morning.'

'I want to do it now.'

Ursula's hands rubbed the inside of the cup beneath the spray of water, which thumped against the bottom of the sink and made Sasha's head throb. She grabbed the cup and slammed it down on the counter, turned off the tap.

'In the morning!'

Ursula looked forlornly at the mug. 'Perhaps I should leave.'

'To go home?' asked Sasha hopefully.

'I don't think I'll be able to afford a hotel. Maybe a hostel or a refuge will take me in.'

'Oh, stop playing the victim, I'm not going to throw you out!' Sasha dropped on to one of the stools at the counter.

'Tomorrow, I'll go next door and apologize to Stuart.'

'No, stay well away. We're in enough trouble as it is without you intimidating the victim.'

'I'm just trying to do the right thing,' said her mother in frustration. 'But you stop me at every turn.'

'Please don't do the right thing, don't do *anything*.'

Sasha's voice rose in irritation. 'It was your meddling that got us into this situation in the first place!'

Ursula swallowed, and when she spoke her voice was choked with upset. 'If that's the way you feel about it.'

'I do, I'm sorry, but I do feel that way!' Ursula sniffed, tears fell down her cheeks, and Sasha instantly felt ashamed. 'Come here.'

She took her mother in her arms and they held each other. Sasha kissed Ursula on the side of the head. 'I didn't mean to shout, I've just got a lot going on at the moment.'

'You care about what you do, any fool can see that. But maybe occasionally you might want to apply those detective skills of yours closer to home. Because things are not right in this house.' Ursula stepped back to rip a piece of kitchen towel from the holder and dab at her cheeks. 'They're not right at all. Now, if you'll excuse me, I'm going to bed.' She walked to the door. 'Good night, Sasha.'

36

'Lydia, it's me, open up!' Karin knocked loudly on the door of Lydia's flat on the estate. 'I know you're in there.'

An old woman who lived a couple of doors away stood watching on her doorstep. 'She'll be asleep most probably.'

'The curtains are still closed,' Karin said.

'She's a lazy cow, that one, she never rises from her pit till the afternoon.' The woman peered around the estate. They were two floors up, with a clear view of the paved walkway below. 'Mind you, there are a few around here who would happily stay in bed all day if they could, and probably do.'

Ignoring her, Karin cupped her hands against the glass. There was a slight gap in the curtains, but it was so gloomy inside that she couldn't see a thing.

'Lydia!' She banged on the door again. 'It's me!'

Looking over the balcony, Karin saw a pair of young

men she recognized, the local drug dealer and his mate, sitting at their usual position on the railings at the edge of the estate, and she looked away quickly.

'I told her it's useless,' the neighbour said to a middle-aged man when he came along the balcony with shopping bags. 'It's like trying to wake the dead.'

'I'm really worried about my friend, Lydia,' Karin told him. 'She's not answering.'

The guy kneeled at the door to lift the letter box and peer inside. 'There's someone on the floor.'

Other neighbours came to see what was happening as Karin crouched at the letter box. She could just about make out a leg, and saw one of Lydia's filthy trainers, a skinny ankle, sticking out from behind the sofa.

'We need to get in there!'

'Stand back,' said the man and he put his foot to the door and kicked. It shuddered, but didn't move. 'I need help here!'

Another man joined him, more neighbours gathering to watch now, and the two men synchronized their kicks. The door flew open and smashed against the wall.

It was hot when Karin rushed inside, as she knew it would be – Lydia always kept the windows shut even in the summer, and the flat smelled of rotting food and body odour. The neighbours who came in after Karin did little to disguise their disgust.

'Open a window,' said the old neighbour. 'Let some clean air in.'

But someone else said, 'Don't touch anything, leave everything as it is.'

Karin went straight to Lydia on the floor. She was wearing an old sleeveless T-shirt and there was a syringe sticking out of one bony shoulder. When Karin felt for a pulse, she couldn't find one. Lydia's face was dry and waxy, her mouth slightly open.

'No, no, no,' said Karin, feeling how cold her hand was, and how stiff her wrist, and she pulled Lydia into her arms. 'Call an ambulance!'

'It's too late for that, if you ask me,' said the old woman. 'But I suppose we'd better go through the motions.'

'I don't think you're meant to touch the body,' suggested another neighbour.

But Karin didn't listen. She cradled Lydia in her arms and whispered again and again into her ear. 'I'm so *sorry*, I'm so *sorry*, I'm so *sorry*.'

37

The Fifth Day...

Jerry pushed Karin along the dark, narrow corridor that ran along the spine of the farmhouse. In the gloom, she glimpsed ugly black-and-white photos hanging on the peeling wallpaper. She nearly lost her footing on the moth-eaten carpet as he shoved her into a kitchen.

It was a small room, unbearably hot compared to the chill of the cellar, and sourly lit by another bare bulb. A solid oak table filled most of the space, a chair on either side of it, and along the walls were stacked cardboard boxes filled with bits of metal, jagged panels of glass and plastic, rusted tools and broken appliances. A cabinet full of chipped brown crockery leaned against one wall. The ancient lino was tacky against the soles of her shoes, and in the places where it was torn, she saw worn flagstones beneath. Flies buzzed around the stained porcelain sink, which was full of plates and pans, and the net curtains at the window were so dark with grime that it was impossible to see into the night. On the wall, an old boiler ticked and puffed, roaring intermittently into life, the blue eye of its pilot light a single spot of vibrant colour in the drab room.

Karin didn't notice all these things that first time, or even the second, but she would spend many hours sitting with Jerry in that kitchen and would come to know every dismal inch of it.

'Sit.' He pushed her down into one of the chairs. Years later, she would still be able to close her eyes and recall in her mind's eye the surface of that wooden table. Her fingers would know the location of every scratch, groove, nick and gouge, every imperfection, as if it were a map of the inside of Jerry Swann's skull.

A broken cardboard box sat on the chair opposite and Jerry picked it up and threw it into a corner. Something inside smashed when it hit the floor, but Jerry didn't care. He fell into the chair and placed the knife in front of him, making a lot of tiny adjustments to the angle until he was satisfied it was just how he wanted it. When he took off his glasses, his eyes were tired pinpricks set deep in dark sockets.

'First things first.' He cleaned the orange lenses on the flap of his sweat-stained shirt. 'All the windows are locked, and the doors, so there's no point in trying to escape. You're going nowhere. It's just us here. I can do anything to you, or to those others, and there's nothing you can do about it, do you understand me?'

Karin wished Becky was beside her, she'd know the right thing to say. 'Please... let us go.'

'I haven't decided what to do with you yet. I may just keep you all here, or do away with you.'

'Why... would you do that?'

'Because I can, because no one can stop me.'

His head twitched, some kind of a nervous tic. Karin clenched her teeth. She didn't want to cry, didn't want to scream, or do anything to make him angry.

'Why... why am I here?' she asked faintly.

'I think you're the *one*.' She didn't know what he was talking about. 'When I climbed in the van everyone was talking, *chat, chat, chat*, screaming, shouting, making noise, but you were sitting quietly, Karin, and I knew, I *knew*, that you would listen to me.'

Dizzy with fear, Karin hardly dared to breathe. The blackened pipes on the walls seemed to uncoil silently like snakes, to slip around her waist and wrists, forcing her tighter into the chair.

'How... how do you know my name?'

His top lip curled in a revolting smile, revealing a perfectly straight row of small teeth. 'Because I know everything. Like I know that she doesn't like you.'

'Who?' asked Karin, bewildered.

'That other one, the tall one. Miss Perfect. The one who thinks she's better than the rest of us. If she was chocolate, that one, she would eat herself.'

'I don't know who you—'

'I don't like the way she treats you.'

She was shocked to realize he was talking about Becky. 'She's my friend.'

He snorted, as if he didn't believe her. 'I've met people like her before, oh, the world is full of them. People who pretend to like you, who tell you how you're going to be together for ever, but the truth is, they can't wait to get away. There's a word for people like that.' His hand slapped on the table, making the knife jump and Karin flinch. 'They're called *liars*!

'I saw you in that van, I saw the way you looked at her, but she will never love you the way you want her to. Can't you see that? Oh, she's too high and mighty. I've met her type many times, people who leave you high and dry the first chance they get.' He gave her a sly look. 'Like your father, he left you, he didn't look back.'

She blinked in shock. How did he—

'We're the same, me and you. Because people leave us behind. They smell the desperation on us. Our trouble is, we love too much, Karin, as if love was a crime!'

She didn't like the way he kept talking as if they were the same, as if it was him and her against the world, and wished he would stop.

'But I'll be your friend.' His fingers walked across the table towards hers. 'Can I be your friend, Karin?'

'I... don't...' She didn't know why he wanted to be her friend, and was terrified of what would happen if she said yes. Maybe she would have to stay up here with him all the time. She wouldn't ever be allowed to go back downstairs to the others… to Becky. She didn't know what Jerry wanted, she was scared and confused, and wished she could run or scream or grab the knife.

'Let me be your friend, let me, let me.' He said it again and again in a whining voice. 'Please let me, please, Karin, let me, let me, let me.' The fingers crept closer. 'Let me, let me, *let me.*'

When his hand almost touched hers, Karin cried out and snatched hers away. He grabbed the knife, the blade scraping noisily across the wood as he lifted it.

'If you don't want to be my friend, what's the point of you?' he snarled. 'If you don't want to be my friend, I may as well kill you now.'

She was terrified, she didn't want to die, and heard herself whisper, 'I'll be your friend.'

'Thank you.' Jerry looked relieved. 'Thank you.'

He replaced the knife and composed himself.

Karin bit back her fear. 'I'm your friend, I promise I am.'

He smiled. 'As we're friends now, call me Jerry.'

'Yes.'

'Yes, Jerry.'

'Yes, Jerry.'

His head twitched. 'I'm so glad because friends tell each other everything, don't they, and I've waited so long to have a friend to talk to. I have so much to tell you, Karin.'

'Tell me what?' she whispered.

He leaned forward, and a big smile lit up his face.

'Tell you about all the people I killed, of course.'

38

When she arrived at the estate, Sasha suited up into coveralls. An officer at the scene volunteered a shoulder to lean on while she slipped on the protective overshoes.

Ajay walked towards her between the police vehicles parked along the slip road, ignoring the clot of onlookers on the other side of the police tape, local residents who had come to enjoy the goings-on. A television van was pulling up outside the estate, no doubt the first of many. The disappearance of Lucas – abducted in broad daylight, only yards from his school – had sent the press into a feeding frenzy. Media people were pouring into town.

'Feeling better this morning, Mrs Dawson?' asked Ajay.

He clearly hadn't heard yet about Kev's assault on Nelson and she didn't fancy going into all the grisly details now, but word would soon spread.

'I didn't get much sleep last night,' she replied, which

was true enough. When she'd finally got into bed beside Kev, she had tossed and turned, and when she eventually nodded off, she dreamed she was sitting in an empty auditorium listening to Sammi's anxious singing. She awoke exhausted to find the bed empty; Kev had already left for work.

Ajay examined her forehead, making a face of mock disgust as if the bump, barely more than a red mark now, was something shocking. 'I haven't seen anything so grotesque since my personal trainer grew a man-bun.'

'The *tiny* injury to my head will have almost disappeared by tomorrow,' she told him, 'but you'll still be ugly.'

'You're still as sharp as a pin, but you may need to get your eyes tested.' Ajay squeezed her shoulder. 'How's Kev?'

'So,' she said in exasperation, 'everyone knows.'

'Are you kidding? It's all anyone's talking about. Your life is so much more exciting than ours, Sasha, it's all sex and violence. I thought people were meant to slow down at your age.'

'You got the violence bit right, at least.'

They continued across the concrete walkway, past the underground garages, to climb the stairs to the second floor, their conversation bouncing off the walls.

'Lydia's death looks like an accidental overdose, she still has the syringe in her arm, but I thought you might want to take a look.'

'Who found her?'

'Your friend, Karin McCarthy.'

She was irritated by the suggestion. 'She's not my friend.'

'She says she came this morning to see Lydia because she was worried about her after what happened on Marine Parade yesterday.'

Sasha stopped at the top of the stairs to recall her last sight of Lydia – her angry tears in the back of a patrol car with Karin – but also because she was sweltering after climbing two steep flights on a baking hot day.

'Was Lydia traumatized enough to go back on the gear?' she wondered out loud.

'Karin didn't get an answer when she knocked on her door so a neighbour kicked it in,' continued Ajay.

They stooped beneath the tape at the inner cordon, which was set up on the balcony, where officers stood chatting with CSIs in Tyvek suits.

'Did you trace Matt Foster's phone number?'

'It's pay-as-you-go and switched off, but we'll find out where it was used. CCTV from Marine Parade hasn't provided much information about our mystery man. We've searched various databases for that name across the county and beyond, and checked on the PNC for Matts and Matthew Fosters, including Matthews with one *t* and two, for drug arrests or convictions, and frankly nobody fits the bill. We were hoping to get more information from Lydia this morning.'

Sasha stopped outside the door to the flat. 'Tell me she at least gave us a description.'

'She was all over the place last night, Sash. DCI Vaughn told us to wait till this morning when she'd calmed down.'

It was disappointing, but Sasha understood the reasoning; Lydia was difficult to talk to at the best of times. Nerves frayed from a restless night, she stared at her mobile when it rang, trying to work out the initials 'RHS' on the screen, wondering in her tiredness why the Royal Horticultural Society was among her contact numbers. Then she realized it was River Hill School. 'I don't know what this is about.'

'Might as well answer it now.' Ajay shrugged. 'Lydia's going nowhere.'

'Is Craig with Karin?' she asked.

'He's gone with Lolly to that drug support centre in Basildon where Lydia met Matt Foster. It's called Inspire.'

'Do they know what's happened here?'

Ajay held up a finger, *good point*. 'I'll call him now to make sure.'

When he walked off, she lifted the ringing phone to her ear. 'Sasha Dawson speaking.'

The call was from the teacher who had left a message the previous day, who asked if Sasha was available to talk about 'Angel's situation'.

'I'd love to. When were you thinking?'

'Can you come in this morning?'

'I'm sorry.' Sasha wondered what the teacher would think if she knew she was dressed in a polyethylene suit and overshoes, and standing a few feet from a dead body. 'It's really not convenient this morning.'

'It won't take very long,' said the teacher. 'Apologies for the short notice, but I think we should talk as a matter of urgency. We take bullying very seriously here.'

'Well, we agree on something, at least.' Sasha was going to say no, but placed the phone to her shoulder and called over to Ajay. 'Can you cover for me if I nip off a bit later? There's something I need to get sorted.'

'You're the boss, boss,' he said.

She told the teacher she'd get there in an hour and then went inside. The council flat managed to be simultaneously sparse and untidy. There was one small room comprising a living area and kitchenette and, behind that, a bedroom and a tiny bathroom. The front room was hot and dark behind closed curtains. In the kitchen was a grubby freestanding cooker, with frayed wiring plugged into a socket spotted with burn marks and electric rings thick with greasy stains; a counter with a peeling laminate surface. The interior of the fridge smelled of sour milk. The doors of the knackered-looking cupboards sagged on their hinges, the sink was filled with grimy pots and pans, a plastic bin bulged with tins and fast-food packaging. Sasha had visited many grim flats and houses in her career, homes blighted by poverty and neglect, and the sight never failed to make her feel a sadness for the people, like Lydia, for whom every day was a struggle to survive.

In the living room the furniture was old and flimsy. Stuffing spilled out of numerous tears in the sofa. A card table had fallen on its side beside a small television on a footstool.

Lydia's body was stretched out behind the sofa. She lay on her back, arms flung out at her sides. There were sticky patches of blood on the side of her head and smears at head height on the flecked wallpaper. A syringe sagged in her shoulder, the skin surrounding it already turning black from necrosis. Lydia's T-shirt had risen up across her stomach and they saw blue-purple discolouration around her sides where livor mortis had set in, the blood settling in the lower part of her body after her heart stopped pumping.

'There's a spoon in the sink with a scorch mark beneath it,' said Ajay. 'And open drawers and cabinets. The contents look disturbed. Someone could have been searching the flat for something, of course, but Lydia doesn't strike me as the tidiest of people.'

Sasha knew the spoon would have been used to liquefy the heroin injected into Lydia's arm. She heard forensic staff place tubs of equipment on the balcony ready to get to work, and told officers inside the flat to be thorough in their search. They could find evidence of the identity of Lydia's boyfriend, Matt Foster, the man Karin had identified as Lucas's abductor – fingerprints, forensic material, maybe even an address scribbled on a scrap of paper – but she somehow doubted it.

She and Ajay crouched near Lydia's body on the brown diamond-patterned carpet. 'Poor woman.'

Sasha considered whether yesterday's pursuit of her mysterious boyfriend, and his possible involvement in the abductions of Sammi and Lucas, had tipped Lydia back into drug use – and an overdose.

'It could be accidental,' said Ajay, playing devil's advocate, 'or she tripped and hit her head on the wall in a stupor, or intended to overdose.'

'Any of those could well be the case.' Sasha pointed at the position of the syringe. 'But never in all my years have I known an experienced user to inject into muscle tissue before. We need a post-mortem ASAP, Ajay. This afternoon, if possible.'

'On it,' he said.

Sasha said, 'Now be so kind as to point me in the direction of Karin.'

Leaning against the door of a police van, Karin straightened as Sasha approached. 'I don't understand how this could have happened. Lydia was clean, she hasn't touched drugs for almost two years. If she was using again, I would have known, she would have come to me for help.'

'We'll need to wait for the results of the post-mortem before we can rush to judgement, but at this stage we're treating Lydia's death as suspicious.'

'Suspicious?' Karin stared. 'You mean it wasn't an overdose? Was it the man who took Lucas? Did he kill her in revenge, Matt whoever he is?'

'Why would he do that?' asked Sasha, interested.

'I don't know, for what happened yesterday.' Karin looked in shock. 'I just don't understand why she would be murdered.'

Sasha changed the subject. 'How are you feeling?'

'First Simon is almost killed, and now Lydia has been... I don't know what to think.'

Sasha had asked how Karin felt, not what she thought. Her face was a blank, frozen in pain, much like it had been when they had sat together late at night in the station corridor all those years ago.

'It's hot enough without having to wear this bloody thing.' Standing beneath the pounding sun, Sasha pulled the bunching hood of the suit away from her collar. 'I saw you both arguing in the car at Marine Parade yesterday.'

'Lydia was very upset. I did my best to comfort her, but she was terrified that her boyfriend wouldn't want to see her again. And she blamed me for telling you about him.'

'Karin.' Sasha looked at her carefully. 'When did you last see Lydia?'

'I came back here with her at eight last night, something like that, and offered to stay. But she wouldn't let me, she was still angry about what happened. She said she wanted to be alone in case he called.'

'And you went home,' said Sasha.

'No, actually.' Karin swallowed. 'I met somebody.'

'Who was it?'

'That's personal.'

'Two kids are missing, Karin, and Lydia is dead.' Sasha was running out of patience with Karin's evasiveness. 'Who did you meet last night?'

'Why, do I need an alibi?' she snapped. 'It was a man... an acquaintance. I went home to change and met him at about half eight, quarter to nine, in a hotel bar on the seafront. We were together until about half ten. Plenty of people would have seen us there.'

'And you didn't see her after that?' Sasha asked. Karin shook her head, looked away. 'Where would she have got the drugs from?'

'There are people around here, dealers she knew.' Karin glanced nervously around the estate. 'I thought she'd left them all behind, I honestly believed she was starting to move on with her life, but obviously not.'

'I'm sorry, I know you and she were close.'

'She was my best friend, I guess.' Karin glanced down at her phone. 'After Becky.'

Lydia had just died and even all these years later Karin still spoke about Becky as if she was still alive.

Karin nodded at Sasha's forehead. 'I hope you weren't hurt too much.'

'This?' Sasha lifted her fingers to the bruise. 'Comes with the territory. But the man who did it, this Matt Foster or whoever he is, said something to me just before he tried to stuff my head into the slot of a fruit machine, he said, *you'll know the truth about her*. He could have been talking about Lydia, he may even have meant Michelle, but I don't think he was, I think he was talking about you.'

Karin glanced sharply at Sasha. 'Why would you think that?'

'Sammi was abducted near your home and Lucas is your pupil. This has something to do with you, Karin. Has anybody tried to make contact with you, have you had any unusual interactions recently?'

A look passed across Karin's face that Sasha couldn't read, and her eyes flicked restlessly across the crowd of onlookers behind the tape, as if there was someone she was looking for, someone she wanted to see.

'Nobody.'

'Messages, calls, texts, letters. Something to do with the Bad Place.'

'Nothing.'

Karin's fingers touched the pocket where she kept her phone. There's something you're not telling me, thought Sasha with irritation, you're hiding something.

You'll know the truth about her.

'You've never spoken about the time you spent alone with Jerry Swann.'

'You make it sound like I chose to spend time with that monster,' Karin said with sudden anger. 'He chose me to sit with him every night. Not any of the others, not Simon or Paul or Lydia or Michelle, not Becky... *me*. It wasn't my choice. Nobody will ever understand how it felt being alone with him hour after hour, as close as you're standing to me now, believing I would be killed at any moment. Forced to listen to his... sick *memories*. I don't know what you're insinuating, but whatever it is, you're wrong. I was his captive. I wasn't his friend, I wasn't his muse, I wasn't his *accomplice*.' Her voice cracked with emotion. 'Nobody can comprehend how terrifying it was for me. Lydia didn't, or any of the others, they had no idea. The only one who has ever understood is Becky, she's the only one.'

Sasha looked at her carefully. 'Becky died, Karin.'

'Yes.' Karin swallowed. 'Look, I want to help, but I don't know who's taken Sammi and Lucas and I don't know why all these bad things are happening. I wish they weren't, how I wish they weren't.' She pulled her bag tightly over her shoulder. 'I've got to get to work.'

'I've got to go to the school myself, do you want a lift?'

'No, I'll go my own way.' Karin turned away. 'As I always have.'

39

The Inspire Drug Support Centre was situated in an office above two shops off the High Street in Basildon.

The downstairs door was unlocked when Craig and Lolly stepped over the small pile of post on the mat to climb the steep, narrow stairs. Lydia had met her mysterious boyfriend at the centre, Sasha had told Craig, and his details could be on file there.

'Hello?' called Lolly, and a bulky middle-aged man in a denim jacket and jeans appeared at the top of the stairs holding a cloth and a bottle of furniture cleaner.

'Can I help you?' he asked, looking surprised.

Lolly and Craig showed their warrant cards. 'Detective Constables Chambers and Power.'

'I'm Jon Wilson, one of the counsellors here.' The man examined their identification carefully and handed it back. 'You're lucky I'm in so early.'

'What is it you do here, exactly?' asked Craig as they walked into what looked like a residential flat converted into a public space. He looked around the room with its dirty dado rail, cornices and ceiling rose, the jumble of plastic chairs, and the walls filled with public health posters about drug and alcohol abuse, mental health issues and STDs.

'We try to help people who identify as having a drug problem,' said Jon. 'We assess them for treatment, arrange for substitute medications and rehabilitation, and we provide practical support.' He sprayed the handle of a door with the cleaner, rubbed it with the cloth. 'And, of course, people with drug dependencies can have somewhat disordered lives so we give them advice about employment and family and law issues. Basically,' he said, 'we help in any way we can.'

'That's really cool.' Lolly nodded at the chairs placed in a broken circle around the bare room. 'And you have group therapy sessions here?'

'We do small groups. It can be useful for addicts to learn from each other's experiences and problems.' He looked at them both. 'What is it I can help you with?'

'A woman called Lydia Tide came here,' said Craig.

'Why, yes, we know Lydia.' Jon hesitated. 'Has something happened?'

'She's dead,' said Craig with a bluntness that made Lolly wince.

'That's terrible, how did she…'

'She may have overdosed.'

'Wow, okay.' The man looked shocked. 'I really liked Lydia, she was a funny lady.'

Lolly felt for him. 'I'm really sorry.'

'As you can imagine, we're no strangers to death around here. The lifespan of addicts can be appreciably lower than for the general population, but that's really knocked me for six. I thought Lydia was clean...'

'We're waiting on the post-mortem result,' said Craig.

Jon sighed and started moving around the room again, briskly squirting the top of a chair and pulling the cloth along it. 'So what is it I can do for you?'

'Lydia had been seeing someone in the last few weeks,' said Lolly, 'a fella she met in one of your group sessions.'

'I don't know anything about that.'

'We're keen to talk to him. His name is Matt, or Matthew, Foster. That's what she called him, anyway.'

They heard the front door open downstairs. Jon nodded to a small office behind the main room.

'We should talk in private.' He stepped aside as Craig and Lolly went in. 'I'm afraid I can't just give out details of our clients like that.'

'Clients?' Craig laughed. 'That's what you call them?'

'Well, yes, that's exactly what they are.' He smiled. 'What would you prefer we called them?'

Put on the spot, Craig thought about it. To break the tension, Lolly pointed at a smear of fingerprints on the woodwork. 'You missed a bit.'

'Thanks.' Jon pointed the nozzle and the spray hissed over the surface of the door. 'You're probably thinking, *what the hell is he doing,* but I'm afraid our cleaning budget has been halved, local authority cuts and so forth, so we're forced to do some of it ourselves, otherwise it just gets filthy.'

'You're very good,' Lolly said cheerfully. 'You can do my flat as well, if you like.'

'I'd give you a very reasonable rate, but you have to provide the apron.'

Lolly giggled, just as the office door opened and a middle-aged woman came in. 'Oh.' She looked surprised. 'What are you doing—'

'I'm sorry, Kathy,' Jon said quickly. 'We're just having a quick chat and then I'll be right out.'

The woman blinked. 'Are you sure you should be—'

'Do you mind getting us a coffee?' He turned to Lolly and Craig. 'Or tea, perhaps?'

'Not for me, fanks,' said Lolly, and Craig shook his head.

'I promise we won't be long.' Jon smiled warmly at the woman and shut the door in her face. 'Kathy's a nice lady, but a bit set in her ways. Excuse me a moment.'

When he slipped outside, Lolly whispered fiercely to Craig, 'Try and be nice to people.'

'I'll do that,' he said, 'if you cut out the flirting. Someone has to stay professional.'

'That's a bit rich coming from you, mate!'

Jon came back into the room and said, 'Sorry about that. Look, I've got to be somewhere else. We've got a bloody budget meeting, yet more financial firefighting, so can we get this over with?'

'If you could give us the names of the people at your group therapy sessions, we'll be gone.'

Going to an open filing cabinet, Jon flicked through the folders inside. He frowned and pulled one out, examined it, and then placed it in a satchel.

'A lot of our clients are people who have fallen foul of the law. As you will appreciate, many of them can go to extreme lengths to feed their addiction. We hear a lot of nasty stuff in this place, there's regrettably a lot of criminality, but we're not here to point the finger. What we provide is a safe space, somewhere our clients can come and not feel threatened that they're being judged, or will be reported to the police.'

'I get all that,' said Craig shortly, 'but a woman has died and her death may well be connected to the disappearance of two teenagers.'

'I read about them,' said Jon.

'Yeah, of course you did,' said Craig, getting more impatient. 'Because it's been all over the news. It's why it's so important we speak to this Matt Foster. We need his contact details and the details of the other participants in Lydia Tide's group sessions.'

'*If*, of course, this chap is one of our clients.' Jon elbowed the cabinet shut. 'Believe me, I'm not trying to be difficult, I just can't give you a name right now.'

Craig was about to reply but Lolly nudged him and asked, 'Why not, Jon?'

'For one thing, I don't participate in any of the groups so the name is not immediately familiar to me – Matt Foster, you say? – and because what you're asking is above my pay grade. I'm not trying to be obstructive but I have to get authorization from my managers. You know how it is, we have a duty to protect the privacy of our—'

'Clients, yeah.' Craig rolled his eyes.

Jon bent his wrist to look at a chunky watch. 'I'm sorry, but I've got to go.'

'They must pay you counsellors well,' said Craig, nodding at the fancy timepiece.

Jon held out his wrist so that Craig could get a better look. 'Family heirloom. It's a Breitling Colt, a lovely thing, used to be my Dad's. He loved this watch.' He picked up the satchel and went to the door. 'I'll come back to you with those details, I promise. Lydia was a nice lady, she was a fixture around here. I still can't believe it.'

'This is someone she believed she was having a romantic attachment with.' Craig followed him into the main room. 'Someone she'd have been spending a lot of time with. He shouldn't be too difficult to identify.'

'Bye, Kathy,' Jon called over his shoulder at the woman, who stood watching them from a kitchen area at the rear of the converted flat. 'See you soon.'

'Fank you,' called Lolly with a wave.

They followed Jon downstairs into the bright sunlight and stood together on the pavement.

'Let me talk to my bosses.' Jon shook hands with Craig and then Lolly. 'I'm sure we can help, but there are hoops to jump through.'

'Just to reiterate,' said Craig. 'We're not just talking about a suspicious death, but also the abduction of two children. This man Matt could very well provide information about their whereabouts.'

'Understood.'

'Can we give you a lift anywhere?' asked Lolly.

'You know what...' Pulling the satchel tighter over his shoulder, he lifted his face to the sun. 'It's good to walk on a beautiful day like this.'

40

'Thanks for coming in,' said Angel's teacher.

It had been harder than Sasha thought to slip into River Hill. Security had been tightened, as it had at all local schools, but reporters were standing at the gates interviewing concerned parents and she saw Jim Haskell was there.

Becky's brother had become a go-to angry voice for the media, giving many interviews demanding that Karin be removed from her teaching position, and petitioning that the police reopen the inquiry into the events at the Bad Place. Sasha wondered if Karin had already got in to work, or whether she had been told to stay away.

Now, she slipped into a seat in the classroom, hoping to settle the matter of Angel's bullying quickly and get back to work, hopefully well before the post-mortem on Lydia was completed. 'Will this take long?'

The teacher closed the door Sasha had left wide open. A class had just finished and the corridor was flooded with pupils and staff rushing back and forth.

'I know what this is about,' said Sasha as the teacher, a woman called Emily Mirpuri, sat down. 'And I just want to say that I'll back whatever action you decide to take, as long as it's proportionate.'

She was livid about Tilly's behaviour and keen to know what the school was intending to do about it, but at the same time she didn't want Tilly to be suspended. Sasha knew how difficult the teenage years could be for girls, and how easily friendships could turn toxic. The bottom line was, she just wanted the bullying of her daughter to stop.

'Well, that's good to know.' Emily moved papers about on the desk. 'Just to fill you in, I'm head of pastoral care here, which means it's my job to look after the well-being of all of our pupils. So I want to help Tilly *and* Angel.'

'Angel is very upset about what's happened.'

Emily's eyes lifted to the bump on Sasha's forehead. 'She hasn't been in school for the last couple of days.'

'She's not been well,' lied Sasha, 'but she'll definitely be in tomorrow. I've told her to stay out of Tilly's way and try not to inflame the situation, but it would be good to have assurances that the matter will be dealt with promptly.'

'That's exactly what I wanted to talk to you about. How we can ensure together that nothing like this happens again.'

'Happy to do anything to help. And, of course, you'll be speaking to Tilly's mother about this, too.'

'I've already done so.'

Sasha liked the way the conversation was going. The teacher had no doubt delivered to Tilly's mum some hard truths about her daughter's behaviour.

'I don't want Tilly to be punished too much, it's such a difficult age. Their wiring's still a bit scrambled.'

Emily gave Sasha a long look. 'I think we're talking at cross purposes, Mrs Dawson. Tilly isn't at fault here.'

'I know you have to be even-handed, but if you don't mind me saying, I think you're being too tolerant of Tilly's behaviour. Angel told me what's happened.'

Emily frowned. 'I don't know what Angel has told you, but that's not our understanding of the situation. Angel and a number of other girls have unfortunately been sending Tilly abusive messages and photos and memes, and intimidating her in the school grounds.'

Sasha stared. 'Excuse me?'

'Angel and her friends have been bullying Tilly,' repeated Emily Mirpuri, 'and sending her abusive messages. Last week they followed her all the way home, shouting threats and insults. She only just managed to get in the door, and was very shaken by what happened. She genuinely believed she was in danger of being physically attacked.'

'That's not possible.' Sasha bristled at the suggestion.

There was some kind of miscommunication occurring. 'She would never... Angel isn't the kind of girl who would instigate something like... like...'

She remembered from her own school days how difficult it was to keep up to date with who had fallen out with whom. Solid friendships hit the rocks and new ones formed very quickly. It was a period of turbulence and change, feelings were hurt easily and emotions ran high. But Sasha had never bullied anyone in her life, she could hardly bring herself to raise her voice at work, and found the whole idea of it repugnant. The idea that her daughter could be a bully was alarming and shameful.

'It can't be. I mean, I'm a police officer! You need to look again at what's been happening.'

'Mrs Dawson, Angel sent Tilly quite a few messages, many by Snapchat, which were intended to disappear as soon as they were viewed. However, Tilly had the presence of mind to screenshot them.'

Opening a folder in the same way Sasha had done many times herself in the interview room, Emily placed before her printouts of the texts, in which her daughter accused Tilly of being a slut, a bitch, a whore, and other delightful things. Sasha couldn't believe that Angel would do such a thing.

'Angel has also been showing Tilly a lot of relational aggression.'

'What does that mean?'

Sasha tried to keep the irritation out of her voice, worried that the teacher would think Angel was a chip off the old block, but she was absolutely seething. With herself, with Kev – and with her daughter. No wonder Tilly's mum had given her the cold shoulder on the street the other morning.

'She's excluded Tilly from certain social groups at school by spreading hurtful gossip about her.'

'Gossip?'

'Lies,' said Emily. 'And sabotaging her friendships.'

'I don't know what to say.'

'We're not talking about exclusion yet.'

'Exclusion?'

'We're a long way off from that, but it's important we stop this behaviour in its tracks. Angel's a popular girl, the staff here like her, even if she can sometimes be a handful.'

'A handful,' Sasha repeated.

'Up until now she's always had good relations with her peers. But Angel's so desperate to fit in that she can be easily led. There are some very strong personalities in her new group of friends who will have encouraged her down this road. They can be a bit... wild. The sad truth is, rivalries sometimes get out of control.'

Sasha was gobsmacked. 'I don't understand how this can have happened.'

'Sometimes there are other factors at play.' Emily leaned forward. 'How are things at home?'

'Absolutely fine,' Sasha said quickly. 'Things have been manic at work for me, and her dad's been a bit... preoccupied. But we've always been a merry band.'

She blushed beneath Emily's penetrating gaze, feeling as if she was being judged. Where the hell was her husband? Why wasn't Kev here with her?

'I hope Angel feels better from whatever it is that's been ailing her,' said Emily, turning away when she heard an email drop into her computer.

'She'll be in tomorrow,' Sasha repeated. 'I'll make sure of that.'

It was annoying the way Emily was distracted, watching something on the screen.

'Have a gentle word with Angel about her actions,' said the teacher, absorbed in whatever was happening on her computer. Sasha heard someone shout on the speaker, the sound of shocked giggles. 'And let's take it from there.'

'I definitely will. My husband and I have always been careful to teach Angel the difference between right and wrong...' When Emily turned to her in surprise, Sasha asked, 'What is it?'

'One of the pupils has emailed me this link.' The teacher turned the monitor on the desk to face her. 'You may want to look at it.'

She saw it was a video embedded on a social media site and her heart leapt when she recognized her garden and patio on the screen. Sasha watched shaky camera phone footage of Kev throwing a punch at Nelson, who went flying, saw herself leaping up from the lounger. She heard the screams of shock and excitement from Angel and her friends.

Sasha stood. 'I've got to go.'

Slipping out of the school gates, she hardly noticed there were more parents there, and protesters with placards, as she pushed through the crowd.

'There she goes,' she heard someone call, and glanced up to see Jim Haskell pointing at her. 'There's Detective Inspector Sasha Dawson. How many more kids need to go missing, luv, before you get your act together?'

She ignored him as he began to clap slowly with ironic disdain, *clap, clap, clap*, encouraging the parents to do the same, and raced to her car, her shirt clinging to her spine beneath the hot, merciless sun.

41

Karin had received a call asking her not to come in to school while the headmaster consulted with governors, but she couldn't bear the thought of sitting at home, staring at her phone willing Becky to message her again, and after lunch she headed into work.

She sensed trouble as she approached the gates and saw the crowd. A group of parents stood in angry discussion with the headmaster, and right in the thick of the altercation was Jim Haskell.

He'd never liked her, not even when they were kids. He had resented her being friends with his sister, and never liked it when she was at his house of an evening, or staying over. *Why is she here again,* he had whined to his mother one morning, *she's always here!*

And when Becky didn't come home from the Bad Place, he had laid the blame fully at the feet of the survivors, and fought for years to get the investigation into the circumstances of her death reopened, a campaign that only gained traction among a small coterie of true crime zealots. But it didn't stop him bombarding Karin with legal letters demanding that she reveal publicly what had occurred between her and Jerry when they were alone.

Please be my friend, said Swann. *Let me, let me, let me.*

Hesitating on the pavement, she was about to turn back when someone shouted, 'There she is!'

The parents surged forwards, a camera team keeping pace alongside them, to surround her:

'We don't want you here!'
'You're not welcome!'
'Stay away from our children!'

These were people who had always been so friendly. She had met them at parents' evenings, sports days and other school events; some of them even sent Christmas cards. One mother she'd chatted with over a glass of mulled wine at the winter fair waved a placard in her face:

SACK MCCARTHY BEFORE
MY KIDS ARE NEXT!

And then the mob of parents parted and Jim Haskell stood directly in front of her, pushing someone out of the way to allow a camera to get into position behind his shoulder.

'First my sister died, and now two kids have gone missing, including a pupil from your own class. An innocent lad, a blameless lad. And now I hear from reporters Lydia Tide was found dead this morning, and *you* found her.' Haskell played to the crowd, getting it riled. 'Tell us, Karin McCarthy, just what is your connection to these kidnappings?'

Pressed in on every side, Karin couldn't think. 'I don't know what—'

'These good people don't believe you're a fit and proper person to be near children. It's a disgrace,' – his voice lifted angrily – 'a *total disgrace* that you're allowed to remain at school!'

'Shame on you!' shouted a parent.

He grabbed a man and woman from the crowd and pushed them forward. Karin was shocked to recognize Lucas's parents.

'Here's a mum and dad who trusted you with the safety of their son.'

The man and woman glared at Karin. Tears bulged in the mother's eyes, her voice cracked. 'Please tell us where he is.'

'I don't know.' Karin's voice was faint. 'I swear.'

'What have you done with him?' said the father, and his despair sent angry murmurs through the mob.

Jim spoke directly to the camera. 'I've always said there was something not right about the way my sister died, but nobody listened, and now look what's happened.' The parents jeered. 'Because this woman, whom my sister loved and trusted, has never told the world what happened between her and Swann. She's not a fit and proper person to be around children!'

The crowd surged. Karin was jostled, someone shouted in her face. She stumbled and was about to fall when a hand grabbed her arm and pulled her through the angry mob. The headmaster pushed everyone out of the way, clearing a path for her towards the school gates. The parents followed, hissing, snarling, shoving, until the gates opened with a buzz and Karin was pushed inside. They clanged shut behind her and the headmaster led her across the playground – pupils stared out of the windows at what was happening – and into the building.

She sat shaking on the sofa in his office while he went to fetch her a glass of water. Karin felt for her phone in her back pocket and saw that another message had arrived:

i miss u

BeXxx

She tapped a response with shaking hands:

Please, who are you??

Xx

Karin waited for the circles to pulsate at the bottom of the screen.

'You know what I'm going to say.' The headmaster returned to the room with a glass of water, and she quickly put her phone away. 'It's unwise for you to continue in your job for the time being. Your presence is causing considerable disruption.'

'You can't believe that I had anything to do with Lucas's disappearance?'

'Of course not. Karin, you're the same excellent teacher you always were, but right now you're a flashpoint. We can't have that kind of behaviour outside the gates every day. I want to invite the media when we say a prayer for Lucas in tomorrow morning's assembly, but—'

'I want to be there,' she insisted.

'The cameras will all be trained on you.'

Karin couldn't argue with him. She couldn't continue, not if she was somehow implicated in the kidnappings – not if it put other children in danger. And now, with what had happened to Lydia…

Karin wished she had never gone to the estate last night, wished she had stayed away…

'I understand, I'll go, I don't want to cause any more trouble.'

Her phone vibrated again, and she held her breath.

u dont ♥ me no more
u ♥ that police bitch
BeXxx

She typed:

No!!!! I love you!!!!
XXXX

The headmaster frowned at her inattention. 'Karin?'
She stood, heart pounding, waiting for the reply.

...

...

...

prove it
u have 2 make a choice

42

The Ninth Day...

Karin lay in Becky's arms.

'I know it's hard, but you are being very brave.'

'But why does it have to be me?' Karin pressed herself against her friend on the concrete floor of the basement. 'Why do I have to be the one who goes upstairs?'

It was easy to lose track of how long they had been there. With no window and the constant light from the bulb, the days and nights all merged into one, and it was only because Jerry Swann took Karin upstairs every evening at dusk and brought her back down again in the early hours that they had any sense of passing time.

The kids were cold and starved and exhausted, and slept as much as they could on the dirty blankets, but Karin didn't have that luxury. She felt fear and revulsion at the thought of having to go upstairs with Jerry every night, she didn't want to be near him, she didn't want to be his friend, all she wanted to do was stay in Becky's arms. But in the evening, they would hear the lock snap and Jerry would take her to the table in the kitchen where she would be forced to spend hours listening to his mad ramblings.

He told her about all the people he had 'disappeared', all the people he had harmed – the people he had killed.

Jerry spoke for hours about the terrible things he had done, and went into excruciating detail. He explained what he did to the men and women who had displeased him, crossed him or been unkind, the random people he had followed home and murdered. He had killed his own mother too, he said, and she was buried beneath the smooth floor of the basement, the empty sockets of her skull filled with hard concrete. Karin daren't tell Becky about that.

Nothing existed during those hours except for Jerry; it was as if the pair of them were totally alone in the universe. All she heard, as the last of the evening light faded and black night closed in, was his voice, talking of madness and murder. All she saw were those small, moist eyes behind the orange lenses, as he spoke about the people he had strangled, stabbed, bludgeoned and smothered.

'Oh, darling, you're doing so well,' said Becky, stroking her hair. 'And it gives us a chance to get out of here. Does he ever leave the room?'

'He never leaves the table.'

'You have to get him to leave you alone, even for just a second, and then you can *do* something.'

Karin wanted to cry. 'He won't, I can't.'

But her friend took her hand. 'You can do this, Kaz, I know you can, you can get us out, which is why you're my best friend.'

Karin felt a hard knot of gratitude clench in her chest. Everyone lay still, but she knew Simon was the only one who was asleep. The cellar was filled with the stench of his feverish sweat as he tossed and turned. Everyone else was thinking about what would happen to them. Jerry couldn't keep them down here for ever, but neither could he let them go home; if he did, he would go to prison. Nobody wanted to say out loud what he would have to do with them.

'He likes you. Why does he like you?'

'He doesn't,' Karin said quickly, because she didn't want it to be true, she didn't want to be his friend.

'Then why does he always take *you* upstairs?'

He had smelled her loneliness, because he was also desperate to love and be loved. *We love too much, as if love was a crime!* But Jerry was mad, he was repulsive. It made Karin sick just thinking about it. She was nothing like him – nothing!

'You have to gain his trust.' Becky lifted herself on to an elbow. 'Be nice to him, and then get us out.'

'But how?' Karin asked miserably.

'Run away, get help. There'll come a time when you'll get a chance and you *must* take it.' Karin let out a fearful sigh, but Becky said again, 'I love you, and I *know* you can do it!'

And Karin knew then that she was capable, because Becky had told her she was.

They listened to Jerry moving about upstairs, as he did all day and night. Sometimes, when he had delivered Karin back to the cellar in the early morning, his restless footsteps moved back and forth for hours afterwards.

'You have to get us out, Karin. We're all counting on you, *I'm* counting on you. If you get us out of here, I'll love you for ever.'

Becky's words made her conflicted. Karin wanted to be free, of course she did, but a small part of her would be disappointed if they did escape, because she knew she'd never again be able to spend so much time with Becky, never again be able to stay so close to her side. This was a bad, terrible place, but at least they had each other.

'I will,' Karin whispered. 'I'll get us out of here.'

Lydia's voice came from across the floor. 'Can't you hit him over the head with something and then climb out the window?'

'He keeps the knife on the table. He'd kill me on the spot, like he did all those others.'

They all fell into silence, thinking about the people Jerry had killed. It was six or seven, or maybe more. The way Jerry spoke about the murders was confusing. Karin didn't know if it was because she was so tired, but the circumstances of what happened and who died seemed to change all the time. Nothing he said seemed to make sense.

'We're all going to die if you don't do *something*,' Michelle said, and Paul began to weep again, but they had all grown tired of his tears. 'Oh, shut up, won't you?'

'There's going to come a time, and it might only be a split second, when you're going to have a chance to get to a phone, break a window and climb out, I don't know what it is, but you'll know when it happens.'

And when Jerry took her upstairs that night, Karin knew she had to act quickly, she had to get them all to safety. She had sat with him for so long that the dull grey of morning had begun to gnaw at the edge of the net curtain. Karin was exhausted, mentally and physically, so tired she could hardly think, and Jerry's monologue had become a burble in her head.

Her eyes must have closed because he rapped on the table. 'Stay awake!'

'I'm sorry, I'm so... tired.'

'Perhaps you like listening to her more than me.' Jerry's head twitched. 'Maybe you're a liar, like the rest of them, and you don't like me. Maybe you're not my friend.'

'I'm your friend, Jerry,' she said. 'Honestly I am.'

He considered her carefully. 'Who's your *best* friend, me or her?'

Karin didn't want to upset him, but she couldn't betray her love for Becky. 'You both are.'

'If she's such a good friend, then why didn't she tell you about that party she went to?'

Karin stared in shock. Her eyes lifted to the pipe on the wall dropping into the floorboards, and she realized he heard everything they said in the cellar. That's how he knew her name, and that her father had left her. Her heart leapt in terror; she wondered if he had heard them talking about escaping.

'Are you really my friend, Karin?' His fingers tapped the table irritably near the handle of the knife. 'Maybe you're like all the others and you've been lying to me all this time. Maybe I can't trust you, maybe you're just pretending to like me and you really want to leave me.'

A muscle ticked in his jaw, his lips quivered, and she decided that she had to do something, make some kind of gesture – or he would kill her, kill all of them. Despite every cell in her body screaming with disgust, she reached across the table and laid her fingers on his, forced herself to hold his gaze. He shuddered with pleasure.

'Of course I'm your friend, Jerry. I'll always be your friend.'

'I really don't know what I'd do without you,' he whispered.

His fingers rubbed hers. Jerry's touch made her skin crawl. It took all her willpower not to snatch her hand away from his clammy grasp.

'Friends do things for each other,' she said.

'Like what?'

'My friend Simon is ill.'

'He's not your friend.'

'He needs to go to a hospital.'

He twitched. 'That's not going to happen.'

'If you were my friend, Jerry, you'd help him,' said Karin. 'You said you would do anything for me.'

'I said I would do anything for *you*, I didn't say anything about him.'

'If you would do anything for me, then please let me take him to the hospital.'

'If I let you go now, we couldn't be friends any more.' He licked his lips. 'But there is something I'll do for you.'

His small eyes glinted behind the lenses. Her heart began to clatter in her chest. Whatever it was he was going to say, she didn't want to hear it.

'I'll kill Becky for you.' He reached for the knife. 'I'll do it right now, if you want.'

'Why…' She found it difficult to breathe. 'Why would you do that?'

'Because she's not your friend, not really. She lied to you about that party, and if she lied about that, she's lied to you about other things. She doesn't know how to love like us, Karin.'

Karin knew he would do it in a heartbeat. He'd go downstairs and kill Becky. All Karin had to do was say… *yes*.

'Please…' she said, and his eyes flashed in hope. 'Please, don't.'

'Why not?'

'Because… I don't want you to.'

'Are you sure?'

'Yes.'

His head twitched. 'I think you want me to do it.'

She could barely breathe. 'No.'

'I think you do.'

'I don't. Please, Jerry,' she pleaded quietly. 'Please don't do it.'

He took off his glasses to consider her carefully.

'You have to go back downstairs now.' She pressed her hands against the table, ready to rise, grateful that another long night was over, but then he grabbed her wrist. 'But if you change your mind, let me know.'

43

'Can you get them to take it down as soon as you
can?' Sasha said into the phone as she let herself
into the house. 'I'd be grateful if you did.'

'We're working on it, DI Dawson,' said the woman in
the Essex Police press office. 'But I'm afraid the footage
has already gone viral, so it's popping up on all kinds
of sites.'

'Bugger!' Sasha slammed the door and went to the
bottom of the stairs. 'Angel, can you come down here?'

Vaughn would go ballistic when he saw the video
of Kev decking Nelson, if he hadn't already. The last
thing they needed right now, in the middle of a stalling
investigation – with two children missing and one
witness dead – was footage uploaded on to the internet
showing the husband of a detective inspector assaulting
a man.

'Thanks, please let me know when it's down,' she said
into the phone, then killed the call. 'Angel, down here,
please!'

Sitting with his legs over the side of an armchair in

the living room, Denny looked up from his phone.

'What are you doing here?' she asked him.

'They sent us home early because there were too many reporters outside.'

'Angel, I'm waiting!'

'I'm doing something!' came the response from upstairs.

'I don't care,' shouted Sasha. 'Come down here right now!'

Her son slipped off, sensing the imminent arrival of a full-blown row, in the way animals sense storms building in the atmosphere. Clutching a tea towel, Ursula watched her in silence, knowing better than to contribute her thoughts.

Sasha dumped her bag on the floor and threw her jacket at the banister, where it sagged untidily. When Ursula went to hang it properly, she snapped, 'Leave it!'

Sasha was pouring herself a glass of cold water from the fridge dispenser when Angel finally made a sullen appearance.

'You lied to me. You knew the school was going to contact me about the bullying so you threw the blame on Tilly.' Sasha felt her anger build. 'I can't believe you did that.'

'Whatever she said, I didn't do it.' Tears filmed Angel's eyes. 'I swear.'

'No wonder you didn't want to go to school, no wonder you didn't want to show your face.'

'What's going on?' asked Ursula finally.

'Well, let me tell you, Mum. It turns out Angel is a mean girl, a persecutor, an oppressor, a *bully*.' Sasha dared her daughter to contradict her, but Angel didn't reply. 'What I don't understand is why you would do such a thing?'

'It all got out of hand,' Angel said miserably. 'My squad thought it was funny to send her some texts. It's not all my fault, it was the others, too.'

'I don't care about any of those other girls,' said Sasha. 'Oh, wait, I do! Because one of your lovely friends who was here last night videoed your dad hitting our neighbour and uploaded it on the internet!'

'It's not my fault Dad's a total fruit loop. It's no wonder I'm the way I am!'

Sasha placed the glass on the counter with a trembling hand. 'You will apologize to Tilly for your appalling behaviour.'

'I could be totally innocent and you wouldn't believe me,' said Angel. 'In your mind I'm always the bad child, the naughty one who does bad things. I'm always *such* a disappointment to you.'

Sasha liked to think she was the kind of person who gave her children positive reinforcements, and tried not to be critical – and the teacher had told her to speak gently to Angel about what had happened – but she felt let down and very cross, and she heard herself say, 'Yes, you are.'

Angel burst into tears.

Sasha instantly tried to backtrack. 'I didn't mean it like that.'

'Yes you did! You hate me!'

'It's just... this is not who you are, Angel, you're better than this.'

'Why is it always me who gets it in the neck?' Angel shouted. 'Oh, yeah, of course, it's because you love Denny more than me, you always have.'

'That's ridic—'

'And you loved Jake more than you love either of us.'

'No...' Sasha gawped at her daughter, shocked, horrified, barely able to speak. 'That's not—'

'Because he's dead, because he's always going to be oh-so-perfect, and he'll never make trouble for you like the rest of us imperfect people!'

The accusation twisted in Sasha's chest like a knife. She spoke quietly but her words were laced with anger. 'I can't believe you would say something so hurtful.'

'Sasha...' warned Ursula.

'How *dare* you say that, how dare you bring Jake into it!'

'You're on everybody's side but mine!' screamed Angel. 'You never see the good in me!'

'That's not true.' Sasha said shortly. 'I love you. I'd give you my last breath if you needed it. But you've let me down, Angel, and you've let yourself down!'

'You think I'm a bully and a hateful person.'

'If the cap fits,' Sasha spat. 'I could just about accept

it if you told me the truth, but you lied, you said this was all Tilly's fault. And all the while you were sending her nasty messages. I saw them, Angel, and they're disgusting!'

'She sent me texts, too! Why are you taking her side in this?'

'Sending vile texts, calling her names, isolating her from other friends. Chasing her home! This isn't you!'

'Nobody likes Tilly, she's not cool.'

'She's not cool?' Sasha snorted. 'Who the hell do you think you are? Listen to yourself. You and Tilly were good friends, best friends, you loved her like a sister, and it hurts me to see how you could be so hateful.'

'How would you know who I am? You're never here! You're always working. Some days I don't even see you, because you're out of the house before I'm up and come home when I've gone to bed!'

Sasha gave herself a moment before she said anything else she would regret. 'I'm sorry about that, but there are two children missing, kids the same age as you, and their parents are very distraught.'

'Then maybe *I* should go missing,' said Angel, in floods. 'Maybe then you would finally pay more attention to me!'

Sasha gasped. 'I can't believe you've said that.'

'If the cap fits!' spat her daughter in bitter triumph. 'If I had normal parents, you know, who wanted to spend actual time with their actual daughter, a mother who actually liked me and a dad who wasn't going *la la,* maybe it wouldn't have happened. You think I'm a bad person, you think I'm as bad as those criminals you love putting in jail so much!'

Sasha tried to take the heat out of the confrontation, but knew it was too late. 'I don't think you're a bad person but I think you've been swept along by a bad crowd.'

'You think I'm a weak bitch! Well, you know what, it takes one to know one!'

'That's enough,' Sasha screamed.

The doorbell rang and Sasha stomped past her daughter and down the hallway, hoping it was Kev. But she recognized the shadow on the other side of the stained-glass immediately and the door swung open to reveal Nelson. She saw with a bitter satisfaction that his nose was red and swollen.

'You realize the whole street can hear you,' he told her.

'Fuck off, Nelson,' she replied.

But then Angel pushed past her.

'And where do you think you're going?'

'To see friends!' her daughter said over her shoulder. 'What do you care, anyway?'

'Come back here, please!' Sasha called. 'Right now!'

Without turning, her daughter held her middle finger high in the air and stormed off. Sasha felt her anger deflate like a balloon. Nelson was still standing on her

335

doorstep – and she took great delight in slamming the door in his face.

In the hallway, her mother's lips were pursed in disapproval.

'*What?*'

'You were too stern,' said Ursula.

Sasha needed to get back to work. She was frustrated and angry about her confrontation with Angel, and didn't like the way her mum was looking at her.

'How would you feel if I'd done that when I was a kid?' Sasha whipped her jacket off the banister. 'Bully a girl, turn people against her, chase her home hurling threats and abuse. You would have gone ballistic. I hate bullies, Mum, I absolutely detest them. I meet them every day at work, weak dickheads who think it's fine to use intimidation and violence, and to find out that my own daughter...'

She covered her face with a hand, exhausted.

'All I'm saying,' Ursula said quietly, 'is that shouting is not going to help. She's a good girl, she's your daughter. What she needs is an arm around her shoulder.'

'And she'll get it. *When* she apologizes to that poor girl.'

'Can I have a fiver?' asked Denny, appearing at the top of the stairs.

'No, you can't.' Denny was about to slope off when Sasha asked, 'Did you know Angel was bullying Tilly?'

Denny thought very carefully about his answer. 'Maybe.'

'Then why on earth didn't you tell me?' she said.

'I ain't a snitch,' he said.

'Be nice to your sister,' said Sasha wearily. 'She's going through a difficult time at the moment.'

'Yeah.' Denny favoured her with the full force of his sarcasm. 'I'll be sure to be as nice to her as you just were.'

When Ursula retreated to the kitchen, Sasha called Kev on his mobile. He needed to know about this, he needed to get his arse in gear and get involved. But, of course, it was switched off. So instead she found his work number – she hadn't called it in months – and phoned that.

'Hi, is Kevin Dawson there, please?' she asked.

'I'm sorry, who?' said the woman on the switchboard.

'Kevin Dawson, he's your Shipping Administrator.'

'I'll put you through.' After a few seconds she came back on again. 'What did you say his name was again?'

'He's worked there for years, but never mind.' The woman was obviously new. 'Can you put me through to his assistant, Madeleine Morris?'

Madeleine came on the line moments later. Sasha had met the girl at a couple of Kev's work functions and really liked her.

'Maddy,' she said, 'it's Sasha Dawson!'

'Oh!' There was genuine surprise in her reaction. 'Mrs Dawson, how are you?'

'I'm very well, Maddy,' she said. 'Is my husband there?'

There was a bit of a pause. 'Mr Dawson?'

'Yes,' said Sasha. 'You know, Kev.'

'Well, um, I'm afraid I can't help you.'

'I have to speak to him urgently, Maddy, and he's not answering his mobile. Is he in a meeting?'

'He's, uh… well…'

But then Sasha saw Craig's number flash on her phone. 'I'm sorry, Maddy, I've got to go. Can you get Kev to phone me as soon as possible? Thanks!'

She answered Craig's call and didn't even give him time to speak.

'I just popped out,' she said, and flew to the front door, 'and I'm on my way back right now.'

44

When she charged into the incident room, Ajay, Lolly and Craig dropped what they were doing to follow Sasha to her desk. They waited patiently while she kicked off her shoes, threw down her bag and fired up her desktop.

'I'm capable of doing something and listening at the same time, guys.'

'Okay, so the post-mortem results are in.' Ajay flicked to the right page in his notebook. 'The pathologist says the angle of the entry of the needle into Lydia's shoulder was odd, as we thought. An experienced user would have slid the needle into a vein at a narrow angle, but this one was stabbed in at ninety degrees high up on the deltoid, straight into muscle and skin tissue. My glamorous assistant will illustrate.'

Craig reached across to his own left shoulder with his right hand to press the top of a pen into it, bending his wrist to show how awkward and difficult it would have been for Lydia, or anyone else, to inject at such an angle. Ajay continued to read from his notes but Sasha's attention was caught by the sight of Vaughn massaging his temples as he spoke on the phone in his office.

'Bruises on her arms and shoulders...' continued Ajay, reading from his notebook. '... estimated time of death...'

Lolly agreed. 'She was seen at the estate gone eleven...'

Vaughn slammed down the phone and met her gaze with a scowl. Sasha snapped back into the room. Craig and Lolly waited for her to respond. What Ajay had been saying was important, perhaps critical to the investigation, and she cursed herself for losing the drift, but...

'Excuse me a moment,' she said and marched to Vaughn's office.

He motioned for her to come in. 'Shut the door.'

'I expect that was about me.'

'Congratulations, the press office tells me your husband's fist fight is breaking some kind of online viewing record. They're spitting feathers upstairs. They take a very dim view of the husband of a senior officer *attacking* another man, and are worried that the incident will bring the force into disrepute.'

'It was just a bit of handbags.'

'Bloody hell, Sasha,' he snapped. 'I told you to go home and relax – the last thing we needed is for your rowdy party to go viral. Two teenagers are missing! One of them was snatched outside a school in broad daylight – a bloody school! – and now Lydia Tide is dead. I've got parents and politicians and journalists calling every two minutes. I keep repeating that I've got my top team on the case, but I'm beginning to wonder. Come on, Sasha, get your bloody act together.'

She spoke quickly. 'One of my daughter's friends filmed the video on her phone. Yes, it makes for uncomfortable viewing, and yes, I'm deeply embarrassed, but Kev was let off with a caution and it'll all be forgotten in a day or two. Reprimand me, replace me, do whatever you want, but you're right about one thing.' She jerked a thumb over her shoulder at the incident room. 'That *is* a top team out there, Vaughn. They're dedicated professionals and I can assure you they're all working flat out.'

Vaughn sighed heavily. 'Replacing you will send off all the wrong signals. But you need to get some traction on this investigation.'

She nodded. 'Shall I go now?'

'Yes,' he told her. 'Please do.'

But Sasha hesitated at the door, eager to get one thing off her chest. 'Just so you know, it wasn't a rowdy party, it was a quiet family barbecue.'

He stared at her and she shut the door quickly. When she got back to Ajay and the others, she said tensely, 'You have my undivided attention.'

'The post-mortem revealed contusions on Lydia's arms and shoulders where someone grabbed her,' continued Ajay as if nothing had happened. 'She died from a traumatic brain injury hitting her head against the wall. She was injected after she died.'

'Time?'

'The pathologist estimates around midnight.'

'A neighbour said he was walking his dog past her flat at about a quarter to midnight,' said Craig. 'And heard her arguing with someone inside.'

'A man or a woman?'

'They didn't hear, but another neighbour said she saw a woman walking across the estate at around the same time. The neighbour said she recognized her from the television coverage.'

'Fucksticks,' said Lolly.

'Karin!' Sasha exclaimed. Karin McCarthy's name kept cropping up again and again. First, in the disappearance of Sammi and Lucas, and now as a person of interest in what was about to become a murder investigation. Her butter-wouldn't-melt act was wearing very thin. 'Craig, go and pick her up.'

He was about to leave when she shoved her feet back in her shoes. 'Wait, I'm coming with you.'

Sasha had cut Karin enough slack, she'd bring her in herself.

45

The message arrived just as Karin was turning the key in the lock.

did u kill Lyds? 😨

She dropped her keys and stared at the phone as the ellipses pulsed on the screen...

...

...

...

did u?

Karin typed in the reply, her fingers moving across the screen so quickly that what she wrote was gibberish, and she had to keep correcting herself. The text flew off with a *whoosh*.

No!!

Why would you say that?

When it had gone, Karin let herself inside and slammed the door. There was something different about the quiet hallway, but she was so focused on her phone that she barely noticed what it was.

...

...

...

U no Y

She couldn't bear it any longer, typed...

Please can we meet? XX

Hit send.

Becky would look different now, of course, she would be a full-grown woman, but they would both recognize each other instantly. Most likely there would be tears and recrimination, but then they would fall into each other's arms, sobbing with relief and happiness.

And then Karin would be able to explain – finally explain – what had happened in the Bad Place, she'd have a chance to tell Becky about the terrible mistake she had made, about the guilt and shame she felt, and how lonely her life had been without her.

They had a chance to begin again, to be together.

Waiting for the ellipses to pulse to show her that Becky was about to reply, she felt a faint breeze on her neck, and realized there was a draught coming down the hallway. From where she stood, Karin could see that the back door had been forced open in the kitchen.

Her phone vibrated in her hand.

> we will meet v soon
> & u will make a choice
> BeXxx

'Bex?' she called as she went into the living room. After all these years, she was back. Karin didn't know how but she had returned. She was here. Becky was somewhere in the house.

'Hello?' she called in hope, but also in fear, because she knew deep down that what she wanted so desperately was impossible. Becky was a long time dead. 'Becky, please come out.'

She walked back into the hallway and stood at the bottom of the stairs. There was no sound at all except for a car passing on the street outside. And then she heard it – a creak on a floorboard upstairs.

'Becky?' she called. 'Is that you?'

She took out her phone and with shaking hands wrote a message:

> Are you in my house?
> I know you're here xxx

The message flew away.

She peered up at the gloom of the landing. Her fingers pressed against the smooth banister.

'Bex, I know you're up there. Please, come down.'

The dim landing swung slowly into view as she climbed the stairs, one careful step at a time. The narrow landing was empty, but the door to her bedroom was ajar. It had been wide open when she left the house this morning and she saw that the curtains, which she had opened, were now closed.

'Becky.'

She moved carefully across the landing and opened the door to see, in the darkness of the room, the photograph of Becky she kept on a chest of drawers; it was the only one she had of her. It was the last thing she saw before she turned the light out at night, and the first thing she saw in the morning. Karin heard, or imagined she heard, Becky's excited breathing in the shadows.

She felt her phone vibrate against her fingers.

Oh Kaz

...

...

...

'I'm here, my darling,' Karin said in a trembling voice, and stepped inside. 'Where are you?'

But the phone buzzed softly again and again as messages dropped on to the screen.

i cant b bex u no that

...

...

...

Bex is DEAD!!!

...

...

...

& u will pay 4 what u did

And then hands grabbed her shoulders, spinning her around, sending the phone flying from her hand, and she was slammed into the wall.

'Becky!' she cried.

'Don't you say her name!' said a man's angry voice. Shaking her violently, screaming into her face. 'Don't you dare say her name!'

46

'Angel,' Sasha said into her phone, 'you've made your point. We both said things in the heat of the moment that we regret. Please give me a call, baby, tell me where you are.' She killed the call. 'A word to the wise, Craig, don't ever have children.'

'My girlfriend says she doesn't want kids,' said DC Power, accelerating along the road. 'She's a model and actress and says it's a lot of work to get back into physical shape. She doesn't want her pelvic floor to be shot to pieces.'

'I've given birth to three kids, so let's not venture much further into this conversation. And, anyway, you'll be too busy cracking heads at the National Crime Agency to have children.'

He blushed, obviously remembering what he'd told Lolly while Sasha was listening on the two-way in the park.

'You know what.' He flicked up the indicator to make

a right turn into Karin's street. 'Despite what I said, there is one good thing about working down here.'

'The rides on Adventure Island,' she said.

'No.' He shot her a sideways look. 'I like working for you.'

'Craig.' Sasha turned towards him in the passenger seat, genuinely touched. 'You don't know how much it means for me to hear you say that. But they won't let you anywhere near the Flying Squad or whatever with that kind of snowflake attitude, you'll have to toughen up a bit.'

'No word of a lie, I reckon you're a nice lady...' She watched him rock his head from side to side, weighing his next words carefully. 'Maybe you're a bit all over the place sometimes, but everyone in the MIT likes you, and we know it's been a difficult week. Fact is, you're the best boss I've ever had.'

She cuffed him softly on the arm. 'You're winding me up.'

'I'm not,' he said, pulling into the street. 'I've learned a lot from you already.'

'Like what?' she said, fishing.

His eyes moved back and forth as he tried to think of something. 'The way you're so calm under fire.'

'Ha, I don't think that's quite true, but I'll gladly accept the compliment. Over there.' She pointed at a space at the kerb as they drove slowly along the narrow winding road, and he pulled up outside Karin's house and cranked the handbrake. 'Just do me a favour and spread some of this charming Craig-love to some of your other colleagues.'

And then they heard a scream from inside the house, and a man's bellowing. They whipped off their seat belts and jumped out of the car.

Craig flew to the front door, shoulder first, hoping the momentum of his run would send it flying open, but he rebounded off it, wincing. Sasha was already on her phone calling for backup. He kicked the door again, with no success.

'The glass, Craig!'

Sasha nodded at a pane in the bay window as she barked into the phone. He picked up a big stone from beside the path, pulled the sleeve of his jacket over his fist and smashed it into the glass, rearing back as jagged shards flew everywhere. He knocked out a bigger hole in the pane with an elbow until he was able to reach inside and unlock the window. As soon as he scrambled over the sill, he heard scuffles upstairs, and shouts.

'Police!' he called as he pounded upstairs. 'We're coming!'

And when he swung into the bedroom, he saw Jim Haskell with his hands gripping Karin's shoulders, slamming her again and again against the wall.

'Where are they?' he roared. 'What did you do with those kids?'

Craig grabbed him, pulling him away, but Jim shouted as he tried to fight him off. 'Get off me! Get away! What happened! Tell me!'

Sasha came into the room to crouch with Karin, who had slid down the wall. Jim lashed out at Craig, but his clumsy swing sent him spinning and he was slammed face down on the floor.

'Stay still now,' Craig told him as he pressed him to the floor and then looked up at Sasha. 'Everything good there?'

She checked Karin over, nodded. 'We're good.'

'What did you do to them?' Jim screamed at Karin. Tears flooding down his cheeks, his face twisted in impotent fury. 'Why did you do it? Why?'

47

'She knows where that missing girl is,' Jim Haskell told Sasha in one of the interview rooms in the custody suite. 'And the boy, I'm sure of it.'

'What makes you think that?'

Jim folded his arms to stare sullenly at Sasha and Craig. If he felt remorse for attacking Karin, he didn't show it; all the tears and anger were gone now, replaced by an implacable contempt.

'Because everyone knows that you interviewed all that lot. Michelle Dormand is the girl's godmother, Karin McCarthy is the boy's teacher. Simon Parkin is in a coma and Lydia Tide is dead, for God's sake. That mob are all in it up to their necks!'

'What I really don't understand is why you dislike Karin so much?'

'With respect, I don't think there's anybody on Earth who knows more about the Bad Place than I do.' He snorted bitterly. 'Listen to me, calling it the Bad Place, like everyone else. Makes it sound like something exciting, don't it? Like a rollercoaster ride, or a scary movie.

But the fact is, my sister was killed in that cesspit, *murdered*. And when Jerry Swann was shot dead the whole investigation was wrapped up in a little bow. How very convenient; Swann died, he was guilty, case closed. But there are so many questions about that place still, a gaping hole in our knowledge of what happened on the night Becky died. Things *she* ain't told us.'

'Such as?'

'For one thing, she spent hours every night with Swann but she's never spoken about what they talked about.'

'He told her about all the people he said he'd killed.'

'All night, every night, that's all they talked about?' He scratched his chin. 'Doesn't seem likely to me, and we only have her word for it. They could have left the house together, gone for a meal, or to the pictures, for all we know. She could have met someone else up there – a relative of Swann's, an accomplice, a pen pal. Someone who's out there now, snatching kids! That copper Carrington once told me he never trusted her version of events, even he reckoned she was hiding something. So what really went on up there?' Sasha was listening carefully, which made him grin. 'I can see you're wondering about it, too.'

'She was just a frightened young girl,' said Sasha. 'The same as Becky.'

Jim made a sarcastic face. 'Even as a teenager that Karin was as needy as hell. Clingy like you wouldn't believe. Always around our house, turning up out of the blue, hanging around like a bad smell. She'd go into a meltdown if Becky even said hello to someone else. I told my sister, *Becky luv, get rid, or you'll be stuck with her for ever*. But she didn't want to upset the girl, because that was the kind of person she was, she was too nice.'

'Karin isn't on trial here,' Sasha reminded him. 'We're here to talk about why you broke into her house and assaulted her.'

'I'm not pleased with myself, I lost control, but you could say the ends justify the means. I went there with the most honest of intentions. To try to get her to come clean about the disappearance of those kids. But when I got there—'

'And broke in,' said Craig.

'When I walked around her nice little house, full of her nice little things, all the knick-knacks and personal items, it made me angry,' said Jim. 'Because those are the kind of things Becky will never enjoy. She'll never have pretty things, she'll never have items to love and cherish. And I found a photo of Becky in her bedroom. Her photo – in that woman's bedroom!' He grimaced. 'And it made me feel *sick*. So, yeah, I got angry, and with good reason, and when she came home I lost it. I'm not proud of it. But maybe I could have found out where those two kids are, if you hadn't turned up. If I had, you'd be treating me like a hero right now, instead of a criminal.'

'You're going to be charged with criminal damage and assault. Was it worth it, Mr Haskell, just to frighten an innocent woman?'

'Innocent?' He clucked his tongue in distaste. 'Do me a favour. She's guilty of something. Everyone knows it.'

'Who's everyone?' asked Sasha.

'There are others like me. Journalists, true crime buffs, experts who have spent years studying this stuff. They all agree that something about the Bad Place stinks.'

'And you're in contact with these people?' asked Craig.

'I get letters and emails from around the world. There are forums, online places you can go where it's all they talk about. There are some very strange types out there, let me tell you, but also people devoted to uncovering the truth about why my sister died.'

'And how far would you go to find out the truth, Mr Haskell?'

He smirked. 'You're trying to pin that murder on me now? Nice try, luv, but I was tucked up in bed with the wife.'

Sasha studied him. The man she'd chased into the arcade was tall. Jim Haskell was of average height and sliding badly into middle-age, with a bulging beer gut. He didn't look like he could run more than twelve yards on a good day.

'Look, what can I say? You got me bang to rights for the assault and the criminal damage – I hold my hands up to that, it was a moment of madness – but can I go now? There are some media interviews I've lined up for this afternoon.'

Sasha smiled across the table. 'There are certain administrative procedures to complete before you can go but I'm afraid our custody officers are rushed off their feet this afternoon. I'm sure they'll get around to you eventually.'

48

Before Karin's interview, Sasha stood outside the room texting her mother to find out if Angel had come home, but sensed Craig pacing restlessly behind her.

'Out with it.'

'I'm a trained investigative interviewer, I've got all my accreditation,' he said. 'It sends off the wrong signals if you're always in there with me.'

She glanced up. 'Earlier you said I was the best boss in the world.'

'There's a problem here,' he said.

'Wait, let me just do this.' She finished the text, considered it, then deleted the whole thing. There was no point in sending it, her mother probably hadn't even turned on her mobile in five years. 'And what's the problem?'

He turned away. 'It doesn't matter.'

'Come on, Craig.' She dropped the phone back in her bag. 'Don't go coy on me now.'

'Nobody doubts your dedication or determination.' He jerked his head towards the room where Karin sat waiting. 'But in the circumstances, ma'am, I think it's best if you leave this interview to me.'

She raised an eyebrow. 'Oh, it's ma'am now, is it? And you were so lovely earlier.'

'You and Karin McCarthy, you have a history with her. Maybe you don't see her clearly enough.'

'What are you talking about?'

'Everyone knows you met her on the night of Becky Haskell's death. You feel like you let her down.'

'Oh dear, this is like that time we fell out over Brexit.' She tried to keep her reply amiable but felt herself bristling at the suggestion. 'Thank you for your input, Craig, or since we're being so formal about it, *Detective Constable* Power, but I'm afraid this will be an argument you'll lose, what with me outranking you and everything. And, just for the record, I'm not distracted in the slightest.'

Her phone rang and she saw it was her mother.

'I'm going to have to take this,' she said quickly and touched the screen. 'Yes, Mum.'

'You'll be glad to know I'm leaving.'

'What, where are you going?' Sasha saw Craig watching her, so she walked away in an effort to get some privacy, but the interview room was on a busy corridor, and everywhere she stopped she was getting in someone's way. 'Never mind.' There were more important things to attend to. 'Is Angel there?'

'She hasn't come back.'

'Do you think you could hang on until she comes home?'

'I'd rather not,' said her mother.

'Then will you at least wait till I get back?' she asked.

Her hope was that she'd be able to convince her mum to stay until Angel turned up. It was absolutely typical of Ursula to leave on the one day when it would be useful to have her there. Kev wasn't answering his mobile, and Sasha didn't know if Angel even had her keys. The last thing she wanted was for her daughter to return home, not be able to get in, and disappear off again.

But her mother's terse replies suggested she was still smarting from being told off about Nelson and the row with Angel. 'Well...'

'I'll get home as soon as I can,' Sasha said. 'I promise.'

When she headed back to Craig, Lolly Chambers was with him.

'Let's ask Lolly what we should do,' said Sasha, still annoyed at Craig's earlier remarks. 'Lols, do you think it should be me or you who goes into the interview room with Detective Constable Power? He says that where Karin is concerned, I'm... compromised.'

Lolly looked uncomfortable at being put on the spot. 'It's not really my place to say.'

'If only one of us here was senior enough to make a decision about who goes in. *Hmm.*' Sasha tapped a finger thoughtfully against her chin and then made a shocked face. 'Oh wait, *I'm* a senior officer.'

And then she pushed past Craig and into the interview room.

'Thanks for waiting, Karin.' Sasha dropped into a chair. Her DS came in and sat beside her while she flicked noisily through her notepad.

'We've interviewed Jim Haskell and I can confirm he's going to be charged with assault and criminal damage. Plus, we're doing intel checks and searching his home and business premises, but there's no evidence to suggest he's involved in the abductions, or in Lydia's death.' Sasha looked up. 'How are you feeling after the attack?'

'Shocked,' Karin said, 'and a little bit foolish for thinking...'

'Thinking what?' asked Sasha when she didn't finish the thought. Karin shook her head and Sasha once again got the feeling there was something she wasn't telling her. 'Do you know why he did it, Karin?'

'He's never liked me.'

'No, he doesn't, does he?' said Sasha. 'I'll be honest with you, Karin, I don't like *him* very much. He strikes me as a bully, one of those men who has all these angry emotions pent up inside him, and then, *boom*! He's been looking for an excuse to lash out for years, and unfortunately you were the target. Nevertheless, he's convinced you're keeping a secret that explains why Jerry Swann killed Becky, and why Sammi and Lucas are missing, and I have to say I agree with him. Is there something you want to tell us, Karin?'

'There's nothing.'

'Do you know why we were coming to see you, myself and DS Power? Because a witness on Lydia's estate saw you heading towards her flat last night, gone midnight actually, which is around the estimated time of her death. You told me that you didn't see her last night.'

'I was disappointed that we had argued earlier, Lydia was upset, she isn't... she wasn't strong.' Karin glanced between Sasha and Craig. 'I went there to clear the air between us and see how she was coping.'

'You went to her flat.'

Karin shook her head. 'I got to the estate and changed my mind. It wasn't a very good idea to go there, it would only have ended in a row and I couldn't face that, so I went home.'

'Are you sure? Because there was no sign of forced entry at her flat, Karin, which suggests she opened the door willingly to whoever went there. It was someone she knew.'

'Where were you earlier in the evening?' asked Craig.

'With a man.' Karin told him. 'And when I left him I went to Karin's estate.'

'Where were you with this man?'

'At a hotel on the seafront.'

Craig clicked open his ballpoint. 'And who was this bloke?'

'I'd rather not say, he's married.' Craig's pen remained

poised over his notepad as Karin turned back to Sasha. 'Am I being accused of something?'

'We have reason to believe Lydia was murdered. She was attacked, or was involved in some kind of struggle and died, and then she was injected in an effort to make her death look like an overdose. A neighbour heard shouting in her flat, around the time you were seen on the estate, and there was no sign of forced entry.'

'Your fingerprints are all over her flat,' said Craig.

'They would be,' said Karin quickly. 'I've been to Lydia's flat many times.'

'I'll ask you again,' said Sasha. 'What did Lydia tell Matt Foster about you? What do you think he meant when he told me, *you'll know the truth about her?*'

Karin's voice was a whisper, 'I don't know what that means.'

'Most people would have run a mile from Lydia. Her life was so chaotic and unhappy, I imagine she could be very draining. But you always helped her, Karin, you always stuck by her, why is that?'

'Because she had no one else. She was vulnerable and easily led. It wasn't her fault she was like that. Maybe if Jerry Swann hadn't climbed into our minibus that day, her life would have turned out differently.'

'A lot of lives would have turned out differently, that's for sure.' Sasha smiled sadly. 'Maybe you kept her close because she was unpredictable, a wild card, and she knew something about you, something she told Matt Foster, something that made you kill her.'

'I didn't kill her.' Karin looked at her steadily. 'She was my friend.'

Sasha drummed her fingers impatiently on the table.

'Sammi and Lucas are missing, Karin, and there's something you're not telling us. It all keeps coming back to you, doesn't it? Someone is trying to get your attention, and the sooner you tell us why, the better chance we have of getting those kids home safely. Because we're running out of time now, and to be honest, I'm losing patience. Tell us what all this has to do with the Bad Place.'

'I don't know.'

'You're lying.' Sasha's voice rose sharply, making Craig glance at her. 'What happened at the Bad Place?'

'Becky died. That's what happened.'

'Why did she die, Karin?'

'Because she was murdered in cold blood by a psychopath!' Karin shouted. 'Because she didn't get away.'

'How did Jerry Swann get her, Karin?' asked Sasha quietly. 'You and the others have always maintained she was with you all when you escaped. But something happened to her, something awful, and she never made it into the woods. Did she trip? That's what investigators have always presumed. Or she went back into the farmhouse for some reason, or maybe she never got out at all.'

Sasha heard Karin's breath quicken.

'All of you have maintained that Becky escaped. Maybe all these years you've been mistaken. Or maybe...' Sasha let a moment pass. 'Maybe one of you is lying.'

Sasha knew Karin wanted to say something. She opened her mouth to speak. But then she cleared her throat and said, 'I've no idea. Am I free to go?'

'Yes.' Sasha stood. 'You can leave.'

49

While Craig showed Karin out of the building, Sasha headed back to the incident room to fetch her things.

'Where are we with that blue Mazda?' she called to Ajay as she put on her jacket.

He lifted his fingers from his computer keyboard. 'No reports of any stolen Mazdas as yet, and we're working as fast as we can on the CCTV footage in the streets around the abduction.'

'I'm popping out again,' she told him. 'It can't be helped. Hold the fort for me.'

He waved without looking up from his screen. 'Missing you already.'

Lolly came towards her as she picked up her bag. 'You okay, Lols, you look like you've seen a ghost.'

'I think I did.'

Lolly's untypical reticence made Sasha wary. 'Out with it.'

'I chased up that fella Jon Wilson from the drug

support centre, the one who was going to get us details on Lydia's mysterious boyfriend, Matt, yeah?'

'And what did he say?'

Lolly grimaced. 'That's the thing… I phoned the centre again, asking to be put through to Jon, and there is no person of that name there.'

Sasha stared. 'What are you telling me?'

'There's no Jon Wilson who works at the centre, he don't exist.'

'Then who the hell were we talking to?' asked Craig, coming back into the room.

'Alright.' Heart sinking, Sasha dropped her bag back on the desk. 'Tell me what you know.'

'There was a woman there, remember her?' Lolly said to Craig. 'She was called Kathy, and she's a volunteer at the centre. When I phoned that Jon to chase up the details on Matt Foster as he'd promised, she answered the phone and she said he recognized him as one of their *clients*, which was why she was surprised to see him in the admin office. He left us in there for a moment and went outside to apologize to her, said we were parole officers, and he needed privacy.'

'Son of a bitch.' Craig turned quickly to Sasha. 'He acted like he had every right to be in that room.'

'And who did she say this man was?'

Lolly swallowed. 'She didn't know his surname but knew him as… Matt. He'd attended group therapy sessions there several times.'

'Matt!' exclaimed Sasha, as Ajay drifted over to listen. 'Lydia's mysterious boyfriend?'

Lolly looked wretched. 'All his details are missing from the centre.'

'He was a very good liar, he was walking around like he owned the place,' said Craig, as if that excused it. 'And he was…'

Craig and Lolly shared a guilty glance.

'And he was *what*?' asked Sasha.

'He was cleaning. Wiping down surfaces. Handles and chairs and stuff.'

'Getting rid of evidence,' said Ajay. 'His own fingerprints.'

Craig shuffled uncomfortably from one foot to another. 'And he took a file from a cabinet.'

'What's the betting that it's the file with his personal details on it?' Sasha dropped her head into a hand. 'And he did all this while you were standing there talking to him?'

'He was very convincing.' Craig bristled. 'What were we meant to do, ask for his ID?'

'Yes, actually,' Ajay said. 'That would have been a good place to start.'

Craig folded his arms tight against his chest. 'Well, we didn't.'

'So our main suspect covered his tracks in front of you both!' Sasha didn't want to blow her top in the middle of the office, it wasn't her style, but she was seething.

'As you know, Craig, I'm not the kind of person who goes about pointing fingers. But, in the circumstances, it would be nice if, just this one time, you tried to show just a tiny bit of contrition.'

Craig stared at his shoes.

'Sasha, I'm so sorry,' said Lolly. 'I'm mortified.'

Sasha jabbed a finger towards Vaughn's empty office. 'Earlier today I was singing your praises to the DCI, telling him what a good bunch you are, how professional and dedicated and bright. What on earth am I meant to say to him about this?'

'I really am—'

'Lolly.' She chopped the air with a hand. 'I don't want to hear it, I'm so very annoyed right now. Nobody breathe a word of this to DCI Vaughn. Let me do it. Goodness knows I'm already in the doghouse.'

'His personal details may also be kept on computer there,' said Ajay, tactfully filling the tense silence. 'You know how these local authorities are with data protection, but he'll have been referred. There'll be a digital trail.'

'All his details will probably be false anyway.'

'Bring me solutions, Craig, not problems,' snapped Sasha.

'I'll get back to them.'

'No. Lolly's already spoken to someone there, she can do it. I want you to talk to Ian Carrington about his father's memories of the Bad Place.'

'You already did that.'

'And came away with nothing, which was a mistake. Peter Carrington told Jim Haskell that he didn't trust Karin McCarthy's version of what happened when they escaped from the cellar, that Becky escaped and was recaptured by Swann. The likelihood is that he also told his son, Ian, of his suspicions, so let's leave no stone unturned.'

'He might not even be there.'

'Ian Carrington told me he saw his old man most afternoons.'

'Anyone could go and do that.'

'It'll get your shorthand speed up.'

'You're sidelining me,' said Craig. Ajay nudged Lolly's elbow, *let's leave them to it*, and together they sloped off. 'I'm sorry about what happened at the drug centre, but it wasn't just my fault.'

'We'll discuss that later,' she said shortly, thinking of Sammi, thinking of Lucas, and how she was letting them down again. 'Right now I need you to go there and come back with as much information as you can.'

Her face was like thunder and Craig knew better than to push it, so he walked off in a huff, whipping his jacket brusquely off the back of his chair.

Sasha stomped over to Ajay. 'I went too far.'

'They fucked up, they deserved it.'

'I'll stay.'

'Do what you have to do, we've got everything

covered here. If there's any developments, I'll ring.'

She didn't need telling twice, went to her desk and grabbed her bag. 'You'll hardly know I've gone.'

'The sooner you're gone, the sooner you're back.'

50

'Can I help you?'

Craig was waiting impatiently in the empty reception of the Tarpley Care Home when a young nurse clutching a pair of fluffy towels came over.

'I'm here to see Ian Carrington.' He flashed her his warrant card. 'DC Craig Power.'

'Ah,' she said. 'Peter's son.'

'I was told he'd be here.'

Craig Power wasn't in the mood to be hanging around the reception of an old people's home in case some fella, who may or may not know something about stuff that happened decades ago, should happen to swing by. This whole Bad Place business was a distraction and a total time-suck.

'I'm just off to check on Peter now, why don't you take a seat?' The nurse gestured to the empty reception desk. 'I'm sure someone will attend to you soon.'

'Why don't I just come up with you since you're on the way?'

'I don't think we allow just anyone to wander around the building,' she told him. 'Good try, though.'

'I'm not just anyone, though, I'm a police officer.' He flashed his best winning smile and took the towels off her. 'Tell you what, I'll even make myself useful by carrying these.'

'I'm not sure you should,' said the young woman, but she didn't put up much resistance, and together they walked to the lift.

When they got to the room, Craig was shocked to see how withered and frail Peter Carrington was. Sasha had described how the old man had been rendered mute and unresponsive by a massive stroke, and the nurse had tried to warn him on the way up, but he still wasn't prepared for the sight of the hunched and twisted figure in a wheelchair.

'How are you doing, Mr Carrington?' said Craig loudly. 'I'm Detective Constable Craig Power. I'm police, just like you.'

The old man didn't react at all, he just stared out of the window, his only movements a slight shudder in the jaw that seemed to sit lopsided on one side of his face, and a tremble of the gnarled hands in his lap.

'Can he hear me?'

'Oh, yes, sure he can. I bet you're looking forward to Ian getting here, aren't you, Peter?' The nurse fussed around his wheelchair, tucking in a blanket, wiping the moisture clinging to the corner of his eyes, making sure he was comfortable. 'I hope when I'm your age I'll have someone visit me so often.'

Craig wandered to a tallboy cabinet to look at all the photos. 'He comes every day?'

'Sometimes twice.' The nurse placed the towels at the bottom of the bed. 'He's a good son, very attentive to his dad. Peter is his world.'

Craig scanned the rows of framed photos. He picked one up to look at Peter Carrington in his prime, taken at some work function. He was the life and soul of the party, broad shoulders flung back and barrel chest puffed out, belly bulging, a pint slopping in his hand. Craig could tell his loud, braying laugh would lift the fringe off your forehead.

Peter was surrounded by other coppers, detectives from another era with moustaches and gelled hair, wide patterned ties and cheap suits. They loved being police, these men, you could see the pride and swagger in the way they held themselves. Craig would have loved to have been in plain clothes back then, when everything was less complicated. Those were the days when you could go to work in the morning and look forward to making some juicy arrests with the boys, get stuck in, bang a few heads together, rather than spend all day hunched over a monitor watching endless CCTV footage.

He picked up the photograph and examined it closely, glancing at the old man to make sure it was the same person. It was difficult to reconcile the big, barnstorming beast of a man in the image with the slight figure, a whisper of his former self, in the wheelchair. Back in the day, Carrington had looked the business. He wore his lustrous hair swept arrogantly back on his head, the knot of his tie was bloated as big as a cravat and there was a medal with the legend 'P' around his neck, a fancy Breitling Colt watch on his wrist...

A Breitling Colt watch on his wrist.

Craig put down that photo and picked up the others, examining them quickly as the nurse crouched in front of Peter Carrington.

'There you are,' she told the old man. 'You're all ready for Ian now.'

He found a photo on the back row of Peter and a woman, presumably his wife, and a teenager. Craig stared at it. He recognized the boy immediately.

'And look, Peter,' said the nurse in a sing-song, 'here he comes now!'

Craig went to the window, careful to stay out of sight, and looked out. He saw the large man he had spoken to at the drug support centre, the man who identified himself as Jon Wilson, but was also known as Matt Foster – and now revealed as Ian Carrington – walking along the leafy pavement towards the building.

Craig stepped back. 'Will he have to sign in?'

'Oh, he'll come straight up, we all know Ian here.' There was uncertainty in the nurse's voice. 'Has he done something wrong?'

'He's a person of interest in a police investigation,' said Craig, wondering if the old man knew what they were talking about. Peter Carrington's jaw jerked occasionally, but other than that he was unresponsive.

'How long will he stay?'

'An hour, forty-five minutes, perhaps?'

'I need you to go downstairs and tell me when he's on his way up.' Craig took out a card with his number on it. 'Don't treat him any differently on the way in, don't come up with him, and don't let anyone else up either. For the time being, this floor is off limits.'

'Shall I tell him you're here?'

'Just let me know as soon as he gets into the lift.'

She grabbed the handles of the old man's wheelchair, intending to move him, but Craig told her, 'There's no time for that.'

When she had gone, Craig took out his phone and called Lolly. He left the room, listening to the soft boom of the lift's mechanics as the nurse headed to reception, and walked along the corridor in the opposite direction. It turned a corner, leading to a stairwell. He stood there, out of sight of the lift, waiting for her to answer the phone. Peeking around the corner, he heard the elevator reach the ground floor, saw the green downwards arrow above the door turn to 'G'.

Lolly's voice was brisk. 'DC Chambers.'

'I need you to get some units to the Tarpley Care Home.' His heart raced. 'I think I may have our man.'

'Who?' she asked. 'The abductor?'

'Yeah.' He heard the lift door close downstairs. 'Ian Carrington is our friend Jon Wilson. Just get here now, he's coming to see his father, and has no idea I'm here. Whatever you do, don't come in all sirens wailing. When he goes into the room, I'll meet you in reception.'

'Okay, mate,' said Lolly. 'Just wait till we get there.'

'Will do.'

'On the way!'

He killed the call, looked around the corner, saw the LED display above the lift change from 'G' to an upwards-pointing arrow. The lift began to ascend. Craig's phone flashed silently and the nurse said, 'He's on his way.'

'Thanks. Just to repeat, nobody comes up.'

Craig put the phone away and waited. The lift door opened at the end of the hallway and he heard the soft pad of feet on the carpet. Pressed against the wall, he held his breath, worried that Carrington could somehow sense his presence. There was a long moment when he couldn't hear a thing, and part of him was tempted to sneak a look, but then the door to Peter Carrington's room opened. He heard a voice say, 'Hi, Dad, it's me!' The door closed.

Craig peeked around the corner. The corridor was empty. It would be easy enough to get to the lift, or he could take the stairs. He crept along the carpeted corridor, briefly putting his ear to the door of Carrington's room, heard Ian saying, '… really proud of me, Dad…'

Then he walked towards the elevator, intending to meet Lolly downstairs. She'd only be a matter of minutes. He stabbed the button and the door opened wide.

But Craig thought about those guys in that photo, those old-style coppers. They wouldn't have waited for backup, they wouldn't have tiptoed around the place until other police arrived to steal their thunder. They were men who took the bull by the horns. It still rankled that he'd put in all that effort to chase Simon Parkin only for other officers, Lolly included, to bring him to the ground.

Also, he'd been made a fool of by Ian Carrington once before – and that really hurt. What if Carrington knew Craig was there, and that other officers were on their way, and took the opportunity to climb out of the window of his father's room? What Craig needed was a result with which to impress Sasha Dawson; if ever he needed to earn a feather in his cap, it was now. He'd make sure Ian Carrington stayed in that room till Lolly and the others turned up.

He let the lift door close and walked back to Carrington's door. Sucking down a deep, steadying breath, he stepped inside.

Craig enjoyed the shock on the man's face when he saw him, and in that moment he knew instinctively that Carrington had taken those kids.

'Hey, Jon.'

Ian swallowed. 'Hello again.'

'Oh wait, you're not Jon, are you, or even Matt, you're Ian Carrington.' He nodded at the Breitling on Ian's wrist, the one he'd worn when they had met previously. 'And just for the record, it looked better on your old man.'

Sitting holding his father's hand, Ian gently replaced it in Peter's lap and stood up.

'It's nice to see you again,' he told Craig, 'but you'll have to excuse me, I've got somewhere I have to be.'

Craig held up a warning hand; he really didn't want to have to subdue him. 'Stay back, please.'

But Ian moved surprisingly fast, and he was strong too, grabbing the lapels of Craig's jacket and swinging him. Craig's feet lifted off the floor and he smashed into the door. All the breath left his chest, and before he could get his wits together, the ground rushed away from him again and he was pushed face first into the door of the cabinet. The glass shattered. He felt a sharp stab of pain just below his eye as a shard pierced his cheek. The photos clattered to the floor as he crashed into them, and then his body was wrenched in a different direction.

Stunned, unable to get his wits together, Craig was pulled towards the open window two storeys above the ground.

51

As soon as Ursula saw Sasha come in the door, she took off the apron and folded it, offering it to her daughter in a kind of formal handing-over ceremony. Sasha threw it on the stairs.

'It's all too exciting for me here,' her mother said.

Her cardigan was folded neatly over the handle of her trolley case by the door and she was wearing shoes, not her slippers.

Sasha didn't like the idea of her mum just upping and leaving, going goodness knows where – to her useless sister's or even making herself homeless. 'You can stay, you know you can. I didn't mean what I said last night, I was just a bit stressed.'

'Your mum doesn't feel welcome here.' She heard the slap of sandals on the parquet and then saw her father walking from the kitchen with a mug of coffee. He wore his usual cargo shorts and baggy top and his deep tan was mahogany against the white walls and china mug.

'Dad!' she said, surprised. 'You're here! Is Angel home?'

'I'm sure she'll turn up,' said Ursula. 'Once she's stopped sulking.'

'Do you mind both hanging on till she gets back?'

'We'd rather not. I'd like to get home as soon as possible. To be honest, my nerves are frazzled. There's an unhealthy tension in this house.'

'I'll bring the car round.' Her father drained the mug, placed it in Sasha's hand and patted her on the cheek. 'Goodbye, sweetheart. She's coming home with me. Thanks for having the old girl, but be nicer to your mum next time, aye?'

'Your father needs me,' said Ursula when he'd left. 'The flat will be an absolute tip by now and... well, coming here has taught me that perhaps things aren't so bad at home. He's not perfect, but it's not a war zone like here. Your family are in and out of this house like ships in the night. Angel, Denny, Kevin... you.' Her mother looked around sadly; once she left, it wouldn't take long for the house to become hopelessly untidy. 'This is a lovely home, but what's the point of it if you can't all enjoy each other's company?' Ursula telescoped the handle of her trolley case, whipping it around in her hand, and gave Sasha a brave smile. 'I'm sure you try your best as a mother.'

'I am a good mother!' Sasha called in irritation as Alec loaded his wife's case into the car. 'I am, and we're a happy family. Don't you worry about us, you get back to your sea view and your lager!'

Her parents waved blandly as they drove off.

Sasha looked at the time, anxious to get back to work; it was unfair to let everyone else shoulder the workload. She saw that Vaughn had emailed her about some meeting he wanted her to attend to reassure local worthies about progress in the investigation. Maybe with the description Craig and Lolly would provide, they'd be able to get an e-fit of their main suspect to the media this afternoon.

But right now Angel was her priority. It wasn't like her daughter to go AWOL for so long. Sasha phoned her again but the call went to voicemail so she left a message, because there was nothing else she could do.

'Call me back, Angel. I'm very sorry if I shouted at you...' She winced. 'I *did* shout at you, and for that I apologize. I just want to make everything better. Give me a ring as soon as possible. *Please*. Love you, bye.'

Sasha wanted to phone the mums of her daughter's friends, but realized she didn't have any numbers. She hardly knew Angel's new crowd.

There was one number she had, though. Tilly's mum, who had ignored her on the street the other day, might know some of the other parents. Sasha would bite the bullet and also take the opportunity to apologize for Angel's behaviour. To her surprise, the call was answered.

'Hi,' she said, speaking as quickly as possible. 'It's Sasha Dawson, Angel's mum. I know things haven't been so great between our kids, but I was wondering whether Angel was with Tilly right now?'

Tilly's mum said, 'Never call this number again.'

The call went dead. Sasha stared at her phone, wondering how they had got into this situation. She didn't like confrontation, didn't like falling out with people even at work, and hated feeling as if she was the bad guy. She went through some other numbers, the parents of Angel's former friends from nursery and primary school. No one she spoke to had the faintest clue where Angel could be. In most cases, Angel hadn't seen their kids for years.

And where was Kev when she needed him, why was she having to do this on her own? He should be here, helping locate their daughter, he should be doing *something*. You'd better answer the phone, she thought as she rang his number, you better bloody had, boyo. The call connected, she heard his phone ring once, twice – and then drop into voicemail.

'Bloody hell!' She threw the phone in her bag, slammed out of the front door and drove the Spider up towards Southend Airport – wriggling out of her jacket as she steered, the fierce afternoon sun heating up the leather interior – to where his firm was based at a nearby industrial estate.

'I'm here to see Kevin Dawson,' she said, striding into reception.

The young receptionist glanced at the sweat pouring off Sasha's forehead. 'Where does he work?'

'He's in Shipping.'

The girl tapped at a keyboard with long blue nails. 'And who shall I say is—'

'Tell him Sasha is here, his wife. I've been here plenty of times before, I know his office, I can just go straight up.'

'I'm afraid I can't let you do that.' The receptionist frowned at the screen. 'I don't see him on the system. What did you say he does again?'

'He's in Shipping, on the third floor,' repeated Sasha, trying to keep smiling, despite the girl's clear incompetence.

But then she chided herself for being so unkind. The girl must be new and still didn't know who anyone was.

'Hi, Tyler!' waved the receptionist as a man walked past. 'You have a good afternoon!'

So she knew Tyler, whoever Tyler was, and during the entire time Sasha was standing there, waiting for her to find Kev on the computer – how hard could it be? – the girl nodded and smiled at umpteen people who walked in and out. Kev had worked there six, nearly seven years now. He was a handsome guy, and charismatic when he wanted to be, and Sasha couldn't understand how the girl didn't know who he was.

'How long have you been working here?' she asked her.

'Three months. How time flies! I can't find him on the system. Why don't you take a seat while I make some calls?'

Sasha didn't have the time. 'Why don't I go and see him?'

She went to the lift and punched the button.

'You can't just—' called the girl.

But Sasha slipped inside and kept her finger on the third-floor button, giving a little wave goodbye as the doors trundled closed. When the lift arrived on Kev's floor, she followed the corridor until she came to the open-plan office. A man she didn't recognize was sitting at Kev's desk, they must have had a move around, but she was relieved to see Madeleine sitting just inside the door, leafing through a magazine.

'Mrs Dawson!' she exclaimed. 'What brings you here?'

'Oh, Maddy, thank God you're here. Where's Kev? It's very important I speak to him.'

Maddy carefully closed the magazine. 'Would you… like to sit down?'

'I just need to speak to Kev,' she said, getting bad vibes. 'Is he here?'

'Mrs Dawson.' Maddy looked at her oddly. 'He hasn't worked here for four months.'

Sasha felt like all the oxygen had been punched out of her. Maddy said Kev had resigned from the company, had just upped and left, giving no reason.

Minutes later, she stumbled out of the lift, ignoring

the receptionist, and into the hard, bright sunlight. She took her phone from her bag and, with shaking hands, called Kev's number again.

It went to voicemail, of course it did, but Sasha didn't mind, because she was happy to leave a message. 'Call me back, you fucking bastard, and tell me where you are!'

And a couple of minutes later, as she climbed into her car, intending to go back to work, he did.

52

Craig grabbed the side of the cabinet to stop himself getting dragged towards the gaping brightness of the open window, but the heavy wooden surround smashed down on top of him. His head became a fog of incoherent thoughts – he may have blacked out – and then he felt the weight of the cabinet lifted off him.

Ian Carrington heaved Craig to his feet and swung him into the wall. Craig tried to twist in his grip but the big man was too strong, and he took a punch in the stomach. All the breath wrenched from his chest, he dropped into a crouch to protect himself. A knee lifted into his face, his head whipped back. He took another blow to the cheek. He hardly knew where he was, or how to stop getting hurt, and only dimly registered Carrington's screams of fury.

Blows rained down on him, pounding into his head and stomach and chest, as he tried to lift himself into a position where he could fight back. He raised his arms to defend himself, but he was becoming too slow, too sluggish. Pain crackled around his body, his nervous system felt like it was on fire.

His legs buckled, he fell to his knees. Blood poured down his face, blurring his vision. His fingers found one of the fallen photo frames on the floor and he swung it upwards with as much strength as he could muster. He heard the glass shatter beneath Carrington's chin, and his attacker staggered back.

Craig was dimly aware he'd given himself a chance – maybe the last one he'd get – and knew he had to get up, he had to act, or he was finished. Carrington was strong, and the cruel rage inside of him was a terrible fuel, giving him strength and purpose.

But Craig didn't, or couldn't, move. Lolly would be coming soon, his muddled brain told him, she'd arrive with other police. They were in the lift, on the stairs, outside the door – they'd burst in at any moment. He wanted to slide to the floor.

'I'm sorry you had to see this,' cried Ian Carrington. 'I really am.'

Craig didn't know who he was talking to, but then saw Peter Carrington watching. The old man's eyes were wide in terror, his mouth agape in a silent scream.

'One of the things you always told me was to finish what I started.' Trying to rise, Craig's fingers scrabbled to find purchase on the thin carpet, but the room spun. 'You told me, *don't let the bastards grind you down, boy, never let them win.* This is my gift to you, Dad.'

Craig felt Ian lift him under the arms and saw the intense light of the window fill his vision. He was dragged past the old man, whose tongue bulged obscenely in his gaping mouth as he tried to talk.

Nnnnnn, Peter Carrington moaned. *Nnnnnn-nn!*

And Craig heard something else as he was hoisted over the window sill two floors above the concrete car park. His mind struggled to make sense of the sound... alarmed voices from below.

As his shoulders were pushed out, Craig squinted at the harsh sun in his eyes. People below were pointing up and shouting, cars screeching to a halt. He heard doors slam, the rustle of the leaves in a tree. A breeze cooled his burning face.

He was about to be hurled out. Ian was shifting his body into position, pushing his torso ever further over the sill and into empty space.

Inside the room, the old man's eyes goggled, his body shook. Craig saw the wisps of grey stubble on his neck, the drool bubbling on his chin. *Nnnnnn. Nnn. Nnnnnn.*

The old man was trying to say something – kill him or let him live? – as his son lifted Craig's legs, causing his body to tip backwards into bright sunlight.

Someone below screamed.

His upper body dangled out of the window. He instinctively snatched at the window frame to stop himself falling out head first.

Craig glimpsed figures rushing into the building. A familiar voice shouted, 'Hold on!'

All he could do was pluck at the peeling wooden frame with his fingers. But then Ian was prising them away. One of Craig's fingers was wrenched back sharply – and his body shrieked with pain.

'Let go!' Ian whispered.

Craig took an elbow hard in the nose and his head snapped back, his vision exploded into static. One hand was forced off the frame, and Ian turned his attention to Craig's other hand, wrenching at the fingers.

Nnnnnn Nnnnnn. Nnn.

'You're nearly there,' Ian hissed urgently. 'Just let go now.'

The last fingers lost purchase on the wood.

Craig felt as if he were suspended in space for a split second as the small of his back pivoted on the edge of the window frame – he sensed the door in the room crashing open – and he tipped backwards.

And fell.

53

When Sasha drove past, she saw him sitting in the window of the café. She parked up and stomped across the road, holding up her hands as if to say, *what the hell, Kev.*

But he didn't react, didn't look embarrassed or defensive or even angry; he blankly watched her yank open the door. When Sasha charged inside, the lady behind the counter gave her a sympathetic smile, as if she was a harassed mum picking up a child late from school.

'What's going on, Kev?' she asked him.

But Kev looked a ghost of the big-hearted, exuberant man she'd married, the man with whom she had shared some of the greatest experiences of her life, and the worst. She dropped into the chair opposite him.

'Talk to me,' she urged him, but he just gazed out of the window, watching the world go by. At the cars zooming past, the dribble of surf climbing the narrow pebble beach and receding, and the tourists walking the coast road towards Chalkwell, beneath the blue, blue sky. His silence was exhausting, and she'd had enough of it.

'Kev…' she began, but a waitress appeared and asked if she wanted anything.

Impatient for her to leave, Sasha smiled. 'Not for me, thank you.'

'What about you, Kev, another one?' The woman picked up his empty mug but he shook his head.

Sasha moved aside the ketchup, salt and pepper, and the laminated menu that sat between them like a barrier.

'So,' she snapped, 'do you want to tell me what's going on?'

He shrugged. 'I wasn't enjoying the work any more, not really, so I quit. But I was too embarrassed to tell you, and I didn't want you to worry. I got myself into a bit of a situation where I was leaving the house every morning and pretending to go to work.'

Her face burned. She was intensely annoyed that he'd been lying to her all this time. 'I don't understand. Money has been coming into our joint account.'

'From our savings. I was waiting for you to notice, but you never did.'

She shook her head, incredulous. 'And what have you been doing all this time?'

'I'll come and sit here, mostly. They're nice, they let me stay for as long as I want, or I'll walk around town. Some days I do nothing but walk.'

She wanted to be nice, to be sympathetic, he was in pain, he wasn't well, but she didn't understand why he'd been lying to her all this time. They were a team; they used to be a *team*.

'If you wanted to give up work, why didn't you tell me? I wouldn't have stood in your way.'

'I didn't want to because, I don't know...' He shrugged. 'You're busy and I didn't want you to worry.'

All the anger and frustration drained from her and was replaced by a terrible sadness. She thought again of the rambunctious guy she'd married. The devil-may-care optimist, the charming joker, the keen sportsman, the tender lover – the brilliant, loving dad. And she wondered again what had happened to that man, what had become of them both.

She pulled her fingers across the surface of the table, giving herself a moment to ensure that, when she spoke, her voice was steady.

'And why here? Why this café?'

'You know why,' he told her softly.

Sasha looked around again and the place became more familiar. The tables and chairs in the long white room were a refreshing aquamarine colour, and the huge windows at the front gave a magnificent view of the estuary.

'Why don't you tell me?'

He smiled. 'I remember we used to come here as a family, before...'

She was about to interrupt, but shook her head, *go on*, knowing he was about to say something she needed to hear.

'We never talk about what happened,' he said. 'But I think about it all the time now. All the time. Why do we never talk about it?'

Her eyes met his. 'Because it's *hard*.'

'There's something I need to tell you and you're going to hate me for it.'

'I'm not going to hate you, Kev.'

'You will.' Emotion made his voice tremble. 'You're going to despise me. There's something I never told you. And all these years the knowledge of it has… I'm finding it… hard to live with.'

'Tell me,' she urged him.

'I shouted at him.' His face contorted in pain. 'Just before it happened. I was trying to get the buggy down, you know how complicated that thing was, and he was running around me, laughing and playing, being silly, just being Jake, you know? It had been a long, exhausting day, hadn't it?'

'It had.'

'It was pissing down all day, do you remember, the other kids were moody, and me and you had been bickering, we were all tired and miserable. I couldn't get the buggy down and Jake wouldn't listen, he just kept running in a circle around me, and I shouted at him, I told him not to be so bloody stupid and to stand still, but when I tried to get hold of him, he squirmed away and ran further along the pavement. I shouted at him to stop, I was bloody angry, *Jake, come back here now!* And then—' He shut his eyes. 'That car came out of nowhere, it mounted the pavement. And he... he...'

He dropped his head. Sasha watched his shoulders heave as he wept.

'You are *not* responsible.' Biting back her own tears, Sasha reached across the table to take his hand, but he moved it away. 'It was an accident.'

'I was angry with him. I shouted at him.' He gasped. 'And then he died.'

'I see this all the time at work, Kev. People beating themselves up because life isn't like some movie. People who get to the hospital too late to say goodbye to a dying relative. Women who regret they didn't kiss their husband on the morning of their final day together because they didn't want to smudge their lipstick. Life is messy. We often don't get to say goodbye, we don't get to tell our nearest and dearest one last time how much we love them. Sometimes we shout, sometimes we are unreasonable and grumpy and preoccupied. Yes, you snapped at Jake, but it was just a moment. He died knowing you loved him dearly.' She nodded at the ceiling. 'And you know what, he's looking down on us right now and it's breaking his heart to see you so unhappy, to see how this silly thought has become all twisted inside of you. I don't hate you, Kev, I love you, and it hurts to see you in such pain, and I wish you had spoken to me about it earlier.'

She looked down to see tissues on the edge of the table, discreetly placed there by the waitress or someone, and she pushed them towards him.

'I think about him all the time.' Kev blew his nose. 'I miss him so much.'

Kev had dragged her through her darkest, lowest days, and all this time he'd bottled up his own grief, trying to be strong for her, for everyone, and the seed of this one toxic notion had steadily grown inside of him. He had weaponized that last angry moment to use against himself, until that single wretched memory had overwhelmed all the good ones. It had isolated him from the people who loved him the most, and she felt a lump in her throat at his pain.

'Our little boy is never coming back,' she said, taking a moment to compose herself. 'I wish more than anything that he was, but he's not going to. And I couldn't bear to lose you, too. We miss you, Kev, all of us, Angel and Denny and me – we need you. We want you to come back to us and be happy and strong. None of us could care less about your silly job, or about bloody Nelson, we just want *you* back.'

'I'm sorry.' He pushed the heel of a hand into one eye to try to stop the tears. 'I'm so sorry.'

'We're going to get you help,' she told him, and when she finally managed to find his hand, he clung to her fingers. 'Somebody you can talk to about your feelings, to help you get back on your feet. But I hope you feel you can talk to me, too, and you'll let me help you. First thing we're going to do is ring the doctor and—'

Her phone rang and her first instinct was to reach for it, but she froze.

'Get the phone,' he told her, trying to compose himself. 'It may be important.'

'*This* is important, Kev. You're the most important thing to me.'

'I'm not going anywhere. I promise.'

She smeared her wet cheeks with the back of her hand and rooted in her bag, not really wanting to answer it, and pressed the screen.

'I have your daughter.'

She thought she'd misheard. 'Excuse me?'

'I've got Angel,' said a man's voice, and a terrible dread washed through Sasha.

'Wait a moment.' She felt faint. 'Give me a second.'

She placed the phone to her shoulder – Kev was looking out at the sea – and slid out of the chair. 'Sorry,' she told him, trying to smile. 'It's a work thing.'

Outside, she stood on the hot pavement beneath the relentless sun. 'Who are you?'

'Just worry about this – I have your daughter.' A jolt of shock made her shudder. 'And if you tell any of your cop friends, I'll kill her, along with those other two, the Sammi girl, the Lucas boy.'

A siren roared past on the road. She eventually managed to speak. 'What do you want?'

'I want Karin to suffer for what she did to my Dad.' She recognized Ian Carrington's angry voice. 'I want you to bring that bitch to me.'

54

When Craig Power's eyes opened, Lolly Chambers placed a calming hand on his chest.

'You gave us a bit of a fright, mate.'

Craig pulled himself on to his elbows on the floor, wincing at the stabbing pains in his sides. 'Where is he?'

She waggled the end of his tie, which had been shredded by glass. 'Honestly, Craigy, you're an even bigger mess than usual.'

'Where—'

'We just missed him. A couple of us gave chase but he legged it down a fire escape. We're looking everywhere.'

Craig sat carefully. 'Help me up.'

'Maybe you should lie there for a moment, you're not looking so hot right now, mate.'

'Help me *up*,' he insisted. Lolly offered a steadying hand as he climbed to his feet, careful not to make any sudden movements in case he had fractured any ribs or broken any limbs. He slowly raised his arms and legs one after the other, like a marionette, carefully scanning his body to discover which parts shrieked with pain, which hurt like hell and which merely throbbed. 'Where's Peter Carrington?'

'Moved to another room,' she told him. 'I think he's under sedation.'

Craig looked out of the window and felt nauseous. If Lolly had arrived a second or so later, his broken body would be sprawled across the car park two floors below.

'You cut it fine.'

She made a face. 'Let's have a race right now to see who can get upstairs fastest.'

When Craig pulled up his shirt, instinctively attempting to tighten his sore abs in front of Lolly, there were bruises and abrasions. In the mirror, his bloody face was a criss-cross of lacerations where it had smashed into the glass cabinet.

'Ouch.' Lolly grimaced at his middle finger, which was swollen and sticking out at an unusual angle. 'It looks broken. That's a shame, you use that finger a lot. We'll wait for the paramedic and then get you to hospital.'

He walked to the door. 'No time, we've got work to do.'

'Don't be ridiculous, Craigy, you need to get to the ED.'

'This building is full of nurses who can clean me up and put a splint on my finger.'

'Sasha and Ajay will go mad if I just let you go.'

'And neither are here,' he said shortly. 'So let's just get on with it.'

'Don't make the mistake of thinking I'm really impressed that you're being so brave and manly, yeah,' she told him. 'Because I ain't in the slightest.'

They walked down the two flights of stairs, Craig clinging to the metal banister, finding his feet. Lolly tried not to notice the way he grimaced every time he lifted his left leg.

'I don't get it. Why's everyone so keen to get back to work? If it was me who was nearly thrown out a window and saved in the nick of time by an attractive and talented colleague, I'd get a sick note and snuggle on the sofa watching *Extreme Cake Makers* for a few days.'

'I'm feeling better already,' he said.

'Course you are.'

'Do we have an address?'

'He lives up in Rochford, units are on the way there now.'

The reception was filled with officers and staff, and when Lolly went to get an update on the pursuit of Ian Carrington – he had given officers the slip in the tangle of streets behind the care home – Craig walked towards the door.

'Wait.' She hurried over. 'Where are you going?'

'To Carrington's home,' he said. 'Text me his address.'

'Oh no.' She jumped in his way. 'Not until we get you seen to.'

He sighed. 'Get me a couple of painkillers and I'm good to go.'

'Right now, yeah,' she told him angrily, 'you look like something out of a horror movie. The Walking Craig.'

'Sasha would do exactly the same. I'll call her on the way.'

'She's not about,' Lolly told him.

'What are you talking about?'

'She's not gone back to the office and nobody can get in touch with her.'

'You're joking, right?'

'Wish I was, mate. Everyone's running around getting as much intel on this Ian Carrington fella as they can, yeah. There's a property search under way. We're looking for second homes, lock-ups, garages, anywhere he could have taken those kids. It turns out Carrington worked as an agent at a lettings agency.' She looked at his battered face and said, 'You totally owe me for saving your neck, so get yourself checked out, get that finger seen to, and then maybe I won't drop you in it with DCI Vaughn.'

'He's a nutcase, he came right at me.' Craig swallowed, and for a moment she thought he was going to burst into tears. 'I didn't know what hit me.'

She touched his arm. 'He got lucky, coz I can't imagine

anyone getting one over the Power Man. We're gonna go get him, but first we have to clean you up.' Lolly caught the eye of one of the staff. 'Can someone take a look at my colleague?'

Craig's fingers trembled at his side. He'd had a fright, his body was probably going into shock, and it was wrong to let him shrug off the attack, but she knew there was no stopping him.

He moved the hand out of sight. 'One of these days, I'm going to come to your rescue.'

'Bound to happen sooner or later, innit, I'm always getting myself into stupid situations. I'll call Ajay and tell him you're okay. But when he sees that face of yours, he ain't gonna agree.' One of the staff came over with a first-aid kit, snapping on disposable gloves. 'I'll tell them you've gone straight to Carrington's home.'

She was about to walk off when he reached out to touch her. 'Thanks, Lols, I really thought I was a goner.'

'Oh, Craigy.' She smiled up at him, feeling his fingertips brush against hers. 'You don't have to fank me. I mean, you did all the hard work.'

55

'He has my daughter, he's got Angel.' The phone was laid on the passenger seat of her Spider as Sasha pulled to the kerb. When she still hadn't got a response on the speaker, she put it to her ear. 'Are you still there?'

Parked at the end of the street with the roof up, Sasha could see the front of Karin's house, with part of the bay window boarded up where Craig had smashed it. A couple of reporters were standing outside now, but thankfully they didn't see her.

Karin said, 'I'm very sorry.'

'He told me that if I want to see her alive, I have to bring you to him.'

'Who?'

'His name is Ian Carrington, he's the son of Peter Carrington, the detective who was in charge of the Bad Place investigation. Do you know him, Karin? Have you ever met him?'

'The son?' Karin sounded bewildered. 'Why would I?'

The way Carrington had spoken had left Sasha in no doubt that he was prepared to kill – and more than capable of doing it. All her training screamed to her that she should call it in, hand it over to Vaughn and her team, let them take charge, but her instinct – her terror for her daughter – had led her here. Talking to Karin now, she felt weirdly calm.

'He told me to bring you to him, said if I involved any of my colleagues he'll kill Sammi, Lucas... and Angel.'

'You said he wants me,' said Karin. 'So take me to him.'

Sasha was finding it physically difficult to breathe. It was baking inside the cramped car with the roof up, and she was scared. 'I can't ask you to do this, but she's my baby...'

'I understand. We'll bring them home together, I promise.' The curtains moved in Karin's bedroom. 'I can see you. I'm coming out.'

The line went dead. Sasha squirmed in the heat. Her mind whirled with thoughts of Angel held against her will, petrified, vulnerable, bewildered, and she had to force herself to remember Sammi and Lucas too.

Her phone rang, making her jump, and she saw it was Vaughn. She couldn't talk to him. If she told him what was happening, he'd persuade her out of recklessly taking the matter into her own hands, he'd command her to tell him where Carrington was keeping those kids. She'd be shunted to the fringes of the investigation, forced to wait for news of whatever operation was launched to rescue the three teenagers. But the confrontation at the Bad Place had ended in a girl's violent death, and she sensed Carrington would kill those kids at the first sign the police were approaching the house. Sasha couldn't take that chance.

Kev's guilt that he'd shouted at Jake moments before his death and her own furious argument with her daughter flooded into her mind, and she felt sick. *Oh, Angel, I'm so sorry. Please forgive me.*

Breathing deeply, and against her better judgement, she answered the phone. 'Hello, Vaughn.'

'Where are you?' he said angrily.

'I'm sorry. Something's happened.' She closed her eyes. 'I can't explain right now.'

'Are you kidding?' She heard phones ringing all around the incident room. 'All hell has broken loose here. We have a suspect, Ian Carrington.'

Her heart leapt. She prayed that Carrington didn't think she had told her team about him. Maybe for some reason he had broken cover. Sasha dreaded to think of what would happen if they were already closing in on his location…

'Do you have him in custody?'

'Not yet, we're on the way to his house in Rochford.'

Sasha felt a sick kind of relief. The address Carrington had given her was up near Wallasea. She may have a head start, at least.

'And you,' Vaughn was saying, 'need to be here.'

'I can't come in.' She tried to shake the tension from her voice. 'There's something I have to do.'

'Hold on.' Her response had caught him off guard, she heard the background noise fall away as he took the call into the privacy of his office. 'What's going on, Sasha?'

The reporters rushed towards the house when Karin appeared outside. The door of a van parked along the street swung open and a camera crew jumped out. Karin walked quickly towards Sasha's car, head down, shoulders hunched.

Sasha said, 'Sorry, Vaughn, I've got to go.'

'Sasha, talk to m—'

As soon as she cut the call, she began to pluck at the casing of her phone with her nails. Karin ran towards her, the reporters and the camera team snapping at her heels.

'Karin,' they called as she bolted for the car, and Sasha leaned across the passenger seat to open the door. 'Is it true you were attacked? What about the arrest of Jim Haskell, Karin, what can you tell us about that?'

Karin climbed inside, slammed the door. Sasha took the SIM card out of her phone and twisted it between her fingers, ignoring the journalists rapping at the passenger window, firing questions. She edged open the driver's door and dropped it into the grate of a drain – no going back now – then turned the key in the ignition and swung the car out from the kerb as quickly as she could without mowing down any journalists.

'Where are we going?'

'Out of town,' Sasha said, accelerating up the road.

'Why is he doing this?'

'Revenge, I think. His father was discredited and hounded from the force. Peter Carrington's bungling got Becky killed, and he also made a number of other mistakes in the investigation. The day before you all escaped, he took part in a house-to-house search and personally spoke to Jerry Swann. He was at the Bad Place, Karin, he could have saved you all.'

'Yes.' What Karin said next made Sasha stare in shock. 'I saw him there.'

56

The Twelfth Day...

Jerry took Karin upstairs at knifepoint and sat her at the table in the kitchen. He fell into the chair opposite, pressing a finger under his glasses and into one moist eye. She saw how weary he was, how gaunt, all those sleepless hours catching up with him.

Karin too was disorientated. She had no idea what day it was, or the time. The thin wash of light struggling in through the thick net curtain gave no clue. The hours she spent with him were like an endless nightmare from which it was impossible to wake, and she submitted to the ordeal numbly.

'You look tired,' she said.

'Not sleeping properly, things on my mind.' Jerry adjusted the glasses on his nose. 'Ask me about the fella at work. About what I did to him.'

This is how it always began. Karin would have to ask him a question and then he would tell her at great length about one of the murders he'd committed, going into excruciating, horrific detail about it.

'Please, Jerry,' she said without enthusiasm. 'I'd like to know about the man at your work.'

'There was a fella I worked with, this was a long time ago now, and he... he displeased me. He wasn't courteous, he wasn't friendly, he looked down his nose at me... thought he was a cut above, but he was a liar and...'

He lapsed into silence.

'So you killed him...' Karin prompted, because that was how the sentence usually ended.

'Yeah, I did, I...' She watched in astonishment as a tear rolled down one of Jerry's cheeks, and he smeared it away quickly. 'It's all coming to an end.'

'What is?'

'All of it.' His head twitched. 'They're looking for you lot, you're all over the papers, the TV, the radio, they're looking everywhere.'

'Then maybe...' Karin whispered, 'now is the time to let us—'

'What?' he snarled. 'Let you *what*?'

Karin wanted to finish the sentence, *let us go*, but she was too scared of Jerry's reaction. The dirty nails of his fingers scratched the table, close to the handle of the knife. It could be that he had decided to kill them all, dig up the cellar and bury their bodies alongside the cold bones of his mother.

'I'm sorry, I didn't mean to—'

'I'm scared, Karin,' he told her.

Then he stood suddenly and went to the sink, leaving the knife on the table. So close to her that she could just pick it up. She wondered if this was the moment Becky had told her about, that split second of opportunity. In her mind's eye, Karin saw herself snatching up the blade and plunging it into his back – but she had no idea if she was capable of doing it. Jerry had killed people, so many people, and he wouldn't hesitate to murder her if she faltered.

He found a dirty glass on the cluttered draining board. Water thundered into the sink. He drank the water and slumped back in the chair.

'I'm scared about what will happen to me. I made a... big mistake. I didn't mean to do it, I was walking past and I saw the minibus and... I don't know why, I just climbed in. I didn't think about what I was doing. I brought you all here and now I don't know what to do.' His tears spattered on the gnarled wood of the table. 'I'm so sorry, I'm so, so *sorry*.'

Karin wondered if Jerry was playing a trick on her, if it was all a cruel joke.

'They're going to punish me, they're going to put me in prison!' He looked pathetic, vulnerable. Sobs wracked his body. 'They'll lock me up and throw away the key. The other prisoners will be unkind to me, they'll be mean and cruel, they'll make me suffer! I didn't mean to do it, I made a mistake!'

'You made a mistake,' she repeated, bewildered.

'I went out with the knife, because I wanted to do something *bad*, I always imagined I could, and I saw the minibus. I didn't even know what I was doing. I climbed in and drove it here. But it was wrong and stupid, I know that now!'

'Then just let us go,' she urged him. 'We won't tell anyone. We just want to go home.'

'But you will,' he wailed. 'You'll tell them about me and I'll go to prison. Oh, what am I going to do?'

An incredible possibility dawned on Karin.

'Jerry.' Karin waited till he lifted his eyes to hers. 'Those stories you told me, did you... did you kill all those people?'

His head dropped shamefully to the table.

'I wanted to,' he whispered. 'In my head I've done it many times.'

'What about your mother?'

'She lives in Eastbourne,' he said miserably.

The truth made her want to laugh out loud. Jerry wasn't dangerous at all. All those stories he told her about the people he killed – his mother, the people at work, the ones who crossed him, the women he followed home – he had made them all up. It was all a fiction.

He was a liar.

Jerry lived in a fantasy world where he was a dangerous hunter, a killer. He desperately wanted the world to be scared of him. But the truth was that he was a total loser.

'Please,' he whined. 'You have to help me.'

She stared in astonishment. 'Why should I?'

'Because you're my friend, because we understand each other, because we're the sa—'

'I'm nothing like you,' she spat. 'Nothing!'

He flinched in surprise at her outburst.

And then a knock on the front door made them both freeze. They stared at each other for a long moment, until Karin said, 'Aren't you going to answer it?'

'I don't know who it is.' He scraped back his chair and went to the window. 'Nobody ever comes here!'

She had never seen him in a panic like this. In the dull light, his gaunt skin was as yellow as wax. He gingerly pulled the net curtain aside and reared back quickly.

'They saw me,' he said, anguish in his voice.

He placed the knife in the sink and went to a drawer and took out a small bunch of keys.

'Please, I beg you,' he pleaded with her, and did his best to wipe the tears from his eyes. 'Don't say anything.'

Karin watched him unlock the front door, heard voices on the doorstep. Careful not to make a sound, she went to the kitchen door. In the reflection of a mirror on the wall in the hallway, she glimpsed Jerry with two men.

One of them was a tall, fat man in a grey suit and the other wore a police uniform.

'… And I'm Detective Inspector Peter Carrington,' said the big man loudly. 'We're going door to door in the area. I can tell you, your house isn't easy to find.'

'Yes,' said Jerry, 'I'm a bit out of the way.'

'That's an understatement.' The detective laughed. 'Anyway, we're speaking to people about those teenagers who went missing.'

'Yes,' stammered Jerry. 'I heard about that, it's a terrible business.'

'We're trying to track the movements of a white minibus that was seen being driven in this part of the county... are you okay, sir?'

'I'm sorry, I've been chopping onions!'

'I always let the wife do that kind of thing,' the detective said amiably. 'I've no talent for cooking.'

This was her moment. All Karin had to do was step into the hallway and reveal herself to the police and it would all be over. She'd never have a better opportunity to get them all home.

But she also knew that she wasn't in any danger, none of them were, because Jerry was a harmless fantasist – and it gave her a notion. The idea was terrible and scary – and *wrong* – but part of her wanted to stay with Becky for just a bit longer. Because who knew what would happen when they returned to real life?

'I'll keep my eyes open day and night, Inspector,' she heard Jerry say. 'And let you know if I see any suspicious vehicle activity in the area.'

'That's good to know, you're a gentleman.' The detective dabbed at his sweating brow with his fingers.

'Bloody hell, it's hot today and I've built up a bit of a thirst. May have to pop into one of the locals on my way home!'

Karin went quietly to the drawer Jerry had just opened and found it was full of stuff. Old envelopes, a ball of string, a screwdriver – she thought briefly about taking that, but didn't know how it would be useful – and screws and a pair of nail clippers. There was a broken set of false teeth, a doorstop and a notebook, paper clips and envelopes, a magnet. And below that, buried at the bottom, was a spare set of keys. They looked exactly the same as the ones Jerry had taken earlier. Karin recognized the one for the front door, and there was a long one that she knew would unlock the cellar door.

She slipped them in a pocket, then went back to the door where she heard the detective say, 'Anyway, better get on, sorry to have kept you.'

'Good luck,' said Jerry. 'I hope you find the person who's taken those children, and enjoy your drink.'

The policeman winked. 'You can rely on me, sir. Good night.'

In the reflection of the mirror, Karin saw the detective salute Jerry, who shut the front door. He leaned his forehead against the glass in relief as he locked it. She returned to her chair at the table just as he came back in, looking deathly pale.

'Thank you, my love,' he said.

'What did you say?' she asked in shock.

'Thank you for not saying anything. You're a good friend to me and I haven't forgotten that I made you a promise.'

She didn't know what he was talking about. 'I want to go downstairs now, please.'

'I'll take you down.' He lifted the knife from the sink, but all its terrible power over her was gone. She knew there was no need to be scared of it, or of him. Because Jerry hadn't murdered anyone, and she believed he never would, he simply wasn't capable of it. Karin and the others could all walk out of this place right now.

But she wasn't ready to go yet.

When they left this bad place, their lives would change, the world would return to normal, she didn't know when she would next get to see Becky, and Karin was desperate to spend just a bit longer with her.

That's all she wanted, just a bit longer.

Just one more night and then they would all go home.

57

Lolly was running out of the lift when her phone rang and Ajay said in a low, urgent voice, 'Where are you?'

'Here now!' She pulled open the glass doors and rushed into the office to find DCI Vaughn standing in the middle of the room barking orders at the Major Incident Team.

'What have I missed?' she whispered to Ajay.

'Nearly everything.'

'Who have we got at Ian Carrington's house?' Vaughn asked the assembled detectives, analysts and officers.

Lolly put up her hand. 'Crai... DC Power is on his way there now, sir.'

'How is he?' Vaughn asked.

'Raring to go.' She cringed inside at not telling Vaughn the full extent of Craig's injuries, but didn't fancy being on the end of one of the DCI's legendary tellings-off. 'He's expecting your call.'

Vaughn thrust a piece of paper into her hand with a name and number on it. 'This is Ian Carrington's estranged wife, speak to her now, find out as much as you can about the man in the next twenty minutes.'

'I'll do it,' said another detective as Lolly tried to untangle the knotted lead of her phone headset.

'No, DC Chambers has a talent for people.' Vaughn clapped his hands. 'You all know what you're doing, get on with it.'

'One more question, sir,' said one of the civilian researchers. 'Where's DI Dawson?'

A cloud passed across his face. 'That's a good question. Unfortunately, right at this moment, your guess is as good as mine.' He gave Lolly an intense look as she struggled with the headset. 'As soon as you can, DC Chambers. DS de Vaz, with me.'

Ajay followed Vaughn into the meeting room – despite the sweltering heat inside, they closed the door to keep out the noise of the fierce activity coming from the incident room – and punched a number into the call conferencing device that squatted like a crab at the centre of the table.

'I'm here,' said Craig, immediately picking up at the other end.

He'd gone straight to Ian Carrington's home in Rochford, a small town three miles north of Southend. It was only a twenty-minute drive to where Jerry Swann's Baden Place farmhouse had stood at the edge of the Wallasea Island wetlands, before it was bulldozed.

'How are you feeling, Detective Constable Power, I hear you've been through the wars.'

'I'll live,' said Craig.

'Good man.' Vaughn pulled his tie low. 'So what have you got for us?'

'There's no sign anybody has been kept here, or even visited. It's very small, there are two floors, a kitchen, living room, one bedroom, an upstairs bathroom, but no cellar; a garden the size of a postage stamp. It's rented. Very tidy, very impersonal. All the furniture came with the place, and Carrington hasn't put much of an effort into making it a home. He's been here for eighteen months, according to immediate neighbours, and was quite open about splitting from his wife and family. They have no idea what, if anything, he does for a living. One neighbour said they saw him this morning, getting into a car – and yeah, it was a blue Mazda – but he hasn't been sighted since.'

'What do they make of him?'

'The usual. Nice bloke, if reserved. Doesn't go to the local pub, keeps himself to himself, all that. Someone said he looked a bit haunted, but put that down to his family problems.'

'Are there garages nearby, or a lock-up?'

'Not connected to the house. If you turn up any rented spaces on your online searches, let us know.'

Vaughn tapped his fingers together impatiently, lifted his gaze to the incident room. Men and women rushed backwards and forwards across the office, or were hunched over phones and computers, building a comprehensive digital portrait of Ian Carrington from various databases.

'What else have you found?'

'Plenty, and I mean plenty, of documents. Folders, files, all relating to his old man's dismissal and the Bad Place.' Craig paused and they could hear the rustle of paper. 'Tons of it, actually, he's totally obsessed. There's a laptop, too. We had a quick look. I'm no expert, but it looks to me as if he has different email accounts under different names. From what I can tell, he was the guy who was encouraging Paul to groom Sammi, and there's correspondence with Jim Haskell, too. We're bagging it up now and... hang on a moment.' They heard Craig having a muffled conversation with one of the officers who was searching the house, and then he came back on the line. 'And we've found keys.'

'Keys?'

'Sorry,' said Craig. 'Say again.'

Ajay leaned towards the speaker. 'You found *keys*.'

'About a dozen sets of keys in numbered envelopes. A lot of them are new and shiny, or don't look used. Copies, maybe.'

'He worked for a couple of years at a letting agency that specialized in local countryside properties,' Ajay told his two colleagues. 'Farmhouses and holiday homes.'

'Look for addresses,' Vaughn shouted to Craig. 'On the computer, or written down somewhere. Addresses related to those keys and numbers.'

'Got it.'

Vaughn turned to Ajay. 'We need a map of everything in that area between the River Crouch and the River Roach.' There were towns and villages, tiny hamlets, in the flat countryside north of Southend – Rochford, Hawkwell, Paglesham, Ashingdon and Canewdon among them – before the Crouch joined its tributary, the Roach, at Wallasea Island and then flowed into the North Sea. 'I want a proper map, DS de Vaz, a big one made of paper, so we can spread it out. I really don't want to fiddle with a laptop.'

'What if we don't have one?'

'Southend Museum is next door,' Vaughn told him.

Ajay rapped his knuckles on the interior glass window to get the attention of one of the support staff in the office, and they spoke for a moment before she rushed off.

'Yeah, okay, we've got something.' Craig said when he came back on the speaker. 'There's a notepad with various addresses in it, they all look like properties in the area.'

They heard him turning pages as he reeled off the addresses, which were spread out across the countryside over a radius of four or five miles.

'Some of those are in the middle of nowhere,' Vaughn told Ajay. 'We'll need GPS coordinates.'

'There's not a lot for me to do here now, sir. I'm in the area already, let me check some of those addresses.'

'Thank you, DC Power, we have that covered. Continue to coordinate the search at the house.'

There was a sound on the other end of the phone that sounded like a snort of annoyance.

'Did you say something, DC Power?'

'Sorry, sir,' Craig said. 'Just dropped my pen.'

One of the MIT detectives knocked on the door and came inside. 'Sir, you might want to come and look at this.'

They went back into the incident room where someone was pointing a remote control at a screen on the wall.

Lolly was at her desk, hunched over a pad, writing as quickly as possible, taking down everything Carrington's estranged wife was telling her. 'That must have been terrible,' she said occasionally into the headset, or, 'Poor you.'

One of the detectives rewound the footage they had seen on a news channel and turned up the volume. A shaky camera raced towards Karin McCarthy as she left her house; they saw reporters jostling her, barking questions about the abductions, heard the slap of footsteps on the pavement. Karin bolted across the street and jumped into a roadster, Sasha's familiar Spider Veloce, which accelerated up the street, making the reporters scatter.

'Well.' Ajay grimaced. 'That doesn't look good.'

'Bloody *hell*, Sasha, what are you playing at?'

Exasperated, Vaughn pointed at one of the team. 'Speak to Chelmsford and get a helicopter in the air, two would be better. Detective Constable Power has a list of addresses he's found, he's on the speakerphone in the meeting room.'

'What addresses?' asked someone.

'Carrington has a list of properties and sets of keys. Get him to send the addresses to North Weald.' The National Police Air Service's Essex base was near Epping. 'A 'copter will cover a lot of ground far more quickly. Make sure it has thermal-imaging equipment, so we'll know immediately if there's anybody in those properties.' Vaughn was about to walk away, but changed his mind. 'And someone contact the agency where Carrington worked. Find out about which rentals he was responsible for. In the first instance, we're looking for empty properties.'

'There could be dozens of them, hundreds.'

'Then you had better get on with it.' He stabbed a finger at someone walking past. 'And where do you think you're going?'

'To the toilet, boss.'

'Then hurry it up!' Vaughn furiously clapped his hands, hurrying him along, and shouted across the office. 'If anybody else needs a piss, go now, because no one leaves here till those children are located.'

He glanced over at Lolly, who gestured that she was wrapping up the call. Vaughn pointed at the meeting room, *we're in here,* and she nodded. When he went back inside, an enormous map of South Essex was laid out across the table.

'Where was Jerry Swann's Baden Place farmhouse?'

Ajay pointed at the remote area of Essex countryside where the Roach forked from the Crouch. 'Near here.'

'Wallasea Island was flooded over a decade ago and is now a nature reserve. There's not much there now, but there'll be abandoned properties. If Ian Carrington is making some kind of grand statement about the Bad Place, then wherever he's holding those kids... if they're still alive...' Vaughn circled the area between the two rivers, the Crouch and its wide tributary, with a magic marker. '... will be in that area.'

Lolly came inside. 'Okay, so I just spoke to Ian Carrington's ex. They split a couple of years back due to his irrational behaviour. Ian had always had a love-hate relationship with his old man. They were close when he was a kid, they were a very happy family, but when Peter was let go from Essex Police his personality changed. Peter became difficult to live with, he didn't cope very well with his early retirement, all the shit he got from the press, and many of his old colleagues cut off contact. He went into a spiral and was arrested a couple of times for domestic abuse, but his wife refused to press charges. The whole thing had a massive impact on Ian, who fell out with his father, yeah? But Ian's ex says that when his mum died, Ian went to pieces. He got it into his head that his father had been the victim of a witch-hunt and that the public hadn't been told the whole story of what happened at the Bad Place.'

Her pen hovered over the notes as she tried to make sense of her handwriting. 'And when his dad got sick, Ian saw it as his sole duty to look after him. He'd been a property surveyor but lost that job, and then worked at a lettings agency and lost that too. He spent more time looking after his old man than his wife and kids, and then he started dossiers on Karin McCarthy and the other kids from the Bad Place, started investigating them, finding out all the personal details of their lives. When Ian's wife confronted him about it, he got irrational and flew into violent rages. Things fell apart and she threw him out of the marital home. He seemed to be under the delusion that he would return home when, and only when, he'd restored his father's reputation.'

'Sounds like a man in freefall,' said Ajay.

'Innit.'

Vaughn looked thoughtfully at the map. 'What the hell is Sasha playing at, Ajay?'

Ajay was surprised. Sasha was relaxed about her team calling each other by their first names and encouraged them to do so, at least in private. But Vaughn was a stickler for rules and tradition, he had never been addressed by the DCI as anything other than his rank, and the unexpected informality clearly showed how concerned Vaughn was for his missing officer – and friend.

'Why did she leave the office?'

'She couldn't get in touch with Angel.'

The two men stared at each other and Vaughn said, 'If you're trying to make me nervous then you're doing a good job. When I spoke to her on the phone she sounded evasive... and scared. And now we discover she's gone to pick up Karin McCarthy. Can we get a ping on her phone?'

'We've tried already,' admitted Lolly. 'But it's switched off.'

'Wherever Carrington is, she's on her way there, isn't she?' Vaughn thumped the table. 'Bloody Sasha, why does she always do this to me?'

'I'm in the area already,' said Craig on the speaker-phone.

'I thought we'd lost you, Detective Constable,' said Vaughn in exasperation.

'Nobody cut me off,' said Craig. 'I'm closer than any-body else. And I've just counted, boss, there are a dozen addresses on the list, and only eleven sets of keys.'

'Which one is missing?'

'It's a property near Wallasea, close to where Swann used to live. It's got to be worth checking out. I can get there before any helicopter.'

Vaughn stood. 'Then what are you waiting for?'

58

Sasha and Karin stood on the verge of a narrow, winding road in the middle of a flat landscape of brown fields, trees and scrubland, looking up at a derelict farmhouse.

Bushes and weeds pushed against the front door of the plain grey front of the building. The lower windows were boarded up. Half the tiled roof was missing. Fallen chunks of masonry were embedded in the hard churn of mud and grass on the overgrown drive. A creeper spread across the brickwork, reaching into the shadows that fell across the front of the crumbling facade.

This place, once a home, had been abandoned years ago.

There was a holdall in the boot where Sasha kept emergency bits of kit – a change of clothes, a spare Tyvek suit and overshoes, exhibit bags and notebooks, even a roll of police tape – and she unzipped it, took out a flashlight and a telescopic baton. Standing behind the raised lid of the boot, they couldn't be seen from the upper windows, where the sunlight reflected off shards of jagged glass.

She handed Karin the long metal flashlight. 'In case we can't see anything.'

Karin slipped it in the back pocket of her jeans.

'What do you think?' Sasha pushed the baton up the sleeve of her shirt, crooking her elbow slightly so that it wouldn't fall back down. 'Can you see it?'

'Will we need that?' asked Karin.

'Let's hope not.'

She slammed the boot shut and turned to the abandoned house, which was surrounded in every direction by trees and fields; behind it, in the distance, were the wetlands of Wallasea Island. An airliner left a trail across the sky above them. Maybe it was her imagination, but Sasha wondered if she heard the staccato thrum of a helicopter somewhere far off.

'Are you ready?'

'There's something you need to know,' Karin told her as they looked up at the derelict building. 'He sent me texts, pretending to be Becky.'

Sasha didn't understand. 'Becky's a long time dead.'

'I was confused, I wasn't thinking straight...' She shook her head dismally. 'I thought... I wished it could be her.'

'What did he say?'

'He warned me... Becky warned me... I had to make a choice.'

'A choice? What kind of choice?'

'We're about to find out.'

'And what about the Bad Place, Karin?' Sasha said. 'Something happened there, something you haven't told me. Something that makes Ian Carrington hate you.'

'We're wasting time.'

Karin stepped towards the farmhouse, but Sasha grabbed her arm.

'My daughter is in there! Tell me now!'

Karin said quietly, 'Whatever happens, make sure the kids get out.'

Sasha didn't like the sound of that. 'We're all leaving, we're all going home.'

Conscious that her team could turn up at any minute, and not wanting the whole situation to turn into a stand-off – she thought again of Becky's horrific death – Sasha stomped quickly towards the building.

'Let's go in.'

Screeching gulls wheeled in the sky as they approached the front door, stepping out of the sun and into the cool interior. The hallway was dark, dank and musty and the floor was covered with fallen plaster and litter – old cans, broken glass, sodden cardboard stained with white mould. Scratching noises came from somewhere near, mice scuttling behind the walls.

'This place is unsafe, careful where you step.'

There was a kitchen to the left as they came in the door.

'He's here.' Karin stopped to look at the empty room.

'The layout is the same as the Bad Place. The kitchen was at the front as you came in, like this, and there was a narrow central hallway past the stairs. There'll be a door that leads to a cellar. I know he's here.'

Sasha led the way to a door behind the stairs, as Karin had predicted. It was ajar, a soft light came from behind it, and they heard Carrington's voice.

'Let me go down first.' Sasha stepped forward. 'Ian!'

'Down here!' he called back casually.

'Mum!' shrieked Angel from below and Sasha's nerves spiked, she had to physically stop herself rushing down the rickety stairs. The rotting wooden steps, soft with damp, bowed beneath her feet. Despite the endless sunshine beating down on the world above, it was cold in this room beneath the earth and the bare brick was chill to the touch.

When she got to the bottom, Sasha saw Ian Carrington standing behind three straight-backed chairs. Tied to them with masking tape were Sammi Manning, Lucas White and Angel Dawson.

'Mum!' Angel screamed. 'Please!'

'Hello, Angel.' Sasha tried her best to sound calm and in control of the situation, despite the terror she felt for her child. 'Has he harmed you?'

Angel shook her head. 'I just want to go home.'

'Lucas?' she asked the boy, who nodded, tight-lipped but trembling, trying to stay strong. Tears bulged in his eyes.

'Sammi.' Sasha smiled at the ashen-faced girl whose disappearance had led them all here. 'We're going to get you home, all of you, okay?'

They all began to speak at once:

'He says he's going to—'

'Please, get me—'

'I want to go!'

'Shut up!' Ian lifted a hand to reveal a long knife, and they whimpered. 'Is she here? Did you bring her?' Sasha walked further into the small, dreary room, the low ceiling only inches above her head, and he barked, 'That's far enough. *Where* is she?'

'Why do you want her?'

'She has a choice to make,' Ian told her.

'And then these kids can go?'

'That very much depends on *her*,' he said impatiently. 'Once again.'

Sammi started to say something, but Sasha put a finger to her lips, *let me handle this.*

'Karin,' Sasha called.

Karin came down the stairs and stepped into the cellar. Ian couldn't take his eyes off her.

'I've thought about this moment for a long time.' He looked almost relieved. 'I never thought we'd meet, not like this.'

'We're here now, so say what you have to say, and then we can all go home.' Sasha nodded at the kids. 'All of us.'

'This is nothing to do with you, so stay out of it.'

Pacing, Ian waved the knife dismissively. 'And move – further – back.'

Sasha edged back. She was too far to be able to lunge forward and disarm him by bringing the baton down on his wrist. All she could do was maintain eye contact with the three teenagers. Smile at them, try to give them silent encouragement that their nightmare would soon be over. She prayed, for Angel's sake, and for the sake of the other two kids, that's what would happen.

'Did you like my messages? They were so much fun to send.' Ian looked very pleased with himself. 'I sent you one as a joke and never for a minute thought you would believe it was Becky, but you really fell for it. You needed to believe, with every fibre of your miserable being, there was a chance that your friend was still alive, despite everything. You really are a sick, sad little girl, aren't you? And then, I thought, well, it's a good way of telling you what will be expected of you.'

'Why are you doing this?' asked Karin. 'What do you want?'

'There has been a massive miscarriage of justice and nobody seems to care in the slightest. My father has been maligned, his good name trashed, his reputation destroyed. He was hounded out of the job he loved, his health suffered. When I was a lad he was a good father, the best, but after it happened, he became... volatile. His family suffered... *I* suffered. My mother died early thanks to the stress of it all. And the hate he received, oh you wouldn't believe the hate, it was as if he cut Becky's throat himself.' Ian's voice was choked with emotion. 'When all he tried to do was *save* her.'

'Swann killed her,' Sasha told him. 'He's the only one responsible.'

'And he died – he never faced justice for what he did. He was never able to tell us how the Haskell girl came to be in that cellar, how she was there but those others managed to escape. Nobody's ever answered that question. *Why* was she there?'

'Swann must have chased after her, caught her...' Sasha glanced at Karin, who stared down at the floor. 'And dragged her back there.'

Ian shook his head. 'I made it my business to find out where the blame lay, I did the job that you people should have done. I ingratiated myself with Paul and Lydia, using different identities, of course.'

'You encouraged Paul to groom Sammi Manning.'

He shrugged. 'It didn't take long to discover what a pathetic man he is, with a certain predilection for young girls, and of no use to me. It was easy enough to set him up. In the same way, I rather enjoyed mowing down Simon when he got in my way.'

'You gave him the burner phone to keep in contact with Sammi.' She glanced at the girl. 'And then used it to lure Sammi on the night you snatched her.'

'I practically told him on which night to throw the

phone away and where. He has a highly suggestible personality.'

'And you murdered Lydia.'

'No.' He shook his head. 'That's not true, but her death is of no consequence to me, they all bear responsibility for what happened to Dad. Michelle, Simon, Paul, none of those other survivors knew how the Haskell girl came to be in that cellar, but their ignorance made them culpable. And I got to the truth, eventually, because Lydia knew who was to blame for the girl's death, and my father's disgrace.' His eyes slid to Karin. 'Isn't that right?'

'What do you *want*?'

Ian snarled. 'You got Becky killed, you destroyed my father and my family, you have got away with your deception all these years. I'm going to show the world just what you're capable of.'

Sasha said, 'Ian, we can get you help—'

'Shut up!' He stepped behind Angel and grabbed a fistful of hair, pulling back her head to hold the knife at her throat.

Sasha lifted her hands in terror. 'No, I'm sorry! Please, you don't have to do that, Ian, I won't interrupt again.'

The knife trembled at Angel's throat for a moment and then Ian rested it on her shoulder.

'I've nothing to lose now, my family is gone, my career, and Dad is... he's a husk, a ghost, his life is as good as over.' He pointed the knife at Karin. 'No one leaves this room till I hear you say it, till I hear the truth about what happened to the Haskell girl. You're going to tell me and everyone here what you did. I want justice for Dad, finally, for the world to know that what happened was *your* fault, not his.'

When Karin spoke, it was in a whisper. 'No.'

'Lydia is dead, Ian,' said Sasha, 'and Simon is in a bad way, but we don't have to take this any further.'

'I told you, I didn't kill Lydia, why would I? I found out everything I needed to know from Lydia. She told me the truth about Karin, and about what really happened to Becky, because she saw it.' Flecks of spittle gathered at the corners of his mouth. 'She saw it all.'

'Then you already know the truth.'

'Everyone must know.'

'Jerry killed Becky,' said Karin.

'Oh, he pulled the blade across her throat, yes, and I'll do the same to all these kids if you don't admit what you did.'

'There were a number of reasons for Becky's death.' Heart pounding, Sasha stepped forward, but as soon as she did Ian began to pace, tapping the knife restlessly against his thigh. 'The inquiry highlighted a number of failures in the investigation, your father went into that house without following proper procedure.'

'I told you to shut *up*! Everyone here has to listen to Karin. All of us here, these kids – Michelle's daughter, oh yeah, Lydia told me that, too – and your favourite pupil and the nice police officer's daughter, I want them all to know the truth. And then when you've told us, finally, you're going to make a big decision, one I think you'll appreciate. So you tell us all, Karin, what happened on the night you all escaped... and just why Becky was left behind.'

Sasha said, 'Ian, this isn't getting us—'

'Enough!' shouted Karin. 'I'll tell you what happened.'

59

The Thirteenth Day...

That last night with Becky was the best of her life; they spoke for hours about the future they would share when they were finally free. Whatever happened next, Karin knew, they'd be best friends for ever.

Becky was so pale and thin, there were rings beneath her eyes, and Karin knew she was losing hope. 'That's if we get out of here.'

'We will!' Karin could barely hide her elation. The keys she had stolen from the drawer in the kitchen were snug against her leg in her pocket. She so dearly wanted Becky to know that they were all already safe, that Jerry was no danger, he was just a scared, confused man, and they could walk out of this place any time they wished. But she also felt sick with guilt at her deception. 'I'm going to get us out tomorrow.'

'Do you promise?'

'I do.'

Karin briefly considered if she could leave it another couple of nights before they left this place, but everybody was so weak and ill; Simon especially was in a bad way. Later tonight she would confront Jerry. She would tell him they were leaving, that she was going to let her friends out of the cellar and take them home, and there was no doubt in her mind that he would be too afraid to stop her.

She'd tell Becky and the others she had grabbed the keys off him and faced him down, and they would all be so happy and grateful. But she could never tell them that when the police had turned up yesterday, she had stood on the other side of the kitchen door, within touching distance of the detectives, and done nothing to alert them.

Karin worried that when this was all over and Jerry was questioned, he'd tell the police that she was there. But she'd say she was bound and gagged and heard nothing, or that Jerry had threatened her. It would be her word against his, and Jerry was a liar and a fantasist, he probably already had a reputation for it, and she would surely be believed. Jerry was so weak and pathetic that he probably didn't even know any more what was the truth and what was lies.

His stories about killing people were a joke, *he* was a total joke.

But Karin also worried that Jerry wouldn't want her to go back upstairs now she knew the truth about him – that all his boasts about killing people were a figment of his muddled imagination – and she felt the keys burn against her leg. If she didn't manage to go upstairs, worse, if he took someone else, she would have to pretend that he'd dropped them on the way out of the cellar. Maybe, and she didn't even want to consider this possibility, he wouldn't come down at all. He may decide to leave them locked up here for ever, let them all rot, too afraid to do anything else. But she didn't think so. Jerry was too scared of the consequences of his actions, and she dismissed the notion from her mind.

The others, weak and starved, were asleep; everyone slept as much as possible now. They had been trapped in this room for nearly two weeks and those early nights when they had struggled to rest under the constant glare of the bare bulb had long ago given way to exhaustion. It meant Karin was able to enjoy Becky's companionship. Her friend was awake beside her, and needed her.

'I'll always remember how brave you've been,' Becky said. 'I'll never forget.'

Karin's heart felt like it was going to burst with happiness, and she pressed closer. Becky's unconditional love was all she had ever wanted. She so desperately wanted her friend to have a glimmer of hope, and heard herself say, 'I think I know how we can escape.'

'How?'

'I know where he keeps his keys, and I can get them, I'm sure I can.'

'When?'

'I'll get them tonight.'

'I know you will.' Becky laid her head on her chest. Karin stroked her long hair, running her fingers through all the kinks and knots.

She heard the soft exhalations of the others curled on the floor. Karin was desperate to stay awake to enjoy Becky's company till morning, but she was shattered, and her body flattened against the hard concrete, her eyelids grew heavy. Holding her closer, Becky stretched her arm over her waist.

Karin barely felt Becky's fingers touch the keys in her pocket.

'What's this?' she asked.

'What's what?' asked Karin groggily.

Becky sat up and shoved her hand into Karin's pocket and took out the keys. 'What are these?'

Still drifting up from the edge of sleep, Karin struggled to think of a reason they should be there.

Becky dug her fingernails into Karin's arm. 'How long have you had these keys?'

'Ouch, you're hurting me!'

'How *long*?'

'Since today,' said Karin quickly. 'I was going to tell everyone, I swear! I wanted to wait till I had had a little sleep!'

'Why would you do that?' Becky stared in incomprehension. 'Why didn't you tell us? Were you even going to say anything?'

Becky climbed to her feet, as the others stirred.

'Please, Becky,' whispered Karin. 'Let me ex—'

'You lying cow!' Becky jangled the keys. 'How could you do such a thing? How could you be so fucking *weird*? We could be out of here already! We could be home!' She went around waking everyone up. 'We've got keys, and we're getting out of here right now!'

'How?' asked Michelle.

'What?' Paul rubbed his eyes with his knuckles.

'I'll tell you after. Let's just get out!'

When they tried to wake Simon, he was insensible. 'We'll have to carry him.'

'He's too heavy!' said Paul.

'Then everyone will have to help him out!' Becky went to Karin and hissed in her ear. 'I will never forgive you for this. I never want to see you again, do you hear me – *ever*!'

'Please.' Karin's mind whirled. 'Let me explain. Let me, let me… let me.'

She tried to grab her friend's hand, but Becky shook her off angrily.

'Everyone come here,' she whispered, examining the keys. 'I think this one is for this door and there's another one, which looks like it's for the front door upstairs. But we're not going to have much time. If none of them work upstairs, we'll have to break a window. Michelle, you go first and open the door upstairs. Paul and Lydia, make sure Simon gets out. I'll be right behind you.'

Michelle nodded and slipped the key into the keyhole. The door unlocked with a soft click, and swung open. They all stared up the dark steps for a moment and then Michelle ran up. Paul and Lydia, lifting Simon between them, followed her out.

Karin and Becky were left alone in the cellar. 'Bex, please let me—'

But Becky pushed her towards the door.

'Go!' There was a look of disgust on Becky's face that made Karin's insides clench with despair. 'Just you wait till I tell everyone what you've done, you sicko!'

'Please, I love you, you're my friend.'

'Not any more I'm not. I've had it with you! I totally hate you for this!'

Karin was in tears. 'You're not being fair!'

'What kind of person would...' Becky looked at Karin as if she were a total stranger. 'Just go!'

Karin couldn't believe Becky was being so unfair, so cruel and judgemental, and anger surged inside her. She went through the door—

'Wait!' called Becky. 'What are you—'

—and slammed it in Becky's face.

There was a bolt on the outside of the door and Karin slid it across, locking Becky in.

'What are you doing?' shouted Becky on the other side. 'Open the door, open it!'

'Tell me you'll be my friend!' Karin called, heart hammering in her chest. 'Promise you won't leave me!'

'Just open it!'

'Tell me!' screamed Karin.

'I'll be your friend.' She could hear the panic in Becky's voice as she desperately pounded on the door with her fists. 'I promise! Please open it!'

'Liar!' Karin knew they could never be friends again, Becky would hate her for ever now, and she couldn't bear it. 'You're lying!'

'I'm not!' Becky sounded terrified. 'Please let me out! You can't leave me!'

'I'm sorry,' said Karin, crying. 'I'll send help, I promise!'

She ran up the stairs, ignoring Becky's frantic shouts, and found Lydia standing at the top.

'Where's Becky?'

'She's coming, keep moving!'

Lydia peered down the darkened staircase. 'Where is she?'

'She's right behind us! Come on!'

They heard Jerry's footsteps upstairs and Karin pushed Lydia along the hallway, where Michelle was tearfully scrabbling with the keys at the door.

She dropped them on the mat. Terrified, Paul was crying. Nobody looked behind them to make sure they were all there.

'Come on!' Paul cried, Simon's head lolling on his shoulder.

Michelle snatched up the keys and found the right

one and slipped it with a trembling hand into the lock. A light went on above them, Jerry's shadow appeared on the wall at the top of the stairs, and they began to panic. The key turned, and Michelle pulled the door open to reveal the night.

'Run!' she screamed and they raced out of the house, bolting for the dark woods on the other side of the overgrown drive.

'Into the trees!' shouted Lydia.

The five of them ran as fast as they could. Stumbling into the trees, weeping with fear and hope, consumed by the panic that Jerry was in pursuit and could grab them at any moment, they tore through the undergrowth to freedom.

Nobody looked round to check that Becky was with them.

But Karin stopped for a moment at the edge of the trees to look back at the farmhouse, and the shape silhouetted at the door.

She was sure Jerry gave her a sad wave goodbye.

60

'Y ou locked Becky in the cellar, knowing he would kill her!'

'I made a terrible mistake.'

'You executed her!'

'No! I was angry and upset, I felt rejected. I thought Jerry Swann was harmless, incapable of killing anybody, and he would flee and Becky would be left alone. I thought the police would come and let her go. He was just a liar, I never imagined in a million years that he would—'

'He murdered her for you,' spat Ian. '*This is for you, my love!* His words weren't intended for Becky, but for you. It was a declaration of love, and you've known that all these years.'

Tears rolled down Karin's face. 'Yes, he killed her for me. He thought I was his friend, the only one he had. But Becky was my friend, I loved her more than anything, and he couldn't bear that, like I couldn't bear her not loving me any more. And I've had to live with the guilt and the shame of what I did ever since.'

'Say it,' Ian said. 'I want to hear you admit what you did.'

'I'm responsible.' Karin's voice cracked as she turned to everyone in the room. 'Becky was killed because of me.'

'You loved her so much you made sure she was murdered,' Ian said quietly. 'An innocent girl died because of your capriciousness, and an innocent man's reputation was destroyed. My dad lost everything – his job, his dignity. You didn't just kill Becky, you ruined his life, too, and my mother's, and mine! The truth is out at last, but the damage is already done.'

'Ian, please.' Sasha stepped closer to the three teenagers tied to chairs in front of him. 'Let those kids free.'

But he ignored her. 'And you killed Lydia too, I expect, because you knew she had betrayed you to me.'

'No.' Karin shook her head. 'I never killed her, I would never do that.'

'You're a liar, just like Swann.'

Karin dropped to her knees, bowing her head. Tears spattered on to the flagstones. 'I told you what happened, and I'm glad. Go ahead, I want the world to know. You've got what you wanted, so please let them go.'

'Oh, no!' he said in triumph. 'The world needs to see what you're capable of.' He stepped in front of Karin, lifting the tip of the knife under her chin so that she was forced to look up at him. 'I told you, you have a choice to make. Two of these children will walk out of here, but one of them must die with me, and you're going to choose which one.'

Sasha maintained eye contact with Angel, who shook in terror, but she struggled to control her own spiralling panic.

Shaking her head in disbelief, Karin whispered, 'I won't do that.'

'Who are you going to leave behind?' Ian placed a hand on the shoulder of each teenager in turn, making them cry out in terror. 'Michelle's daughter... or your favourite pupil... or the policewoman's kid?'

'Why is Angel here?' asked Sasha quickly. 'What has she got to do with any of this?'

'That's a good question.' He scratched his cheek with the blade. 'When he could still talk, my father told me everything about what happened on the night of Becky Haskell's death, DI Dawson, even his brief encounter with you. You were just an upstart probationary PC but you had the temerity to challenge his authority in front of his colleagues. Oh, he remembered you. Every single moment of that terrible night was burned on his brain.

'So I knew perfectly well who you were when you visited him at the home, and it was such a delicious piece of symmetry that it was you who came. And when I saw you and Karin together, it gave me an idea. It didn't take much to find out about your son and your husband.' He cupped the back of Angel's neck, making her go rigid with fear. 'And, of course, your darling daughter.'

Despite her fear for Angel and the other kids, Sasha had to remain calm. If they had any chance of getting out of here, it was vital she stayed focused. Feeling the baton press against her forearm beneath her sleeve, she had to get closer to Ian.

'Two will live, one shall die down here. Come on now, Karin, it'll be just like old times for you, deciding who should be left behind to die. Which of the youngsters is it going to be?'

Sasha stepped forward. 'Ian, please…'

Ian put the knife to Angel's soft throat. 'Back,' he barked, '*now*!'

Heart pounding, Sasha stepped backwards, her eyes never leaving her stricken daughter's tearful face. Whatever happened next, she would be there for her, for all the kids.

'Make the decision.' He paced angrily, slapping the blade against the backs of the chairs. The teenagers squeezed their eyes shut. 'Who dies? Make your choice now or I'll kill them all.'

Karin planted her hands on the cold flagstones. 'You can't ask me to make that decision.'

'Why not? You sacrificed Becky, you didn't think twice about it, you just have to do it again.'

'Please just let them go! I was a stupid little girl,' she told him, 'and I'm going to tell the world what I did. I know that's what you want.'

'I've told you what I want.'

Karin heard Becky's voice in her head from all those years ago.

You'll get an opportunity and you must take it.

'I can't,' she muttered dismally.

'Can't what?' said Ian.

I know you can do it.

She lifted her eyes to his.

'You're right, I'm responsible for Becky's death and I'll never forgive myself, but do you know what else nobody knows?' She grinned at him. 'Not even Lydia knew this... I was there when your father came to the doorstep of the Bad Place. I was in the kitchen and I could have ended the whole nightmare right then, I could have walked out in front of him. He would have gone down in the history books as the man who saved us all from the Bad Place. Becky would have lived and everyone would think of him as a hero. But I never did, and do you know why, Ian?' She climbed to her feet. 'Because I was too scared.'

'You're a liar!'

'He was drunk and no good for anything. Even from the kitchen I could smell the alcohol fumes coming off him.'

'That's a disgusting thing to say,' Ian cried out. 'You're nasty!'

'I'd rather hide in that kitchen than reveal myself. It made my skin crawl just to see him. He was a mess, he was no better than Jerry. And when I met him afterwards

I realized I was right, because he was so unpleasant. My heart goes out to you, Ian.'

'No,' whispered Ian. 'What are you—'

'Did he hit you? Did he make your life a misery? I bet he did, I bet you dreaded him coming home late at night, barely able to put the key in the door, coming in angry and drunk.'

'Don't you talk about him like that,' he hissed. 'Don't you *dare!*'

She glanced at Sasha, *be ready*.

'My mum was the same, Ian, she was a violent drunk. What did he do to you, Ian?' He blinked at her in shock. 'Poor Ian, look what he made you.'

I know you can do it.

'He didn't... he didn't mean it, the pressure, it...' Ian smeared away the tears streaming down his face. 'I'm going to count to three and if you haven't chosen by then you'll be sorry... *One.*'

'Ian, don't do this.' Sasha shifted the weight of the baton in her sleeve, but he was still too far away. If she lunged at him, he would still be able to fatally stab one of the kids. 'It's not too late.'

'*Two.*'

Karin came closer. 'That's why he made mistake after mistake in the investigation, that's why he was drummed out of the police, and it's why he couldn't save Becky in that basement – because he was a blundering drunk!'

'No!' Ian stepped towards the chairs. '*Three!*'

Karin stepped right up to him, getting in his face. 'A useless, pathetic, vicious drunk!'

'Liar!' he screamed.

His hesitation gave her a fleeting moment to grab his hand that held the knife, twisting the wrist as hard as she could. But he effortlessly swung her into the wall, pulled back the blade—

'No!' Sasha let the baton drop from her sleeve into her palm, extending the steel rod at its core with a soft click, and stepped forward to smash Ian across the back of the shoulders as hard as she could. The knife flew out of his grasp as he crashed to the floor.

'We're going to get you out!' she told the kids, dropping into a crouch at Angel's chair.

'Mum!' cried Angel, desperately straining against her bonds.

'The knife!' Karin kicked it towards her, and Sasha used it to cut through the tape tying Angel to the chair.

On the floor, Ian groaned. He rolled on to his front, hands clawing at the dusty tile.

When Angel was free, Sasha told her, 'Go!'

But her daughter helped her tear the tape off Lucas. 'Get out of here!' she repeated, but Angel didn't listen. 'Just run!'

As Karin freed Sammi, ripping the tape with her bare hands, she heard a groan and glanced over her shoulder to see Ian lifting himself on to all fours. The three teenagers scrambled up the stairs and Sasha followed them.

Karin was just behind her. 'Keep going, I'm here.'

'Mum!' Angel let out a scream and Sasha turned at the top of the stairs, saw Ian Carrington staggering behind Karin.

Knife still in her hand, she waited for Karin to rush past, but instead Karin told her urgently, 'Make sure they're safe.'

And then she shoved Sasha, causing her to stagger backwards through the open door. 'No!'

Karin slammed the door in her face, sliding the bolt home on the inside.

'Karin!' Sasha shouted, pounding on the door with her fists. 'Open up!'

She heard Karin's body thump against the door as Ian smashed her against it, and heard his rasping voice.

'I wanted to humiliate you,' he told Karin. 'I wanted to make you suffer for what you did, but now I'm just going to kill you.'

Sasha heard Karin cry out. She slammed her fists against the cellar door as the kids disappeared into the glare of sunshine. A moment later, a familiar face appeared.

'Over here,' she screamed, slamming her shoulder against the door again and again as Craig Power ran to her. 'We need to get this open – *right now*!'

61

His hands around her neck, squeezing so tightly that she couldn't breathe, Karin felt her life ebbing away and knew there was nothing she could do about it.

She and Becky would finally be reunited in death.

Pressed against the wall, an explosion of shape and colour filling the inside of her skull, his fingers digging into the meat of her throat, her thoughts became sluggish.

What little light there was in the room seemed to dim, so that all she could see was Ian Carrington's grimacing face, like an angry mask; lips curled back in concentration, teeth clenched. She felt his hot, panting breath on her cheeks as his strong hands tightened inexorably around her neck. One of her feet twisted off the edge of a stair but, pinned against the brick, she was unable to fall.

She was dimly aware of voices on the other side of the door and a ferocious pounding against the wood. *Karin,* the voices called from very far away, *we're coming.*

But it wouldn't be soon enough.

There was a pipe sticking out of the brick at her

side and when her fingers brushed across it, it moved. Karin plucked at it, feeling the way it rattled in the loose cement.

Vicious thuds made the door shake. Once, twice, three times. The wood bulged and the rusted bolt shuddered, but the door held fast.

Ian's face was pressed close to hers. *Me and you*, his voice was like an echo from another room, *we'll die together, me and you.*

And she realized – maybe it would be her final thought – that those three kids, Sammi, Lucas, Angel, were alive, and he couldn't touch them now.

They were alive because of what she did.

And right then, Karin knew she wanted to live, she realized she didn't want to die like Becky, not now, not like this, and the knowledge was like a burst of cool air on her burning face, like a door opening in her mind.

Her friend was gone and she missed her. Karin would never stop missing Becky. But she had told the truth about what she had done, the world would finally know, and it was like a weight lifted from her shoulders – she would endure the consequences.

Ian Carrington's snarling face swam in her vision. His features seemed to splinter into fragments. She saw one squinting eye, his angry red gums, a flash of an incisor, all swimming behind a starburst of juddering, spinning swirls and shapes on the surface of her eyes. Her neck would snap at any moment and she would be dead.

The door bulged and thudded.

We're coming, someone shouted. *Hang on!*

Karin wanted to breathe, more than anything she had ever wanted before. What she did to Becky was a stupid, impetuous, childish thing, born of a moment of madness, and it was wrong. But she didn't deserve to die, not like this.

I'm so sorry, Becky.

She would never forget what she did, or ever forget her friend.

But I want to live.

She frantically pulled at the pipe but it wouldn't come away from the wall, and in a panic her fingers found the metal cylinder of the flashlight in her back pocket. She fumbled at it, felt the weight of it in her palm, and with her last ounce of strength lifted it over her head, and smashed it into the side of Ian's head.

He stepped back in surprise, his twitching hands lifting from her throat; his heels disappeared over the edge of the wooden stair, and then he fell away. She felt the steps judder beneath her feet as he crashed down the stairs, rolling head over heels, his skull hitting the flagstones, and the last thing she saw as he came to a rest was the way his neck jutted at a strange angle.

Just as the door flew open.

And she blacked out.

Goodbye, my darling Bex.

I love you.

62

Michelle was sitting staring into space when she got the call from Alan Manning to say he wasn't coming back to work.

'Of course,' she told him. 'Really, Alan, take off as long as you like.'

'I mean I'm quitting, Michelle.'

If she was honest with herself, she had been expecting something like this to happen. It was the best possible news that Sammi had returned safely. Michelle wasn't ashamed to say she burst into tears when she heard it on the radio. It would have been nice, a common courtesy, if someone had thought to ring her personally, but despite that, she was relieved and thankful. She had been determined not to contact Alan, Jessica and Sammi, appreciated that they all needed to take a breath. But Jessica had already texted Michelle to tell her to stay away. Sammi was in a bad way, Jessica said, and they wanted to spend time together, just the three of them, after Sammi's traumatic experience, and so on and so forth. It was a blow, but Michelle understood that Jessica was still angry about what happened at the press conference.

Sitting at her desk, she listened now while Alan made his excuses. Sammi needed peace and quiet, she was crying all the time and afraid of outsiders – it wounded Michelle to be called an *outsider* – and wanted to spend more time with her parents.

Michelle sipped from her mug.

It had been a dream of hers that Sammi's return would be a new beginning for them all. Alan and Jessica would finally tell Sammi that Michelle was her mother – maybe she had already found out. It wasn't like she wanted Sammi to come and live with her or anything, she just yearned for her daughter to know the truth, and then they could all move forward. But she knew now that the Mannings intended to freeze her out of Sammi's life completely, so his resignation from the company was hardly unexpected.

Still, it was a bitter pill to swallow. Alan would be difficult to replace, and he had been a comfortable presence in Michelle's life, like a favourite pair of slippers. Men had come and gone, and in many respects, Alan had been a better husband to her than any of them.

She was getting tired of his pathetic excuses now – he felt terrible about the whole thing, he had enjoyed working with her all these years, blah blah blah – and Michelle wanted to get him off the phone. Then her assistant poked her head in the door and said, 'There are police officers here to see you, Michelle.'

'Alan, I'm going to have to go now.' Michelle calmly

sipped from the mug. 'Please give my love to Jessica and... to Sammi. I'm so relieved that she's back, Alan, you don't know how much.'

There was silence on the other end, and she knew he felt awful. Well, good. She didn't know when, or if, they would speak again.

In many ways, it was a shame that things had turned out the way they had. Simon was still seriously ill in hospital, although Michelle had heard he was on the mend, and Paul was in big trouble with the police, as well he should be, the disgusting toad. And Lydia was... Lydia was gone.

Karin had a man in her life, some businessman from out of town – wonders never ceased! – and it occurred to Michelle that she had always really looked forward to the evenings they all reunited. The truth was that, despite all her success, she was lonely and she had known those people – Karin, Simon, Paul, Lydia – for many, many years. She supposed the survivors of the Bad Place would all finally be forced to go their own way now, and the knowledge hit her hard.

But she was kidding herself that things could possibly remain the same – she heard her assistant, Jenny, talking to the officers outside – because she knew everything was about to fall apart. Michelle didn't know when she would get to see Sammi again; her latest marriage was disintegrating, her husband had lawyered up and was making threatening noises about her fortune; but all that was small potatoes compared to what was about to happen.

Michelle opened a drawer, took out a bottle of vodka and poured more into the mug, just as DI Sasha Dawson came into the room with the handsome black detective whose name she couldn't remember. The criss-cross of cuts and bruises on his face only made him even more attractive.

She stood. 'DI Dawson.'

'This is Detective Constable Power,' said Sasha.

'If only I were a few years younger,' Michelle murmured as she shook his hand.

'Excuse me?' said Sasha.

'I said, of course, it's Detective Constable Power. Please, sit, both of you.'

As DI Dawson made herself comfortable, she looked around the plush office, clearly admiring the way it was decorated in bright pastel colours. Pleased, Michelle sipped from the mug.

'I know why you're here.' She was conscious that she was slurring. It was possible that she was actually quite drunk and it was only – her eyes lifted to the clock on the wall – eleven in the morning. What with everything that was happening, it was probably best to ease up on the vodka. 'I've been waiting for you to come for some time, actually. I don't think any of us want to make a big song and dance about it, so I'll just say I'm so very sorry about what happened to Lydia.'

Sasha Dawson gave her that infuriating smile, the one that made you want to confess everything immediately. 'Can you tell us what happened?'

Michelle wagged a finger. 'Oh, you're very good.' She reached into the drawer to take out the bottle and add a last splash of vodka to the mug. 'I would have liked to have been your friend, DI Dawson. You have this way about you. I see you and I think everything's going to work out fine.'

DC Power scraped his pen across his notebook but it had run out of ink, and Michelle offered a biro from a drawer.

'Thanks,' he said.

'You're welcome.' Michelle winked at Sasha. 'You're very lucky to be able to work with this handsome man, I can tell you. All I ever got to look at all day was Mr Wishy-Washy, Alan Manning.'

'Tell me about Lydia,' prompted Sasha.

Tears bulged in Michelle's eyes. 'I didn't mean for it to happen, I honestly didn't. Lydia was freaking out, she was being so mean to Karin, and I couldn't stand it any more, so I got this idea to cheer her up, help her relax. I thought I'd get her some smack, or whatever they call it. Just a little bit, just as a one-off.'

'But Lydia had been clean for some time, you know that.'

'Yes, I suppose she had.' Michelle eyed Sasha guiltily. 'But I thought that just this once wouldn't hurt, not if it... helped her calm down. So I found this young man, a dealer, he was on her own estate actually, and bought the stuff and went to her flat.' She lifted her arms. 'I went to cheer her up, I swear, but we got into this silly argument. Lydia could be... intolerable. She started making all kinds of accusations about Karin, that she was responsible for Becky's death, that she had locked her in that cellar... and I just got so cross. There was a bit of pushing and shoving, it was nothing really, but you know what she was like, as light as a feather, and I must have pushed her harder than I thought. She stumbled on her tatty carpet and hit her head on the wall.

'I couldn't believe it, I couldn't wake her... she was *dead*. It was just my luck.' Michelle pulled tissues from a holder on the desk to soak up the tears clinging to her lashes. 'I had the heroin on me, in a little wrap thing, but I didn't have the faintest clue what to do with it, so I had to look it up on my phone, one of those idiot guides on how to prepare and inject it. And then I didn't have a syringe, so I had to search the flat, looking here and there, and I found one at the back of a drawer, because that's just typical of Lydia's bad faith to have kept one, just in case. I followed the instructions and injected it, I stuck it in, but I was shaking like a leaf. I suppose I made a terrible mess of it, yes? I bet I did.' She sipped from the mug. 'How did you...'

'Your car was parked nearby and caught on camera,'

said Sasha. 'And when the dealer was arrested on another matter, he gave us a description.'

'I'll be honest with you,' Michelle sniffed, 'it's a weight off my mind that you know. I guess you'll want me to come to the station. When shall we go?'

'Let's go now,' said Sasha Dawson gently.

'You had better read me my rights, that's what happens, isn't it?'

'Michelle Dormand,' intoned DC Craig Power, 'you do not have to say anything. But it may harm your defence if you do not mention when questioned something which you later rely on in court. Anything you do say may be given in evidence.'

'I could listen to your lovely voice all day,' Michelle told him.

'You may have to,' said Craig.

'Funny, too.' Michelle drained her mug. 'Jenny!'

Her assistant poked her head in the door. 'Yes, Ms Dormand?'

'I'm popping out, and... I may be some time.'

'Yes, Ms Dormand.'

Michelle plopped bits and pieces back into the drawer of her desk and looked dismally at Sasha.

'I had hoped that one day Sammi and I would be the best of friends. I had this dream that she would see me and think, there she is, there's my *real* mum, and I'm so very, very proud of her. That's not going to happen now, I suppose.'

63

'**H**e's doing my head in! Mum, tell him to stop!'
'You tell him,' said Sasha, who'd been staring at the menu for what seemed like minutes.

'Mum! He's hitting me under the table.'

'No, I'm not!' said Denny in disgust. 'Because if I did, my foot would rebound off your big, flabby knee and hit me in my own face.'

'He's lying,' said Angel. 'Ouch, he just did it again!'

They were all sitting at a table in the same café where they used to come regularly as a family, and where Kev had stayed all day when everyone thought he was at work. It had seemed like a good idea to come here together, but now Sasha was not so sure. Everyone was tense and irritable, Kev was quiet, and this place, as lovely as it was, just seemed like another reminder of what they had lost, *who* they had lost.

'Denny.' Conscious of the other customers giving them dirty looks, Sasha kept her voice low. 'Leave your sister alone, she was recently abducted and held hostage by a dangerous maniac, and has been through a very traumatic situation.'

Angel gave her brother a superior smile. 'The doctor says I may have post-traumatic stress disorder. And every time you act like a complete knob and kick me in the leg, it triggers me.'

'Bull. Shit.' Denny was annoyed at being outmanoeuvred. Sasha knew that Angel would use her ordeal to torment him for a long time to come, probably until they were both pensioners, and there was absolutely nothing he could do about it. Sasha glanced at Kev, who was gazing at the white tips of ocean surf breaking on the strip of sand on the other side of the road.

Denny reached into his pocket. 'What's the Wi-Fi password here?'

'No phones,' she told him again. 'We're enjoying a family day out.'

'Wait, all day? Nobody said anything about all day!'

'Kev?' Sasha said, trying to sound cheerful. 'What do you fancy?'

He looked up in surprise at the sound of her voice and turned his attention back to the menu.

'There's nothing here I want,' Angel said.

Denny shrugged. 'I just want an ice cream.'

'You're not having an ice cream until you've eaten properly,' insisted Sasha. Honestly, it was like he was still six years old sometimes.

Then Angel screamed – Denny had pinched her under

the table – and they all jumped, making the cutlery bounce. The other customers looked annoyed.

'There are people here trying to enjoy a nice meal, so let's try and keep the noise down.' Sasha leaned across the table. 'Kev, feel free to have a word with your boisterous offspring.'

But Kev threw down the menu and jumped out of his chair and headed towards the door.

'Where are you going? Kev!'

He disappeared out of the door.

'Where's Dad gone?' asked Denny anxiously.

'He's gone mental again, hasn't he?' said Angel.

Sasha had thought he was on the mend now that he was getting help. She wanted to go after him, but didn't want to leave the kids, and felt upset and annoyed. Kev clearly wasn't back to his old self, not yet, and Angel was still recovering from her ordeal. They shouldn't have come here. As bright and cheerful as the café was, they should have just gone for fish and chips.

Sasha impatiently stabbed a finger at the menu. 'Just pick something!'

'Can you imagine how calorific this food is!' cried Angel.

'Where's Dad gone?' said Denny again. 'Can we go after him?'

'Don't worry about him,' Sasha told him. 'We're here and we're all going to *enjoy* ourselves.'

Denny waved the menu in her face. 'There. Is. Nothing. I. Want.'

Sasha was ready to admit defeat and take them all home, order in a takeaway. She knew Angel and Denny would jump at the chance, but as soon as they got through the door they would find excuses to drift off to their rooms. Angel would sit on her phone, Denny would play a computer game, she would hear him yelling to his friends on his headphones, and Sasha would watch that new series on Netflix. Kev would come home in his own good time, and she'd try to talk to him then. He wasn't well, she had to remember that, he needed time. But a moment later, her husband came back in the door with ice creams.

'Budge up,' he told Sasha. 'These will keep us going!'

'Yeah!' said Denny, grabbing one. 'That's more like it!'

He handed around the cones and they all licked them, even Angel, who had forgotten to worry about how fattening it was.

'Mmmm,' said Denny, 'this is *sick*.'

'So here we are again,' Kev said to Sasha.

'Here we are again.'

Sasha surreptitiously tried to wipe away a tear crawling down her cheek.

'Mum,' said Denny, rolling his eyes. 'Don't embarrass us.'

She tried to laugh it away, but felt an ache in her chest at the thought of how close they had come to disaster. She had almost lost her daughter, and would never have been able to forgive herself.

'I can't help it.' She laughed as she dabbed at her eyes. 'I can't believe we're all here together... the four of us.'

'The five of us,' Angel told her. 'Because Jake is here too.'

'Yes, he is.' Sasha looked around the table, at Denny and Angel and Kev, and was overwhelmed by the fierce love she felt for them all; it was like a physical pain. And for Jake, too, who would always be in their hearts. When Kev slipped his hand into hers, she was certain she was going to start ugly crying.

'So,' said Denny, 'now we've done the family bonding bit, can I look at my phone?'

Sasha couldn't remember the last time they'd all laughed together, but they did now.

Cramming the last of the cone into his mouth, Kev waved to the owner behind the counter, and said, 'Come on, everybody, let's go and get some chips.'

They walked outside and across the road to the thin sliver of beach. With Angel and Denny talking animatedly ahead of them, Kev pulled Sasha close.

'Thank you,' he said.

'Don't leave us again.' She was still emotional. 'We miss you too much.'

He kissed her on the forehead. 'Not a chance.'

And then he put a finger to his lips, *watch this*, and crept up behind his daughter, and while she was talking to Denny leaned over and bit the top off her last bit of ice cream.

'Dad!' she screamed, and her brother laughed like it was the funniest thing he'd ever seen, and Sasha laughed too.

And right at that moment her phone rang and she stopped to fumble in her bag for it. She saw it was a call from the office. Her thumb hovered over the screen, ready to accept the call. But when she glanced up, they were all standing looking at her, Kev and Angel and Denny.

'No phones,' they chorused.

She felt the weight of it in her hand, watched the screen flash angrily for her attention, and then lobbed it into the sea.

It sank with a plonk.

Denny and Kev doubled over in laughter.

'Mum!' screamed Angel. 'I can't believe you did that!'

'Oh well,' said Sasha Dawson. 'That call will have to wait.'

Acknowledgements

Sasha Dawson will return, as they say in those movies. But while you're still here, let me mention some lovely people who really helped in the writing of *The Bad Place*.

I ask Michael Gradwell and Inspector Kevin Horn endless questions about police procedure and they are both unfailingly helpful and patient; the same goes for Senior Paramedic Jason Eddings and his medical guidance. I'm grateful to Robert Colby-Blake and Christopher Langdon at Southend Museums, and to Graham Beale for his technological expertise. Crispin Bonham-Carter and Jason Butler kindly spoke to me about bullying in schools.

I'm lucky to have Jamie Cowen at The Ampersand Agency fighting my corner, and the same goes for Rosie and Jessica Buckman at The Buckman Agency.

Many thanks to my brilliant editor Laura Palmer and all the other lovely and talented people at Head of Zeus. Special mentions must go to Vicky Joss, Nikky Ward, Flo Hare, Sophie Robinson, Dan Gronewald, Vicki Reed, Chrissy Ryan, Christian Duck, Jenni Edgecome, Jon Appleton – and Mark Swan for his terrific cover.

As usual, lots of friends and family encouraged and supported me in the writing of *The Bad Place*. I really couldn't have written a word without the endless love and patience of Fiona and Archie, or the warm companionship of my four-legged assistants Jason and Gracie.

About the author

Mark Hill was a journalist and an award-winning music radio producer before becoming a full-time writer. He lives in London. Visit him at *mkhill.uk*, on Twitter *@markhillwriter* and Facebook *@MarkHillAuthor*.